A Year

Of a Thousand

Casts

I hope you enjoy the story. Unplug & sling a line !

Fantasy books by Jason L. McWhirter

The Lands of Kraawn
The Cavalier Trilogy
The Cavalier, book one
The Rise of Malbeck, book two
Glimmer in the Shadow, book three
The Shadow Knight Books
The Shadow Knight

The World of Corvell and Belorth
The Steel Lord Series
BannerFall, book one
Banner Lord, book two
The Chronicles of Corvell
The Glimmer Blade

The Five Lands
The Unbroken Gate
Stone Blood

Non-Fantasy books by Jason L. McWhirter

The Life of Ely

A Year of a Thousand Casts

Published by Twiin Entertainment
www.twiinentertainment.com

Cover/Photo manipulation by Mario Teodosio
All other images by Jason L. McWhirter

AUTHOR'S NOTE

This is a work of fiction. Names, characters, places, and incidents are the product of the author's imagination or are used fictitiously, and any resemblance to actual persons, living or dead, and events, is entirely coincidental. The actual fishing destinations are real, the lodges and locales, although their names were changed, were based on a combination of research and the authors imagination.

DEDICATION

This book is dedicated to my wife, Jody, and the thousands of other nurses out there who spend their life helping others. Specifically, I'd like to honor pediatric medical personal who endure the difficulties of navigating children and their families through some of the most trying situations you can imagine.

I would also like to dedicate this story to anyone who has lost a loved one, someone so close to them that they thought they would never be able to move past the pain associated with their passing. May you eventually find peace.

And lastly, I'd like to dedicate this adventure to all the fly-fishing aficionados out there, past, present, and future. May you forever experience tight lines, beautiful scenery, and the comradery of like-minded individuals.

A Year of a

Thousand Casts

A Story of Love, Loss, and Healing

Jason L. McWhirter

Prologue

Jena O'Malley was numb. Not the kind of numbness you get when your dentist pokes a needle in your gums. It was much deeper, more profound, as if the air around her had become an impenetrable fog. The sounds in the room were muffled, like someone humming with a pillow over their face. It felt like she was under water, like she was drowning in a deep sea. It wasn't just her consciousness that was drowning, but her heart as well. It hurt, like an ache rising from her chest and lodging in her throat. She didn't know if the pain would ever go away.

A hand gently squeezing her leg drug her thoughts through the haze, the sound of Rob's voice, her husband's friend speaking at the podium, suddenly breaking through her miasma of pain. Glancing over, she gave her mother a forced smile, the feeble attempt failing to lighten the dark cloud surrounding her. Her mother smiled back, her own eyes glistening with fresh tears. Her look was one of concern, but she said nothing, tapping Jena's leg, the subtle gesture reflecting more love than any words could in that moment.

Jena looked to the stage of the tavern they had rented for the night. It was Chris's favorite drinking hole. They had been there together many times, the smell of aged leather booths, beer, and the cleaning disinfectant the bartender used to clean the long mahogany bar, bringing her a sense of nostalgia. She was barely containing herself as it was that nostalgia that hammered home the fact that she would never experience this bar with her husband again. She couldn't count the number of nights they had sat together at the old wood tables listening to singers test their skills on open mic night. They had sipped cocktails and quietly talked as the sounds, some pleasant and others not so much, of amateur musicians filled the bar. She took a deep breath as another wave of emotion washed over her. She glanced at her best friend, Brook, who was sitting next to her, hoping to find something there that would ease the pain. Brook squeezed her other leg and wiped tears from her cheeks. She too was hurting, having known Chris for over twenty years when Jena had first met her at the hospital. Brook had taken another job as a nurse at a nearby hospital but she had still been a part of the O'Malley's lives for half of her life.

6

A Year of a Thousand Casts

Jena looked from her best friend to Rob on the stage. She wanted to listen to him. To hear what he was saying, to hear what her husband's friends had said previously. She wanted to remember this day, to hold onto their words, to cherish them. She wanted to be able to pull forth the memories that people had of her late husband, to add them to her own memory bank. But she was struggling to rise above the despair. It had been four weeks since Chris had succumbed to pancreatic cancer, and yet it felt like yesterday. She blinked, tears dripping freely down her red cheeks, the simple movement a door in time taking her back to the man she had loved for over twenty-five years. His voice found her, and the image of his wavy dark hair and exuberant smile briefly broke through her pain. But then he was gone, the image of his shrunken and withered body replacing his vigorous persona, his enthusiasm crushed under the boot of a ruthless disease that killed so many. She could still hear his slow ragged breathing, and feel his hand touch her as his eyes closed, his last words, a gentle whisper, *I love you*, escaping through his cracked and dried lips. Then he was gone.

Grief struck her and she sobbed, her shoulders shaking as she lowered her head. Her mother held her leg tighter as more people around her, friends and family, cried along with her. Her mother reached over and gently touched her tied back red hair, pulling her head against her chest as Jena sobbed. After a few moments she pulled away and looked up at the podium, her face grief stricken, her glistening eyes finding Rob as he paused, his expression matching her own. His dark brown eyes found her and for a moment they shared their grief. Rob was Chris's best friend. They had grown up together in Gig Harbor, Washington. And although Rob had moved to Portland, Oregon to start his own law firm, they had talked often and hung out when they could. They were like brothers, and Chris's death had had a profound impact on Rob.

Rob spoke of Chris's love for life. He spoke of his tenacity and his love for his friends and family. He did his best to express Chris's view on how he saw his place in the world. And everyone present knew that Rob's words were not just kind rhetoric expected to be heard at one's wake. Chris represented the best parts of everyone, and they all knew it. He was smart and hardworking, managing to create a small graphic design business that made good money and yet gave him the time to indulge in his many hobbies. He loved to build things of wood, make beer and wine, and dabble in the stock market. He was a voracious reader and cared deeply about the environment. He was the kind of guy who washed out every glass container, removing their metal or plastic tops before recycling them. Everyone in attendance knew that Chris was the best kind of friend. He would do anything to help out a buddy. He was the first one there if you needed help moving and he was the last one leaving if you needed help with something around the house. Chris could fix anything, and he never shied away from helping a friend who needed his expertise. Chris spoke kindly and was rarely one to rush to anger. He was leaving behind a loving sister and her two children, all of whom lived in Spokane Washington.

Jena wiped the tears from her eyes, her focus fluttering from Rob's words to her own memories, some meshing together as his stories elicited memories she had forgotten. Rob's speech inevitably ended with Chris's love for fly-fishing. Smiles momentarily broke through the melancholy in the room as people fondly remembered Chris's passion. Every one of them had inside stories regarding her husband's fly-fishing antics. Jena was convinced it was more of an addiction than a passion. Her husband was a fanatic when it came to fly fishing. Jena was pretty sure she had a solid foundation of the sport just from hearing her husband constantly speak of it. She knew basic entomology and what weight rods were used for specific fish. She knew about catch and release practices and what rivers in the state were the best. But she had only fished with him a few times, something she now greatly regretted. Their summers had been filled with camping and hiking, but she had never really indulged him by learning how to fly fish. She would read by the lake, looking up occasionally as he smoothly cast a dry fly to rising fish. It looked so effortless, and she did enjoy watching him. It had reminded her of the fishing scenes she had seen in the movie *A River Runs Through It* with Brad Pitt. Occasionally he had convinced her to try it. She realized instantly it was not as easy as he had made it seem. He was calm and patient with her, but in the end, she would get frustrated and give up. She remembered his smile as he took the rod back from her. He would always say, "*It will come, just be patient. Once you get it, you will get it.*" She had never spent much time trying to understand what he had meant, but now as his words floated through her memories, she wished she would've made more of an effort in trying to understand why the sport spoke to him as it did.

Jena was so wrapped up in her own thoughts that she hadn't noticed the end of Rob's speech. People were already getting up and heading to the bar to get drinks. Chris had wanted his memorial service to be a celebration, and his friends were damn sure they were going to give him one. There were eight bottles of his favorite expensive scotches lined up on the bar, as well as the makings of Irish car bombs, his favorite shot.

"Honey, it's time to get up," her mother said softly, her hand still resting on her leg.

Jena wiped her tears and nodded, standing up slowly, her mother rising next to her. She looked around, not sure where to go or what to do. Even though her husband had been adamant about having a celebration, there was no possible way she could partake. A smile to her felt as strange as breathing underwater.

She looked at her mother, "I don't know what to do."

"I know, baby." Tesa, her mother, looked at her with deep sadness, her faded blonde hair long and wavy, the light grayness tempered by a layer of dye. Jena wished her father could be with them, but he had died of a heart attack five years ago. His death still weighed heavily on her, and now, as she looked past her mother, remembering his kind smile, her heart hurt even more. Looking back at her mother, it was obvious by her expression that she wanted to take her daughter's pain away, but she simply didn't know how. "Let's just go to the bar and be with Chris's family and friends."

"Okay," Jena nodded numbly and followed her mother to the bar.

Brook was behind her and she reached for her hand, squeezing it as they moved through the crowd. Laura, Chris's sister was in front of Tesa, both of her children and her husband before her as they all made their way to the bar. Jena, although she didn't see Laura and her family more than a few times a year, was quite close to Chris's sister and her two kids. They talked on the phone often and Chris's death had hit his sister's family really hard, just as it had everyone else. There was no one else left in Chris's family, his parents having both died five years ago. Terrance, Chris's father, had smoked all his life and died of lung cancer. His mother, Merith, just withered away after her husband's death, dying of a broken heart two years later. Other than his sister's family, Chris had no family left to mourn his death.

A Year of a Thousand Casts

Many eyes were cast her way, some obviously feeling as she did, unsure how to celebrate Chris's life. When she neared the bar, she was surprised to see the entire wood top covered with trays of shots. She recognized the plastic cups built for the sole purpose of Irish Car Bombs, Jager Bombs, and other similar shots. The middle held equal parts Jameson whiskey and Baileys, while the other portion held about six ounces of Guinness, the three components quite tasty when taken as a shot. Jena remembered fondly the Irish car bombs she had shared with Chris at this very bar.

Rob's strong voice broke through her thoughts once again and she looked up as he stood on the top of the bar, holding one of the plastic cups in his hands. Various servers took the ten trays and began walking around serving the shots to all the guests as Rob shouted over the quiet clamor. Tony, one of Chris's fishing partners, slid two glasses to Jena and her mother. His eyes were red but he smiled softly, touching her hand as he nodded at the glass. His long hair was unruly and his face covered in days of stubble. He looked rough around the edges but his gentle smile softened his hard exterior.

"You all knew Chris well, so there is not much I need to say here to explain his wishes. After all, the shot glass coming your way clarifies it nicely." Everyone laughed, the somber fog lifting slightly in the room. "Chris wanted us to celebrate his life. And although we all know how difficult that is to do with his death sitting so heavy on us," Rob paused briefly as he looked at Jena, "I for one am going to do my best to honor his wishes. I am going to drink and laugh. We are going to tell stories about Chris and share in our memories. Tonight I want us all to try to imagine Chris sitting at the bar watching us and drinking with us. You all know that Chris loved history and he was an avid reader. One of his favorite historical quotes sums up Chris's viewpoint on life, and I think it's fitting to share it with you now. Once I am done, I want anyone who is willing, to share a quote, a saying, or a brief statement about Chris. It can be something he said or something that just reminds you of him. Then we will make a toast in his honor. Chris had the quote I'm about to share with you personalized on one of his hundred fly rods." Everyone laughed as the servers continued to hand out shots, making sure everyone had one. Even Jena smiled briefly at the thought. The amount of fly gear that Chris had accumulated over the years was something of legend amongst his friends. "It read, *In the end, it's not the years in your life that count.*

10

It's the life in your years, by Abraham Lincoln." Rob paused and smiled sadly. "That quote reflects Chris's life perfectly. He lived life to its fullest and felt deeply about many things. He built lasting relationship with all of us. When Chris was with you, there was no one else in the room. He made us all feel important. He made us all better people. More importantly he was lucky enough to find Jena, someone who could handle his intrinsic enthusiasm for life. Together they built a bond of love that has been a model for us all." Rob paused again as he regained control of his emotions. "Now," he continued, "it is time to hear from others."

"Pain is just an inconvenience!" Martin shouted, one of Chris's high school friends. They had wrestled together and Jena cracked a small smile remembering how many times Chris had said those very words.

"Oh, it's happening!" Torgan shouted. Torgan was a fly-fishing guide that Chris had met in Alaska. They had fished together many times over the last ten years and he flew in just for Chris's memorial service. Everyone laughed as they each remembered the many times Chris had pushed them to do something they did not want to do. It was his favorite thing to say, often preceding a wink and a smile, followed by something they probably shouldn't be doing

"Back, back, back!" Larry added. Larry was the husband of one of the nurses Jena worked with. He had learned to fly fish under Chris's tutelage, as well as how to row a raft down a river. It was the latter skill that initiated the phrase as Chris had often yelled out while directing many friends manning the raft to row back to avoid a rock or to position the boat for another swing through a productive run.

Everyone continued to share their one-line memories and Jena heard them all, her own mind drifting in and out to Chris's words that continued to ring in her head. She was not sure why the words kept coming back, but they replayed in her head over and over again.

Rob's voice gently broke through her consciousness once again. "Jena, did you have something you wanted to add?"

Jena looked up, realizing that she had been mumbling the words to herself. Rob had clearly been watching her. Everyone fell silent, their full shots held in their hands. She choked on the knot in her throat and glanced at her mother. Tesa simply nodded, urging her to speak.

She cleared her throat and looked at everyone surrounding her. "This is very hard for me, but I want to say something." She paused to swallow the lump in her throat, tears moistening her cheeks. "It's not something sappy, but something I wish I understood better. I think it's fitting and I know that anyone who has fished with him, which is likely everyone in this room," she said, pausing as the room softly laughed, "will understand its meaning. I hope someday that I will." She cleared her throat again as she wiped the tears from her eyes. "I didn't seem to have the patience to learn how to fly fish, and the few times I picked up his fly rod I ended up handing it back to him out of frustration. When I did, he would always smile at me and say, *be patient, when you get it, you will get it.*"

No one said anything but everyone in the room lifted their glasses, the fishermen present, which was nearly everyone, smiled wide and lifted their shots higher. Rob, still standing on the bar, smiled at Jena and lifted his glass. "To Chris O'Malley, the best person I know!"

Seventy-three people slammed back an Irish car bomb.

Chapter 1

Jena sat quietly in report, listening to Sara, the charge nurse, give a snapshot on each patient. It had been four weeks since Chris's memorial service and her mind still wandered constantly to her husband, his images flashing through her consciousness like a montage in a movie that was constantly playing. This was her first day back and she hoped that work would distract her. She looked around the breakroom and felt a sense of wistfulness looking at the brown leather couches and seats, all clearly bought from the same commercial furniture store. The buzz of the refrigerator, the board peppered with thumbtack notes, the old white microwave; it was all a comforting blanket for her, but even those familiar props could not dissipate the images of Chris that continued to dance through her mind.

"Jena, did you hear me?" Sara asked, her voice filled with concern.

Jena looked up and blinked. "Um, I'm sorry, what were you saying?"

Besides Jena and the charge nurse, there were three other nurses present in the breakroom. Lonney was fifty-five years old and the most senior nurse. Jena had been working with her in the Pediatric Intensive Care Unit for over fifteen years, and although they were not friends that hung out on the weekends, Jena definitely considered her a mentor. She was a bit heavy set with short black hair brushed with streaks of gray, the hair style prevalent with the older lesbian community. She was perhaps the smartest nurse that Jena knew. The nurse sitting next to Jena on the breakroom love seat was Tory, a young blonde straight out of nursing school. She had been in the PICU for three months and although she was a hard worker, she had a long way to go in her bedside manner. She was not overly rude or harsh. She just wasn't great at empathizing with her patients, and more importantly, with her patients' families. She was very matter of fact, often giving information as if she were reading the back of a medicine bottle. The families in the PICU were often going through the most difficult events in their lives, and a truly skilled nurse needed to be not just knowledgeable in medical procedure, but able to be a caring advocate for the suffering families under her care. It was no easy feat to carry the burden of sick and dying children, as well as the insurmountable grief plaguing their families. It was a skill set that few had and it was what had made Jena so good at what she did. It was also the reason why burnout was so prevalent in pediatric intensive care. The last nurse was Becky and she had been working in the PICU for six years. She was in her early thirties and quite pretty, her red hair pulled back into a ponytail. Jena had liked her positive attitude immediately, feeling a kindred spirit with her outgoing personality.

"I was asking if you were okay in taking room two...we can make you open for admit."

"I'm fine with that," Jena said, although she had not been listening who the patient was. Quite frankly, she just wanted to get to work. The other three nurses had one to twos, each caring for two patients, while Jena, also with a one to two assignment, only had one patient at the moment. But being open for admit was always a bit risky, as you never knew what type of patient might arrive.

"Jena, I don't mind being open for admit," Lonney added, her voice showing some concern.

Jena shook her head. "No, its fine, I got it." Typically the most seasoned nurse, in this case Lonney, got first pick of the patients if they were not there the day before. The other patients were then assigned to the remaining nurses.

"Okay," Sara said, turning her eyes on Tory. "Tory, that leaves room six and seven for you. I know six is a tough one. Let me know if you need anything." Tory let out a slow breath. It was obvious she had known she was going to get that patient. Jena, having been on leave, was not yet privy to who was in room six. "Doctor Espinoza is the attending today. Good luck." Sara got up, signaling the end of the meeting.

Jena stood and started to make her way out of the breakroom when Lonney reached out and touched her arm. Lonney had been at Chris's memorial service and was well aware of Jena's situation. "Hey, you sure you don't need more time? I'm worried about you."

Jena forced a smile. "Thanks Lonney, but it's worse just sitting at home. I need to be doing something."

Lonney pursed her lips with concern, nodding subtly with understanding. "Okay, but I'm here for you. Just let me know if I can do anything to help."

"Thanks."

As she turned to leave her phone buzzed in her pocket. They were not supposed to use their phones while on shift, but it was an unspoken fact that most of the nurses surreptitiously broke that rule. She took out the phone and glanced at the screen. It was Rob, her husband's friend, calling her, the fourth time in two days. She had been avoiding him. She knew that he had to go through Chris's will with her, but she just couldn't bring herself to do it. But she couldn't avoid him forever. She made the decision to call Rob after her shift.

Making her way to room two she saw Conny, the night nurse that had been assigned to that patient, just exiting. Jena did not know her well, their relationship consisted of passing on patient reports as Jena took over her shift. Needless to say they interacted briefly throughout the year. Conny was in her late forties, perhaps a handful of years older than Jena and despite her monotone dialogue she seemed nice enough. She had a bob of straight brown hair and a soft round face.

She smiled warmly when she saw Jena. "Hi Jena, it's good to see you." She paused as if she were going to say something else, clearly struggling with a thought. Jena knew that everyone at the hospital was aware of her husband's death. The moment passed and she looked back into the room. "Ready for report?"

Jena was happy Conny didn't say anything. She was tired of making small talk about Chris's death. Jena nodded and followed Conny to the computer station near the room. Conny pulled out her *brain* from her pocket, common jargon for the piece of paper that kept the report of all her patients. Jena grabbed a pen and her own *brain* and leaned against the computer station counter as Conny began her report.

"We have a failure to fly case," Conny began, "but luckily she is going to be okay. We were told that her neighbor heard her scream and found her lying in her front yard. The mother said she was upstairs folding laundry when she left the room to go to the bathroom. The patient then went to the master bedroom window, which was obviously open. Well, you know the rest."

Unfortunately, Jena did know, seeing many *failures to fly* over her long career. Sadly, it was a common summertime accident. People open their windows to cool down their homes and forget that young children will often press up against the screens to look outside. The screen pops out and the child falls.

"Her name is Lisa," Conny continued, "age three, twenty kilos, with no allergies. She suffered multiple skull fractures as well as a broken right arm. She was found unconscious and came to the ICU intubated. They promptly took her to get an MRI and her brain was fine, other than a small bleed. The neuro team cleared the bleed in the OR but wanted to keep an eye on her. She went to surgery for her arm as well. Her C-spine was cleared and now that she is awake, she is eating and tolerating clear liquids. She got her ICP bolt removed two days ago and we have her on a morphine drip, alternating Tylenol and Ibuprofen PO Q6. She is awake and alert with no neurological deficits."

"What kind of access does she have?" Jena asked.

"PIV in left AC. It's been four days Post OP and her last MRI yesterday showed the bleed was under control."

Jena nodded and wrote that down. "She has had a busy few days."

Conny nodded. "I think she is ready to move to the med-surg floor."

Jena nodded, figuring that was going to happen. "Should I push for that in rounds?"

"I think so," Conny added.

"Ok...What's the family like?"

"They seem fine," Conny added. "The father has been in and out but the mother has been here every day. His name is Jack and the mother's name is Theresa. She is in the room now."

Jena nodded. "Are you back tonight?"

Jena had hoped she was. It was always easy passing on report to the same nurse that had taken care of the patient previously. Conny nodded. "Yeah, I'm on tomorrow and Saturday."

"Great...okay, I'll see you in twelve hours."

Conny nodded, reaching out, she touched Jena's shoulder. "It's good to have you back, Jena. Things are never the same without you."

"Thanks." She was a bit surprised as Conny turned and left. She didn't know Conny that well and it was rare they talked much outside of patient care. But it was nice to know that people on other shifts respected you.

Jena took a deep breath, tucked her *brain* into her pocket, and entered room two. The room was roughly the size of a large bedroom, the patient's bed on the adjacent wall with a bathroom to the left. Theresa was sitting in a chair near her daughter's bed reading a book. She looked up when Jena entered, smiling forcefully.

"Good morning Mrs. Sorana, I'm Jena O'Malley, and I'm taking over for Conny for the next twelve hours."

Theresa stood and they shook hands near her daughter's bed. "Nice to meet you." She had long wavy dark hair, likely in her mid-thirties. She was pretty in an athletic sort of way. She was clearly tired and the stress of her daughter's recent event was written all over her face.

Jena looked at Lisa laying asleep in bed and smiled, turning her gaze to Theresa. "I want you to know that I'm going to take great care of your little girl. I always like to ask the parents of my patients what I can do to make your experience here better. What have nurses done in the past that you liked, and what have they done that you did not prefer? It's my hope that I can better serve you and your family if I understand your needs."

Theresa blinked and clearly did not know what to say. It was something Jena was used to as she knew her opening remarks to family members were not typical. She had learned through trial and error over the years that the best way to be a patient and families advocate was to allow them to express their needs. Many nurses and doctors sidelined that simple concept for their own objectives. Jena just smiled and urged her on. "Have you had any frustrations so far?"

"Well, um, things have been pretty good. I'm just so happy that she is going to be okay...but—"

"Go ahead, and don't worry, this is confidential between us. I just want to provide the best care for you and your family."

This time it was Theresa's turn to smile. "I really appreciate that. My only complaint is sometimes I don't get the information in a way that I can understand. It can be pretty confusing, especially when you are already worried about your daughter."

"I understand and rest assured that that is a common issue. I think I can help though," Jena added with a smile. "We will be doing morning rounds soon. I'm not sure which room we will start at, but when we finish with your case, I will make sure you understood everything the care team talked about. Sound good?"

"Yes, and thank you again."

Jena nodded, noticing Theresa's shoulders relax just a little. It felt good knowing that she could provide emotional support while suffering herself. "You're welcome."

The eight thirty rounds came right on time. Doctor Espinoza was there along with Terry, the dietician, Judy from pharmacy, John from social work, Sara, the charge nurse, Shelly, the hospital supervisor, and Jill from Child Life. The team came to Jena's room and Dr. Espinoza smiled warmly as Jena and Theresa met them at the door. They had both been talking to Lisa who had woken a half hour ago.

"Good morning," the doc said to Theresa. Never one to ask dumb questions, like *how are you doing* to someone whose child was in the ICU, she then looked right at Lisa. "It is good to see you awake. How are you feeling?"

Lisa was still a bit groggy from sleep and the pain medications. "I'm fine," she said, smiling, a bit embarrassed by all the people outside the room.

"I'm happy to hear that," Dr. Espinoza said, smiling back. Then she looked at Jena. "So, how was her night?"

Dr. Espinoza had been at the hospital for four years and Jena really liked her. She was short and a bit stocky, with a firecracker wit and personality. Her black hair was cut short like a boy, but she wore it styled so it accentuated her high cheekbones. Jena thought that few women could pull off short hair, but she was always jealous of those who could. It looked amazing on Dr. Espinoza. She was wicked smart and didn't beat around the bush.

"As you all know, this is Lisa's fourth hospital day. She fell from the second floor of her home causing multiple skull fractures and a broken arm," Jena began. "She had a small bleed that was evacuated and the last MRI showed the bleed was under control. She had surgery on her elbow. Her C-spine was cleared and she is eating and tolerating clear liquids. We have her on a morphine drip and we are alternating Tylenol and ibuprofen. Her intake and output are equal, she's had no fever, and all other systems are within defined limits. She continues to be neurologically intact. The night went well and I see no reason to keep her in the ICU."

Dr. Espinoza nodded. "You think she is ready for the med-surg floor?"

"I do." Lisa was doing great and typically when a patient was on the mend, they were sent to the med-surg floor to prepare them to leave the hospital. They didn't want to occupy an ICU room when it wasn't necessary. Lisa would be going home soon and the med-surg floor was the best spot to facilitate that transition.

"Very good," Dr. Espinoza agreed. She then glanced at the pharmacist, Judy, asking her to change her morphine to a liquid dose. "Anything else?" she asked, looking back at Jena.

"I think she could use some help from Child Life to provide some activities for her to do."

Jill from Child Life entered the room, stepping closer to Lisa's bed. She smiled warmly. "I can help with that. Lisa, what kind of projects do you like to do?"

Lisa was embarrassed and she looked at her mom for reassurance. "Go ahead, honey," Theresa urged, "tell her; it's okay."

"Well," Lisa said shyly. "I like coloring books, especially if they have mermaids."

Jill smiled. "Okay, I'll see what I can find for you. Sound good?"

Lisa nodded her head.

"What do you say honey?" her mom added.

Lisa looked at Jill and pulled the covers closer to her face. "Thank you."

Dr. Espinoza smiled and looked at Theresa. "Do you have any questions?"

"What time will they move us?" Theresa asked.

"Probably within a few hours," the doc said. "Jena will help you with that."

"What about when we go home?" Theresa asked. "What care will she need? I'm worried about this bleed. Do we have anything to worry about?"

"The neuro team evacuated it and are happy with what they saw in the MRI. The neuro team will see her again on the med-surg floor. They will keep you until tomorrow at the earliest and they will make sure you get home with good care instructions and close follow up. We see no neurological damage. She is going to be just fine."

Theresa let out a deep sigh. "Thank you so much."

"Of course," Dr. Espinoza said with a gentle smile. Then she looked at Jena. "It's good to have you back." Her smile softened some, turning from reassuring to caring. Then she pivoted and left, the team following.

When they were gone Jena looked at Theresa. "Do you have any questions?"

"I don't think so," she said, holding her daughter's hand. "I'm just glad she is going to be okay."

"Me too."

A half hour later, Sara, the charge nurse, found Jena at her computer. "Hey, you have a new patient coming from the ER."

"Okay, what do we know?" Jena only had one patient and was open for admit, so she knew that any new patient would be hers.

"The labs are pointing to cancer, likely leukemia," Sara said, her voice changing from business to one of a caring friend. "We can have Lonney take him if—"

"I can do it," Jena said, shaking her head. "I'll be okay."

Sara's lips tightened and she took on a thoughtful expression. "Okay." She didn't sound convinced. Taking on newly diagnosed pediatric cancer patients was one of the hardest things to do, and with the loss of Chris, that pain would still be simmering at the surface. Sara was clearly worried. "He is seven and coming up now from the ER. He will need a central line with sedation. Espinoza has a call into oncology now and they will likely do a bone marrow biopsy while he is sedated."

It was standard protocol. Jena nodded. "Okay. Are we putting him in room three?"

"Yup."

"I'll get it ready."

"Sounds good," Sara said as she turned and left in preparation for the new patient.

Fifteen minutes later, the new patient arrived, with his mother and father in tow. The ER nurse escorting him was a veteran named Jonathan. He was a reserved gay man in his mid-thirties who had been in the ER for nearly ten years. Jena had always liked him and was impressed with his calm bedside manner, as well as his confidence. The tech with him was Paul, a young 'wannabe' firefighter. He had been at the hospital for less than a year and was actively trying to get hired as a firefighter. Many of the nurses liked working with Paul, likely due to his boyish good looks and muscular physique. He was the epitome of a high school quarterback. Jena didn't know him well, but despite his age, he seemed skilled enough.

They brought the gurney into the room and began to take off the cardiac leads and oxygen probe. Jena smiled at Jonathon as she moved to the parents, introducing herself.

"Hello, I'm Jena and I'll be taking care of your son. If you don't mind would you please have a seat over here," she said, pointing to the chair-bed against the wall, "while we get Mason settled in and transferred from the ER equipment to ours. Jonathon will give me a report and Dr. Espinoza will be in shortly to introduce herself and talk with you about his care." She smiled reassuringly. "We are going to take good care of your son."

The mother's eyes were red and swollen. She had clearly been crying. The father's face was tense, firm, focused, like a man pushing through the last hundred yards of a marathon. Jena had seen it before, the gambit of emotions that people feel. In this case, the mother was despondent, crushed by her son's likely diagnosis. The father had pushed all pessimism away and was focused on what they could do to heal his son. This man was a fixer, someone who was used to mending broken things.

The father reached out and shook Jena's hand. "I'm Scott and this is my wife Liv." He looked at his son and back to the chair behind him.

"Go ahead, have a seat. Once I get him settled in, we can talk more." Scott nodded and gently pulled his wife to the chair against the wall while Jena turned to address Jonathan. "Hi Jonathan. What's the report?"

Paul, the tech, continued to remove the ER's leads while Jonathan looked up at Jena. "This little guy is Mason and he is seven years old. He was brought into the ER late last night as the parents noticed he had not been feeling well for several days. He was fatigued and had flu-like symptoms. He was very pale and was having a hard time eating without vomiting. He was lethargic, so tired that he could barely get out of bed. When these symptoms didn't improve, they brought him to the ER.

Jena nodded. They were typical signs of cancer. "And the labs?"

Jonathon listed off the numbers. "His white count was 3, red count was 2.5, his platelets 120, hematocrit 28, and hemoglobin 8."

Jena pursed her lips. They were not good numbers and definitely synonymous with leukemia. "Okay, thanks."

He reached out and subtly touched her hand. "It's good to see you back at work," he whispered. He knew better than to say anything else, so he simply squeezed her hand and let go. She appreciated the kind gesture.

"Thanks."

Jena looked at Mason. He was pale white and awake, but his eyelids were heavy with fatigue. "Hi, Mason. I'm nurse Jena and I'm going to be taking care of you today. I'm going to hook my equipment up to you but there is nothing to worry about, okay?"

Mason had a flop of unruly blond hair. His eyes were red and puffy. "Will anything hurt?" he whispered softly.

"Nope," she answered as she attached the cardiac leads to the monitor. She gently touched his arm. "I'm going to take real good care of you, kiddo. You only have one job," she said, smiling, "and that's to rest."

Once everything was hooked up, Mason was already asleep and Jena turned to his parents. She pulled up a chair and sat next to them. She tried to look reassuring. "I'm so sorry you are going through this but I want you to know that I'm going to take good care of Mason. You guys are in good hands and we are going to do everything we can for your son. What's going to happen next is that Dr. Espinoza will come in soon to introduce herself to you and get you started on Mason's care. You'll really like her. She is extremely knowledgeable and will be a good fit for this diagnosis. In the meantime I'd like to ask you some admit questions. Would that be okay?"

"Yes, that would be fine," Scott said, his voice strained as he looked at his son's bed.

Jena smiled and stood next to the computer near the bed. She was just getting ready to get started when Dr. Espinoza entered. She went directly to the parents and sat in the chair that Jena had just left.

"Mr. Weller, Mrs. Weller, my name is Doctor Espinoza. I'm am so sorry your family is going through this. Being admitted into the PICU can be a scary experience and we will do our absolute best to ease your transition. I want you to know that I am a straight shooter and I will always tell you what I think, no matter how difficult it may be to hear. I hope you're okay with that."

Scott wiped a tear from his eye as Liv squeezed his hand tighter. Jena looked at them and could tell that the father was close to losing control. His wife sensed it as well and took over. "I'm Liv and this is Scott. So," she said softly, "does he have cancer?"

Dr. Espinoza's eyes narrowed as her expression grew serious. "Based on the labs, it is very likely, although we'll know for sure in a few hours."

"How will you know?" Scott managed to say.

"Oncology will come up and take a bone marrow biopsy. We'll know more when we get the results back on the biopsy. But we'd like to start him on treatment right away."

"Will it hurt our boy?"

"No, we will sedate Mason for the procedure. We need to get blood into him to help with his low blood counts. That's our first priority. Once we do that, the oncology team will come up, we'll sedate Mason, and they'll perform the biopsy while I get a central line in." Dr. Espinoza looked over at Jena who was still standing at the computer. "Jena here is one of our best nurses. She will guide you through the process. But if you have any questions please don't hesitate to ask. We are a team here, and we work together in order to give the best patient care. Do you have any questions so far?"

"How long will he be sedated?" Scott asked, the last word coming out garbled as he fought to maintain control. But the dam had broken and his emotions exploded out of him, deep sobs racking his body. Liv wrapped her arm around him as he sobbed into his hands.

They had all seen this happen many times in their careers but it never got easier. It was not uncommon for the fathers to start off stoic, maintaining emotional control to try and project a sense that everything was going to be okay. But when that control finally slipped through their fingers, it often resulted in a powerful expression of emotion. It was always so difficult to watch. Jena pushed the knot in her throat down and focused on Dr. Espinoza, glancing over at Mason to make sure he was still asleep.

Dr. Espinoza leaned forward in her chair and softly touched his knee. "He'll likely be sedated for around an hour. I know this is extremely difficult, and I wish I could say something to make the pain go away. But we are here for you." Then she stood. "We'll get to work in a few hours. But for now, be with your son." Dr. Espinoza stood from the chair and left the room.

Jena sat back in the chair. Scott was still crying as Liv held him, tears flowing freely down her cheeks.

"I didn't think I had any tears left," she said.

"I like to think of tears as pain leaving our body," Jena said. "Don't try to fight them, let them come, it will be better for you."

"We were going to go camping this weekend," Scott interjected, "and now, he might have cancer. He's only seven. This isn't fair. This was the trip where I wanted to teach him to fish," he said as he struggled to fight back the tears.

Scott's remark hit her hard and she struggled to control the sudden wave of emotions that came over her. She blinked as images of Chris showing their unborn son how to fish flashed through her mind. They were never able to have children and despite their decision to stop trying, the pain of that loss was always there, ready to rise to the surface. It was not uncommon for her to visualize what their son or daughter would've looked like and to imagine Chris being the wonderful father she knew he would be. Losing Chris was incredibly difficult, but knowing that she had no piece of him left, hit home harder than she had expected. If they had been able to have a baby, perhaps she could see Chris's eyes in their son, or his wide charismatic smile in their daughter. But it was not meant to be, and now he was dead. She would never see those special nuances again, whether from him or the child they were not able to conceive. She would try to hold onto them in her mind, but she knew that over time, even those images would diminish like ripples in a pond. It was her greatest fear that she would forget the sound of his voice and the smell of his skin. And now, seeing this father's emotion as he pondered the seriousness of his son's illness...watching the pain in his eyes as he realized he might never teach his son to fish, nearly broke through the substantial wall she had erected over a twenty-year pediatric career of controlling her emotions.

To be a successful PICU nurse you had to learn to compartmentalize your emotions. If you could not, then you would burn out from the difficult experiences you endured. Her lower lip quivered, but like a blink it was gone, her trained will pushing the knot down. Regaining control, she dissipated the images of Chris and refocused her attention on her patient.

She leaned in closer to them. "I will help you both through this. It's going to be hard, but we all need to be here for Mason. We can continue with the admit questions later. Why don't you take some time with your son and I'll be back in twenty minutes. Would that be okay?"

Liv nodded and continued to hold onto her husband. Jena stood up and left the room, quickly reaching up to wipe the tear away that had pooled in the corner of her eye. She blinked and cleared her head, rebuilding the mental wall that had protected her from the pain of her job for as long as she could remember. It was not uncommon for the wall to come crumbling down at home, or in the car on the ride home, but she never let it crack at work. She owed it to her patients to be strong. But there were more cracks this time, her solid wall fractured with Chris's death. She pushed the thought away, glancing back at Mason one more time before leaving the room. The little boy would be her strength.

* * *

Jena sat in her car and gave herself permission to let the tears finally flow. She had done a miraculous job keeping the wall up at work, even when Scott and Liv received the news that their son had leukemia. She had kept it intact when Mason learned he had cancer and that he wouldn't be able to go fishing this weekend. But now, alone in her car, she let the emotions break through the dam. She missed her husband...she hurt for Scott and Liv...she hurt for Mason who had a long road of chemotherapy and likely radiation before him. He might survive, and then again, he might not. She cried as she thought of the prospect of her, or another nurse, washing Mason's cold body, putting him in a shroud to take to the morgue. She cried as she thought of his parents and family mourning for him, just as she mourned for her husband. Most people had no idea of the things

26

PICU nurses had to do. For many, it would be enough to emotionally crush them. Jena had dealt with this pain in many ways...crying in cars, seeing a counselor most of her career, and venting to her nurse friends. But even with those outlets, the grief would sometimes manifest itself as it found cracks in her armor. Even Chris had had a difficult time in helping her through her ups and downs as a pediatric critical care nurse. He did his best, being there when he thought she needed it. But in the end, he simply couldn't understand what she was going through. He was quite good at bringing energy and joy to any situation, and he was a good empathetic listener, at least until she was done talking. Then his immediate response had generally been to try and fix the problem; after all, he was good at that. Chris fixed stuff. But most of the issues she faced at work were not fixable. Sometimes she just needed a supportive ear. But now, as she cried in her car, she would do anything for his warm hug and his desire to bring her comfort by solving her problem.

This was not the first time she had lost control in her car. Finally, when she had cried herself out, she wiped the corners of her eyes with her tissues, took a few deep breaths, and started her car.

Once under control, Jena called Rob on the way home from work as she had promised. Whether she was ready to talk to Rob about Chris's will was still undecided, but she knew it had to be done. Besides, Rob's practice was in Portland, only a few hours away. She knew he would have to plan a weekend to meet with her and she felt guilty for stringing him along the last few weeks.

Rob picked up on the second ring. "Jena, hi."

Jena was speaking through the Bluetooth in her Honda Accord. "Hi Rob, I'm driving home from work. Can you hear me okay?"

"I can. I'm glad you called."

"I'm sorry it's taken me so long to call you back," Jena tried to explain before Rob cut her off.

"Jena, listen, it's okay. I completely understand. But we do need to meet. I have a lot to discuss with you."

"Yeah, I figured. I'm off this weekend but I feel bad–"

"I'll be there tomorrow," Rob interrupted. "And don't feel bad. Chris entrusted me with a lot of information for you, and I'm more than happy to do it. Plus, it will be good to see you. How does tomorrow, at your house, around noon work?"

"That would be great...thank you so much, Rob, for everything."

"Of course. I'll see you tomorrow." And Rob hung up the phone.

Jena clicked the Bluetooth off and let out a deep sigh. She had had a tough day at work, but she had a strange feeling that tomorrow was going to be worse. She was dreading going home to a quiet lonely home, but then remembered that Brook, her best friend, was meeting her. Since Chris's death it was a rare night that her friend did not spend with her, making sure she was not alone. As she thought of her friend's car in the driveway, she noticed her shoulders relax some. Her mind then drifted to Mason's mother, remembering the slight drop to her shoulders as she calmed under Jena's comforting words. If she could provide just a moment of peace for a mom going through the worst experience in her life, all the while suffering herself, then perhaps she could still perform her job at the level she had before Chris's death. Just for a moment she felt better knowing she was helping someone else slog through the mire of pain.

* * *

Jena woke the next day after a fitful sleep. It was late, nearly ten, the sunlight breaking through the crack in her curtains, the beam of light shining across her bed. Looking over at Chris's spot on the bed, a deep sadness filled her, as it had every day since his death. There was no one lying beside her, Chris's pillow plumped and lacking the disheveled 'slept on' look. The emptiness of her bed reflected the emptiness in her heart. She rolled on to her side and stared at the empty side of the bed, the light from the curtains painting his pillow a golden yellow. A gentle smile briefly cracked her melancholy, remembering how he had always complained that the light shone right in his eyes. Then she remembered she would never hear those complaints again, or smell him near her, his body a comforting scent that made her feel safe. A lone tear rolled down her cheek. She had no idea how she was supposed to move on. Everything she saw, did, heard, reminded her of Chris, reminded her of what she would never experience again. How was she supposed to continue to work and help parents going through the pain of injured and dying children when she couldn't even compartmentalize her own suffering? The events at work yesterday highlighted this struggle. She didn't know what she was supposed to do.

Letting out a deep breath, she wiped the tear away and pulled herself out of bed. Going through her normal morning routine, she brushed her teeth, showered, and put on leggings and a matching workout top. Rob was going to arrive soon and she knew it would be a difficult meeting. A good long run afterwards would help settle her soul, at least she hoped it would.

Brook had slept in the guest room and was long gone, having to go to work early. They had drunk several glasses of wine, a jammy Zinfandel from the Sonoma area. Jena was feeling a little groggy, and although she was grateful for Brook's company, she felt bad that she was likely going to work a bit foggy herself.

By the time she had her morning coffee and had eaten a bowl of oatmeal with strawberries, the doorbell rang. Putting the dishes in the sink she walked through her living room and opened the door. Rob was looking at her with a soft smile. He was tall, with short brown hair parted on the side, silver wire framed glasses giving him the look of a GQ model advertising Prada glasses. Rob had always been Chris's most handsome friend. He didn't say a word. He stepped in and embraced her with a strong hug. Holding her for a few moments he stepped back, his eyes rimmed with moisture.

"It is good to see you," he said.

"Thanks...you too." Seeing him stand there with red rimmed eyes reminded Jena that she was not the only one suffering. Chris had had a profound effect on everyone he had met, and his loss had left a significant hole in the lives of those he was closest to. And Rob was his best friend, despite the fact that he was not much of a fly-fisherman. Their friendship went much further back; growing up in Gig Harbor they started first grade together. Many years of playing sports and chasing girls together had formed a strong bond between them. They were close after high school as well, even after Rob had moved to Portland to start his law firm. "Come in." Jena stepped aside and Rob entered. He was carrying a brief case and he set it on the dining room table adjacent to the living room as Jena went into the kitchen. "Can I get you some coffee?"

"Sure, you know how I like it." It wasn't a question. In fact how he took his coffee was something of a joke between him and Chris. Chris had drunk his coffee black and had often teased Rob that his was more like a dessert.

Jena looked back and smiled. "Four sugars and heavy cream, I know."

Rob smiled as he opened his briefcase and took out his computer, along with several folders. Plugging in his computer he powered it up and logged on.

A minute later Jena came in and set the coffee on the table next to him.

Rob looked up. "Thanks. Why don't you have a seat?"

Jena nodded and sat next to Rob. There was a knot in her throat as anxiety about the meeting began to rise to the surface. She didn't know what to say so she opted to say nothing as she sipped her own coffee.

Rob took a deep breath, removed his glasses, and wiped his eyes. Then, putting his glasses back on, he looked at her poignantly. "Okay, I know you have been avoiding this. The very nature of a will is always extremely difficult. It's the finality of it that I believe hurts the most. I have prepared hundreds of wills, but now, since this loss of life is so close to me, I think I finally understand how my clients have felt." Again, he let out a deep breath to calm himself.

Jena was touched by Rob's sentiment and her eyes welled with fresh tears in response, but she didn't bother to wipe them as she knew more were to come. The knot in her throat now felt like a fist sized rock, her heart pounding as she tried to swallow more coffee. She was nervous, sad, scared, all at the same time. Chris was dead and Rob's presence re-emphasized this immutable fact.

"Jena, I normally have a system for this type of thing, but this is uniquely personal and it's leaving me at a loss as how to start."

Jena reached over and put her hand on his. "Rob, it's okay," she struggled to say. "Just do it like you normally would."

Rob gulped, releasing an anxious smile. "I'll try, but this is unlike any will I've ever prepared." He let out a deep breath. "Okay, let's start with the finances. Jena, if you don't want to, you will never have to work again. Were you aware of Chris's financial practices?"

Jena knew that Chris had owned a successful graphic arts business, building websites, doing work for advertising agencies, as well as any digital artwork that came his way. He worked alone and loved it that way. Running his own business allowed him to travel and fish. He could work while on the road if necessary, which he often did at night when they had traveled to various locations to fish and camp. She knew he had done well, making as much or more than she made as an RN. She also knew that he loved to dabble in penny stocks and other stock market commodities. She was never interested in finances and had left all that up to him.

"Chris did all the finances," she answered. "I knew we did well."

Rob smiled. "Jena, you likely only saw your personal and joint accounts. But Chris didn't just do well in the stock market, he did fantastically well investing your money in various companies over the last fifteen years." Rob paused and looked at his computer. "Your home is paid off, and besides what you now have in your checking and savings," Rob continued, checking his computer again, "you have over three million dollars invested in various stocks. To be exact, you have three million three hundred and forty-five dollars in stock assets."

Jena sat back in her chair. "Are you serious?" She knew that Chris had paid off their house, but had no idea how much money he had made in the stock market. Every time he had brought up his dabbling in stocks, he had done it as if it were a joke, something fun he did on the side. She typically laughed it off and ignored his comments, not interested in the buying and selling of stocks from some weird company she had never heard of.

"I am. You are set for life. We can go over all the details of the money later. Did you know about the trusts that Rob set up for your niece and nephew?"

31

"I did," Jena said, still reeling from the amount of money she now had. Chris had always been good with money but she had had no idea how successful he had actually been.

"Well, ten years ago Chris opened two trust accounts with your bank, adding money into those accounts every month since. They are to be given to your niece, Jessica, and nephew, Shane, when they turn eighteen for the express purpose of college. Were you aware of this?"

"Yes, since we were not able to have children," Jena added, the infertility monster causing her to pause before she could finish her sentence.

This time it was Rob who reached over and touched her hand. He didn't say anything, knowing full well their struggles with infertility. There was nothing to say other than to give her comfort.

Jena swallowed and continued. "We had agreed to set up the accounts for his sister's two children."

Rob nodded and removed his hand. "Each of those accounts is now worth one hundred thousand dollars."

Jena's eyes widened at that. "I had no idea he was investing that much. That is amazing."

"Yes, that is quite a gift for them. Other than that, all of Chris's assets and belongings are now bequeathed to you. Do you have any questions so far?"

Jena shook her head.

"Now, this is the hard part and I'm not sure how to do this, so I'm just going to start from the beginning. Is that okay?"

Jena nodded.

"Okay, when Chris received his diagnosis and we all found out that his cancer was likely terminal, he set something quite extensive in motion...for you. He knew that his death would be difficult on you, to say the least, and he has..." Rob paused, struggling with the right words as he looked at his computer screen, "created a plan to help you deal with his death, and hopefully learn to be happy and love again." Rob looked at Jena. "Those were his words exactly."

"Ummm, okay," Jena said, not sure where Rob was going.

Rob took another breath. "Jena, are you aware that Chris had created a bucket list of places he wanted to fish before he died?"

"He had talked about places he wanted to fish all the time. But I never saw an actual list."

"Well, he created one..." Rob paused again, "and he wants you to finish it."

He sat back in his chair as if he had been holding onto some burden, and now, as he said the words, it had been lifted. He simply looked at her, his eyes unreadable.

Jena tilted her head in confusion. "I don't understand."

Now that Rob had finally been able to share Chris's most important wish for his wife, his words flowed freely. Leaning forward, Rob looked intently at Jena. "Chris wants you to finish his bucket list. He wants you to travel to the places he never had time to visit, and fish them, spreading his ashes at each location along the way."

Jena took a sharp breath, her hand coming to her mouth as tears again welled in her eyes. She was moved, sad, scared, and angry all at the same time, the gambit of emotions hitting her like a freight train. She didn't say anything for a while, and neither did Rob. He was clearly letting her process the information.

Her first reaction was defiance. "What? How can I do that? I don't even fish. I have a job," she blurted. Then it turned to anger. "How can he ask this of me? I can't do this." Then it morphed into bewilderment. "How many places are there? What exactly does he want me to do?" And then to sadness. "He wants me to sprinkle his ashes? Rob, I don't know...this is so—"

"Crazy!?" Rob interjected.

She stopped her rampage, tears streaking her cheeks. "Yes."

"I know it is, but he was adamant." Rob took another deep breath. "Jena, he knew this would be hard for you, so he has made videos on thumb drives to be played at various intervals throughout this process." He reached into his briefcase, pulled out a Tupperware container, and opened the lid to reveal seven thumb drives, each marked with a number. He picked one out that was labeled number one. "As per his instructions, I'm supposed to play this recording for you now."

Jena let out a cry as her hand came to her mouth, fresh tears rolling down her cheeks. "I don't know if I can watch them."

"I know it's hard, but I'm here with you. We'll do it together."

"You haven't seen them?"

Rob shook his head. "No. He wanted me to watch this one with you. But the rest are for you and you alone."

Jena looked away, took a deep breath, and wiped her eyes with trembling hands. After a few moments she had regained enough control to look at Rob. "Okay, let's watch it."

He nodded and placed the thumb drive into the USB port on his computer. A few clicks later he looked up at her. "You ready?"

"I think so."

He turned the computer to face her and adjusted his chair so he was next to her. He reached out and held her hand while his other hand went to the mouse. The screen was black when he looked at her, gripping her hand tighter. She nodded and he clicked the mouse.

The screen flashed and Chris was suddenly there, looking back at them. At this time in his diagnosis he had just started chemotherapy. His once long and wavy hair was gone, his tan skin now pale like a baby's. But no matter what toxins they were pumping into his body, they could not destroy his luminous smile. Jena could tell he was in his office.

"Hi, my love," he said with a smile. "If you are seeing this video then this fucking cancer has kicked my ass. I know you are hurting and that you don't know what to do with yourself. I know this because that's how I would feel if it I were sitting in your position. By now, Rob should've explained to you what I want you to do. I know it seems crazy. But I've thought a lot about this. Everything I'm going to ask you to do is not for me, it's for you. After all, I'm fucking dead, so I'm either in Heaven being berated by God who is pissed I never believed in him, or I'm energy flowing through the universe, or I'm simply nothing. Who the fuck knows? All I know is that I'm not there with you, and that my absence is causing you pain, and that is something I cannot tolerate. Jena, I want you to be happy. I want you to love again. I want you to live your life to its fullest." Chris paused as he lifted a glass of scotch, a few ice cubes jingling. He smiled as he toasted the camera, taking a sip. "I probably shouldn't be drinking this,

34

*but fuck it, if I don't have much time, I might as well drink the good
stuff. Anyway, I want you to go on a learning quest, an adventure that
will help you remember me, and at the same time let me go. It will be
a magnificent journey. Rob has already told you that you don't need to
work if you don't want to. His firm will manage the house while you
are gone."* Chris smiled again as he took another sip of scotch. *"Now,
I have some requirements that you must do during this trip, and you're
not going to like some of them. You ready?"* he asked, picking up a
piece of paper and looking back at the camera. *"One, you have to
learn to fly fish. Now, I know you've tried it before and got frustrated.
But what did I always say to you?"* Chris stopped and looked
poignantly into the camera.

Rob looked at Jena, his knowing eyes telling her to repeat the
words.

Jena looked at the image of Chris and recited the words.
"Once you get it, you'll get it."

*Two heartbeats later Chris nodded his head, as if he actually
heard her. "Yup, that's it. Once you get it, you'll get it. In good time
you will know what that means. Now, I know you can do it. You are
the most incredible person I have ever met. You heal and help
families through their most horrible tragedies. You deal with death and
dying on a level that simply amazes me. You teach people how to care
and love on a level that I have never experienced. If you can do all
that, you can fly fish. Two, you must fish at every location on the list
that Rob provides you. Each spot is a location that I wanted to visit but
was not able to because cancer kicked me in the balls."* Chris laughed.
*"Well technically, it kicked my pancreas. Anyway, the locations are all
over the world and they make up the dreams of any addicted fly fisher
person. Each journey will be extensive, exciting, trying, wonderful, and
frustrating, but so much more. Three, you must drink a scotch and
smoke a cigar at each location after you've caught a trophy fish. Now, I
know you don't like scotch or cigars, but this you are doing for me. I
want you to imagine I am there with you, at that moment, enjoying
these vices as I revel in the excitement of the catch. It is an experience*

that I want you to hold on to. It is something that will forever connect you to me. Four, you are to find a spot or task at each location that you know I would love, but likely, you would not. It could be an old bar, a sportsman's hotel, a fly shop, anything. When you are there, I want you to imagine what I would do and say. Five, I want you to meet one interesting person at each location. And I want you to tell them the story of what you are doing and why. Six, you are to learn one major life lesson at each location. Keep a journal of all this. Write it down so that you can process it later and better accept all that's happened. And lastly, you are to sprinkle my ashes at every location. Now, I know that this all seems so crazy. But you know that the impossible, the crazy, they are just walls built by others to slow their own progress. We O'Malley's climb those walls. I have other video messages for you. You need to watch them in order as you travel from one location to another." Chris stopped and leaned closer to the camera, a mischievous look on his face. *"And don't you try to watch them early."*

Chris laughed and Jena cried softly, remembering the sound and cadence of his voice which again evoked so many wonderful memories. Rob squeezed her hand again, wiping the tears away from his eyes.

"Well, honey, I love you, more than you know. The hardest thing about me dying is knowing I won't be able to see you again, to hold you, to laugh with you, to take care of you. You need to do this, and although I can say you need to do this for me, the reality is, you need to do this for you. I want you to be able to process my death by embracing the pastime that I loved almost as much as you. I know it sounds weird, but trust me, once you get it, you will get it." Chris lifted his scotch glass, winked, and drained it. *"I love you."* Then he reached over and clicked the mouse, and the screen went black again.

Jena didn't say anything. The room was quiet except for her gentle sobs. Rob let go of her hand and reached his arm around her, hugging her close as they cried together.

A Year of a Thousand Casts

* * *

"You have to be fucking kidding me!?" Brook said as she leaned back in the bar stool. While Brook was at work, Jena had called her hoping they could meet for drinks after she got off. After the reading of the will, Jena had a lot to process and she desperately needed to talk to her best friend. They had met at The Bachram, the Irish bar that hosted Chris's memorial service. Jena was unsure if she wanted to go back so soon, but then felt that perhaps it was appropriate to do so considering the topic of conversation. Backram was an Irish word that meant boisterous or rambunctious behavior, which seemed fitting for the bar. They had loved the place for many years and learned that it was aptly named, having partaken in some wild drinking nights.

Jena took a sip of her gin and tonic and shook her head. It had taken her a few minutes to explain the entire situation to Brook, and to her surprise, Brook did not interrupt once. "No, I'm not kidding, he wants me to travel the world and fish the locations he never got to fish."

Brook let out a breath and brushed her shoulder length dark brown hair over her ears. Jena had known Brook for nearly twenty years, having worked together when they first started their careers. They had become friends immediately. Jena loved Brook's crass humor and energy and Brook was drawn to Jena's emotional strength. Brook always joked that she was more guy-like than most guys and she needed Jena's emotional fortitude to remind her she had a vagina. Brook had been married for ten years but got a divorce after her husband had cheated on her. It had been a rough split and Brook swore she would never give her heart to a man again. Brook was now swiping right and dating more guys than Jena could keep track of. She joked that she should open a curbside hot dog stand as she was now an expert on wieners. Brook was short, like a gymnast, with a strong cross-fit build. Her brown hair had streaks of blond and red, the color accentuating her bright green eyes. She had a strong Greek heritage giving her an olive complexion and a long classic nose. She hated her nose, but Jena thought it gave her a unique look. Besides, guys never noticed her nose, her large breasts capturing their attention every time.

"I need to pee and process this information," Brook said as she stood from the bar. They were sitting at the long bar facing a well-stocked wall of liquor, most of the shelves lined with whiskey, bourbons, and scotches, the main reason why Chris had loved the place so much. Jena nodded, reaching for her drink as Brook walked off.

Jena sipped her cocktail and wistfully ran her hand over the wood bar, the mahogany glistening from the thick layer of resin. Her hand felt every scratch as it stopped on the dovetail joint. Tears welled in her eyes as she remembered how Chris had always appreciated the craftmanship of the bar. She could hear his voice explaining what a dovetail joint was, the excitement in his voice over such a trivial thing always bringing a smile to her face. She wiped the tear from the corner of her eye before it spilled down her cheek, looking elsewhere, hoping to distract herself from the pain in her heart. But everywhere she looked reminded her of him...the bottle of Talisker Scotch on the high shelf, the stage where he attempted to sing *You Lost that Loving Feeling*, from the movie *Top Gun* on open mic night. His rendition was not great, but she could still remember the feeling she had as she watched him perform, a wide smile on his face, and not a care in the world. She had always envied his confidence.

Brook plopped down in the seat next to her, pulling Jena from her reverie. Brook smiled and looked at Jack, the bald-headed bartender who was part owner of the place. "Jack, two Irish car bombs." Jack looked up from mixing a jack and coke and nodded as Brook looked back at her friend. "What are you going to do?"

"I don't know—"

"The hell you don't! That was a rhetorical question. Of course you are going to do it," Brook said adamantly as she slammed down the rest of her whiskey sour.

"Brook...it's not that easy. I have a job, a house, respon—"

"Don't you fucking say it," Brook argued. "Your responsibility is to honor your late husband's dying wish, and to get out and have some fun...to have some new experiences!"

Jena sighed. "I know," she said resignedly, not the least bit hurt by her words. Jena, long ago, had gotten used to Brook's harsh

38

demeanor. She actually appreciated it. Brook always said what she thought, whether you wanted to hear it or not. "It's just so much."

"Hell yes, it is. It's crazy, it's fantastic, it's a lot...but it's so Chris," Brook added. "It will be good for you. You need something...something to guide you right now. You can't just go back to your normal world and expect things to be the same."

"So you think I should quit my job and just take off?"

"How much money again do you have?"

"Over three million dollars, not including my retirement." Brook whistled. "Fuck yes! Quit. You've done your part and more. It's time to take care of yourself."

Just then Jack set three Irish Car Bombs on the bar. Jack was in his late sixties, but was handsome in a Clint Eastwood kind of way. He had known Chris for many years and was proud to have opened the bar for his wake. He had shut down the bar for the night at no cost. That was the kind of loyalty that Chris had earned in life.

"On the house," he said, pushing the shots and half-filled glass of Guinness closer to them, the third shot near him. "And, if you care about my opinion," he added, "you should do it."

Clearly Jack had been listening in on their conversation.

"See," Brook said, grabbing the shot glass. "He's not just rugged good looks. He has some common sense." Brook held up her shot glass and looked at Jena, her eyebrows lifted in a questioning expression. "Well?"

Jena reached for her glass and paused in thought as she held it before her. Deep down she had known all along that she was going to do it. She had to. She couldn't not do Chris's last wish. It was just the thought of it all was so overwhelming. She had to learn to fish. She was going to have to travel all over the world by herself. It would be physically and emotionally demanding. But perhaps Chris was right. Maybe it would help her heal. Then she looked at her friend. "You know I have to do it. I just wanted your confirmation," she added with a knowing smile, lifting the shot higher.

"Fuck yeah!" Brook explained. "To new adventures!"

Jack lifted his own shot. "To healing!"

Jena's eyes glistened with emotion at Jack's words. He was rough around the edges but Jena had learned over the years that he had a soft spot. She clinked her glass to theirs. "To Chris!"

They all dropped their shots in the glass of Guinness and slammed it back.

Chapter 2

"Hello, Dear, it's so good to see you." Chris laughed at his joke. "Come on, you know that is funny." He replaced his smile with a subtle grin. "Well, if you are listening to this, then you have decided to take on the adventure. I knew you would. But then again, what choice did you have?" Chris said, laughing again. "I mean who would not complete a dead man's last wish?"

Jena leaned back in the leather couch, shaking her head at his crass humor, a full glass of Caymus Cabernet in her hand. It was an expensive bottle but it seemed appropriate for such a serious event. After she had decided what she was going to do, she had called Rob. He had told her that thumb drive number two was supposed to explain her next steps. So, the next day, she had cracked open a good bottle of wine, sat in front of the computer, and inserted the thumb drive in the USB slot. Anxiety of what was to come filled her heart as she listened to her late husband.

"First things first, my love," he began. "You need to learn to fly fish. In order for you to truly understand the sport, which will really help you heal, you need to be able to fish. I know that sounds weird, but I believe it to be true, and I'll do my best to explain why. But remember, in the end, I can't explain the connection between fly fishing and personal growth...it's something you have to experience. All I can do is try and explain what the sport has done for me. As you know, the five steps of grief and healing are denial, anger, bargaining, depression, and acceptance. Now, you are likely in the shock and denial steps, with the ever-looming head of depression breaking through the muck to pull you down." Chris smiled, raising his eyebrows. "Pretty poetic don't you think?"

Jena let out a laugh and a cry at the same time, tears rolling down her cheeks. Chris had always been so good with words.

"I just believe that learning to fish will help guide you through the healing process, and every step of your adventure will get you closer to the seemingly distant goal of acceptance. There are many things about fly fishing that drew me to the sport. The serenity of the surroundings, the hunt for that elusive fish, the art of casting and fly tying, and the reward of catching a fish as a by-product of hard work, research, practice, and tenacity. All of those things brought me a zen experience that is hard to explain. I dream of the surface 'take' as a winter steelhead explodes from the water to grab a skated fly that I tied and designed myself. In my mind's eye I can see the strike indicator drop below the surface, the summer Methow sun hot on my bare skin as a twenty-inch cutthroat grabs my stonefly nymph. I can feel the lift of my rod tip and the weight of the fish on the end, the strong head shakes sending reverberations through the rod and into my hands." Chris closed his eyes for a moment and sighed, remembering the feeling. After a few heartbeats he opened them again and smiled. *"I'll fish a hole for hours with no luck just because it looks 'fishy'. Every time I see fishable water, I look at it from a fisherman's perspective. I know you know many of these things as I'm sure you grew tired of me talking about them. But now I want you to try and grasp the feelings I experienced. I want you to hold onto them and feel what I felt. In so doing, I think it will help you heal and adjust to my absence while allowing you to hold onto memories of me as you move forward in your life."*

"I doubt that," Jena mumbled, taking a large swallow of wine.

As if he had heard her, Chris said, *"Now, I know you find that unlikely. But I need you to buy in to this experience for it to work."* He paused as he reached off camera and lifted a wine glass. *"Now, if I know you, you are holding a lovely glass of wine as I speak. So I thought I'd join you."* Chris sipped from his glass.

Jena wept again, the thought of never drinking a great bottle of wine with him overwhelming her. Wine was a big part of their lives together. They tasted wine whenever they could and Chris got so into it that he started making wine as a hobby. He took another long drink, smiling as he savored the dark red wine, and began again. It was all she could do to wrestle the sobs down so she could hear him.

"So here is the plan. I have a guy, a friend named Hans who lives on the northern section of the Skagit River. He owns a small convenience store there but the reality is he just fishes most of the day, well, every day. I want you to go and see him. I want you to ask him to teach you to fly fish. He has a small room above his store that he rents out to fisherman. I'm sure he will let you stay there indefinitely. Now, just so you know, he is a bit rough around the edges. He doesn't like most people, and he's a bit crotchety towards even the ones he does like. When you get there, he may give you a hard time. Just roll with it and persevere. Rob has the address and Sten will help you pack the right gear. One other thing. I want you to save some of my ashes and return to the Skagit River at the end of your trip. I thought it would be nostalgic for you, and me I guess, to spread my ashes in the very river where your journey started. Now, I know you have a lot of questions, but unfortunately I am unavailable to answer them." Chris laughed and lifted his glass, slowly savoring the wine. When he was done, he gave her his mischievous smile. *"I'm sorry I'm making light of this, but Phyllis Diller once said, A smile is a curve that sets everything straight. I think it's quite fitting. Oh, I almost forgot. I need you to stop the video right here. I have a small continuation that I want you to play for Hans when he decides to help you, which I'm betting that he will. I know you can be convincing, so make sure you convince him. So, stop it here. It's not long, but make sure you don't try and get a sneak peek. Until next time, my love,"* he said, lifting his wine glass. He took another big sip and smiled. *"I love you. And good luck!"* He winked at her. *"Stop the video...NOW."*

Jena was crying softly as she cradled her wine glass near her chest. Reaching up, she stopped the video, although there was a strong urge to let it continue as Chris sat there smiling, waiting calmly for her to do as he requested. She was sure if she waited another ten seconds, that he would start whatever message he had made for Hans. It was difficult, but she honored his request.

She had barely processed most of what Chris had said, her mind gleaning fragments from him that she would never see again; his soft eyes, bright smile, and infectious laugh. After a few moments to gather herself, she drained her wine glass and set it on the table, leaning back into the soft leather couch. She let out a deep sigh and thought about what he had said. She was not prepared for what he had proposed. The idea of picking up and moving to some small shithole above a convenience store, all the while trying to convince some grumpy man to teach her to fish, just didn't sound all that appealing. There were so many things to do. What was she going to do about work? Rob had said that his firm would take care of the house while she was gone, but just the idea of asking him to do that was so crazy.

She rubbed her face with both hands in frustration. "What have you gotten me into?" she mumbled. Then she remembered one of the phrases that Chris's friend had said at his wake. He had yelled out, *Oh, it's on!* It was something that Chris had said quite often, and she smiled, hearing his voice echo the words in her mind. And for some reason, it made her feel better about the prospect of starting this crazy adventure.

Two days later Jena had an appointment with human resources at the hospital. She knew Tamara, the HR representative she was meeting, and was confident that she would do whatever she could to help Jena with her leave of absence. And as it turned out, the meeting went better than expected. Tamara had told her that she could take a year leave of absence and would be guaranteed a job at the PICU on her return. The only drawback was that she could not guarantee her same shift. But Jena had been prepared for that and left Tamara's office feeling much better about leaving.

On her way out of the hospital she stopped in the cafeteria to get an espresso. The cafeteria food was mediocre at best and Jena generally avoided it. But there was a small espresso stand that made a good latte. They used Stump Town coffee, one of Jena's favorites. The cafeteria was a large open space, with three different kitchens along the far edge, the rest of the room filled with long rows of tables and blue and gray plastic chairs. The entire area was blanketed in a blue and gray carpet to match the chairs. There was an unattended salad bar as well as a grab and go station. They also had an attended kitchen that served various meals depending on the time of day. Jena was heading to the espresso bar located at the far end of the room. The room was generally quite busy, and today was no different. There were lots of operating room personnel about, their turquoise scrubs and booties easily identifying them. There were visitors about as well, some eating in small groups, likely family members visiting someone. Chatter filled the space as people talked as they ate their food. As usual, Jena smelled the odor of fried oil and potatoes. It always seemed to smell like a fast food joint, which was strange because as far as she knew the cafeteria had no fryer.

"Jena!"

Jena stopped and saw Theresa, Mason's mother, the young boy recently diagnosed with leukemia, walk towards her from a nearby table. "Oh, hi," Jena said. She refrained from saying *how are you*, as she already knew the answer to that question. "Getting a bite to eat?"

Theresa looked around; her face scrunched up in what can only be described as disgust. "Yeah, but it's not that great."

Jena smiled. "No, it's not. If I can give you some advice, eat from the grab and go area or the salad bar. The sandwiches aren't too bad and it's hard to mess up a salad."

"Oh, okay, good to know. When are you working next? We really enjoyed having you as our nurse the other day. Mason liked you as well. He keeps asking for nurse Jena."

"Ah, thanks, I appreciate that." She didn't respond to her question right away and changed the subject. "How is that tough guy handling the radiation?" she asked, her face now a mask of concern.

Tears immediately welled up in Theresa's eyes, but she managed to stay in control. "He's doing okay, better than we are."

Jena nodded. "Being sick is often harder on the loved ones than the patient."

A Year of a Thousand Casts

Theresa nodded and wiped her eyes. "They say we are heading to the med/surg floor in a few days to finish out the radiation and chemo. I hope we can take him home soon."

"There can be great success with radiation. You hang in there for him."

Theresa nodded numbly. "So, will we get you as our nurse again before we go to the med/surg floor?"

Jena shook her head. "I'm so sorry but I'm actually taking a leave of absence. I just met with human resources. I was going to finish out my shifts but in light of a recent situation they are letting me leave now."

Theresa looked confused. "Leave of absence? If you don't mind me asking, why?"

Jena didn't want to lie to her and she didn't know how to sugar coat it, so she didn't bother trying. "I recently lost my husband."

Theresa went wide eyed, her hand coming to her mouth as she let out a breath. "I'm so sorry, I had no idea. Here I am begging for you to be our nurse...I feel horrible."

Jena reached out and touched her arm, giving Theresa her best reassuring smile. "It's okay, you had no way of knowing." Luckily, she had been able to voice her loss without any new emotions rising to the surface. Perhaps the hospital unconsciously put her in work mode, the wall that kept the stress at bay solidifying every time she entered the automatic doors. "I'm going to take some time to heal."

Theresa nodded in understanding. "I imagine what you do is extremely hard at the best of times. But taking care of sick kids and grieving families while processing such a hard loss...is...well, I just can't imagine."

Jena needed to get away before her self-control came crumbling down. "I'll be back in a year. I just need some time." She put on her best smile. "You be strong for Mason. Perhaps I'll see you again, but let's hope it will be at the grocery store instead of here."

Theresa forced a smile. "Deal." Then she reached out and hugged Jena. "Find your peace." Then she let go, giving her a warm smile before turning back to her table.

Jena left, deciding she would stop to buy coffee on the way home rather than wait awkwardly in line at the espresso stand. It had been a difficult conversation, but then again, whenever people spoke of death and tragedy it always was. Jena was used to it, but most were not. She could speak of death in a casual conversation. Most people had no background or experiences that allowed them to speak of the finality of death in such a way, at least when it pertained to a loved one. It was one of the reasons why PICU nurses needed to voice their issues with other nurses, or a shrink. Jena had taken comfort from both many times. Most other people had a hard time being comfortable discussing the topic. She hoped that Theresa would not have to deal with the stress of talking about the death of her son, that her family would not suffer the loss of their child like so many had before her. She hoped Mason would go into remission and live a healthy life. But for now, she had to push those thoughts aside. It was time for her to focus on herself. It was her time to mend her soul. And as she had helped so many others deal with loss, she hoped that she, in turn, could be a conduit for her own healing. Time would only tell.

* * *

"Okay," Sten said, "what weight rod would you likely use for a trout stream?"

They were in Chris's study, which wasn't really a study as the only thing "studied" in the room was fly fishing. One wall was dominated by a large fly-tying desk. It was quite beautiful, the old wood well cared for, the aged oak stained a golden red. Chris had found the dilapidated desk at a garage sale and spent two weeks in his shop bringing it back to its former glory, as well as adding his own bells and whistles. He had built a new shelf that occupied the entire length of the back of the desktop, the interior lined with many small shelves and cubby holes, all presently stuffed with fly tying materials, most of which appeared to be dyed feathers and animal hair. He had built another series of drawers on the right of the desk adding another sixteen inches to its length. Chris had done such a skillful job with the additions that they looked as if they had always been a part of the desk.

You had to look closely to even see the seam where he had extended the length of the desk's top to cover the new shelves. A fly-tying vice was attached to the edge of the desk, a light with a flexible tube hovering over it.

Typically, the desk was a mess, its top covered with various materials as Chris had worked on the fly of the day. But now it was empty, cleaned up long ago when Chris had been admitted to the hospital. The desk's emptiness was a poignant reminder of the vacancy Jena felt in her heart every time she looked at it.

Tearing her gaze from the desk, Jena looked at Sten, scrunching her eyes as she thought. "What size trout are we talking about?"

Sten smiled and shrugged. "Mostly ten to sixteen inchers, with a possibility of a fish in the low twenties."

"If I was throwing dry flies, I'd go with anything between a three and five weight. But for streamers, throwing a medium sink, I'd likely do a five, maybe a six." Jena lifted her eyes in amusement. "I'd need a little back bone to turn over those heavy streamers and sculpin patterns."

Sten shook his head and laughed, nearly spitting his beer out. "You know, for one who doesn't know how to fly fish, you sure can speak the lingo."

This time it was Jena's turn to laugh. "I have listened to Chris talk about fishing for the last twenty years. I may not be able to cast, but I do know something about the sport."

Sten lifted his beer in salute. "Yes you do."

Jena raised her wine glass and they tapped them together before drinking. They were sitting on the ground of Chris's study, his gear spread out all around them. There were rod tubes, reel cases, fly boxes and more. The walls were covered with pictures of Chris and his friends holding various fish, their smiles so pronounced that you'd think they were holding an academy award. The closet was filled with fishing clothes and boxes filled with more gear. It looked as if Chris had bought an entire store of fishing gear and crammed it in one bedroom. Besides the fly-tying desk, the only other furniture was a worn leather chair the color of cinnamon, a side table and desk lamp next to it. There were a few fly-fishing magazines scattered across it but what caught Jena's attention was a candle, the glass black, the words Vanilla Tobacco written across it in gold writing. She had bought it for Chris before he was diagnosed, the memory of the candle's aroma bringing a smile to her face, replaced in a blink by a wave of melancholy.

Sten noticed. "Are you okay?"

She took a deep breath and exhaled. "I'll be fine," she said quickly, trying to convince herself. "It's just that everything in the room reminds me of him." She grabbed one of the rod tubes on the ground, holding it so Sten could see it. "You see this rod?" she asked, "I gave it to Chris on our wedding day. He didn't want an expensive ring, so I went to a fly shop and spent over fifteen hundred dollars on this rod and a matching reel. I tied a fifty-dollar ring to the end of the fly line." She smiled. "He was so excited he nearly forgot to take the ring."

Sten chuckled. "I wish I knew you guys back then. I would've loved to have been there to see that."

"Me too," Jena whispered as she reverently held the rod in her hands, her thoughts drifting to their wedding, the best day of her life.

Sten massaged his long brown unruly beard, and not knowing what to say he took a long swig of his beer. But then he surprised her. "I think of him all the time. When you've had the pleasure to know someone as amazing as Chris, their absence is even more profound, creating a massive void left empty by such a huge personality that is no longer with us." Sten scratched his beard and looked intently at Jena. "But you know what is great about a void in your heart?"

Jena was pretty sure she knew where he was going, but she didn't want to spoil the moment. "Tell me."

"They can be filled again." Sten ran both his hands through his hair and sighed deeply. He had spent many years fishing with Chris. And although Jena was not a fisherman, she understood that the bond between fly-fishing friends was quite strong. It was obvious that Chris's death had had a profound impact on Sten. He looked up again, his green eyes serious. "Jena, you are not alone. We will all help you. I think this new adventure will help ease your pain. I think that was Chris's plan all along."

Jena wiped the corner of her eyes. "Thanks Sten. I appreciate all your help."

Sten nodded. "Now, what color streamer would you use on a dark cloudy day?"

Jena laughed and thought about the question, accessing her data base of knowledge acquired by many conversations she had had with her late husband. But she couldn't bring any answer forth, so she went with a guess. "Well, if it's dark, I'd use a bright color so the fish could see it."

Sten shook his head. "Generally, bright colors, especially flies with gold or silver, need the sun to reflect off them to really bring them to life. There is an old fly-fishing rule, and although it's not always true, it's a good one to remember. Dark days dark flies, bright days bright flies."

Jena nodded. "Okay, got it."

They spent the rest of the evening sorting through gear and drinking while Sten quizzed her further.

* * *

Two weeks later Jena was on the road, Chris's Toyota Tundra packed with all the gear she would likely need. She had gone back and forth on whether to take her car or Chris's truck, opting for the latter due to the large amount of gear she was bringing with her. She knew it was going to be tough, as everything about the vehicle elicited so many memories. But she rationalized her decision by realizing that everything reminded her of Chris, and avoiding the memories was like trying to catch a fly with chop sticks. She figured she might as well hit the grieving process head on, and that meant not avoiding things that brought forth the memories that caused her emotional strife.

Sten had helped Jena pack the proper gear. Some of it she was familiar with, and others, well, she was clueless. Sten had also taken her to several stores to buy more, one a local big retailer, the other a small fly shop. She needed waders, boots, fishing clothes for various weather conditions, as well as her fishing license. But when it came to the actual fishing gear, Chris had provided all that she needed, and then some.

She was already two hours into the drive and had successfully made it through Seattle and Everett with minimal traffic. It helped that she had left at three in the morning. She hadn't been able to sleep anyway and was eager to start her journey, despite her anxiety to do so. She still couldn't believe what she was doing. She had taken a year leave of absence to fish in locations all over the world, finishing Chris's bucket list for him and depositing his ashes each step of the journey. She was now heading to some cranky old man's home on a north Washington river to convince him to teach her to fly-fish. Why Chris picked this Hans character she had no idea. Clearly, he had his reasons. Why couldn't one of his fishing buddies, like Sten, teach her?

She sighed and glanced up at the old flies dangling from his visor. They were obviously used up but despite their ill condition, she imagined Chris's hands working effortlessly at his bench creating them. She had always been so impressed with the beauty of his creations and she laughed out loud, hearing his voice in her mind's eye as he named them. He would bring her a new fly and say things like, *"This is called the O'malley Ghost, and it's going to slay some steelhead."* Chris had always said that any serious fly-fisherman was not only a fly tier, but they should always name their creations. He would sometimes name the flies after his friends, or even their dog, Macallan, who had died a few years back from a heart defect. Chris had named the puppy after the scotch of course. The pain they experienced after that loss had been tremendous and neither of them had been ready to raise another puppy. Since they had not been able to have children, they had dumped all their love into their little fur baby. His death hit them both much harder than either of them had expected. Then when Chris got diagnosed the idea of another dog got swept further under the carpet. Perhaps, someday, she would be ready for a fur baby again. He had once named a pretty fly the Jen-in-ator, after the terminator. And as the memories floated through her mind she ran through the typical gambit of emotions. She went from smiles associated with the fond memories to a crushing sadness at the weight of her loss, then followed by anger as she thought of her world without Chris.

She blinked away the tears, dabbing her eyes with her hand. Sighing deeply, she looked out at the river to her right. The two-lane road was lined with a canopy of trees and she had not seen a house for thirty minutes. The highway snaked through the woods, the river appearing and disappearing from view as it more or less followed the road. She had made it through the small town of Leroy and was nearly at an intersection called Rockwood. According to the GPS on her phone, Hans's country store was another twenty-five minutes past Rockwood near a dam on the river.

The river was stunning, with huge boulders and clear, dark turquoise, water. The access looked tough, with steep rock walls or dense woods protecting the river from most weekend fishermen. Chris preferred the rivers that required great effort to get to, thus rewarding you in return for your effort. There would also be fewer people on the river. It looked to Jena that this particular river was just that type.

Turning up the radio, she attempted to lose herself in the lyrics of Taylor Swift, the playlist from her phone ringing in all her favorites. Ten minutes passed in a blur; her mind occupied by the music while images of Chris continued to flash through her mind like the slide show at a family reunion. Arriving at Rockwood, she was temporarily distracted as she surveyed the little town. It wasn't really a town at all. There were a few cabins and run-down trailers leading up to an intersection that allowed you to go straight, over a bridge that spanned the river, or left, taking you further upstream. Jena knew from her GPS that she would be turning left. There was a gas station, a small tavern, and what looked like a country motel called the Sleepy Inn. It looked small but quaint, and Jena thought it could make a good plan B if sleeping above Hans's store didn't work out.

If she was honest with herself, she was nervous to meet the man. Chris had not painted a good picture of him, which was the source of her anxiety and the nagging question in her mind as to why Chris wanted her to learn from the crotchety man to begin with. And what was she to do? Just walk into his place and say *Hi, I'm Jena. My husband, Chris, who you know, is dead, and he asked me to come here so you could teach me to fish.* It made no sense. Did Hans know she might be coming? Chris had not hinted that he did, but then again it

52

was just something Chris would do. It was obvious he had some motive to send her to the man, and perhaps he had already spoken with Hans about his plan. If not, it would be a strange introduction. Jena sighed and looked at the GPS on her phone. Well, she thought, she didn't have long to wait. Turning left, she drove past the Sleepy Inn and headed towards the answers to her questions.

Twenty-four minutes later she clicked on her blinker and turned right into a small parking lot, six stalls lined up before an old country store. The wood building was two stories and the vertical planks were an aged white. An old faded sign above the distressed wooden door read *Stumpies*. The lower level was clearly the store while the top floor must have been the small apartment that Chris had spoken of. She turned off her car and looked up through the sunroof, the fir tree branches above swaying gently in the breeze. She shook her head, feeling a mixture of anxiety and frustration as she reached for the door handle. She felt like the car door opening signaled the start of her epic journey.

As she opened the dilapidated wood door, a bell above it announced her entrance. An old woman with a long gray ponytail sat behind the counter reading a magazine titled *Fine Woodworking*. She looked up and set the magazine down, smiling at Jena as she stepped to the counter.

"Hi," Jena said, a little uncomfortably. "Is Hans around?"

The woman stood from her stool. "He's on the river. Is there something I can do?"

"I need to speak with him about the loft upstairs. Do you know when he'll be back?"

She shrugged. She was likely in her early seventies but there was something about her that belied her age. Perhaps it was her bright inquisitive eyes or her confident posture. "He usually comes back after the morning bite." The woman looked at her watch, a turquoise and silver piece that reminded Jena of Native American jewelry she had seen before. "My guess is he'll be back by one."

That was two hours away.

"Okay, well, is it okay if I wait?"

"Sure," she replied, "but if it's the room you want, I can take care of that, although he usually only rents it to people he knows. How did you know about it?"

Jena didn't know how to respond, so she went with a version of the truth. "My husband was a fly-fisherman. He fished up here quite a bit and that's how he became friends with Hans."

It was obvious that the woman was curious, perhaps noting her use of past tense in referencing her husband, but she didn't push further. "Well, Hans doesn't have many friends." She chuckled, "so your husband must be something special."

"Yup," Jena said awkwardly, looking around the little store to distract her.

The woman picked up on her unease and moved the conversation in a different direction. "Well, my name is Irma. If you want to waste some time until Hans comes back there is a trail around the side of the building. It goes down to the river."

Jena silently thanked Irma for not pressing the conversation. "I'm Jena, nice to meet you, Irma...and thanks, I think I'll do that. Let me grab a few snacks first."

Irma nodded. "I'm not going anywhere," she said, smiling warmly.

Jena smiled back and went to a cooler to get a beverage, grabbing a bag of sunflower seeds on the way. She always chewed them as a nervous habit and Chris hated the mess they made. She smiled briefly as she thought about the many times he had heckled her when he found them in the cracks of his seats. She took a Gatorade, paid Irma, and headed around the side of the building. It was nearly eleven now and the summer sun was trying to break through the light layer of clouds, its rays casting fingers of light through the canopy of trees as she made her way down the dirt trail to the river. It was only sixty yards or so, the trail steep at the end, emerging onto a bed of river rock, the raging river no more than a stone's throw away. The riverbed was littered with downed timber, some aged white by the sun. The far side of the river was a steep bank, its edge lined with boulders, log jams, and thick foliage. A mixture of huge fir and cedar trees surrounded her, their limbs reaching out like arms to embrace her. She loved the forest. It calmed her. They had spent many years camping, and she always felt that a few days in a desolate forest felt like a weeklong vacation.

She walked across the rocks, meandering through some old logs to get closer to the river. The sound of the turbulent water made her smile, the sound comforting, like a warm blanket on a cold night. She had always loved that sound, sitting on a log or rock deep into a book while Chris had fished. It was a very nostalgic feeling, perhaps more now than ever. She found a big rock to sit on, and opening up the bag of sunflower seeds and Gatorade, she gazed at the running water before her, her mind occupied by more memories of Chris drifting through her consciousness.

After a few introspective minutes, she shook the memories away and looked intently at the river. There was a decent run in front of her, with shallow fast water dumping into a pool lined with rocks, some big enough to cause the water to boil around them. The inside seam, where the slow water meets the fast water, looked particularly like good trout holding water. The tail-out was short, moving quickly into another fast run of shallow water that meandered a few hundred yards upriver where it disappeared around a bend. Jena heard Chris's voice in her head as she examined the fishing hole before her. Jena had learned from Chris that that tail-out would be a good spot to fish, although this hole, as the fishermen called them, being so close to the road and easily accessible, was not likely very productive. At least that's what Jena figured based on her meager knowledge. She surprised herself that she was able to read the water, and smiled fondly at the memories of Chris's long fishing diatribes. He would have explained to her the nuances of where fish might be located in various water conditions. She wouldn't have any idea how to fish it, but she did know where the fish would likely be. Anger and frustration suddenly interrupted her reverie and she was back to feeling like she was making a big mistake. But just as quickly, images of Chris saying, *Oh, it's on,* with a twinkle in his eye, made her laugh out loud. Her emotions were all over the place. She had a very real feeling that the next six months were going to be one big emotional roller coaster ride.

A Year of a Thousand Casts

Looking at her watch she realized she had a few hours before Hans returned. She had just popped a few more handfuls of sunflower seeds into her mouth when she just caught a glimpse of a fish splash from the surface right on the inside seam where the fast water meets the slow current. Her eyes widened and she laughed. The fish didn't look big, but for some reason she saw it as a positive omen. Right when she was questioning her course, a fish rose from the water, in her mind proclaiming an answer to her questions. *Yes, you are on the right path. Don't worry, you will make it through this.*

Then she got a crazy idea. She had tons of gear in the car and a few hours to herself. Why not give this fishing thing a try? Making up her mind, she gathered her snack and drink and walked briskly back to her car. She was actually excited, thinking she was doing something spontaneous and a bit unlike her, just as Chris would've liked it. She couldn't count the number of times they were on some trip when he had asked her to pull over so he could scout or fish some run he saw on a new river. She had loved that about him. He was always so spontaneous, especially when it came to fishing.

Opening up the door to the canopy on her truck, she dropped the tail gate and looked apprehensively at all the gear. Suddenly her idea didn't seem that great. She was pretty clueless on where to start. Taking a deep breath she thought of her many talks with Chris and her recent discussions with Sten.

"Okay," she said out loud, "if I'm on a trout stream and I don't know what to expect, a five weight was always a good place to start."

She knew the "weight" of the rod had nothing to do with its actual weight. It had to do with the weight of the fly line the rod was generally paired with. The weight of the rod was also correspondingly connected to its power, thus the size and strength of the fish you were targeting. If you were targeting salmon or other big game fish, a five-weight rod, although possible if you were skilled enough, would make it tough to land that fish without breaking the line or rod. Jena knew that a five-weight rod was a good all-around weight on an unknown trout stream.

Jena took out the rod and reel. The reel had line on it and was ready to go. She looked and saw it had a leader attached to the fly line already. She put the rod together and strung the line through the eyelets, leaning the rod against the side of the truck.

"Okay, now what?" She knew she needed a fly but had no idea what to put on. She browsed the files in her mind and went through what she knew. She was either going to use dry flies that float, or wet flies that sink. She knew there was no sink tip on the fly line. If there were, there would've been a section of line ranging from four or five feet up to fifteen that was dark in color and heavier. The purpose of the sink tip was obviously to sink and push the fly underwater. She also remembered that casting a heavy fly and sink tip was very difficult. The fish she saw had come out of the water, and although she had no idea if it was feeding on something on the surface, it seemed logical based on her present skill to tie on a dry fly.

She went through all of Chris's fly boxes and remembered a few things that Sten had taught her. She knew that there were flies that represented bugs exactly, and there were others that Sten had called "attractors". Those particular flies didn't look exactly like a bug but they were designed to attract the fish in an attempt to entice a strike. She remembered Sten saying those dry flies were generally bigger and brighter in color. She grazed through his boxes and finally settled on a fly that she thought was pretty. It was a little longer than her fingernail with an orange head, yellow body, and what looked like various feathers wrapped around it to represent legs. The "wings" were white and seemed much larger than actual wings.

She smiled as she held the fly up. "I'm going to call this the Orange Pegasus." Chris had often named the flies he had created and she had always thought that to be endearing. He had spoken often that real fly-fisherman name their flies, so she figured, even though she never tied the fly herself, that she should honor that tradition. Her thoughts sparked a sudden feeling of sadness. She sat down on the tail gate and put her hands over her eyes, willing the tears to retreat back to the depths of her consciousness. Taking five deep breaths she finally pulled her hands away and looked around to make sure no one was watching. She wiped away the dripping tears, held the fly up again, and said, "you can do this." She solidified her resolve, ready to move forward with her first fly-fishing experience.

Taking a deep breath she stood and grabbed the leader attached to the fly line in one hand, the Orange Pegasus held in the other hand, and stared at both. Now what? She thought. The only knot she knew at this point was the standard surgeons knot. But she also knew there was something called a tippet that you tied onto the end of the leader. It was the tippet that you then tied to the fly. The function of the tippet is to allow the fly to float invisibly in the water. She remembered that a new leader right from the package tapered to the proper size depending on what was purchased. But she had no idea if the leader she held was new or old, having been cut back to a shorter length as new flies were added. She looked at the leader carefully and noticed that the last two feet were thinner than the rest and there was a small knot attaching that section to the leader. Perhaps that was the tippet and it was ready to fish. She sighed, realizing she just didn't know enough. But she wasn't going to stop now. Making up her mind, she connected the fly to the end of the tippet with the only knot she knew. She found a pair of clippers attached to Chris's waders and used them to snip the excess line from the knot. She picked up the rod and attached the fly to the clip that was connected to the rod near the reel seat, winding up the slack line until it was tight. She shut the tailgate and canopy door, locking it before picking up the rod.

"Okay, what am I missing?" she asked herself.

She had no idea what she was missing so she shook off the doubt and made her way back to the trail. Moments later she was standing on the rocks at the river's edge looking at the "hole" before her. She had very little idea of what to do next.

The fish she saw had jumped no more than ten feet from her. She figured even if she couldn't cast the line, she should be able to throw it that far. Thinking back to the few times Chris had tried to show her to cast, she tried her best to recall the steps. She pulled some line from the reel so there was about five feet hanging by her feet. She unhooked the fly from the clasp at the reel seat and pulled some of the slack through the eyelets until there was about ten feet of line hanging from the tip of the rod.

"Okay," she said, "let's do this." And with that, she lifted the rod and attempted to *throw* the line into the water. It landed in the water alright, but with a massive splash. The fly floated slower than the line and came down last amongst a coil of fly line.

"Damn," she swore, knowing that if there was a fish anywhere near, it was likely spooked off by her sad display of casting. She focused again on her memories, trying to pull forth Chris's words in regard to casting. Small clipped sound bites rose to the surface...*keep the tip up, don't use so much wrist, finesse it, don't throw it.* It was a jumble of memories and none of it made much sense. But she tried again. Keeping the rod tip up and her wrist stiff, she pulled the rod back and the line zipped off the water, the fly striking her near her neck. Luckily, it hit her collar, and not her actual skin.

"Shit!" she swore, setting the rod down to try and free the fly. Then she remembered that Chris had always made sure the barb on the hook was pinched down. In most places it was illegal not to do so as it was quite difficult to remove a barbed hook from a fish's mouth without doing damage to the fish, and equally so it was just as tough to remove the fly from your own flesh. Luckily, the barb had already been pinched down and she had no problem removing it from her clothing. She was glad she was wearing her sunglasses. A fly to the eye would not be a fun experience.

Picking up the rod, she tried again, this time angling the tip slightly away from her. She pulled back on the rod and the ten feet of line shot back, then she flicked the rod tip forward and the line arced awkwardly but fell to the water in a somewhat better display, the fly landing near the seam where the fish had jumped. The current pulled the fly downstream for five feet before her line tightened and the fly skidded across the water towards the shore. She scooted down river three or four feet and tried again, the line zipping past her head by a hair as she recast. She swore as she ducked and clumsily tried to adjust her body to start her forward stroke. But when she did, the line tightened as the fly stuck to a downed log behind her.

"Damn it!"

She set the rod down and unhooked the fly from the log, setting it on the rocks near the rod. Picking the rod up, she tried again, determined to get a decent presentation. Chris had always talked about presenting the fly properly so as not to spook a fish, especially if the water was clear and you were casting to fish you could see. She knew the terminology, but executing the maneuvers were an entirely different thing. A proper presentation helped the fly land softly, mimicking the natural landing of a bug on the water. She knew that keeping the fly drifting down river without drag from the fly line was the goal, but actually creating that scenario was turning out to be quite difficult, and extremely frustrating, which is exactly how she felt when she had tried it with Chris on numerous occasions. It was also the reason why she never continued to try.

And just for a moment her mind drifted from memories of Chris to her father. He had always told her that good things rarely came easily. She had heard those words from him her entire life, but they really became meaningful when she was in nursing school. It had been the hardest thing she had ever done. On a few occasions when she had expressed her doubt about succeeding to her father, he had voiced those same words. It had kept her going. She missed her father extremely, and when he had passed Chris had been there for her. He had helped fill that void, and now, he too was gone. All the influential men in her life were no longer with her. Her 'rocks' so to speak, were absent from her life. She was alone.

Intellectually she knew she was not totally alone. She had great friends and a loving mother. But the void left behind from losing her father, and now Chris, felt like a huge empty hole. She was sure that some of Chris's reasoning for pushing her to do this crazy adventure was to get her to find some new 'rocks', something concrete to fill the emptiness left behind by his passing. Maybe it wasn't supposed to be a person, but a hobby, like fly fishing. At this point she wasn't exactly sure what his motivation had been. Right now it didn't feel like it was possible to mend the wound in her heart. She hoped he was right.

Picking up the rod, she angled the rod tip up and away, making sure the line was to her right. Pulling the tip back, she let the line unfurl behind her, shooting her arm forward when it looked like all the line had extended to its full length. Lowering the rod tip at the end of the cast, she let the line fall towards the water. It wasn't perfect by any means, but the fly line landed in a halfway decent presentation, and although the leader coiled on itself, the fly actually landed fairly softly.

She let the current take the fly down river picking up the slack in the leader. Just when it was reaching the full extent of the line, she pulled the rod tip back a little to get ready to recast. The fly skidded a few feet upriver and suddenly the water exploded as a fish attacked the retreating fly.

"Holy shit!" she yelped. She was so startled she instinctively leaped backwards and pulled the rod with her at the same time. Luckily, there was very little slack line left so the leader snapped tight and the fish was on, tugging hard on the line. "Oh my god, oh my god," she giggled as she stood there with the rod tip up and the fish pulling on the line. Then she realized she had no idea what to do.

The fish suddenly swam into the faster current and started to take line out as the turbulent water pushed the fish further down river. The reel zinged as she let go of it, afraid if she held on that the line would break. Her heart was pounding as she walked down river, following the fish as it swam into the deeper pool. Once the fish got into the slower deeper water, she was able to reel in the line slowly, the fish getting reluctantly closer to the shore.

"I do hope you have a net," a voice came from behind her.

She was so excited about the fish that she hadn't even heard the man's footsteps. Glancing back, the man, likely in his mid-sixties, was standing behind her in waders. He was holding a fly rod casually angled backwards. He was not smiling, however.

Jena was beaming from ear to ear and the man's stoic expression did little to dampen her excitement. "I don't," she said. "I didn't really expect to catch anything as I have no idea what I'm doing."

The man shook his head. The move was subtle, but held the power of a father gravely disappointed in his son. He leaned his rod against the log nearby and removed the net dangling from his back. It was attached to some type of breakaway clasp at his side.

"Keep your rod tip up and walk back from the shore," he ordered, walking towards the shore near the fish.

"Okay," she said, chastened some but determined to enjoy the experience, nonetheless.

As the fish got closer to the shore it used one more burst of energy to shoot back to the safety of the deep pool.

"Whoa!" Jena yelped, leaning forward as the fish pulled harder. She was holding tight onto the reel afraid the fish was going to get away.

"Hand off the reel!" The man demanded. "Let the fish run but keep the line tight."

Startled by his stern voice, she let go of the reel like she had touched a hot stove. The fish ran and the reel zinged again.

"Tighten the drag," he ordered again, his voice sounding clearly annoyed.

"The drag?!" As soon as she said the words, she regretted them. She suddenly remembered where the drag was on the reel and was angry at herself for not recalling Chris's lessons sooner. The excitement of the fish had caused her to forget the very few things she actually knew. The drag was a knob on the right side of the reel and the more you turned it the tighter the drag became, making it more difficult for the fish to take line out of the reel. It was like the breaks on a car so to speak. If it were too loose, the fish could just run and pull all the line from the reel. If it were too tight, a burst of speed and power could cause the delicate tippet near the fly to break as the drag tightened. One of the many skills of fly fishing was learning the proper amount of drag to safely bring a fish to the net.

He glared at her as she tightened the knob, causing the fish to slow its pull. Stepping into the water, he readied the net. "Now reel in slowly. If it pulls again, let it run, but keep tension on the line by adjusting your drag."

"Okay," she said, holding the fish just outside the deep water. She could see it shake and flip around, the late morning sun reflecting off its glittering scales. She started reeling in slowly, careful to not pull to hard.

"Good," the man said, "now back up and when the fish gets close to the shore, I'll come up behind it to net him. Keep the rod tip up and try to control his head."

Jena nodded even though she really had no idea what he was talking about. But she wasn't about to tell him that. Suddenly she realized how fast her heart was beating. She was tightly clenching the rod as adrenaline rushed through her body. She had held Chris's rod before with a fish on the line. On several occasions he had handed her the rod so she could experience what it felt like to have a fish tug on the other end. But this time it felt entirely different. She wasn't sure why but the level of excitement she was experiencing now was far more elevated than her past experiences.

The fish was tiring and she was able to reel it closer to the shore. The man came up behind it and with practiced ease dipped the net quickly into the water, capturing it within its deep folds. He squatted down and held the fish in the water, the net's rim above the water to keep it from flipping out.

"Set your rod down and come over here to take a look," the man said, this time his voice a bit softer.

She did as he ordered and squatted down along the shoreline to see the fish. It looked to be about a foot long and had sparkling scales and a slight red band running down the center of its body.

"You caught Sparky," he said, looking up at her.

For the first time Jena noticed his accent. It was clipped and sounded Norwegian. *Oh shit*, she thought, *was this Hans?* Then she focused on his words. Sparky? "You know this fish?"

The man nodded. "This hole is generally not very productive," he responded, removing the hook from the side of the fish's mouth. "There are usually just a few smaller fish here, but Sparky seems to like it here a lot. I've caught him many times." Seeing Jena's confused expression, he continued with a slight upturn of his lip.

Was that his smile? Jena thought.

"See here," the man said, pointing to the fish's tail. "Sparky has one big black spot on his tail. The first time I hooked him he was about six inches long."

Jena smiled. "Sparky is growing."

"Yes he is." Then he locked eyes with her. "And that is generally due to the fact that most fishermen have a net with them and know how to safely land and release him." Once he made his point, he looked down, and reaching in he lifted Sparky from the net, holding him lightly in the water, not letting him go immediately. Sparky slowly moved his tail back and forth but didn't bolt for the safety of the deeper water.

"What are you doing?" Jena asked. She had been clearly reprimanded, her excitement replaced by anger, and then a sense of shame.

"He needs to catch his breath so to speak. If you tire a fish out too much, and let him go before he has rested, he can roll over in the water and die. If he doesn't move the water won't flow through his gills, and he'll suffocate. He'll swim away when he's ready."

Sure enough, a few moments later, Sparky snapped his tail and he shot off into the water, disappearing into the dark depths.

The man stood up and his stern demeanor returned. "Now, why were you fishing without a net? You might have killed him trying to release him."

"I'm sorry," Jena stammered, still taken aback by his flinty words. "I don't really know what I'm doing."

"Then you shouldn't be fishing," he said, walking away from her to retrieve his rod. He stopped near her rod on the rocks. "You should pick up your rod before you step on it."

She grabbed her rod and reeled up the slack line, her emotions now settling on a sense of guilt. "I was waiting for someone and decided to try it. I didn't actually think I'd catch anything."

The man picked up his rod and looked back at her. "Waiting for who?"

"You, I think. Are you Hans?"

"I am," the man said, his expression stoic. "Do I know you?"

"No, but you knew my husband, Chris O'Malley."

For just a moment Jena saw something flash across Han's face. It wasn't recognition, for she already knew Hans knew her husband. It was almost like the mentioning of his name solidified something in Han's mind. Han's nodded, his expression softening some. "Come with me."

They entered the store a few minutes later and Irma was still behind the counter. Jena followed Hans past the counter to an old wood door. She had seen it earlier but had no idea where it led.

"Oh, good, you found him," Irma said, glancing up from her wood working magazine.

Jena smiled and was about to say something when Hans spoke. "Put your rod there," he said, pointing to a rod rack near the door. It was empty so she hadn't noticed it before. Hans put the end of his rod in a plastic finger-like clasp, then he laid the rod sideways making sure to secure the tip on a similar plastic clasp. He entered the door, leaving it open as Jena followed his lead, securing her own rod below his.

She looked back at Irma. The older woman glanced up when she saw her pause. Irma smiled and didn't seem the least bit perturbed at Hans's callous behavior. Jena's return smile was forced. But she took a deep breath and entered the room, shutting the door behind her. She felt as if she were entering the principal's office.

Hans had sat down in an old worn office chair behind a desk cluttered with stacks of paper. The desk was L shaped, and the part not facing her was occupied by an old computer, the keyboard so old that each number key was lined with brown dirt the shape of his fingertip. The room itself was about the size of a big bedroom. It was clearly an office. Old fishing pictures covered the worn shiplap walls along with various ancient rods, nets, and what appeared to be baskets. She knew they were old fishing creels, where fisherman used to store their catch of the day. Everything looked like it came straight from a country antique store. The wall to her immediate left was mostly covered by a second smaller desk, its top covered with various fly-tying materials including a small lamp and vice. Jena smiled when she saw it, reminding her of Chris. The room smelt like her grandma's musty knickknack cabinet.

There was a chair positioned before the fly-tying desk. "Have a seat," Hans said, pointing to the chair.

Jena slid the chair around and positioned it closer to the desk before she sat down. His gray hair, hanging in unruly waves, framed his tanned and creased face. Ruggedly handsome, his stolid stare unnerved her.

Jena didn't know what to say to him, so she just started talking to break the tension in the room. "I'm Jena O'Malley. My husband," she stopped. It felt surreal to her to start to speak of him, almost as if he were still with her. Jena continued. "My late husband knew you. He asked me, before he died, to come here and meet you."

Hans sighed and for just a moment, an expression of sorrow passed over his features. But it was gone just as fast as it had shown up. "I'm sorry for your loss," he said. "Chris was one of the best fishermen I've seen. He taught me a lot." He paused as he looked out the only window in the room. It's smudged and dirty panes faced the woods flanking the river. She couldn't be sure but she imagined him thinking of Chris. Looking back at her, he spoke again. "Why did he want you to meet me?" He asked the question as if he already knew the answer.

Here it goes Jena thought. "He asked me to ask you, if you would teach me to fly fish."

Hans let out a deep breath. Jena was unsure if the sigh was a product of frustration, melancholy, or something else. "To what end?"

Jena frowned. "So I can fly fish." She had thought the answer was obvious.

"Of course," Hans said, his tone this time clearly frustrated. "But for what purpose? Why does he want you to learn to fly fish now?"

It was a valid question. Jena rubbed her eyes as she thought of the absurdity of the entire adventure. But there was no way to simplify the situation. So she told him the entire story. He sat back in his chair and listened; his expression just as deadpan as it had been when they met. She finished, adding the part about renting the room above to wrap up the story.

He didn't say anything for a few moments. Then he smiled, the lines around his lips struggling against the rare expression. "That crafty son of a bitch," he said. "He put you in quite a pickle."

Jena chuckled, his smile allowing some of the tension to leave her body. "Yes, he sure did."

"And I take it by your presence that you are taking him up on this fishing bucket list?"

"I am."

Suddenly his smile disappeared, his eyes narrowing some before looking back out the window. She counted at least fifteen heartbeats before he looked back at her.

"I'm an old man set in my ways. I'm not good with people. He must have told you that."

"Not in those exact words, but yes," Jena replied.

"I don't mix words or use them to placate one's emotions," he quipped.

"I gathered that."

The edge of his lip curled up slightly again. She had seen that expression down by the river and wondered if it was one of amusement or something else.

"There are not many people I respect, but Chris was one," he added, pausing as if thinking it over. "I will do this for him. I will teach you to fly fish. But I need you to understand something. Fly fishing is much more than just catching fish. Chris was someone who understood that. I hope you can. I don't want to waste my time."

"I'll do my best," Jena said, unsure of what else to say. "Thank you. One more thing. Chris left me a video that he wanted you to watch with me."

Hans shook his head. "Not now. You can stay in the room upstairs for fifty bucks a night."

"I appreciate that."

Hans stood. "Now, Irma will get you situated. I have to go. Be ready tomorrow at sunup. We can watch the video then."

Jena stood as well, feeling a bit uncomfortable. Hans nodded and walked right past her and out the door. Jena looked around in bewilderment. What a strange guy, she thought. She heard him say a few things to Irma, then the bell over the front door rang, indicating his departure. Jena smiled awkwardly; a bit befuddled. She looked around the room one more time, her eyes scanning the top of the desk.

She noticed a picture frame for the first time amongst the mess of papers. Turning it around, she saw it was an old worn image of Hans when he was young, a little girl sitting on his lap. They were both smiling from ear to ear.

Then her eyes caught something that solidified a lump in her throat, causing her breathe to catch. Under a stack a papers was a letter, the corner sticking out exposing the sender's name. She recognized the fluid script of her husband. She slid the letter out from the stack and confirmed that it was a letter from her husband addressed to Hans. It was already open and she was debating on whether or not she should read it when the door behind her creaked open. She dropped the letter and turned around to see Irma enter the room.

Irma was smiling warmly. Then she noticed the picture frame turned towards her and her expression turned serious. "That is Han's daughter," she said in reverence, stepping closer and looking fondly at the picture, her smile returning. Then it turned to sadness as she looked sidelong at Jena. "She was only eight when she was killed in a car accident. But he doesn't like to talk about it so I better not either." Then her warm smile returned. "It sounds like you are going to be staying with us for a bit."

Jena returned her smile. "I am."

"It will be nice to have some more estrogen around," Irma joked. "Here are the keys to the room upstairs," she added, handing her the set of keys. "The entrance is outside around the corner of the building. There are stairs that lead up to the room."

"Thank you," Jena replied.

"Follow me. I'll show you to the stairs." Irma stepped out of the room and Jena followed. She went behind the counter to a back door, leading Jena outside and around the building. The steps were made from the same aged whitewashed wood. They led up to a landing and another door. Irma indicated the stairs. "Why don't you get settled in." She turned to leave but stopped, turning towards her again. "I'm sorry about Chris. He was a lovely man." She pursed her lips in a forced but reassuring smile, though her eyes reflected her sadness. Then she turned and left Jena to her thoughts.

Chapter 3

"Hi Hans, it's good to see you," Chris said, smiling wide. "I'm sorry, but that joke just gets funnier in my mind."

Hans frowned and looked at Jena.

"I know," she said, "I find it morbid as well."

It was bright and early the next morning. Hans had turned the computer screen around so they could both see it from their seats in his office. Jena had inserted the thumb drive and continued the previous video where she had paused it weeks ago. She was excited to see Chris and hear the rest of his message.

"Now," Chris continued. "If you are both watching this, then you have decided to help Jena learn to fish." Chris's playful expression turned serious. "I cannot thank you enough for this, Hans. She is going to need all the help you can provide for her to accomplish the tasks I've put before her. I want you to know that when Jena puts her mind to something, there is nothing she cannot do. She will not let you down, that much I can promise you."

"We'll see about that," Hans mumbled.

Jena frowned but said nothing as Chris continued.

"So I think it's important that you know where I plan to send Jena. She will need some help preparing her skills for the following locations. These locations are places where I was not able to fish before I died. As you know, each one will require different skills and knowledge. She will have help from local guides, but I'm hoping you can provide a foundation from which she can build upon on her own. I want her to go to Chile to fish the secluded fjords. I would also like her to go to the Seychelles to fish around Alphonse Island, as well as Brazil to fish for peacock bass on the Aqua Boa River. I will send her to New Zealand to fish the South Island. Then I'd like her to hit the

Big Tree Lodge in Alaska." Chris smiled. "Five locations, all with many different species of fish."

"That is quite a list," Hans said.

Jena was silent, overwhelmed at all the locations he was asking her to visit. My god, the Seychelles...wasn't that off the coast of Africa? she thought. She was in shock.

"If I know my wife," Chris continued, "she is in shock right now trying to mull over the difficult task I've provided for her."

Jena cried and laughed at the same time, her hand coming to her mouth as Chris had just described exactly how she was feeling. It made her miss him even more. For just a moment, her mind plunged into a dark pit, her thoughts swirling as she remembered how Chris had protected her, how he made her feel safe, how he loved her for who she was. He was always her best advocate, supporting her during all her work trials and tribulations. Struggling, she managed to pull her thoughts from the muck to focus on Chris's next words.

"Hans, I'm going to need you to prepare her for those fishing conditions. Now, I know that is a difficult task, but trust me when I tell you, she will rise to the occasion. She is the most amazing person I have ever met and I think that once you get to know her, you will agree. I know your circle of trust is quite small, but I believe that Jena will join the select few in that isolated space."

Jena looked at Hans expecting a rebuttal. But he said nothing, continuing to stare at the computer screen.

"I think the best start for this trip is to go big or go home. Jena," Chris said, "I'd like you to start by going to New Zealand in December and then heading to the Seychelles in March. I'll provide videos for each trip, so don't worry about that. Now, do you have any questions?" Chris laughed again. "Just kidding. Sorry, I can't help myself. Hans, thank you again. Jena, you got this...don't look ahead, it

70

will stress you out. Look to the now. Enjoy every moment as you experience it. Remember, we cannot receive wisdom, we must find it for ourselves after a journey." Chris smiled. "I stole that from someone, I can't remember who. I love you, honey. And good luck to you both." Chris reached down and the screen went black.

Han's scratched his head, running his hand through his unruly gray hair. Then he looked at Jena and said two simple words. "You ready?"

* * *

As it turned out, Jena was not ready. There was so much to learn it felt like she was preparing for her nursing **NCLEX**, the national nursing license examination, all over again. That exam was so grueling that it left an indelible imprint in her memory. But, she admitted, at least this was more fun. Hans spent the first week taking her up and down the river, discussing river conditions and reading the water, all the while diving into everything from leaders, tippets, fly selection, presentation, and of course casting.

It was the casting that proved to be the most difficult. Hans was somewhat surprised at her knowledge regarding fishing, considering she had such little skill in actually doing it. Over the years she had gleaned a lot from Chris, but it was more verbiage than anything. She had no idea how to apply what knowledge she knew to the actual sport. She had to learn the basic cast, the roll cast, curve cast, and of course, false casting. Jena had learned there were other more advanced casts but Hans saw no reason to complicate things any more than they already were. If she could learn the basic casting techniques, then Hans said she could fish nearly every condition and situation. They spent most of the mornings and evenings fishing, and at night, Hans taught her how to tie flies. She was not particularly good, but she enjoyed the artistic side of the skill. Designing flies based on various patterns was somewhat stimulating, although the results of her endeavors were not much to look at, and likely incapable of catching fish. But as the weeks flowed by, she continued to work on it,

eventually completing a few flies that received a coveted nod of
approval from Hans. As it turned out, fly tying, despite her lack of
skill, had become something she enjoyed. In a strange way, it helped
connect her more deeply to her husband. Every time she worked on a
fly, she pictured herself standing next to Chris at his own fly-tying desk
as he discussed his recent creation. On more than a few occasions,
Jena had to clear the tears from her eyes before she could see the next
step when tying her own fly.

 Hans was not affable, but neither was he mean. He was serious
and to the point, instructing her in a way that made it seem like he
really didn't care if she succeeded. His demeanor, whether she cast
well or not, was always the same. He was a difficult man to read.
As far as her accommodations, they were definitely rustic, but not in a
fancy ski lodge kind of way. The one room studio had an adjoining
bathroom. Everything was old and well worn, but it did have one
saving grace, a claw foot bathtub stuffed into the corner of the small
bathroom. The bathroom window was positioned in such a way that
when you were sitting up in the tub, you could view the trees behind
the store, small gaps through the foliage allowing glimpses of the river
beyond. After a long day of fishing, she often relaxed in the tub, her
busy mind finally slowing, allowing her body to relax in the hot
soothing water. Her mind always drifted to Chris, images of him
flashing through her consciousness as she willed the water to wash away
her sadness. Despite its warm embrace, the hot water could not
completely pacify her turbulent thoughts. She wondered if it ever
would.

 Four weeks later Jena was standing near the river's edge staring
at a long run, the early morning sun just peaking over the trees, trying,
unsuccessfully, to reach into the canyon carved out by the river. It was
a cold morning, but she was dressed warmly in all the gear she had
bought with Sten. She had spared no expense, purchasing top gear
from Simms, Orvis, and Patagonia. And she was thankful for it now as
the warm sun struggled to fight off the morning chill.

 They had hiked further upriver than ever before, Hans telling
her that there was a secret spot he wanted to show her. Five miles later,

he had directed her down a steep trail towards the river. Some spots were no more than small cliffs, sharp rocks and roots giving the only hand and foot holds. Hans had surprised her by presenting a coiled rope from behind a rock attached to a thick tree, knots tied in the rope every two feet. He had tossed the rope down the small ravine and had begun to make his way down, using the rope to guide him. Their rods were still in their cases, strapped to the sides of their backpacks.

Jena had looked down a bit apprehensively. But then she had thought of Chris, his huge smile reflecting his eagerness to explore and find locations off the beaten path. This was just the sort of thing Chris would love.

She had managed to work her way down the trail, using the rope to guide her over some steep drops, the edges of roots and rocks giving her footholds on the way down. Hans was in his sixties, but he had managed the feat easily enough. She wasn't about to wimp out now. After getting on solid ground, she had walked to the riverbed to find Hans waiting for her, his expression stolid as usual.

"That was interesting," Jena had said.

"That's what I told Chris when he took me here."

Jena had been taken aback. She had assumed this was Han's secret spot. "Chris placed that rope there?"

Hans nodded. "Follow me."

Jena had paused momentarily, her breath caught in her throat as she looked back up the steep incline, the rope dangling from the tree above, the image of Chris climbing down the secret path etched in her mind. She had felt empty, the hole Chris's death had created in her heart a painful reminder that she would never feel his presence again, yet following in his footsteps was in some way a comfort as she forced herself to follow Hans to the fishing hole.

They had walked up the riverbed, countless smooth gray rocks peppered with downed trees and timber surrounding them. Huge boulders and trees formed steep cliffs on both sides of the river. After several hundred yards they were rewarded with finding the fishing hole nestled in the small canyon. Before them was a ten-foot waterfall, the churning water cascading over gigantic rocks worn smooth by the water.

Massive old growth trees loomed over them, their protective branches filled with greenery, the fresh smell of pine permeating the clearing. And now she found herself facing a long run, the water deep from the constant crash of the waterfall, the bottom littered with giant boulders. The run ran for fifty feet, with a fishable seam on the inside and outside of the slow current.

"This is beautiful," Jena said, gazing at her surroundings.

Hans nodded. "Believe it or not, the trout manage to get up that waterfall."

"So the river is fishable further up?"

"It is. But this is the spot I want you to fish. Many of the smaller fish gather here feeding off all the food coming down river. And the bigger fish do the same, sometimes feeding off the smaller fish. I've caught big trout here, as well as monster bull trout, and even a few steelhead on occasion."

"Steelhead? I thought you said they don't run here anymore."

"They don't," Hans replied. "But occasionally you'll get a few, remnants of the runs that used to be plentiful."

Jena had learned that steelhead were native rainbow trout that migrate to the ocean as juvenile fish and return to the rivers to spawn as adults. Their time in the ocean allows them to grow big and strong. They are arguably the most sought-after game fish in the western United States. Hans called them the fish of a thousand casts', as they are so elusive and difficult to catch.

Hans looked at her. "What do you think of the water?" Jena studied it longer before speaking. "It's deep, that's for sure. The inside and outside seams look fishy. There is lots of cover near the bottom, especially near the far shore."

"Fishing techniques?"

"I would think dry flies, nymphs, and streamers could all potentially catch fish here."

Hans nodded. "I want you to practice streamer fishing with a sink tip. Get your rod set up."

Jena cringed on the inside, not so eager to continue her embarrassing struggle of casting a heavy sink tip line. The weight of the sink tip created a sensation that was so much different than casting a dry fly. It felt like she was trying to throw a slinky back and forth, the chunky weight of the sink tip threw off her timing, resulting in clumsy casts. One of the most frustrating things for Jena had been learning to adjust her casting techniques for each type of presentation. Casting a dry fly was much different than casting a two-nymph set up with a strike indicator, which was just a fancy term for a bobber. And casting a streamer with a sink tip was even different still. She had hoped that once she got the basic casting strokes down that the rest would be easy. She had been dead wrong.

She strung up her six weight, pulling the line through the eyelets. It already had the ten-foot section of type 6 sink tip, which was extra heavy. Hans figured if she could learn to cast the heavy sink tip, then she could cast a lighter one easy enough. And by the looks of the deep hole, the extra heavy tip would be just right to get the fly deep in the strike zone.

Once the line was through, she inspected her leader and tippet. The leader was short, about three feet, with another foot of tippet. She had prepared the leader herself and she remembered the 3x tippet was nine pounds. Besides the basic clinch knot, she now knew how to tie the surgeon's knot as well as the non-slip mono loop. Hans said she could get by knowing just those three knots.

She picked up her streamer box and began the process of selecting the right fly. She looked back at the hole, analyzing the water conditions once again. The water was gin clear, with some oxygenated turbulence near the waterfall. The sun was out but it would still be hours before it touched the shadowy section of river. She could feel Hans looking at her as she processed the information.

She pulled out a white and black streamer, a mixture of rabbit fur with a sculpin metal head and a few strands of crystal flash. Now that she was learning to tie her own flies, she was constantly analyzing the thousands of flies that filled her fly boxes. Chris had tied most of them, and considering she now knew the rudimentary skills of fly tying, she continued to marvel at his creations. Sculpins were a small freshwater fish that lived in many river systems throughout the western United States. They looked like the bull head that were often caught in the Puget Sound. Apparently, they made up a large portion of a trout's diet, especially the large fish who preferred a big meal to wasting their energy on a small dry fly. She decided to call this fly the Cop Car Crusader, a fitting name she thought for a white and black streamer. She smiled briefly thinking that Chris would like that name.

Hans nodded, approving of her choice to use a dark bodied fly on a dark day. She tied the fly to the tippet using the non-slip mono loop. That particular knot didn't cinch tight on the eyelet of the fly, allowing for more movement in the water, which better simulated a swimming fish.

She picked up her rod and moved to stand near the top of the pool, Hans just behind her.

"Now remember," Hans instructed, "keep your false casts minimal. Make sure you have some slack line near your feet and just let the weight of the sinking line pull the slack out when you cast the fly."

They had been working all week on the technique, but Jena had noticed little success. The last time they had tried, which was a few days ago, she had seen some improvement, but by no means was she casting smoothly.

She pulled some slack from the reel and let it coil up by her feet, pulling the sink tip line through the rod until the end stopped near the tip of the rod. She angled herself to cast out at about a forty-five-degree angle. The goal would be to get the fly to land in the faster current, the water taking it down stream as it sank. Then as the fly starts to swing across the current through the inside seam, she would begin to strip it in. The technique was called *swinging* for just that reason.

Lifting the rod tip up, she started her back cast, the heavy line jerking the large fly back. She thought to herself, oh shit, here goes that slinky feeling again. Once the line unfurled, nearly reaching its full length, she quickly shot her arm forward, shooting the line past her and out over the water. Letting go of the line, she let the heavy sink tip pull the slack at her feet and the line shot out about twenty feet. The cast was decent, but at the end, the power of the forward movement was more than necessary for the amount of slack, and it snapped back as the slack was used up. The fly shot back and landed in a pile near the tip of the fly line.

"You need more slack line," Hans instructed. "The power of your forward cast should pull the line out until the power dissipates, allowing the fly to land in a straight line."

Jena nodded. She had known that, but executing the movement was a bit harder than simple understanding. She let the line sink and allowed it to swing across the current and through the seam, which was the strike zone. She was just about to strip it in, when Hans spoke again.

"Wait," he said. "Let the fly sway back and forth in the current for a few moments before stripping it in. Sometimes you can entice a strike that way."

She waited, stripping the fly in by jerking the line just after the last eyelet near the reel. The line coiled near her feet as she brought the back of the sink tip to the end of the rod. Then she prepared to cast again.

Performing three more casts, she slowly moved down river, covering the water one cast at a time. She kept making the same mistake, not quite judging the amount of slack line needed before allowing the sink tip to pull the line and deliver the fly. As she moved down river, the width of the hole widened and she was forced to do a few more false casts to get more line out, enabling her to make longer casts. At least that was the goal, but again, executing the maneuvers was much harder than merely understanding them. She made some sloppy casts, the more line in motion causing her to use more power. She stripped in the line again and was getting ready to cast when Hans stopped her.

"Remember, when you false cast with a heavy sink tip, things get sloppy and you get tired. Just cast once, laying the line out. Then, with more slack at your feet, pull the line hard off the water and cast again, letting the weight of the line pull more line out. That way you're only casting twice and getting the same distance."

Jena let out a frustrated breath. "Okay, I'll try it."
She cast once, pulling the line back and using the rod to load the line, and shot it out over the water. The line flung out tight and landed

much lighter, having used up the slack on the rocks with a few yards still remaining. Immediately, she pulled hard and back again, casting a second time. On her forward movement she let the line pull the last few yards of slack out and the fly landed another fifteen feet, clearing the fast current to land on the outer seam.

"Good job," Hans grunted.

It was a good job, Jena thought, smiling to herself. That cast just felt right. She let the line sink and get pulled down river through the current. As it swung through the current, she looked back at Hans. "That felt really good."

Hans nodded and his eyes glanced back down river. Suddenly his eyes widened and Jena looked towards her fly.

"Fish!" Hans said in excitement as they both saw a white glow shoot from the depths towards the fly that was presently swimming in the current at the end of the swing.

It looked like a big one and Jena's heart pounded in her chest as her breath caught in her throat. She was so excited that all her lessons were suddenly flushed down the toilet, her body reacting only to her nerves. She jerked the rod back way to soon, pulling the fly away from the fish at the last moment. In two heartbeats, the fish flashed in annoyance and raced back into the dark water.

Jena stood there, slack jawed, dejected, at a loss for words. She looked at Hans, her face a mix of disappointment, shock, and excitement all at the same time.

"What are you feeling right now?" Hans asked.

"Pissed! Did you see that fish!?"

"I did," Hans said, "but what are you feeling?"

Jena let the line dangle in the water as she thought a bit deeper about her feelings. Her adrenaline was just beginning to abate, but her hands were still shaking. "I feel excited."

Hans nodded. "That is the feeling you want to hold onto. That is why we fish. That is why we spend hours working water for that one elusive fish. That is the drug known as fly-fishing."

"But I just missed that elusive fish!" Jena stormed, still angry at herself.

"That's why you need to put in the time. It will happen again. Recast."

Jena continued to work on her casting, moving further down the run until the faster current slowed and the water began to get shallower. It was still plenty deep and had lots of cover. Her arm was tiring but she finally felt like she was getting the hang of it. Casting once, she let the line unfurl across the slow moving water. Quickly picking the line off the water, she recast again, letting out more line as Hans had instructed. The fly carried the line another fifteen feet and landed at a perfect forty-five-degree angle, the fly touching down just as the line tightened, all the slack gone. It was a perfect cast.

"Did you see that!?" Jena whooped.

Hans nodded as she looked back at him.

Suddenly her line stopped in mid-swing.

"Set the hook!" Hans shouted.

Jena's head jerked back to the water and she lifted the rod tip at the same time. The line went tight and Jena felt a heavy weight on the other end. Suddenly the water exploded and a silver fish, much bigger than the last one, leaped from the clear water.

"Holy shit!" Jena screamed, holding onto the rod with wild eyes.

"It's a steelhead!" Hans yelled; his stoic demeanor replaced by an excitement that Jena had not yet seen. "Keep the tip up! If it jumps again lean into it by leveling out the rod!"

"Okay," Jena responded as the fish ran down river. Her reel zinged as line was pulled out faster than she thought possible. As the fish pulled, the rod tip lowered and she was forced to follow it down river. Hans's words echoed in her mind and she lifted the rod tip. But just when she did, the fish jumped from the water.

"Lower the tip!" Hans ordered as he followed her.

Jena leaned forward as the fish jumped three more times from the water, all the while pulling more line from the reel. "Oh my god, Oh my god!" Jena chanted hysterically as she followed the fish down river.

Just below the run was a shallow riffle that led to faster pocket water, large boulders placed sporadically across the river for at least fifty yards. Beyond that the canyon continued, the river flanked by rock cliffs. If the fish got into that portion of the canyon, she would not be able to follow.

The steelhead burst through the shallow riffle water and found soft water behind a boulder as big as a bathtub. Jena could barely keep up and by this time the fish had taken all the fly line out and she was into her backing. Most fly lines are between eighty and one hundred feet, and behind that is your backing, which was a thin braided line that could be another hundred feet or more. Jena was not sure how much backing was on the reel as it had been loaded by her husband. The rod was a six weight with a large arbor reel, so she had to assume there was at least a hundred feet of backing.

"What do I do?" Jena asked, her voice shaking with excitement.

"Don't let it get into the canyon," Hans said, his earlier excitement now replaced by calm instruction. "Angle the rod tip to the side and try to pull its head closer to the shore. If it runs, let it. You won't be able to stop it with 3x tippet."

"Okay," Jena said. She was afraid she was going to lose it. Moving closer to the fish, she reeled in ten feet of fly line.

She turned the rod on its side and used the tip to pull the fish closer to the shore.

"Gentle," Hans whispered.

Stepping away from the river, she directed the fish from the still water closer to the shore. But once it hit the faster current, it shot off again, like a rocket. Jena lifted the rod as more line screamed from the reel. This time the fish shot across the water, turning around another big boulder and changing directions to go upriver again.

"Rod up!" Hans shouted.

But it was too late. As the fish turned around the boulder, the fly line caught on the corner of the rock. Without stopping, the powerful fish propelled itself upriver as the line dangerously rubbed across the rock.

"You have to get the line off that rock," Hans ordered, his voice tense.

"How?" Jena asked frantically, barely holding onto the rod.

"Get in the water! Now! You're going to lose it!"

Jena didn't hesitate. She stepped into the water, keeping her rod tip up. Lifting her rod tip up and out, she tried to alleviate the pressure of the line on the rock. The fish stopped pulling, maintaining a firm position in the softer current.

She moved steadily across the water, her feet shuffling carefully across the slick rocks. Two steps later and she was up to her thighs. Two more steps and she was in just past her waist. But the angle was much better and she was able to lift the line off the edge of the rock. As soon as she did so, however, the fish must have felt the release of pressure, and it shot forward again, heading for the canyon water.

"Tighten the drag!" Hans yelled. "You have to keep him out of the canyon."

Jena turned the drag knob two more clicks and the line tightened a touch, slowing the fish some. She walked about five feet forward in the water as the fish pulled steadily. He seemed to be tiring some, but it was hard to tell. She was on a shallow rift, deeper water surrounding her on both sides.

Then the fish did something totally unexpected. It turned and bolted right at her.

"Keep the line tight!" Hans yelled.

Jena began to reel as fast as she could as the fish angled right towards her, the slack building in the line.

"No! Strip the line in, its faster!"

Jena let go of the reel and began to strip in the line as fast she could, using her right hand to pull two-foot sections of line in at a time, desperately trying to pick up the slack.

"Holy shit!" Jena yelled as the fish swam right by her, the line zipping through the water as it pulled the neon green line back upriver. Turning around, she followed the fish as it shot back into the shallow riffle water, heading straight for the protection of the deep-water from which she had hooked it. Suddenly her foot struck a big rock, and as she tried to catch herself, her other foot slipped on a second rock. She knew she was falling, but could do little about it. She screamed like a little girl as she fell side long into the cold water, clumsily catching herself before her head fell under the surface. Holding the rod up with her right hand, she used her left hand to push off the bottom and get her feet under her. Standing again, she regained control of the rod as the fish leaped from the surface again, flipping end over end as it struggled with the hook in its mouth. Screaming from the cold and adrenaline, she stumbled forward, trying to maintain a tight line as the fish jumped again, its silver body flashing in the morning sun that was just now penetrating the shadowy glade.

Her face was dripping with water and her eyes were wild, her chest heaving as she panted from the rush of excitement. As she stepped into the shallower water, she edged closer to the shore where Hans was waiting, her rod high and her line tight.

The steelhead had made it into the deeper water and was now holding still, the tight line angled straight down into the dark depths.

"Okay," Hans said. "Keep up the pressure. It's starting to tire."

"It doesn't feel like it," Jena panted, her arms exhausted from her exertion.

"Start to reel in slowly, turning the rod to pull its head sideways. Direct it towards the shore. If it's ready, it will let you. If not, it will run again. Just let it," Hans ordered. "Your tippet doesn't have the strength to stop it and you don't want to break him off."

Jena let out a deep breath, trying to calm her nerves as she slowly reeled, turning the rod sideways to move its head from the deep water. Slowly, the fish obliged, clearly not liking the pull on the side of its jaw. It shook its head a few times, angling for the deep water again, but she used her right hand to tighten the drag a few more clicks.

"Don't tighten—"

Suddenly the fish shot up and leapt from the water, its body shaking violently in one last attempt to free itself from the fly.

Jena yelped as she instinctively lifted the rod tip, trying to keep the line tight. There was a subtle snap and then the fish landed in a splash. And just like that, it was gone, her rod and line slack in her tired arms.

"No!" Jena screamed, looking frantically at Hans. "It's gone!" she yelled, unable to comprehend the loss. She just stood there in shock, staring into the water's depths, her heart still pounding like a war drum. She wanted to cry. She was having a hard time coming to terms with her emotions. The loss of the fish was magnified by the death of her husband, the two events, although completely different, assaulted her in a similar way.

She reeled up the line and walked from the river, tears streaming down her cheeks. "I'm sorry," she sniffed. "I think I need a minute." She turned away from Hans, confused and frustrated at her emotions. Was she sad about the fish? Was the loss of the fish a mirror reflecting the loss of her husband? All she knew was she was pissed, angry at losing the fish and frustrated as to how it made her feel.

Hans said nothing as she stepped next to him near the shore. They both stared at the water in silence, the morning sun glittering off the smooth surface.

After what seemed like an eternity to Jena, Hans finally spoke. "You shouldn't have tightened the drag."

She looked at him, her emotions turning from sadness, to frustration, to anger, and finally to something akin to amusement. "I gathered that," she responded with a wry smile.

"What else did you do wrong?"

Jena thought about it. "I didn't lean in and point the rod tip at it when it last jumped."

He nodded. "The line broke, likely from a combination of a tight drag and the elevated rod tip pulling the line away from the fish. It was just too much tension on the tippet."

Jena was silent as she contemplated her mistakes.

Hans looked at her thoughtfully. "You did good today." She wiped the tears from her cheeks and smiled. It looked like he was going to say something else, but then he simply nodded and added. "Ready to head back?"

She nodded and they gathered their gear in silence.

They spent two weeks working on casting, all the while going over gear, river conditions, entomology, and presentation. She was starting to feel confident in her casting, although casting a heavy sink tip was still her biggest obstacle. But she had improved greatly and didn't tire as fast as she had before. For false casts, which one does to get more line out or to dry a wet dry fly, she really enjoyed the analogy of flicking a paint brush. Hans had told her to imagine she was holding a paint brush in her right hand about shoulder height. He said she should be moving the rod from position 10 to 2, at the end of each stroke, think of stopping abruptly to flick the paint from the brush. That will load the rod and make sure not to start your forward movement until the line is completely unfurled. That way you won't lose your power. She had been practicing the technique for over a month now and it was beginning to feel second nature. At first, she had to look behind her. Now, she could feel the rod and line in a way that allowed her to cast using muscle memory, allowing her to focus on the water and the presentation.

She had caught over a dozen trout from six to sixteen inches, learning how to properly handle and release the fish. But the bigger fish had been eluding her, and the recent feel of that monster steelhead she had lost still haunted her memories. She wondered why she was still so focused on that when just weeks before she could've cared less about catching a steelhead. She voiced her quandary while they fished a known run about six miles downriver from the store.

"I can't stop thinking about that steelhead," she said, looking over her left shoulder to Hans who was fishing about twenty feet down river from her.

Han's lifted the edge of his lip as he shot a perfect cast to the far seam. Lifting his rod high, he kept his line off the current so the fly could drift naturally for at least ten feet before the current took his line and dragged his fly across the run. Sometimes all you needed was a few feet on a good drift to entice a fish to the surface.

"Steelhead dreams, I call it," Hans said. "That was your first taste of a truly magnificent fish. You'll dream about it forever."

She frowned. "Seems a bit melodramatic."

Hans just shrugged and cast again.

Jena was fishing a stonefly nymph under a strike indicator, which was basically just a bobber. It was a bit harder to cast than a traditional dry fly set up, but she was learning to adjust her movements for the various styles of fishing she had been learning. Casting a weighted nymph with a small lead shot, as well as a wind resistant strike indicator was no easy feat. She definitely false casted less, which was a good strategy anyway as Hans always liked to say, *the fish are in the water, not the air.*

"You remember your first steelhead?" Jena asked.

He nodded. "I was thirty, just after..." he paused briefly, interrupting his story. "I was fishing the Queets River," he continued, quickly picking up where he left off. "I was swinging a purple streamer on a slow run when the fish slammed it like a hammer. It was nearly twenty pounds. I'll never forget it," he said, while his eyes followed the dry fly as it drifted through the soft current. Jena could tell his mind was somewhere else, but she didn't push the subject, changing the direction of conversation.

"One thing I've learned is that I had no idea what fly fishing involved. There is so much to know."

"Yup," Hans grunted. "It's the little things that matter. Once you can combine them all, you'll understand the magnificence of the sport."

She nodded, remembering similar words Chris had spoken on many occasions. Memories of him cast a shadow over her thoughts as she walked further downstream, presenting her fly to the inside seam nearly thirty feet away.

That night Jena sat at Hans's fly-tying desk working on her first stonefly nymph. Hans was doing the store's books, somehow making sense of the mess on his desk as he occasionally went to his computer to type a few things. It was nearly eight and the store was about to close.

Irma knocked on the door and entered, her warm smile leading the way as it always did. "Everything is shut down. Here's the cash from the register today," she said, handing Hans a small money bag. Irma looked over Jena's shoulder. "What are you tying?" she asked.

Jena glanced back. "A stonefly nymph."

Irma looked intently, analyzing the fly. "I like it."

Jena smiled. "Thanks."

"You've come a long way," Irma said. "You think you're ready?"

"I think so," Jena said. "But I'm nervous."

Irma squeezed her shoulder. "I have a good feeling about you. You're going to be okay."

Jena was touched. She had spoken to Irma many times the last six weeks and had learned that Irma had lost her husband to a heart attack ten years ago. She had been working at Han's store every day since then. Nothing happened at that store without Irma's involvement. Jena had wondered on many occasions how Hans had survived prior to her employment. She worked the store daily while Hans fished. They both seemed to enjoy the symbiotic relationship, although Jena knew very little about their personal relationship.

"I hope so," she answered gratefully.

Irma grinned, glancing back to Hans. "I'll see you tomorrow," she said.

Hans grunted, not bothering to make eye contact.

Jena was looking at Irma, puzzled as to why she always seemed to take Hans's rude behavior in stride.

Irma winked at her and leaned in, whispering in her ear. "He's just a man. You can't expect much from him." She smiled and turned to leave.

Jena let out a soft laugh and returned to her fly as Irma shut the door behind her. A few minutes later, she decided to press Hans about his relationship with Irma. He had been curt to her on many occasions, but his behavior towards Irma had always bothered her. Irma did almost everything for him and he acted completely ungrateful. His rudeness was beginning to frustrate Jena to say the least. It was obvious that he was taking Irma for granted and yet neither of them seemed to care.

"How did you and Irma meet?" she asked.

"She is a local," Hans said sort of absent mindedly. "They both came to the store a lot. When her husband died, she asked for a job." He shrugged nonchalantly. "The rest is history."

Jena whip finished the end of her fly, tying it off before cutting the thread and applying a small amount of head cement, securing the thread behind the gold bead near the hook eye. Spinning around in her chair, she faced Hans.

"You know, you don't treat her very well."

Hans looked up for the first time, his eyes narrowing. "You know nothing about us."

Jena was tired of Hans's curtness, both to her, but more importantly to Irma. "I don't have to know any more than I do to know that she doesn't deserve to be disrespected." She appreciated all that Hans had done for her, but now it was time to challenge his behavior. Never being one to back down, she pressed the issue further. "Why are you such a cliché? I would've thought that was beneath you."

"Cliché?" Hans muttered. "What do you mean?" His tone revealed he was getting angry.

"A grumpy old man living alone because he can't reconcile the loss of his daughter," she pressed. She knew she might be pushing too hard. But she also knew that if he never talked about his daughter, that the festering wound her death left behind would kill him, and hurt others around him in the process. Years of counseling and trying to wade through a career where you're surrounded by death and dying had made her acutely aware of the healing power of talking about loss. She decided it was now time to broach the subject. "By all accounts Irma has been here for you, and yet you interact with her like she is nothing more than an annoyance."

Hans sat back in his chair, his anger palpable as he looked away from her, his eyes staring out the dark window. Then he looked back at her, his fiery eyes revealing his growing anger. "Don't speak of my daughter as if you understand. Losing a husband is one thing, but—"

"Stop!" Jena said, her voice equally stern, "before you say something stupid. You have no idea what I've seen and done. Do you know what it's like to take care of sick kids for months, only to watch them die? Do you know what it's like to grieve alongside their parents while trying to stay positive for the two other patients I have? I have bathed the cold, lifeless bodies of many children, some no more than a few months old, before handing over their little shrouded bodies to their parents so they can say goodbye to them one more time before I have to carry them to the morgue." Jena had now stood up, her anger escalating as the loss of her husband coalesced with the loss of so many

87

others she had experienced in her life. "I've personally experienced the grief associated with the loss of a child many times. But I have to relive it from all angles. I cry for the child I got to know. I cry for the grieving parents. I cry for the grandparents who don't know how to help their family suffer through the loss. I cry for the parents who are forced to leave the hospital without their child, only to come home to a house filled with their dead child's things. I understand your grief more than anyone," she said, her voice softer as tears streaked her face. "But it does not give you the right to treat those who clearly care for you with disdain. You need to grieve the loss of your child. You need to accept that there are people willing to help you through your grief. You do no one any good by denying your grief, especially yourself. Believe me when I tell you, this is one thing I know about." Jena paused as she regained control of her emotions. "As you said to me today, It's the little things that matter. Focus on the little things around you, and perhaps the big weight on your shoulder will blur into the background."

Then she tossed the finished fly onto his desk and left, leaving Hans in his chair, his expression a mix of anger and bewilderment.

The next morning Jena was up earlier than normal, even before the sun rose over the mountain peaks flanking the river. She heard Irma pull up and open the store at four thirty and decided to head down and help her get the coffee going.

Walking in the side door, she greeted Irma who was turning on all the lights and going through the morning procedures.

"Good morning," Jena said.

Irma looked up from the coffee pots. "Morning dear," she said. "I'm glad you're here. I have something for you."

Jena went to the coffee pots and helped her prepare the beverages for the morning. "Let me help you," she said. "What do you mean you have something for me?"

Irma smiled and went to the counter. She returned with a small package shaped like a box. It was wrapped in birthday paper. Handing it to Jena, she said, "It's for you."

Jena took it from her. "For me? It's not my birthday," she said, clearly confused.

"Perhaps not, but it's the only paper I had. Open it."

Jena smiled and opened the package. Inside was a beautiful wood box. The darker grain of the wood stood out like veins and it was polished brightly. "It's beautiful," she whispered. Opening it, she smiled even wider. It was a fly box, and inside was foam glued to the bottom and top where various flies could be placed. She was impressed with the craftmanship. "I love it."

"Good," Irma said. "It took a week to make," she laughed.

Jena's eyes widened. "You made this?" She couldn't believe it. It was really stunning. It was something that Chris would've loved, both for its purpose and its workmanship. Then she remembered that Irma was always reading wood working magazines and things began to click. She had thought it a strange genre for an old lady to read, but now it all made sense.

"I did. My husband died and he was a wood worker. I sat at home for years looking at his tools and machines. All it did was make me sad. It was last year when I decided I was going to learn how to use the stuff, both for healing and also for remembrance. Now everything I make in that shop has a piece of Bob in it. Strangely that makes me feel better."

Jena pressed her lips together in understanding. "It's not strange at all." She smiled widely. "I love it! Thank you so much." She couldn't help but think that they were both on a similar journey.

"Look on the back."

Jena flipped it over and there was a message that read, *The art of living is the mingling of letting go and holding on.* Jena smiled and looked up. "It's beautiful."

"I didn't make it up," Irma replied. "Some Mr. Ellis said it, or something like that. But I think it's fitting, for all of us." Her meaning was clear, and as if the universe agreed, Hans entered, the ringing bell above the door directing their eyes to the front of the store.

"Good morning," Hans said, his sharp eyes glancing at Irma. Still standing at the entrance with the door part open, he then looked at

Jena. "Get your eight weight and gear. We are going for a drive."
Then he left.

Jena hugged Irma tightly. "Thank you so much."

"You're welcome," Irma said, embracing her back. "You
better go, hon. Hans seems all business this morning."

Jena released her, giving Irma a mock frown. "What's new?"

Irma laughed and went back to prepping the store while Jena
moved to the side door. She had to grab her gear from upstairs.

Ten minutes later they were in Hans's old Ford heading down
river. Jena had grabbed a cinnamon roll from the store, as well as a
prepackaged sandwich and a large coffee. The sandwiches were not
that great, but they tasted somewhat edible after a long day of fishing.
Neither said anything as they drove through the grayness of morning,
Jena looking out at the river she had fished the last seven weeks. She
had come a long way, and if she were honest with herself, she couldn't
believe what she was now capable of with a fly rod. She was no expert
by any means, but she could cast proficiently, and more importantly
she was starting to understand the subtle nuances of fly fishing. And, as
a result, she was having more fun, which ironically also made her
sadder. Why hadn't she put this kind of dedication into the sport
when Chris was alive? Why did it take Chris's death to make her put
the time and effort into learning something that he loved more than
anything? She tried not to dwell on things she couldn't change. She
knew that Chris wanted her to live in the now, to not think about the
future, or to regret the past. She would honor his wishes and do her
best to put one foot in front of the other, and try to enjoy every step
along the way.

She surreptitiously glanced at Hans as they drove silently. He
was staring out the window, his mind seemingly elsewhere as he turned
left off the main road heading towards a town called Arlington. Jena
purposefully said nothing, realizing that after last night it might be wiser
to shut her mouth. It was hard for her, the silence creating an
uncomfortable stillness. Hans didn't seem to be affected by it, and she
silently wished she could enjoy life's moments without accompanying
them with words.

"She was eight when it happened," he said suddenly. Jena was so startled she nearly jolted in her seat. He continued to stare out the front window. "She died in my arms. We were throwing a ball back and forth in our front yard when I threw it a little too high. She just missed it and it went over her head and out into the street. She ran to get it not even looking before she entered the road." Hans paused as he blinked a few times. He was not yet crying but Jena could see the moisture glisten in his eyes. "She wasn't hit very hard, but I'll never forget the sound her head made as it cracked against the concrete. It was my bad throw that caused her death."

"You know that's not true, right?" Jena responded softly.

"Intellectually, perhaps," Hans said after a moment, quickly wiping the corner of his eye before a tear fell. "But the fact remains, she ran into that street because I threw the ball too high."

"I understand the guilt you feel. But it wasn't your fault, nor more than it is a mother's fault when her new boyfriend beats her child to death while she is at work. Things happened, an unfortunate series of events that led to her death. It wasn't your fault, and if you don't forgive yourself, it's going to destroy you."

"It already has."

Jena shook her head. "I see a healthy, fit man before me. You're not dead yet."

"The only time I feel alive is when I'm fishing," Hans said matter-of-factly. "My wife left me a year after it happened. We just couldn't reconcile the pain we were both feeling." He glanced at her for the first time. "I think she blamed me as well, although she never said as much. I needed to get away. I bought the store and the rest is history."

"You've held onto all that pain for over thirty years?" She asked, her voice a whisper.

"It's my way of not forgetting her," he said, the last word coming out a bit high as he struggled to hold back his emotions. Jena nodded. "That is something I can understand," she said, her own mind drifting to images of Chris. "But holding onto pain and guilt are not ways to remember our loved ones. You need to find a healthy way."

"I don't know how."

Jena was surprised at his vulnerability. Jena had begun to think that he was emotionally stunted, but now she was forced to adjust her appraisal of him. He was being honest and open, and she bet that it had been the first time in a very long while.

"I wish I had the answers," she said, just as much to herself as to him. "I'm struggling to find this path right now as well. Chris seemed to think that this journey of mine will guide me to those very answers." She looked at Hans poignantly. "You just need to find the right path."

"Perhaps I've just veered to the right on a new path and I didn't even realize it," he said, the corner of his lip curling up, as it did when he said something that he thought was witty or funny.

Jena smiled back. "Perhaps Chris purposefully put us on this path together."

Hans nodded. "The thought did cross my mind."

"How did you guys meet anyway? I've been meaning to ask you but we've been so busy."

"It was seven years ago," Hans began, as if he had already prepared the story. To Jena, he sounded like a bard of ages past retelling a story to a room full of ale infused patrons. "I was hiking far upstream, past the waterfall that I took you to, when I heard a cheer of excitement come from the river. I was curious as it was rare to find anyone that far upriver. Not to mention I didn't even know there was a way to access that canyon portion of the river. I bushwhacked through the brush and came out over a rock cliff just above that hole where you hooked the steelhead. Chris was there battling a large fish, hollering with joy. I watched him bring a twenty plus rainbow to the net, releasing him with reverence back into the deep water. I surprised him by telling him that was a great fish. He laughed with excitement and shouted at me to join him, pulling out two cigars from his wader pocket."

"That sounds like Chris," Jena interjected, enjoying his story. "No one else could get a stranger to join him for a cigar." Her own thoughts briefly drifted to when she had met Chris. He was in a restaurant eating dinner with a few buddies while she was at the bar drinking cocktails with friends, trying to unwind after a hard, twelve-hour shift. She had smiled at him a few times, noticing his rugged handsomeness. He must have noticed because he simply walked over to her and said hi. He was so confident and honest. She felt that he was genuinely interested in her, not like she was just a conquest to him. She found his carefree confidence to be alluring. And well, the rest was history.

"He told me about the secret rope and path and before I thought too hard about it, I was sitting next to him on a log smoking a cigar. As you know, I'm not that fun to be around and that was completely out of character for me," he added, smiling wryly. "But there was something about Chris that drew me to him. Chris didn't seem to care that I wasn't much of a talker, keeping the topic of conversation on fly fishing. He asked me to join him at the hole and we fished together for the rest of the day. I invited him to stay in the room above the store, but he declined."

"He liked to camp," Jena chimed in.

"That's what he said. We landed some nice fish that day, including a ten-pound steelhead that Chris caught. I had only seen a steelhead on the river on two other occasions. I was happy to be a part of it. I still call it *Chris's Hole.* Over the years after that day, we became friends and fished together as much as we could. We built a friendship and strong sense of comradery around fly fishing. He did stay in the room you are in on a few occasions."

"As he got older, camping became less appealing," Jena added. Hans nodded. "As it does for all of us."

Jena was silent for a few minutes as she thought of her late husband. As she had so many times before, she blinked to hold back the tears. Hans didn't say anything, his mind adrift with his own thoughts.

Finally Hans looked at her. "You know, his enthusiasm for life was quite annoying at first."

Jena barked out a laugh, which nearly became a sob, nodding her head. "I know...right!"

Hans laughed back. "He could always find the silver lining, and for someone like me who was living in the muck of depression, that can be very irritating."

"Maybe you were unconsciously drawn to him as you realized deep down that it was something you needed," Jena said. Hans nodded, mulling over her words. "I know I was drawn to him," she continued. "He was so good at pulling me from the sadness associated with my job."

They drove in silence for a few more minutes before Jena spoke up.

"Where are we going anyway?"

"We need to get you prepared for bigger fish," Hans answered. "We are going after the Coho in the Stillaguamish River."

Jena was excited. She had yet to catch and land a big fish. "Will we be swinging?"

"Yup."

Swinging big flies through runs was still her biggest struggle. Well, it wasn't the swinging part, it was the casting the heavy line and big fly. But she was now arguably proficient, and the thought of hooking into a big salmon was exciting.

Jena lay in the bathtub, the hot water slowly drawing the soreness from her body. She hadn't realized that fishing all day really wore you out. Casting heavy lines over and over again caused her right arm to ache. Her lower back, likely from walking and balancing over slick rocks, felt strained and sore. But the hot water pulled the tightness from her body and she closed her eyes thinking about the day.

She had landed two strong Coho, also known as silver salmon. Both of them really hammered her pink and purple streamer but she fought and landed them with practiced skill. She was proud of herself and as she sat in the tub her mind could still feel the strike and pull, the headshakes of the fish reverberating through the rod to her hands. She smiled as the steam from the water caressed the skin on her face. She was beginning to understand the reasons for Chris's passion, although she still struggled with one main thought. *How was learning to fish going to help her grieve?* Every time she thought about anything to do with fishing, she thought of Chris. How was that supposed to help her? Intellectually she knew that holding onto fond memories of your loved ones was a healthy way of remembering them, and in time the pain would ease as the memories became enjoyable. But emotionally, she was not able to imagine herself moving on, or being okay with Chris's death. She just wasn't ready for that. She had to believe that time would bring her the answers.

A week later, an early Saturday morning, Jena joined Irma to help her set up for the day. It had become an unspoken ritual, both enjoying their newfound comradery. Jena had made it a point to ask her about her late husband, and after a week had come to realize that she wished she had met him. He had been career army and they had retired far off the grid, both wanting to get away and start their new life together in a small town. She was into gardening and he did side jobs helping local community members with small building projects. He loved to work with wood and was an avid hunter and fisherman, although he never delved into the art of fly fishing. They had had a quiet, peaceful life together, until he had died of a sudden heart attack. Irma didn't know what to do with herself and that's when she saw the help wanted sign out in front of the store that had been purchased by a new owner. That owner of course was Hans, and well, the rest is history.

"I hope he pays you well," Jena said as she prepared one of the coffee pots. "You do everything around here."

Irma shrugged. "It keeps me busy and I don't need the money. Bob's military retirement is more than enough. He fought in Vietnam, contracting prostate cancer from that agent orange garbage they dropped all over Southeast Asia. The army paid him for the disease they caused." She sighed. "I find it so strange that he made it through all that only to die of a heart attack." She shook her head and changed the subject. "How about you? Are you going to be okay financially?" Irma had not asked her a lot of questions about Chris, but she was slowly beginning to prick the surface, easing into the discussion knowing that it was all still so fresh for her. Jena appreciated her tact.

"His life insurance policy was pretty significant. And he had invested our money wisely. I'll be fine to say the least."

"Good," Irma said as she finished getting the cash register ready. "So you really leaving us tomorrow?"

Jena clicked the lid shut, turned it on, and joined Irma at the counter. "Yeah, it's time to start the adventure," she said in mock excitement. It came out a bit more sarcastic than she meant it.

"You really not looking forward to it?"

This time Jena frowned. "It's not that, it's just...I can't stop—"

"—thinking about him," Irma interjected.

'Yeah," Jena agreed. "Fly fishing was his thing; it was his passion. I've actually really enjoyed the last two months, but everything that deals with fly fishing just brings memories of him racing to the surface. It's hard."

Irma nodded in understanding as she organized the counter. "That doesn't go away. The only thing I can say is that the pain you feel from the memories lessens over time."

"I know that intellectually," Jena said, "but it's so hard to process it emotionally. Everything is still so fresh, so new. I've been handling things pretty well, but I have my moments where I just want to curl up in a ball and disappear in my pain."

Irma reached over and touched Jena's hand. "I know, and I'm sorry."

The bell above the door rang and they both looked up. Hans entered and gave them a subtle smile. "Good morning, Irma," he said, his tone a bit softer than it had been before.

Jena turned away from Hans and winked at Irma, flashing her a knowing smile. Jena had informed Irma about the conversation they had had about his daughter. They had discussed privately that perhaps Hans was trying to open up more, and to be a better person. Both of them had noticed small changes in the man's attitude. He was less curt and freer with his smiles. He spoke more often and attempted small talk, although it always sounded pretty contrived. But it was a start.

Jena turned around, leaning against the counter. "Ready for our last day of fishing?"

Hans nodded. "You in for a hike? I'd like to end our time at Chris's Hole."

Jena smiled. "That would be great." But internally, Jena was feeling a whirlwind of emotions. Anxiety fluttered to the surface as she thought about leaving Hans and the safety of the world he had created. She realized it was exactly what she had needed. And now, it was nearly over, and she would be thrust into a fishing adventure she was not sure she was ready for.

It was raining when they got on the trail. But they were both decked out in waders and raingear, and despite the annoying drizzle they stayed warm and dry. She had a small fishing pack with lunch, water, and her fly gear, her two rods strapped to either side. Hans was similarly outfitted.

They didn't speak much and by the time they made it to the spot, the rain clouds had dispersed and the sun was shining through the holes left behind. The warmth didn't find them in the confines of the trees but it had turned into a pleasant afternoon, nonetheless.

Making their way down the tricky steep trail was a bit more difficult. Their feet slipped on the wet rocks and roots, and if it had not been for the rope Chris had put there years before, there would be no way they could've made it to the riverbed and the small canyon below. But eventually they found themselves facing the long, pristine hole, and rather than set their rods up, Hans surprised her by sitting on a log and indicating for her to join him. She sat next to him, taking off her pack and setting it on the smooth river rocks.

He had taken off his backpack and had gotten his gear out, but didn't move to string up the rod, opting to look out at the hole before him.

Finally he spoke. "When you hooked that steelhead here, how did you feel?"

Jena gazed at the crystalline waters, images of the steelhead leaping from the water filling her mind. "Adrenaline," she said easy enough. "My heart was pounding. I was nervous, excited, and scared at the same time."

"Nervous about what?"

"I didn't want to lose it."

"But why would that matter? Just a few months ago you could've cared less."

Jena could tell that he was leading her somewhere. "I don't know. I guess it's because I've worked hard. I actually know what I'm doing...sort of anyway," she added with a smile.

Hans nodded. "You do. In fact I'm very much surprised how fast you've picked up the sport. Chris was right, you did not disappoint."

Jena smiled. "Thanks." She hadn't heard much praise from him, and when she had, it came in very short bursts.

"The excitement you felt comes from knowledge," Hans began, starting his lesson like a seasoned teacher. "It comes from the fact that you hooked that fish because of a culmination of skills that you applied to that very action...the choice of the fly, the cast, your presentation, your hook set, the fight itself...it all led to nearly landing that fish." Hans paused as he looked intently at her. "To be a fisherman does not mean you have to catch a lot of fish, it simply means that you desire to chase that excitement. It's your high, it's your drug, it's what drives you to hone your skills further and to put time on the water. To be a fly fisherman is to enjoy the act...to enjoy the process." Then he smiled. "And when you do that, you will start to catch fish. There was no one I knew who understood that more than Chris. He was perhaps the finest fly fisherman I have ever seen. But it wasn't just his knowledge of the sport that made him great, it was the aura he exuded."

"What do you mean?"

"He always out-fished me and it used to drive me crazy. I would fish a run and move down river and then he would fish that same run just after me and land a beautiful fish. I hated it. Then I started joking around with him that the fish just liked him better." Hans paused and laughed, looking at Jena with a marvelous smile. She had yet to see him smile so broadly. It reminded her of the picture on his desk with his daughter. She couldn't help but smile back. "You know what he said to me?"

"What?" Jena asked, engrossed in his story.

"He said, *of course they like me better...the fish can feel my altruistic intent and stunning skill and they honor me with the fight.*"

Jena scoffed. "That sounds stupid, although it does sound like something he would say."

Hans laughed. "That's what I said. But he just smiled and kept fishing. I've thought about it many times since then and have concluded that there was something truthful about what he said."

"Really?" She inquired. It sounded a bit metaphysical, even for Chris.

Hans nodded. "I don't really have a good answer why. I just feel that how we think about something, impacts that something in a very physical way. I think that's what Chris was trying to say. It started to make sense to me when I applied the concept to fishing, but I could never apply it to my life. I want to thank you for opening me up to that very idea."

"I didn't do much," Jena added.

"It was enough. I've secluded myself for a long time, digging a rut so deep that I couldn't even see over the edges." Hans looked at her, his expression serious, his eyes misting over as he cleared his throat. "You gave me a boost."

Jena reached out and touched his hand, squeezing it gently. "You're welcome. I just hope I don't dig the same rut," she said, sighing deeply at the very prospect of such a thing.

"You won't."

"How do you know?"

"You're much more evolved emotionally than I am."

She looked at him to see if he was serious and he was smiling. Jena laughed. "Well that is definitely true." Jena decided to raise a question that had been nagging at her. "I've been wanting to ask you something. When I first met you in your office, I saw a letter addressed to you from Chris. Did he tell you I might be coming?"

Hans's expression grew serious. "He wrote me when he was diagnosed. He never mentioned his plan or the chance that you might be showing up at my door." Jena saw Hans's eyes glisten but she said nothing, waiting patiently for him to continue. Hans cleared his throat. "He just wanted to say goodbye."

"I wonder why he didn't just call you."

"He told me in the letter that he thought it would be easier for both of us if he wrote his words down."

Jena nodded, "I can understand that. Saying goodbye forever is a hard thing to do." By this time her tears were flowing freely as she recalled the night he died. She shook her head, trying to clear the memory. "It's not something I want to think about right now."

Hans coughed uncomfortably and reached into his pack, pulling out a flask and two glasses. "This should sidetrack us," he said as he handed one to her and poured two fingers of an amber liquid in each cup.

"What's this?" she asked.

"Scotch."

"Oh yum," she said sarcastically, wiping the tears from her face. Hans smirked and reached into his bag again, withdrawing two cigars. He handed one to her. "Mmmmm, double yum." The sarcasm was dripping this time.

"You told me that one of Chris's requests is that every time you catch a trophy fish at your locations, that you drink a scotch and smoke a cigar. I thought we'd practice both on our last day."

Jena nodded. "Okay...and despite my earlier sarcasm, I'd like that."

He pulled out a set of matches and lit his own cigar, puffing on it until the end was a glowing amber. Then he set the cigar on the edge of the log and prepared a wood match for her. "Have you smoked a cigar before?"

Jena shrugged. "Not really, although I've taken a few puffs off my husband's." She caught herself, a look of sadness flashing over her eyes. "Off of Chris's," she added softly.

Hans nodded. "Take the cigar in your mouth. I'll light it, and while I do just pull air through the cigar. But don't inhale, just let the smoke exit the sides of your mouth."

Jena readied the cigar in her mouth. "Okay," she mumbled, "go ahead."

Hans struck the match, holding the burning end to the tip of the cigar. Jena sucked in, drawing air through the tobacco, causing the end to flare brighter. "Good," he said, blowing out the match.

Jena suddenly coughed as she accidently inhaled some smoke. "Uhhhh, yuck," she coughed.

"Like I said, don't inhale the smoke. Just draw it in your mouth and exhale."

Jena hacked a bit more and took a sip of the scotch, trying to clear her throat. That didn't work well either and she coughed again. "Oh god," she coughed more, "that does not taste great."

Hans smiled. "It's an acquired taste. Just like in fishing, once you understand all the work that went into making that scotch, it becomes quite enjoyable, and you learn to appreciate the variety of flavors." Hans took a long pull of his cigar, exhaled slowly, then sipped the scotch, looking out at the water.

Jena practiced on the cigar, taking several shallow puffs, afraid of inhaling more smoke. She wasn't a huge fan yet, but she was tasting nuances of spice and leather. She sipped the scotch, swishing a small amount around in her mouth before swallowing the burning liquid.

"Tastes a bit smoky."

"It does, and that's not the cigar."

They sat in silence, puffing on their cigars and sipping from the scotch. Jena was hesitant on both accounts but after a while she got the hang of the cigar, and the scotch became somewhat palatable. The sky had cleared but the sun still could not penetrate the deep canyon.

"What's next?" Jena finally asked, breaking their silence.

Hans swallowed the last of his scotch. "We fish."

"You think the fish are ready to grace me with a strike, honoring my skill and technique?" Jena asked with a wry smile.

"You?" Hans asked, pursing his lips in mock thought, "probably not, but me, absolutely."

Jena laughed, and they both prepared their rods for their last day of fishing together.

Chapter 4

"Hi baby," Chris said as the video clicked on. Chris was filming from his office, sitting in his worn leather chair where he had often sat to read. "Well, I'm sure the last month or so has been quite interesting to say the least. If I know you, and I know I do, you persevered and showed Hans the true grit of an O'Malley. I sure wish I could've been there to see it all," Chris said, a flash of sadness floating across his features.

He quickly dismissed it but Jena noticed it, the subtle change in his demeanor causing a lump to form in her throat. She knew that in all the previous videos he had tried to be upbeat, to instill in her a sense that he was going to be okay, thus she would too. But it was only natural that there would be moments where he would slip. And she had just witnessed the first. "Oh baby," she cried. "I miss you so much. I'm so sorry I didn't learn to fish when you were alive." She was openly crying. Jena felt her nose burn and her heart pound in her ears. Sniffling, she wiped the tears from her eyes as she tried to control the pressure building in her throat.

"I bet you cast well and I'm sure Hans was impressed. I hope you and Hans got along okay. He is a good man. It's just that he has a lot of pain buried away. I was hoping that perhaps you would help him with that. It's in your nature to care for others, which is why I love you so much. I never would've noticed his pain prior to meeting you. But you've made me a better person. I have so many things I want to ask you about your experience, but, well," Chris smiled, "it would be a one-way conversation. If I could ask you one thing, it would be, did you enjoy learning to fly fish?"

"I did baby," Jena wept, wiping the tears from her eyes. She was sitting on her couch, having come home from the Skagit River the day before. It had been strange coming home after being gone for two months. It was comforting, but if she were honest with herself, she already missed Hans's old apartment, the smell of aged wood and clean air still reminiscent in her senses. As usual, she was drinking a glass of wine, a chardonnay from the Napa Valley. Cradling the glass in her hands she held herself tight, tucked into the corner of the soft couch. She wore a pair of comfortable sweats and one of Chris's old worn sweatshirts, his clean smell still clinging to the garment.

"I hope you had fun," Chris continued. "I hope you are beginning to understand why I loved the sport so much. I know you just touched the surface, but perhaps, over time, you will be the fly-fishing aficionado as I am...was...shit," he swore, laughing. "You know how difficult it is to reference yourself as if you are already dead?"

"You'll never be dead to me," Jena cried. Picturing him dead was something she really struggled with. It was easier for her to imagine him on a long fishing trip.

Chris paused and reached off screen, bringing into view a glass of scotch. Smiling, he lifted the glass in salute and took a sip. "So, it's time to plan our first trip. I am starting you off with the trip that I am just dying to go on." He laughed again, his wide smile lighting up the screen. "Sorry, too soon?" Chuckling, he continued. "You will be heading to the South Island in New Zealand to fish for monster brown and rainbow trout. Of all the places on my list, this is at the top. You'll want to bring five and six weight rods with natural tone dry lines. The water is gin clear and the fish are spooky. You don't want any bright fly line. Make sure you have at least a hundred feet of backing as well. Some of the fish there can get up to eight or even ten pounds. Bring nine to twelve-foot leaders with tippets ranging from 3x to 5x. Bring typical trout dry flies like Adams, Elk Hair Caddis, Royal Wulffs, Humpies, and Hoppers. Some Green Beetles or other terrestrial patterns work well too. As far as nymphs go, bring some Pheasant Tails, Hare's Ears, Copper Johns. I'm not sure if you'll be doing much swinging but it doesn't hurt to bring a variety of sink tips and streamers just in case. The weather there is similar to ours so dress accordingly." Chris suddenly smiled. "I just thought about how cool it is that you actually know what the hell I'm talking about."

Jena laughed as she was just thinking the same thing.

"Here is the tricky part. I already have you booked at a lodge called The Forest Lodge. I'm hoping the timing works but I had to book it early as it's popular and small and fills quickly." Chris's face sobered some, his mind clearly drifting to his own thoughts. *"I wasn't sure when I was going to pass,"* he said softly, *"but when I got to the point when I knew, I had Rob arrange it for me, well, for you, I guess."*

Jena sat forward in her seat. "Shit, when did you book it?" she asked out loud, knowing of course that he wasn't listening. She was nervous that she had taken too long up north learning to fish. Had she missed the reservation? Wait, she thought quickly, Rob would've told me if I had. She relaxed some, sitting back in her seat with her wine.

"Their seasons are opposite ours so you'll be heading there during our winter. I booked you a trip for December fifth to the ninth. You'll be back in time for Christmas with just enough time to get ready for your second trip."

Oh god, she thought. This would be the first Christmas without him. She didn't want to think about it let alone actually endure the pain. Maybe she could leave on her second trip right away, skipping Christmas altogether? It was something to think about.

"You're going to love the lodge and the scenery. It's stunning, not to mention you'll be taking a helicopter to some of the most remote locations on the island. That is where I want you to spread my first set of ashes. I trust you to pick the spot that speaks to you."

At the mention of Chris's ashes, Jena looked up at the hand carved wooden box on the mantle that contained Chris's remains. The sides were covered with beautiful etchings of fish. One of Chris's friends had made the box with great care and skill. Jena looked away quickly, not bearing to think about the fact that his once lovely and vivacious form was now reduced to a box of ash. It made her sick and she refocused her attention on the video, trying to shake the thought from her mind.

"I figured you have the money, so why not splurge. You're going to be pampered and fish some of the best locations in the world.

It's going to be amazing. I just wish I could be there with you to experience it." Again, melancholy flashed over his face. But he reeled it in quickly, smiling as if the gesture would push the sadness away.

"Oh honey, I'm so sorry," Jena languished. She now realized how difficult it was for Chris to pass these missions on to her. The locations he was sending her to were places he wanted to fish more than any other places in the world. And now, he would never get to. It had to make him sad. And even more so, it likely hurt him that she would be experiencing the destinations without him. She cried openly for his loss, and hers. Her body flushed with frustration as she realized she would never be able to fish with him, to share their joy of the sport together. Her regret was so palpable that she could cut it with a knife.

Chris spoke softly, addressing her as if he heard her speak. "Baby, this is hard for me. I cannot tell you how bad I want to experience these trips with you. I'm so sorry. I don't want to be sad when I speak with you like this." He smiled again, but this time it wasn't so vibrant. "So Rob has all the details. Also, don't forget my ashes, some scotch, and a few cigars. I will join you by the river, my presence formed from memories of me as you smoke a cigar and sip a scotch by the river side, the adrenaline from catching a trophy fish still coursing through your veins. I may not be there physically, but I will be there with you...right here," he said, tapping the side of his head. "I am always just a memory away. Just close your eyes and I'll be there." He smiled wide, the energy of his vibrant soul glowing through the simple gesture. "I love you more than anything. Good luck." Then he reached over and the screen went black.

* * *

Two months later and Jena was in a rental car driving towards the Forest Lodge. She had taken a short flight to Los Angeles with a three-hour layover, finally getting on a very long flight to New Zealand, landing in Queenstown roughly sixteen hours later. It had been a long flight, but two movies later and lots of naps, she had finally made it to her destination...well close anyway. She had picked up her huge checked bag, which was mostly filled with fishing gear, rented a car, and got on the road by noon. According to her research, and correspondence from the lodge manager, it would be a pretty two-and-a-half-hour drive to the lodge located on the Makarora River, nestled along the edge of Mount Aspiring National Park.

The drive was flying by quickly, the scenery truly magnificent, especially when she had made it to Lake Hawea and a short time later, Lake Wanaka. Makarora Lake Hawea Rd edged both of the stunning lakes and despite her anxiety of starting her first trip, she was mesmerized by the beauty of the place. The water was calm as the sun glistened off its surface, the double image of the mountain peaks in the distance reminiscent of a fabulous filtered Instagram picture.

A horn suddenly blared, snapping Jena from her thoughts as she jerked the car back onto the left side of the road. She had been nervous about driving on the left-hand side of the road, and true to her worries, her muscle memory sometimes pulled her to the right into oncoming traffic. She'd have to be more careful. Luckily, she was only about thirty minutes away from the lodge. Once there, she wouldn't have to worry about driving. Taking a deep breath, she gripped the wheel tighter, setting her nerves for the remainder of the drive.

Once she passed the northern end of Lake Wanaka, according to her GPS she knew she was getting close to the lodge. The road she was on meandered through a beautiful forest, the Makarora River somewhere through the woods to her left. Forty minutes later she had emerged from the woods, the gravel road leading towards an open valley, the picturesque river in the background shaded by mountains from the national park. There was a cluster of trees before her and it wasn't long before she drove into the parking lot.

The lodge was not big, reminding her of an expensive private home you might find in a ski town like Jackson Hole. It was an A frame building with what she guessed were living quarters on either side. The front of the building was dominated by an expansive deck. The open grounds were covered in lush grass and sporadic trees, a farm style wood fence surrounding it, the valley behind it leading to the open riverbed. Everything was so green, many of the trees big like oaks, their branches hanging low and covered with leaves of brilliant jade. Off in the distance, near the river's edge, she saw black cattle grazing peacefully under the peaks of the mountains behind them. She could see a quaint firepit to the right of the main structure with welcoming chairs and what looked like an outdoor kitchen. It was cozy and inviting, just what you would expect from a high-end fishing lodge.

There was a smiling man stepping off the deck to greet her, a cocktail held in hand. She guessed it was the lodge manager she had been corresponding with, although she wasn't sure as she had not seen a picture of him. She put the car in park and stepped out as the man approached.

"Welcome," he said. "You must be Jena."

Jena nodded, returning his smile. "I am, thank you."

He handed her the drink. "Would you like a margarita?"

"Sure," Jena said, taking the glass from him.

"My name is Todd and I'm the lodge manager. Please, don't worry about your things just yet. Let me show you around."

Jena stretched her back. "That would be nice. Do you mind if I use the bathroom first?"

"Of course not. We can start inside then. Please, follow me."

Jena loved his Kiwi accent and guessed that he was likely in his late forties. He had short dark brown hair and two-day old scruff. His skin was tanned and he wore a forest green button up fly-fishing shirt and tan khakis. According to the lodge webpage, Todd was not only the manager but an avid fly fisherman as well, and he certainly fit the part. If one were to pick out a lifelong fly fisherman from a line up, he would look like Todd.

Following Todd, she walked onto the expansive deck and went through huge glass doors that marked the entry into the A frame part of the home. The entire wall facing the river was glass and when they entered, Jena was not disappointed. The ceiling was high and thick dark beams stood out in contrast to the white ceiling. One side was occupied by a huge stone fireplace, the gray rock rising all the way to the thirty-foot ceiling. Surrounding it were comfortable couches and a wood coffee table, all looking as if they were purchased from Pottery Barn. Again, it reminded Jena of an expensive ski lodge. Behind the couches was a long beautiful wood dining table surrounded by fourteen gray leather chairs. There was a doorway on one side and a long hallway on the other.

"Down the hall at the end is the bathroom," Todd said, smiling. "I'll wait here for you."

"Thank you."

Jena found the bathroom easy enough. There were four other doors occupying the long hallway and she assumed they were guest rooms. She had seen a few other buildings on the property and based on what she had learned from the website they were the chalets, offering more guest accommodations.

Todd was there waiting for her when she returned. Jena sipped the margarita. "This is good," she said.

"We made it just as you instructed...lime juice, Cointreau, and tequila."

"It's the best," she said, saluting Todd before drinking again. She had learned many things from Chris, and one of them was how to make a high-quality cocktail. Part of the guest questionnaire she had filled out prior to coming was what kind of foods she liked and didn't, and what drinks were her favorite. She was glad to see they had paid attention.

"How was the drive?"

"It was beautiful. I thought about stopping more to explore, but I really wanted to get here."

"Well it's good to have you. And don't worry, you'll see plenty of beauty in the next few days." Todd looked around. "So this is the main gathering room and dining hall. Everyone is away now, fishing, but this evening the guests generally meet here. We'll have appetizers provided as well as cocktails. The guests will hang out on the deck, by the fireplace inside, or out near the firepit. Then you will all sit around the table for dinner. It's a fun time to hear everyone's fishing stories for the day." Todd pointed towards the door on the other side of the room. "That is the kitchen. Our chef, Lisa, is simply fantastic. You'll meet her later this evening."

"It's a beautiful place. Do those doors lead to rooms?" she asked, pointing down the hall.

"Yup, we have four rooms here and four chalets outside. You have one of the chalets, so you have the space to yourself as well as your own hot tub. You'll love it after a long day of fishing."

Jena thought back to the evenings soaking in the bathtub above Hans's store. She had no doubt that she would be enjoying the soothing hot water. "Do we do a lot of hiking when we fish?"

Todd nodded. "We have different fishing conditions available for different levels of endurance. But, if you're in decent shape, we recommend hiking to find your fish. You'll get into bigger fish, more of them, and the scenery is breathtaking."

"Sounds wonderful." Jena wasn't worried about the hikes. She enjoyed the physical activity associated with fishing and she was no stranger to walking long distances. Hans had taken her up and down the river for miles, even bushwhacking in some spots to get down to the riverbed.

"Let me take you to your chalet so you can look around and unpack," Todd suggested. "If you don't mind me doing so, I can grab your gear and bring it to you."

"Okay, that sounds fine."

Todd led her out a set off French doors onto the back deck, its entire expanse covered by the A frame ceiling made of more stout beams, beautiful steel pendant lights hanging from above. The grass beyond had a few lawn games, one she recognized as corn hole. She had played it many times with Chris.

A wave of sadness suddenly hit her as she imagined Chris walking with her onto the back deck, looking back at her with a wide vibrant smile, his enthusiasm and excitement bringing a smile to her face as it typically did. The image was in slow motion, Chris's form like a ghost as she tried to hold onto the construct in her mind. It was a double-edged sword of course, the image bringing to mind something that she would never get to experience with him, along with the reminder of how he made her feel.

"It's right through that trail," Todd said, stepping onto the grass towards an opening in the hedge. The entire backyard was wrapped in a waist high hedge, various openings leading to the chalets and more grounds beyond.

Chris's image faded from her mind at the sound of Todd's voice. She quickly wiped the corner of her eyes. It looked as if Todd might have noticed the subtle movement, but if he did, he didn't say anything, continuing his tour without pause.

"The property was bought twenty years ago by the owner and converted into a lodge. The chalets are the newest additions having been built five years ago."

"Does the owner live here?"

"He lives here about five months out of the year and then spends the remainder of the year in Oregon guiding the rivers there on our off season. He's a fishing bum like the rest of us," Todd added with a smile.

He led her to a cute building on the right, a small porch welcoming them to a solid wood door. The building was a smaller version of the lodge, an A frame style with living space on either side.

"Why don't you look around and I'll get your luggage. Is the car door open?"

"I think so," Jena said. "Here, take the keys just in case." She handed Todd the keys. "There is a big bag and a smaller carry on. The big bag is heavy. It has all my fishing gear."

"No problem." He reached by her and opened the door to the chalet. "Go on in. I'll be back in a little bit."

Jena entered and smiled. The room was fantastic, a sense of comfort surrounding her. The main room was a small living room with an inviting couch, the cognac leather aged and worn. But it wasn't the aged look you get when gazing at a dilapidated couch on its last legs. It looked soft and comfortable, like you could easily slip into its embrace, the supple leather pulling away the stresses of the day. The couch faced a gray stone fireplace and the ceiling was similar to the main house, wide dark beams met a huge center beam holding up the A frame roof. There was a small kitchen and dining room table, reminiscent of something you would see in a nice condo at a ski lodge. Beyond the kitchen was a set of French doors that led to a small covered deck, a little table and two chairs positioned to look out at the expanse of grass that covered the valley floor. She couldn't see it, but knew the river wasn't too far beyond the field as she could hear its flowing water. To the right was a little two-man hot tub surrounded by a privacy screen on one side. The other side of the deck was edged by a tall hedge providing privacy from the adjacent building. She was thankful for that as she did not bring a bathing suit. But she had no qualms about jumping naked into the tub.

The bedroom was simple and comfortable, the bed flanked by two nightstands. There was a dresser as well as a good-sized closet, all the furniture of high quality. The bathroom was a mixture of gray tile and beautiful wood, the concrete countertop and white vessel sink giving it a nice combination of rustic and modern.

By the time she reentered the living room, Todd was at the door with her things. "Knock knock," he said, pushing open the cracked door. He smiled when he saw her, setting the bag down near the couch. "What do you think of the place?"

Jena smiled in approval. "It's beautiful...so comfortable. I love it."

"Good. So, are you hungry?"

"A little." It was early afternoon and Jena had not eaten lunch.

"I'll have Lisa make you a late lunch. Any ideas what you'd like to do? It's too late to go on an excursion, but I could take you down to the river to explore if you'd like. You can bring your rod. Or you can take a look around on your own, whatever you prefer."

"I think I'd like to go explore the river on my own if you don't mind."

"Not at all," Todd said. "You going to bring your rod?"

"One thing my husband," Jena paused, checking her words once again. "I'm sorry," she stumbled. "One thing my late husband taught me was it was always better to have a rod and not use it, then to need it and not have it."

Todd's face sobered some. "Sounds like he was a smart man." For just a moment it looked like he was going to ask more, but then decided against it. "Can I give you some recommendations on tackle?"

Jena smiled, trying to ease the uncomfortable situation. "Of course."

"Did you bring a six weight?"

"Yup."

"What about a light-colored dry line?"

"I did."

"Okay, rig that up with a Royal Wulf or maybe a small hopper. If you see a fish, be easy on your presentations. The water is really clear and they are quite spooky. If they don't take that, tie on a small pheasant tail as a dropper."

Todd was looking at her to see if she understood what he was talking about. He had no idea the level of her skill and knowledge, but likely assumed she knew something considering what she was spending to fish in one of the best places in the world for trophy brown and rainbow trout.

"Got it," she said confidently. "So do you get much time to fish?"

Todd shrugged. "Not as much as I'd like, but I get my line wet when I can. Why don't you get rigged up and I'll get you a sandwich. Want it in a to go bag?"

"Yeah, that would be great. Thanks."

Thirty minutes later and Jena was walking across the grassy field, passing through a gate that looked like it fenced in the cattle she had seen earlier. She wore her waders and carried her six-weight rod, a small chest pack holding her fishing gear and sandwich. When Todd had seen her net, he had quickly found her a replacement more suitable for the size of fish she might find. She emerged onto the sandy riverbed, walking another couple hundred yards before finding river rocks and downed timber, and finally the clear river.

It was obvious by her surroundings that they were nestled in a big valley, so the river directly in front of the lodge cut through farmland and was relatively flat. She could only guess that further upriver would be the secluded fishing grounds that one could only reach by helicopter. Todd had told her that the water in front of the lodge was not prime water, but occasionally guests would hook into a nice fish. Jena was just looking forward to stretching her legs after a long flight and drive, and to ease her mind into her first fishing adventure.

She walked upriver enjoying the beautiful scenery. It was mid-day and around seventy-three degrees, the skies bright blue and not a cloud in sight. And Todd wasn't kidding, she could see straight down to the bottom like it was glass. Scanning the water, she looked for any signs of fish. She figured it was so clear that she would have no problem spotting one. A mile later and she hadn't seen a thing. She crossed over some big rocks forming a bulwark to the river and giving her an ample view from above. The section of the river before her looked to be between three to eight feet deep, the bottom lined with rocks of various sizes and colors, ranging from light gray, white, and some even black. A few of the rocks were huge, half the size of a car. The current was moving but not turbulent. It looked to be a good spot to possibly hold fish. She stood on a rock and gazed out over the stretch of river, but after a few minutes gave up, not seeing anything that resembled the body of a fish.

Deciding to sit on the boulder, she took out the sandwich and bottle of water. Biting into the sandwich, she was impressed with its flavor. It looked to be fresh cut turkey breast, lettuce, tomato, mayonnaise, and some type of tomato jam. But she could taste rosemary as well, which surprised her in a very pleasant way. Chris would've enjoyed the flavors. He had been quite the cook, enjoying the artistic side of creating unique dishes. Jena loved his food, but she had hated coming home to the mess he had built during his culinary experiments. He wasn't perfect, she had to remind herself. The one thing they argued over was his sloppiness. But now, staring out at the stunning river, she would give anything to come home to his mess again. Feeling morose, she tried to focus on something more positive as she quickly consumed the sandwich. She had to admit that she was excited for dinner. If it was anything resembling the quality of table fare she had just eaten, then she would be in for an outstanding meal.

Drawing her gaze from the stunningly clear water, she drew her small leather-bound journal from her chest pack. She wanted to go over the things that Chris had asked her to do. She had written the list down on the first page, saving the rest of the little book for journaling every step of the adventure as Chris had requested. Opening it to page one, she went through the list once again.

1. Drink a scotch and smoke a cigar at each location after I catch a trophy fish
2. Find an event, or experience, at each spot that Chris would love that I would not. I must experience it as Chris would
3. I am to meet one interesting person at each location and tell them why I am doing what I'm doing
4. I am supposed to learn one major life lesson at each location

"Shit," Jena swore, looking up. *This was going to be hard,* she thought. Not all fishing locations were conducive to meeting the requirements on the list. There were no 'places' here to visit...and what life lessons was she going to learn while fishing in New Zealand? *Damn it, Chris,* she thought, *why are you doing this to me?* Now she was starting to get angry. She just couldn't see how all this shit was going to ease the pain in her heart.

Well, the easy part would hopefully be catching a trophy fish, enjoying the scotch and attempting to enjoy the cigar. It was likely, she thought, that one of the guests or guides would provide her an opportunity to tell them her story. So the difficult requirements asked of her were finding a spot that Chris would enjoy and she likely would not, and learning a life lesson.

Suddenly a rhythmic *whoop whoop* drew her attention up valley. She caught sight of a white helicopter racing down valley heading directly towards her. Turning at the last minute, the pilot expertly maneuvered the chopper towards the lodge, landing gracefully on the field adjacent the building, causing the high grass to blow outward forming a circular pattern as the deafening roar of the blades gradually quieted as they slowed their rotations.

Jena stood on the rock to get a better view. Two guests off loaded the chopper and were met by Todd, who handed them each a cocktail, likely their favorite beverage. They looked to be an older couple and they followed Todd back into the lodge. A few moments later and the chopper was off again, heading back towards the direction from which it had come. Checking her watch, she saw it was nearly four in the afternoon. The guests would likely be coming home in waves, although she was not sure just how many were presently staying at the lodge.

Glancing back at the water, she perused the long deep run one more time. Again she saw nothing, deciding it was time to head back to the lodge and meet some of the guests. She was by no means an extrovert, but neither was she an introvert. She enjoyed meeting new people and she could hold her own making small talk. But she had to admit she was dreading telling her story, worried that voicing the words would cause her emotions to rush to the surface. And she knew she wouldn't be able to avoid sharing her story. Afterall, it was rather unlikely that a middle-aged woman would go on an expensive fly-fishing trip by herself. People were bound to be curious.

A few hours later found everyone in the dining room eating appetizers and enjoying their beverages, countless choices of wines, beers, and custom-made cocktails. The appetizers consisted of grilled prawns, a lovely charcuterie plate, bacon wrapped pineapple, and small skewers of beef tips drenched in some sort of sweet sauce. Everything was delicious and artfully plated.

Jena had made the rounds, introducing herself to the guests. The first couple she met was a father son duo. The father's name was John and he was an executive at Amazon. He was tall and gangly with wide rimmed glasses and wavy salt and pepper hair. His son, Dawson, the spitting image of his father, minus the glasses and the salt in his hair, had just turned eighteen. They had been fly-fishing together since he was twelve and John thought it would be a great birthday present to take his son on this extraordinary fly-fishing vacation. It was pretty clear to Jena that John was giving himself quite a gift at the same time.

There was a single man from Montana, a fly-fishing guide who had always dreamed of fishing in New Zealand. She guessed he was in his early thirties and she had to admit he was pretty handsome. He reminded her of an L.A. surfer, with unruly sandy blond hair and a tan to match the stereotype. His name was Lars and she liked his down to earth personality immediately, reminding her of Chris's friends.

The largest group was four gentlemen from England, old college friends who had made it a yearly tradition to fish together in popular locations all around the world. Their accents enchanted her but what really impressed her was their comradery. They truly enjoyed each other's company, laughing and joking about past exploits, and ribbing each other good naturedly about lost fish or other faux pas. It was obvious to her how excited they were to be on this particular trip.

As she sipped her salty dog, which was her go to drink when she couldn't decide what she wanted, she talked with an older couple from Texas. She realized that this must have been the couple that had gotten off the helicopter while she was out near the river. After she had introduced herself to everyone, she had made her way to the comfort of one of the leather chairs next to the couch that was facing the crackling fire. The couple had sat down on the sofa next to her and introduced themselves immediately. They had a Texas drawl that Jena found quaint but endearing. She guessed them to be in their sixties. Ron was tan with silver hair parted on the side. Lilith equally tan, and her years in the sun had aged her prematurely, though her gray hair was cut in a stylish bob that gave her a contrastingly youthful look. Both were fun and vivacious. Jena learned that Ron had recently retired as a history teacher and his wife, a retired insurance agent, had booked his dream trip to New Zealand to celebrate. It was just the thing she would've done for Chris. The wife was not a fly fisher herself, but she wanted to be a part of his retirement adventure, nonetheless.

"So you came here all by yourself?" Lilith asked. Lilith and Ron were sitting on the couch facing the huge fireplace. Jena occupied the leather chair adjacent to them. The room wasn't cold, but the flickering fire provided a tranquil ambiance.

Jena shrugged. "I did." Up to this point, their conversation had been small talk. Perhaps this was the time to open up a bit. She felt comfortable with them and decided immediately that she would broach the subject. "My husband passed away and this was a trip he had always wanted to make."

Lilith put her hand to her mouth, and sat back in her chair, her eyes sympathetic. "Oh my dear, I'm so sorry, I didn't mean to pry."

Ron, on the other hand, leaned forward, very much interested in what she had said. "I'm so sorry, Jena. If you feel up to it, I'd love to hear your story."

Oh god, Jena thought, *did she really want to bring this up?* Would she be able to maintain control? She had been fine up to this point, but now, Ron's interest had rekindled her pain. She cleared her throat. "Well, since you asked..." she paused, not sure how to continue as a lump grew in her throat. "I'm sorry," she continued, "but this is all still so fresh." She paused again, then began slowly. "Chris, my husband, was an avid fly-fisherman. The sport was his life. He was diagnosed with cancer and died soon after." She paused as she looked at them both. "Are you sure you want to hear the story?" Despite the fact that one of Chris's requirements was to tell the story, she was self-conscious about dumping such a heavy load on someone.

"If you're okay telling it, we'd like to hear it," Ron said, urging her on again as he glanced at his wife. Lilith looked at Jena expectantly as she tightly held her husband's hand.

"Okay," Jena continued. "I have to admit, it is an interesting story."

"Well those are the best kind," Lilith urged softly.

Jena smiled. "Okay, here it goes. So, before Chris passed away, he conjured up this adventure for me, telling me about it after his death through a series of video clips."

This time it was Ron's turn to sit back in his seat. "Wow," he whispered, looking at his wife before returning his gaze to Jena. It was pretty clear that he was thinking about the difficulty he would have watching videos of his deceased wife. "It must be so hard watching the videos."

Jena nodded, her eyes glistening with tears thinking about them. "It is, but seeing his face...hearing his voice...it's all I have left. I'm actually looking forward to seeing the next video."

Lilith still had her hand to her mouth, her eyes reflecting genuine empathy. "How many videos are left?"

"It's probably easier if I just start from the beginning."

Lilith was sitting closest to Jena and she leaned forward and touched her leg. "Go ahead dear, start where you see fit."

116

Jena nodded. "So my husband asked me to finish his fly-fishing bucket list. He wants me to fish all the locations he wanted to fish before he died, spreading his ashes at each location. There was a list of things he wanted me to do at each spot."

"Did you know how to fly fish prior to his passing?" Ron asked, intrigued by her story.

"I did not. He asked me, in one of the first videos, to visit a friend in the mountains and spend some time with him in order to learn the sport."

"And you did that?"

Jena nodded. "Two months of training on a remote north Washington river and here I am."

"How many trips does he want you to make?" Ron asked.

"This is my first one. I have four more to go."

Ron sipped his scotch slowly as he processed her story. "So what does he want you to do at each location, besides fish I mean?"

"Well, that's where it gets interesting. He wants me to drink a scotch and smoke a cigar after I catch a trophy fish."

Ron grinned, lifting his clear glass of golden scotch. "I'll drink to that. Damn," he swore, "he sounds like my type of guy."

She smiled sadly and managed to hold back her tears. She took a deep breath, and continued.

"You don't have to talk about it," Lilith said, seeing Jena's emotional state.

"No, no, it's okay," Jena said. "One of the stipulations was that on each trip, I find someone to tell my story to. You two," she said sheepishly, "are my first audience."

Ron nodded. "Okay, so you need to drink a scotch and smoke a cigar after a trophy fish, as well as tell your story to one person on each trip. What else did that crafty husband of yours devise?"

"Well," Jena continued. "I need to visit one place that he would like but I would not, and try to enjoy it through his eyes. Oh, and I'm supposed to learn one life lesson at each location."

Lilith looked a little confused. "You mean a life lesson learned by fly-fishing?"

"Yeah, I think so," Jena said, although she wasn't totally sure if it had to be linked directly to fly-fishing. "I think as long as it is something learned during the trip then it would apply."

Ron smiled. "Are you looking for a life lesson for this trip?"

Jena cleared her throat, wiping her eyes again. "I am."

"Okay, I have one for you, and it's related to fly fishing," Ron added. "It's something that has driven me my entire life. "Here it is," Ron paused dramatically to build anticipation. "Choose experiences over things." He paused again as he let the words set in. "I chose to be a teacher as a direct consequence of those very words. It is what we do that matters, not what we say or what we own. Fly-fishing is a sport that creates experiences, events that sear into our consciousness, memories that make us who we are. It is the memories we gain that enrich our lives. Besides my wife and family," Ron continued, "there is nothing that has given me more incredible memories than fly-fishing. They fill my thoughts and my dreams."

Jena smiled. "You sound like Chris."

Ron nodded and smiled. "Of course I do. We are kindred spirits." He lifted his glass. "To Chris, a true angler...a man of dreams and experiences...a man not to be forgotten."

Jena felt the rush of sadness again, but she found a place for it, shoving it behind a door, a technique that had saved her many times at work. She lifted her glass.

Lilith raised her glass with a soft smile. "To Chris."

"To Chris," Jena whispered.

They all took a generous sip.

"Okay," Jena said. "No more of this depressing shit. Let's talk fishing."

Jena didn't think it was possible, but Ron smiled even wider.

* * *

The next day Jena found herself buzzing over the tops of the emerald foliage that adorned the mountainous landscape. The *thumping* blades and agility of the R44 helicopter was exhilarating as they flew west towards a high mountain section of river. Justin, her guide, sat next to her in the back while the pilot expertly maneuvered the chopper. She had never before been in a helicopter, and despite her fluttering nerves, she was enjoying herself. Perhaps, she thought, this flight counts as something on the list that Chris would want to visit, or do, that she would not. After all, she never would've agreed to jump into a helicopter if it wasn't for this crazy adventure Chris had planned for her. She suddenly decided that it did count, and did her best to experience the flight through Chris's lens. She imagined his eager eyes as he took in the scenery, anxious to see the crystal-clear waters that housed the massive trout he had read so much about. She found herself forgetting about possibly crashing into a mountain and focused instead on the picturesque landscape. It was easy to imagine herself hiking the stunningly clear river below, hunting for big trout. It was an exciting lens to look through.

Her day had started at 6:30 with coffee and a high energy breakfast of eggs, bacon, toast, and oatmeal. Her guide, Justin, had told her to fuel up as they would be doing a lot of walking. She looked out the window of the chopper and couldn't help but continue to think of Chris, which of course was the point of the entire trip. What she needed to figure out was how she was supposed to remember her husband, while at the same time not suffering from the burdensome pain that weighed on her heart like a pile of rocks. How was she supposed to remember her husband through fly fishing without feeling his absence? She didn't know the answer, and her momentary excitement was again dispersed by her recurring sense of loss. He would never get to experience what she was seeing...what she was about to do. The feeling of regret was nearly overwhelming.

The sound of her guide's voice over the headset jolted her from her solemn reverie. "We'll be landing over there," he said, pointing towards a valley that was quickly approaching. Justin sat next to her. He looked as if he were in his mid-forties, around her own age, with black hair and a neatly trimmed beard. His accent clearly pegged him as a Kiwi but she didn't know much else about him. Short and stocky, his muscular arms indicated that he spent some time in the gym. His serious demeanor seemed at odds with the more cheerful and outgoing personalities of the many fly-fishing folks she had met over the years.

Jena looked down at the sprawling valley, the turquoise river cutting through it, twisting around beds of rocks and patches of trees. The pilot, Gerald, brought the helicopter down quickly, expertly maneuvering it towards a flat expanse of knee-high grass, the river an arrow shot away.

The helicopter rocked a bit as it came in fast. Jena looked apprehensively at Justin and he smiled. "It's okay, we'll be on the ground soon."

Hovering, the chopper slowly lowered and touched down gently onto the grassy field. Justin took off his headset, grabbed his backpack, and flung open the door, jumping out smoothly. To Jena, it looked like he had done that a thousand times. She followed suit, though not as gracefully, grabbing her own pack and climbing out as the powerful downwash from the blades pummeled them both. Keeping their heads down, she followed him away from the chopper as the grass around them futilely fought against the power of the blades' wind.

Justin gave Gerald a thumbs up and just as quickly as he had landed, he shot off into the clear blue sky. Once the chopper was far enough away so they could hear again, Justin smiled at Jena. "You ready for this?"

"I think so," she said tentatively, feeling a little bit out of her league.

Justin could tell she was uneasy and he tried to ease her concerns. "Listen, this is all about having fun. It doesn't matter if you are an expert or a beginner, it's the fishing we are here for, not the catching."

Jena wanted to tell Justin that that was something Chris' would've said, but she didn't feel like getting into her story at the moment. It wasn't the time or place, and besides, she had already told her story to the couple the night before, and quite honestly, even though they had received it with empathetic grace, it had exhausted her. Now was the time to fish.

"So it's tough to catch fish here?"

Justin shook his head. "It's not that, it's just that sometimes people come here thinking they are going to catch hundreds of fish. This fishery is not a numbers game, it's a quality one. We'll get you into some fish, I have no doubt, but whether we get them to the net is an entirely different story."

Jena remembered that steelhead she had hooked and lost, and knew exactly what he was talking about. "Okay," she said, "let's do this."

Justin smiled. "Get your rod strung and we'll get moving."

They had walked a mile along the river's edge, all the while Justin scanning the clear water as they picked their way over rocks and debris. The riverbed was wide and open, most of the debris littering the river's edge in sporadic piles. The temperature was in the mid-eighties and despite Jena's thin summer waders and light short sleeve fly fishing shirt, she was sweating pretty heavily. The sky was clear and blue, with occasional white clouds, like cotton balls, drifting by in the mountain breeze. The scenery was desolate and alluring at the same time. Chris would've loved it.

They passed a number of great pools and tail-outs and Jena was surprised they hadn't stopped to fish a single one. Justin picked up on her confusion. "Our chances go up significantly if we sight cast to fish we can actually see. The fish here are very territorial and it's uncommon to see more than one or two together. If I can't see a fish, there likely isn't one in that hole."

They walked another half mile when Justin finally stopped. They had entered a more forested section, the open valley narrowing to cliffs of trees and rocks, the river's edge scattered with rocks of all sizes. They traversed the river's edge, picking their way over boulders and smaller rocks, their surfaces slick with moss. In most places the river's edge was dominated by pocket water, shallow water rushing around the various sized boulders and rocks. Justin crouched low on a large flat rock. He motioned for her to stay low and join him.

"You see one?" she asked as she stepped onto the rock to his right.

He nodded, pointing towards a deep section of the river against the far bank. "Look there, about three feet up from that log."

There was a log sticking out of the deep water and she scanned the area around it. The water was clear and all she could see were shadows from the rocks that littered the bottom. She guessed it was nearly six feet deep. But she couldn't see a fish. "I don't see it."

Justin looked at her and winked. "Doesn't mean it's not there," he said, smiling. "They are very difficult to see. It's about a sixty-foot cast. Place the fly right in line with that log about six feet in front of it. Let it drift naturally through the current. Be ready," he warned, grinning excitedly. "The take could be a gentle slurp or an explosion. Either way, hold on, it looks like a big one."

Justin scooted aside as Jena unhooked her size 14 Elk Hair Caddis from the fly hook next to the reel, pulling out slack line to prepare her cast. Her heart was pounding as she readied herself for her first cast.

"Stay low so you don't spook the fish."

She nodded as she stood, bending her legs to keep her body low. She was nervous, unsure of her abilities, the pressure of Justin's eyes on her causing her confidence to falter. She false cast a few times

121

to get more line out, looking back a couple of times to make sure she had enough back-casting room. Luckily, the area behind her was pretty open and she wouldn't have to worry about hooking a tree as she pulled out the necessary sixty feet of line. Her hands shook, but her false casts were good, the endless practice allowing muscle memory to take over despite her thumping heart. And as she fell into a practiced rhythm, her insecurities drifted away.

"Good," Justin said softly to her left, encouraging her. "That's about right...set the fly down softly."

Jena nodded as she false cast one more time, the line loading behind her as she shot the rod forward, her left hand pulling the line by the reel to load the line as it zipped out before her. When it reached her desired distance, she lowered the rod tip and the tan fly line settled across the slow-moving current, the fly touching down gently about ten feet in front of the log.

"Damn," she swore, realizing she was a bit far from the log.

"It's okay," Justin interjected quickly, excitement rising in his voice. "Keep it there," he urged as they both watched the little fly drift towards the log. She still couldn't see the fish, but trusted that Justin could. "Mend the line a little," he instructed.

She stood up a little higher and lifted the rod tip up and to the left, picking the fly line off the water and setting it further upriver. Current had a way of pulling the heavy fly line down river faster than the fly, causing it to bow and tug the fly through the current at an unnatural rate. The purpose of the mend was to give the fly a few more seconds in a natural drift.

"Good job," Justin whispered.

Jena's hands trembled as she glued her eyes to the fly. Suddenly she saw something dark slowly rise towards the surface. "I see it!" She said excitingly.

"Keep it there." Justin's tone was tense as the fish lazily rose towards the fly.

She readied herself, everything moving in slow motion as it looked like the fish was just about to slurp the fly off the surface. But two inches from it, the fish suddenly turned away and disappeared again into the dark depths.

"Holy shit, did you see that!?" Jena exclaimed. It was a rhetorical question. Of course he had seen it. "That was so close."

Justin smiled. "Great casting by the way. That was well done."

"Thanks."

"Bring the line in slowly. I'm going to change out the fly."

"You think it didn't like the fly?" Jena asked as she slowly stripped the line in so as not to spook the fish.

"These fish are picky," Justin replied as he dug into his fly box. "If they don't take it the first time, they likely won't take it at all."

"What are you putting on?"

"I tie an Adam's variation with a green body. For some reason they like that color. We have a green beetle that they feed on for part of the year and I think the green body initiates the strike. I call it the Green Lanternator." He smiled at her as he displayed the fly.

"My husband used to name his flies too," Jena added before she realized what she had said.

Justin looked at her seriously for a moment, his earnest expression disappearing quickly as he clearly realized it was not the time to probe further. Her dispirited expression was not hard to miss when just seconds before she had been beaming from ear to ear. "Do you tie?" he asked, tactfully changing the subject.

She appreciated his perceptiveness, and was relieved to change the subject. "A little," she said. "I really enjoy it but I have a long way to go."

He shrugged. "We all do. It's an ever-evolving skill." He finished tying on the fly and tossed it into the river. "Okay, just do the exact same thing again."

She took a deep breath. "Okay, I'll try."

And again she false cast until the line was at the proper distance, setting the line down as the fly landed on the surface. This time her target area was perfect, having placed the fly just before the target zone. But the fly landed a bit harder than she would've liked and she swore again. "Damn, that was hard. Is he spooked?"

"He's still there," Justin replied, looking on intently.

Jena didn't think she would have to mend this time as she had put the fly in the right spot, which was good, as sometimes mending the line could startle a spooky fish. Then she saw it again, the fish rising slowly from the surface.

"There he is!" she said, unable to hide the excitement in her voice.

"He's coming," Justin whispered standing up slowly in anticipation.

Jena watched as the fish opened its mouth, the white inner jaw flashing as it slowly sipped the fly off the surface.

"Set!" Justin yelled.

It all happened in slow motion as her mind registered the event, sending electrical impulses to her brain, which then told her body what to do, which was to pull back and up on the rod tip, setting the hook in the fish's mouth as the line tightened.

Immediately the fish twisted and bolted upriver, ripping the slack line off the water as Jena tried to let it out smoothly while still keeping tension on the line.

"Get it on the reel!" Justin urged as the fish turned direction and shot closer to the bank, pulling the last of the slack line. Jena now had the fish on the reel so she could use the drag to tire it out and bring it to the net. At least that was the goal.

"Oh my god!" Jena yelled as the fish shot up and down river, its powerful head jerking back and forth, tugging on the rod and pulling line from the reel. Justin had already checked the drag so Jena knew it was set appropriately.

"Keep it away from that log!" Justin yelled as the fish shot down river towards it.

Jena's heart leaped into her throat as she saw the fish angle for it. She quickly turned the rod tip down and pulled back, trying to guide its head around the near side of the log. The fish shot by the log, narrowly missing it and catapulting down river.

"Follow it!" Justin yelled in excitement as he jumped off the rock. Jena shrieked with enthusiasm and did the same, stumbling on rocks as she frantically raced down river, water splashing everywhere as the fish swam into stronger current. Her reel zinged as line was pulled from it, both of them trying to keep up with the powerful fish. It was like the fish was on cocaine, ripping line from the reel as it rocketed in various directions, shaking its head violently the entire time. The rod bent precariously as Jena did her best to control it.

"That's a big one!" Justin yelled as he urged her along. "You got this! Keep the rod up and try to keep it out of the current!"

"It's so strong!" Jena responded; her voice frantic as the fish had now taken her into the backing. "I'm in my backing!"

"It's okay! Just stay on it."

And she did, stumbling across the wet rocks as she found solid ground. She was able to move faster now, reeling in the slack as the fish found a deep hole to rest. Racing across the rock-strewn riverbed, she finally caught up to the fish, her line angled down as the fish held deep in a hole behind a large boulder. "He's not moving," she said, panting more from excitement than anything else.

Justin came up beside her, his net held at the ready. "Okay, try to angle its head towards us. Remember, if it runs, let' im."

She nodded as she gripped the rod further up from the reel, angling the tip down and away as she pulled with her right hand. The fish slowly moved out into the current, and when it did, it burst from the water like a rocket.

"Shit!" Jena screamed as she angled the rod tip up, leaning forward at the same time as the fish leaped from the water again, twisting in the air several times as it tried to shake the fly. Her tired hands shook as she followed the fish down river, but her adrenaline gave her the strength to hang on to the fish as it shook its head back and forth under the surface, hoping to dislodge whatever it was that was stuck in its jaw.

"Good job," Justin said, his tone now more sober as the prospect of landing the fish became more possible. "Keep the line tight and try to angle his head towards shore."

She nodded and lowered the rod tip again, pulling slowly, directing its head towards the shore. This time the fish moved with her, swimming with the least resistance towards the rocky shoreline. "He's coming in!" she said, her voice shaking in excitement.

"Good," Justin said, stepping into the water behind the fish. "Keep the pressure steady and start walking back."

Jena was having a flashback of fishing with Hans. He had instructed her in exactly the same way on several occasions. She also remembered the steelhead she had lost, and hoped she was not about to repeat that event.

Suddenly the fish jerked its head towards the deeper water and shot back into the current. The reel zinged again but stopped as the fish swam ten feet away before slowing in the current.

"He's tiring," Justin said, readying the net. "Do it again and bring 'im back towards the shore...just like you did before."

Jena nodded, angling the rod down and towards her. Just as before, the fish followed and moved slowly into the shallower water. It was the first time she really got a good look at it, and she was surprised at its size.

"Holy shit! It's huge!" she exclaimed.

Justin nodded. "He's a big boy. Keep going," he urged as he got closer to the back of the fish. "Ease him in." It bolted three more times, each time the distance shorter as it tired. Jena controlled him each time, easing its head back towards the shore and Justin's net. "You're doing great," Justin encouraged.

She stepped back a few more steps, pulling the fish slowly closer to shore. The fish flipped and turned a few times, like he wanted to bolt back into the depths, but the tension on the line was too much for it in its tired state and decided it needed to rest further.

And that's when Justin shot the net under it and wrapped it in the embrace of its rubber folds.

"Yes!" he yelled.

Jena finally relaxed her grip on her rod. "I did it!" She yelled, her excitement getting the best of her.

Justin looked up and smiled. "You did great. Now come take a look at this beautiful brown."

Jena set her rod on the ground as Justin removed the fly from the brown trout's mouth, all the while keeping the fish under the water and safely in the confines of the net.

Squatting next to him in the water, Jena got a good look at her first fish in New Zealand. He was huge, with a bronze body and darker spots that mottled its back. Its mouth was wide, opening and shutting as it sucked in water to bring in desperately needed oxygen.

"It's beautiful," she said.

"My guess is he's nearly nine pounds. Your first fish and it's a trophy." He was smiling from ear to ear. "Well done."

"Thanks," Jena whispered. "Oh my god, my heart is still pounding."

Justin nodded his head. "It's a good feeling, isn't it?"

Jena couldn't stop smiling. "Is this really a trophy fish?"

Justin nodded. "Most of the fish here will be between three and six pounds, with some big ones in the seven to eight-pound range. Sometimes we'll get one this size, but it's not terribly common. Let's get a quick picture and let him go."

"Okay."

"Take the net and I'll get the camera ready."

Jena held the net while Justin took out his waterproof camera.

"Okay, when you're ready, grab the tail and under his body and lift him up. I'll snap a few pictures. Then set him in the water but don't let him go. Do you know how to release a fish properly?"

Jena nodded. "Hold him softly against the current to get more oxygen through his gills. When he is ready, he'll pull away on his own."

"Yes, good," Justin confirmed. "You ready?" he asked, holding up the camera.

Jena smiled and reached into the net, holding its slick tail. With her other hand, she gently held him under its body and lifted it from the water, raising it towards Justin as he clicked off a few pictures. Her smile was beaming as she put the fish back into the water, holding it softly in the current. His tail swayed lazily back and forth as water moved through his mouth and gills. She was mesmerized by its beauty, but more importantly by how she felt. Excitement flowed through her. She was thankful, and proud of her accomplishment. There was a connection with the fish that she was having a hard time explaining. Her mind drifted to what Chris had said to Hans, that the fish he had caught over the years had somehow honored his skill and dedication by biting his fly. It was a stupid sentiment of course. But now, holding the fish in the water, she felt an acute connection to it. She had to admit his idea didn't sound that stupid at this moment. She felt energized and more alive, and she couldn't stop smiling. Then suddenly, its tail flicked hard and it was gone, its dark body disappearing into the depths.

Jena stood, still smiling as she turned to look at Justin. "Want a scotch and cigar?"

Feeling her excitement, he smiled with her, his white teeth in contrast to his dark beard. Jena thought he looked like the Cheshire Cat. "You serious?"

"What!? Can't a girl smoke a cigar?" she asked.

"Of course. Let's do it."

They sat together on a flat rock looking out over the section of river where she had just landed her first fish. She pulled out two cigars from the pouch in her waders as well as a flask. She handed one to Justin and he looked at her with interest.

"Is it really that strange for a woman to suggest a scotch and cigar?"

"Umm, yeah," Justin conceded. "It's quite rare to find a woman who can cast like you and wants to indulge in a cigar and scotch after a trophy fish, which brings me to my next question," he paused as he glanced at her wedding ring. "Do you have a sister and is she single?"

They both laughed as Jena procured a small lighter, handing it to Justin.

"If you must know," Jena said, "I have not yet acquired the taste for either indulgence."

"Then why do it?" he asked as he lit his cigar, sucking on the end as the tip glowed red, smoke drifting lazily from the sides of his mouth. He had clearly done that many times. "Nice cigar by the way. I love Cohibas."

"Nothing but the best. They were my husband's favorites," she said softly, taking the lighter from Justin and lighting her own, albeit not quite so smoothly. Justin said nothing, enjoying his cigar as he waited for her to continue, glancing at her once before gazing out at the river. She was ready to tell him, so she gave him the abridged version. "My husband recently passed away from cancer. He was an avid fly fisherman. I took a year off of work and I'm finishing off his fly fishing bucket list." She was able to get the words out without crying, which she mused was progress.

He didn't say anything for a bit, his eyes distant as he seemed to be pulling something deep from his own consciousness. "I'm sorry," he finally said, looking at her. "The death of loved ones is a difficult thing to process."

Jena pulled lamely on her cigar, exhaling the smoke as she looked at Justin. "You've lost someone close?"

He nodded. "I was in the New Zealand special forces stationed in Afghanistan. I lost three of my buddies in an IED explosion. Two more later when we came under fire while patrolling. I, uh," he paused as he processed the painful memories. "I can still smell the coppery scent of their blood and hear their screams." He shook off the memories and glanced at the flask in her hand. "What's in there?"

Jena handed it to him. "Macallan 25."

He raised his eyebrows appreciatively.

"Nothing but the best," Jena repeated, her eyes appraising Justin differently. She could now recognize his military bearing, the strength of his body, the ease with which he hiked over the rocks and leaped from the chopper. She could easily picture him wearing camouflage and shouldering an eighty-pound backpack with a rifle in his hands. "I'm sorry for your losses."

Justin took a deep swallow from the flask before handing it back. "And I yours."

They sat in silence for a few minutes, drinking scotch and smoking their cigars. Finally Justin spoke again. "I suffer from PTSD. The only thing I found that helped was fly fishing. It's the only thing that eases my mind, that softens the sharp edges of my memories. Now I dream of a fish exploding from the water as it takes my perfectly presented dry fly. Those memories override the bad ones."

Jena nodded. Then she looked at him quizzically. "But how do you remember the memory of your friends without dredging up all the pain?"

Justin shrugged, glancing at a tattoo on his inner forearm. "I'm still working on that," he added as he winked at her.

She smiled softly. "Well, let me know when you find an answer." She had noticed him glance at his arm and asked him about it. "What does that tattoo mean?" The mark was a semi-colon followed by the letters IGY and the number six. It was comprised of three different colors, teal, black, and red.

His eyes grew more serious as he first pointed at the semi-colon. "The color teal is for PTSD awareness and the semi-colon represents someone taking pause before they kill themselves." He then pointed to the letters. "The color black represents the heavy heart that we carry for those who suffer from PTSD and for those we have lost to suicide. The letters are an acronym for I Got Your." The last thing he pointed at was the number six. "The red is a symbol of blood that has been shed. In military terms I got your six means I got your back. Putting it all together it is a way of saying that if you are contemplating suicide, PAUSE, it's not time, I got your back and will stand by your side to help you through this. My intention for wearing this is not only to remind me of my own journey, but to let my military brothers know that I am here to help."

Jena touched the tattoo on his arm. "Wow, that's incredible." She gave his wrist a gentle squeeze. "I'm glad you're still here."

He nodded, smiled solemnly, and gazed at the river before them. They both sat silently, losing themselves in their own thoughts.

"You know," Justin finally said, "I would've liked to have met your husband. Any man who fly fishes and enjoys twenty-five year old scotch and a cigar by the river is a man worth knowing."

Jena laughed. "That's what every guy keeps telling me."

"I think you brought a piece of him here, with you, just by telling me the story."

"Oh, he is here alright," she smiled, lifting out a small metal vial attached to a chain around her neck. "I know it seems a bit morbid," she said, "but I have some of his ashes with me. He wanted me to deposit some at each location."

Justin took a long drag from his cigar, exhaling the smoke slowly as he nodded his head in understanding. "I have just the spot. Tomorrow, if you'll allow me, I'd like to show it to you."

"Of course."

They sat quietly enjoying the scotch and cigars. Strangely, she was not thinking of Chris. She was thinking of Justin and the pain he had experienced, and evidently continued to experience. In her own life, she had experienced loss and death in a way that few could understand. She had spent countless hours in counseling sessions trying to work through those experiences. But here sat a man who had held his dying friends in his arms, their blood soaking the ground around him. She had no idea if he had sought help. It was not uncommon for men, especially combat soldiers, to think they could handle the stress related to witnessing violence and death on their own. Jena hoped that Justin had not taken on that burden on his own, that he wasn't shouldering the pain by himself. His tattoo indicated that perhaps he had sought help. She shouldn't assume that he hadn't. He was seeking solace through fly fishing, and for him, it seemed to be working. Perhaps it would help her as well. Chris clearly thought that it would. As the old adage says, only time would tell.

"Well, you ready to get some more fish?" Justin asked, snapping Jena from her thoughts.

She smiled and snubbed out the cigar on the rock she was sitting on. "Let's do it."

* * *

The next day started off much the same as the previous, with a 5:30 wake up and a 6:00 hearty breakfast. Jena had been thrilled with her previous days adventure. After that first fish, she had landed five more, losing three before she got them into the net. All the fish had been large and hard fighting, although none were as big as the first. She had to admit that sight casting to fish was much more fun than just fishing blindly. Justin had been a fantastic guide, seeing fish way before she did, despite the clear water. Brown trout were well camouflaged, and on several occasions, she didn't even see the fish until they were close to taking the fly, which of course had just added to the excitement. The guests had spent that evening drinking aperitifs on the back deck, eating dinner, and continuing their alcohol consumption while telling fish stories out by the firepit. Jena still experienced many moments thinking of Chris, constantly reminded that he was not there with her. But she did her best to hide her thoughts, not wanting to tarnish the festive atmosphere with her own melancholy. She caught Ron and Lilith glance her way a few times, their concerned expressions reminding her to wipe the solemn expression off her face. A quick reassuring smile seemed to satisfy them, and although the thoughts of Chris still lingered, she was mostly able to focus on the cheerful excitement of the group.

Justin had told her that the second day of fishing was going to be a little different. They started the morning off with a thirty-minute drive east to a clearing between Lake Wanaka and Lake Hawea. From there they jumped into the helicopter and Gerald took them over Lake Wanaka towards a higher more remote stream. The scenery was even more stunning than that of the day before, especially when they cut through a steep valley, the mountainous cliffs on either side forcing Gerald to maneuver left and right as if he were driving on a go-cart track. Below was a steep canyon and a winding stream. From Jena's vantage point, it didn't look as if there was any place to land as far as the eye could see.

But suddenly, Gerald banked hard to the left and dropped quickly. Just below them was a small grassy field that seemed to appear out of nowhere. Just like before, Gerald set the chopper down smoothly and they jumped out. Justin gave Gerald a thumbs up and he was off in a flash. Jena looked around and couldn't help but experience an immense feeling of solitude, hemmed in by green and rugged mountains, above them the clear cerulean sky. The only sound was the soft rustle of leaves in the gentle breeze.

Justin looked at Jena. "Beautiful, isn't it?"

131

She nodded, mesmerized. "It makes me feel so small."

"Yup," he said. "Okay, get your rod strung up." Then he smiled. "I hope you're in shape. We've got some serious hiking to do."

"No problem. And you're still taking me to that spot?" They had talked the previous day about a spot that Justin thought would be good in which to spread Chris's ashes. She was excited and apprehensive at the same time. She wasn't sure how she was going to feel, sprinkling what used to be his vibrant body in some remote location deep in the mountains of New Zealand. But she was going to find out whether she was prepared or not. After all, it's what he wanted.

"Yup," he confirmed. "But it's not easy to get to."

"Most cool spots aren't."

"That's true. Now, most of the fish we'll encounter today will be rainbows, although it's possible we might encounter a few browns."

Jena got her rod strung up. Justin then tied on a tan caddis and a prince nymph dropper. She liked the dropper set up. The first fly was a dry fly, designed to float on the surface. The second fly, which was tied to the hook shank of the first fly, was a small nymph, designed to sink. The setup offered the fish two choices. If they ate the nymph, the dry fly would sink, acting like a strike indicator. It was a fun way to fish.

Once Jena hooked the lower fly to the fly hook near the reel, they took off, heading upriver. They walked about a mile across a rock-strewn riverbed before entering a more confined section of the river, the thick forested valley walls meeting the river close to its edge. They climbed over rocks and waded sections of the river before coming to a bend, the river having cut out a deep bank on the far side. Behind them were thick stands of trees and dense foliage, giving her very little casting room.

Justin spotted a fish immediately. "You see it?" he said, squatting low and pointing to the edge of the pool on the far side. There were branches hanging over the far edge and despite the fact that it was already nine o'clock, the sun still had not broken into the valley. Jena was looking for a fish in the shadows created by the steep far bank.

"I don't," she said, squinting towards the location.

"Okay, the cast is going to be tough. You're going to have to side cast to get the flies under those branches. Set em' down at about eleven o'clock."

Jena looked at him apprehensively. "I'll try."

She let out some slack and started her false casting, careful to angle her casting up and down river to avoid the foliage behind her. Once she thought the distance was about right, she turned last minute as she brought the flies forward, casting sideways towards the eleven o'clock position. The fly line slapped across the water, and although the location was correct, the two flies hit hard. The presentation was horrible.

"Shit!"

Justin stood up. "He bolted down river."

"I'm sorry," she said as she reeled up the line.

Justin smiled reassuringly. "Don't worry, that was a tough cast. We'll find more."

And as it turned out, he had been correct. The casting and presentation had been much more technical, and even though she had screwed up many times, losing fish and snagging trees, she had still landed six amazing rainbows before two o'clock. They had then continued their hike upriver, finding fish every quarter mile or so. Jena reasoned they had hiked nearly four miles before stopping for a late lunch at a section of small waterfalls cascading down a steep part of the canyon. She was tired and hungry, and ravenously dug into the turkey sandwich.

Justin pointed up the ravine. "Guess what's up there?" he asked with a mischievous smile.

Jena groaned. "Let me guess, your secret spot."

He nodded. "We'll be climbing over big boulders and through some tricky water, but at the top of that is a stunning pool." He saw her apprehensive glare. "Don't worry, it will be worth it."

Ten minutes later they started their climb. The river flowed down what could only be described as a hill of solid rock. They hiked up the rock face, climbing over boulders and wading through sections of current that had worn through the rock for thousands of years. There were sections of pocket water and small deep holes, waterfalls ranging from two to five feet connecting them as they progressed further up the rock face. Justin had spotted a lovely rainbow in one hole and they spent half an hour casting to it, finally getting it to hit a small black Chernobyl Chubby, which was a fly tied with foam, eight legs, and a huge white wing case that allowed it to float in turbulent water. The hole was small, a three-foot waterfall crashing into it causing a white vortex before rushing past them to another small waterfall. Jena was surprised that the fish could move up through the system of waterfalls. She had finally got the fish to rise to her fly, and after a short hard fight, had it in the net for a quick picture. Justin assured her that his secret spot was close.

She was exhausted when they finally reached the location. The hike up the rock face was probably only half a mile, but it had been steep and littered with rocks and boulders, forcing them to slowly pick their way up stream. She wiped the sweat from her face and smiled, gazing at a long stretch of river, the bright sun reflecting off the turquoise water like thousands of twinkling Christmas lights. Where the hike up had been tight and confined, the area before her opened into a small clearing, the long deep pool tranquil and smooth compared to the rushing water cascading down river behind them.

Her senses felt more alive as she took in the scents, smells, and sounds of the pristine surroundings. She closed her eyes and listened to the gentle breeze move through the branches rustling the leaves in a soothing rhythm. She could smell the earthiness of the damp forest as the clean air filled her lungs. Birds twittered in the distance; their calls barely discernable over the rushing water behind her.

Opening her eyes, she noticed a stunning dead tree jutting up from the middle of the deep pool. The thick trunk was as wide as she was tall, the wood aged and bleached silver, its contorted branches reaching up forty feet from the water. Jena wondered how the tree had gotten there, or how it had grown there, if that was indeed what happened.

"That tree, how did it get there?" Jena asked.

"Cool, isn't it?"

"Yes, it's amazing," she said, walking across the rocks to get closer.

"I'm not sure," Justin said. "Some think it had grown here and then the river had changed course, eventually drowning it. Others speculate it had washed down the river in a heavy storm, its roots snagging perfectly against the rocks beneath the surface and allowing it to lodge in an upright position. No one really knows."

"How long has it been here like this?"

"The lodge owner said that he saw it when he had first started fishing here twenty years back, so who knows."

"It's beautiful."

"You think it will work?"

Jena looked at him and smiled. "Yes, it's perfect. Thank you for taking me here."

Justin nodded. "Hey, there are fish here as well." He had a twinkle in his eye.

"Should we fish first?" Jena asked.

"Well, what would Chris want?"

Jena smiled knowingly as she removed the fly from the hook at the reel.

Chapter 5

"Well, how was it?" Chris smiled as he sat back in his soft leather chair. "I can only imagine how the fishing in New Zealand was; it's the stuff that made up my dreams for so long." He paused as he looked intently at the camera. "But the real question is...how are you doing?" His expression turned more serious. "I'm sure this has all been hard on you. Quite frankly, what they say about death and dying is true; it's always harder on the family, on the loved ones that are left behind." He shrugged. "I mean, once you've accepted that life will likely be over soon, it sort of frees your mind from the worry. But while my ashes sit in some box, you are forced to deal with all the emotions associated with my death. And for that, I'm very sorry." Chris leaned forward in the chair. "So, I hope you found something in New Zealand that will help you deal with these emotions. I sincerely want you to be able to build a new life for yourself. I'm hoping that every trip will bring you fresh experiences, each one a new brick to add to that foundation, eventually leading to something solid on which to stand on and face the world." Chris reached off camera and brought a cold glass of beer back into the frame. "What are you drinking? I decided to go with my Tight Lines IPA. It's the last of that batch I made."

Jena remembered it. She wasn't a fan of most IPA's, but Chris's tended to be more fruity than bitter, which she appreciated. Jena was curled up on the couch watching the video from her laptop. As usual, she was cradling a glass of bold Zinfandel, her legs tucked under her. "I'm drinking a glass of Zin, one of our favorites," she said, her throat tightening. "I miss you." Chris looked pale and thin, the results of his treatments. But his genuine smile had always managed to break through the symptoms of that emaciating disease. She remembered those days as if they were yesterday. Despite his pain and weakness he had felt, even up to the last day, he did his best to paint an 'I'm fine' picture. He had been strong for her, and even in death he had found a way to come back and help her.

Chris held the glass up. "I love you, hon. I'm so proud of you." Then he took a long drink and set the glass off camera again. "So little remnants of me are now flowing through the turquoise water of some remote river in New Zealand. The existential part of me loves that idea, and then my rational mind takes over and makes it difficult to process the concept. I mean, right now, as I speak, I'm still alive. But in my mind's eye," he said, closing his eyes, "I can picture you sitting on some log, looking out at the river, a flask of scotch in one hand and a cigar in the other. I see your rod leaning against the log next to you, your shirt wet from the splash of water delivered by a six-pound brown trout you just released."

"Try nine pounds," Jena interjected, sniffling as she forced a laugh. She also easily pictured that actual scene in her mind, Chris's shimmering ghostlike body watching her sharing a cigar and scotch with Justin. He would've liked Justin, and most definitely would've found his military story interesting and poignant. Jena certainly did, and indeed, remembering Justin's words about the pain in losing his friends, in a strange way helped her better process her own pain. Justin had said that fly-fishing was the only thing he had found that could ease the pain of those grim memories. Fly-fishing, for Justin, was the tool that he had used to deal with the trauma he had suffered in combat. The sport created the only distraction that seemed to override his memories of blood and violence that had plagued him when he had returned from combat. It gave her hope that perhaps it would help her deal with her own pain, not just from the loss of her husband, but potentially from the difficulties of her job. She knew that many first responders and some medical personnel suffered something similar called 'vicarious trauma'. When you experience trauma through someone else's lens on a steady basis, it can have a strong emotional impact on your own psyche. She knew from personal experience, that dealing with death, loss, and suffering, on a regular basis has a way of burrowing into your personal life in profound ways. The symptoms of 'vicarious trauma' can create emotional disturbances such as feelings of sadness, grief, irritability and mood swings. It was very similar to the PTSD suffered by many soldiers like Justin.

"I wish I could've been there to see it, to see your face smiling with excitement. I think by now you are beginning to learn about the

rush associated with fly-fishing, with putting all your skill into the act of catching that one elusive fish, and the feeling you get when you accomplish that task." Chris shook his head and smiled, remembering the many times he experienced those very sensations. "I believe that feeling to be similar to a drug. You learn to crave it, to dream of it, to invent new ways to find it, and unlike harmful drugs, this drug brings meaning and joy to your life. It brings a sense of belonging and oneness with nature that heals your body and soul." He grew more serious again. "I hope you are beginning to realize what I am saying is true, and that in time you will feel the same way. Fly-fishing-will-help-heal you," he said, emphasizing the words. "It may be the rush of the hunt that speaks to you more than anything, or perhaps it will be the peace you experience through the environment associated with fly-fishing, or the comradery experienced by fishing with like-minded souls. Or maybe, it will be everything about the sport that brings peace to your heart, as it was for me. For me, everything I did brought forth the memories of catching that trophy fish, and it was those memories that made me feel good, helped me understand my connection with the world around me. It made me feel huge and powerful, and insignificant and little all at the same time. In a very strange way, fly-fishing made me a better person. It was my avenue, my path, to becoming the man that I'm proud to die as." Chris smiled and reached over to grab his beer. "That was pretty good if I do say so myself. Let's toast to my linguistic talent." Chris winked and drank from his beer.

Jena laughed and cried at the same time, raising her own glass to her lips. "Oh, baby, I miss you so much."

Chris set the beer down again and looked intently at the camera. "Okay, let's get down to business. Next up is the Seychelles, an independent country east of Africa and north of Madagascar. Now, you'll want to book your trip sometime between January and the start of May. If you followed the itinerary I provided, you returned home from New Zealand around December tenth. It would be wise to make a reservation at the Lone Island Resort on Alphonse Island. You'll love the place. Now, the fishing here will be very different than what you have ever done, which doesn't say much as you've done very little." He laughed. "You'll be fishing the flats mostly, which is really shallow water for as far as the eye can see. You'll be sight casting to bonefish mostly, as well as various trevallies, permit, milkfish, triggerfish, and more. There is probably not a spot in the world that offers more variety of fish than the Seychelles. It is the hook set that you'll have to get used to the most, as well as the scorching sun pounding down on you. And if you thought brown trout were hard to spot in New Zealand, wait until you're trying to spot that seven-pound bonefish. They can be very difficult to see in the white sandy shallow water. You'll want to bring a variety of tackle from 8 weight rods with 150 yards of backing as well as my 10 weight with 250 yards of backing. For bigger, stronger fish, you'll likely have to use the lodge rods as I don't have any 12 weights."

"Jesus," Jena mumbled. "How big are these fish?"

As if he had heard her, Chris said, "You'll be getting into some very powerful fish, some potentially between fifty and a hundred pounds. You'll have to learn some new techniques but the guides at the lodge will be fantastic. As far as flies go, bring a variety, including Crazy Charlies, Gotchas, Minipuffs, Bonefish Specials, as well as Clouser Minnows. I'd also bring some poppers for the trevally and other minnow imitators like sardine, anchovy, squid, and mackerel patterns. The local fly-shop can help you with all that. You'll be fishing in hot weather and warm water, so bring attire that will keep the sun off your lovely skin." Chris leaned back in his chair. "You ready for adventure number two? Don't forget my ashes. Oh, and the sunscreen," he added with a chuckle.

Jena shook her head, smiling as she remembered the many times he had nagged her to use sunscreen when they were out in the open elements.

"I'd like to be sprinkled in the crystalline waters somewhere, overlooking the massive expanse the Seychelles flats provide. I've heard it's a truly stunning view, like big sky Montana, but in the tropics. Remember, life will give you whatever experience is most helpful for the evolution of your consciousness. Eckhart Tolle said that. You will learn what you need to learn to dig yourself out of the sadness you feel. You will learn to coexist with memories of me and make new

*memories as you allow your life to continue in a fantastic way. That is
my wish. My dreams are now not of fishing, but of YOU, fishing, with
a smile on your face as you live your life to its fullest. I love you."* He
gave her a mock salute. *"Until next time."* He smiled, reached over,
and the screen went black.

Jena blinked away the tears welling up in her eyes. Then she
gave into the crying, openly and unabashedly, the black empty screen a
physical reminder of Chris's absence from her life.

* * *

"Honey, are you sure you want to miss Christmas?" Tesa
asked, her eyes pleading. "It will be so lonely without you."

Jena was sitting with her mother, Tesa, and her best friend,
Brook, at a wine bar she frequented. It was a cool place, with soft
leather chairs and couches, a large black stone fireplace, and various
other wood bistro tables and high brown leather chairs. The center
focus, however, was the long concrete bar along the back wall with
three servers pouring the different varietals of wines they were tasting
for the day. The muted lighting cast a golden glow on the red oak
tables, concrete counter, and amber leather, creating a warm and
peaceful ambiance.

Jena felt horrible leaving her Mother during the holidays. She
just wanted to stay busy, to keep her thoughts focused on the next trip.
She knew that being with her family, and Chris's, during the holidays
would be difficult. She wasn't sure if running away from those
emotions was the most productive thing to do, but it felt right for her at
the moment.

"I'm sorry, Mom, I just don't want to be sitting around drinking
eggnog without him right now. If I stay busy, it helps. And I want to
fulfill Chris's wish for me."

Tesa reached out and touched her arm. "I understand." She
pursed her lips. "I'll just miss you."

"So," Brook asked, changing the subject, "where are you off to
next?"

They had spent the last half hour talking about her New
Zealand trip and they were curious about her next adventure. Jena

shook her head in amazement. "The Seychelles off the coast of Africa."

"The Sey-what?" Brook asked.

Jena smiled. Just a few days ago she wouldn't have known what the Seychelles were either. "It's a country made up of a series of islands off the coast of Africa and Madagascar. I'll be staying at a fishing lodge on one of the small islands, fishing the flats formed by the many small islands in the area."

"What are the flats?" Tesa asked.

"Evidently these islands are surrounded by miles and miles of shallow water, up to my knees, and the many species of fish move into the flats to feed. I'll be targeting those fish."

"Sounds expensive," Brook said, taking a sip of her sauvignon blanc.

Jena lifted her eyebrows at that. "Over ten thousand dollars for a week of fishing. They have to charge me for the entire bungalow even though I'm alone."

"Oh dear," Tesa said.

"Fuck me!" Brook blurted, quickly glancing at Tesa apologetically. "Sorry."

Tesa looked at Brook. "Oh honey, I've heard it all from your mouth before." She laughed.

"I'm glad I don't disappoint," Brook responded. They laughed together. Tesa had gotten to know Brook well over the years and thought of her as a second daughter.

"And, Jena, I'm also glad that Chris made sure you would be financially secure," Tesa said. "He was a good man, one of the best." All three of them were quiet during the solemn moment before Tesa spoke again, obviously changing the subject. "Is this place dangerous?"

"I don't think so," Jena shrugged, glad to shift her thoughts to her upcoming trip. "Unless a tsunami hits us or I get eaten by a shark, I think I'll be perfectly safe."

"And you're leaving in four days?" Brook asked.

"Yeah. The place was all booked but there was a last-minute cancelation for one of the private bungalows. That's one of the reasons it was so expensive."

"So soon," Tesa frowned.

This time it was Jena who reached out to hold her Mom's hand. "I'm sorry I'm leaving you on the holidays. I know its shitty of me, but I don't think facing the holidays without Chris is something I can bear just yet." Jena felt even worse for Chris's sister, Laura. She and her family would usually come down from Spokane to spend a few days with them after Christmas. Typically, after Chris's sister spent Christmas with her husband's family, they would drive down and have a second Christmas with them. But now, with Chris's death and Jena leaving, Laura had decided to keep the family home. Tesa was sad that she would not get to see them and her two kids, whom Jena loved dearly. Since they were not able to have kids, Jena and Chris had dumped their love into their niece and nephew, spoiling them on Christmas and their birthdays.

"Listen," Brook said, looking at Tesa. "Why don't you come over to my place on Christmas and we'll watch the Home Alone movies and drink good wine. Sound good?"

Jena knew that the holidays had been hard for her friend ever since her ugly divorce. Not to mention, her family lived back east and she rarely saw them, even on Christmas. Brook, ever since she had become single, had spent most of the holidays with Jena and Chris. Jena felt bad that she had failed to consider Brook's situation, so wrapped up was she in her own anguish. But hearing her friend's words just reminded her why she loved her so much.

"Really?" Tesa asked.

"Of course, it will be fun."

"Thank you, I would like that." It was clear that Tesa was touched by the invitation.

Brook, not one for being touchy feely, jumped in quickly. "We'll get fucked up!" she said, lifting her glass in salute. She smiled and winked at Jena.

Jena laughed and her mom did the same. They clinked their glasses and drank. Jena mouthed *thank you* to her friend, who nodded back in acknowledgement.

* * *

The flight to the Seychelles was even more complicated than her travels to New Zealand. She first flew to New York where she caught a flight to Paris, France. From there she flew to Mahe which is the only large airport in the Seychelles island chain. She had to stay the night in Mahe in order to take the morning jumper plane to the tiny island of Alphonse. All combined it had taken her just over fourteen hours, not including lay over time. Jena learned that many of the islands in the Seychelles were atolls, which are basically coral islands that have their own lagoons.

She had decided to do some research into the history of the islands. She knew that Chris would have loved to learn about the discovery of the islands. Researching their history made her feel close to her husband. She learned that the first recorded founding of the islands came from the East India Company back in the early 1600's. The French then laid claim to the Islands in the 1700's. In fact, the name, Seychelles, came from Louis XV's Minister of Finance, Jean Moreau de Seychelles. Of course, the first settlers brought slaves with them and it wasn't long before plantations of coffee, sweet potatoes, sugar cane, and maize peppered the main islands. Eventually the English would gain control of the islands in the 1800's, until finally, in 1976 the islands would gain their independence. Despite the English presence, much of the Seychelles' history is still linked to French culture. She found herself excited to visit a place with such a rich history, as well as some of the best fly fishing in the world.

And when she arrived, she was not disappointed. As the small plane maneuvered towards Alphonse Island, Jena was surprised at how small it was. The little airstrip literally split the island in two, the resort on one side with a line of villas and beach bungalows flanking the center structure and pool. The only thing on the island that she could see were the buildings that made up the Lone Island Resort. The resort was surrounded by brilliant green foliage, most were coconut palms with some colorful splashes of bougainvillea, hibiscus, and flame trees. The water surrounding the atoll was aqua marine blue, but it was so luminous that it looked as if there were lights under the ocean shining up. It was incredible. But what really captured her attention were the flats that surrounded the island. As the water neared the island, it got shallow, the flats shallow water like melted glass poured over a mixture of white sand and dark shades, like smudges from a paintbrush. Jena guessed the contrasting dark hues were the coral reefs and water grasses that surrounded the island. It was incredible, small and personal, and so damn remote. She had to admit, she was feeling a bit overwhelmed. After all, this was where the most serious fly-fishermen went to test their skills. She was just a novice in comparison.

When the plane landed there were six golf carts there to pick them up. A few carts had luggage trailers attached and the drivers promptly got to work unloading the plane with their belongings. Everyone was corralled towards the carts and Jena joined three other guests in one of them. The driver greeted them with bottled waters and a smile, introducing himself as Pierre. His aged bronzed skin was the color of most creoles, and his curly black hair was chopped short. He spoke with a unique accent, English, with a touch of French and maybe something else. He was full of energy and had them moving off towards the resort in no time. A family of three accompanied her. The man was likely in his fifties, with tan skin that accompanied his graying hair quite nicely. The wife was a bit younger, with wavy blond hair and oversized sunglasses that made her look like a movie star. Both were good looking and well dressed, a yellow and turquoise summer dress for her and flowy blue and tan linen for him. With them was a young teenage girl. She was blonde and all smiles, oblivious to how much her jean shorts left nothing to the imagination. Jena introduced herself to them and they all seemed nice enough. She was thankful for the water as the temperature was in the nineties.

The white gravel road was shorter than some driveways. They were at the main building of the resort in less than three minutes. Pierre ushered everyone out and they were greeted by three servers in crisp white shirts, The Lone Island logo printed on their chest, which was a whipping fly line over the outline of some tropical fish. She was sure every fisherman here knew exactly what it was, but she had no idea. Soon the other four carts arrived and the rest of the guests joined them. Each server carried trays of drinks and they made their way through the guests, handing out a variety of tropical cocktails, beers, and wine.

A young man in his early twenties greeted Jena. His skin was tanned like brown smooth leather, his wavy black hair fashionably unruly, hanging over his ears. He studied her for a moment before reaching for a drink on his tray. "Mrs. O'Malley, welcome to Lone Island Resort," he said, handing her a margarita. He was all smiles.

"Thank you," Jena said, taking the drink.

He nodded. "Pierre will lead you inside," he said, stepping away to greet another guest.

Jena was impressed. They must have studied the dossiers of the guests to know who they all were, and they had memorized the information. Just like in New Zealand, she had filled out an information form when she booked the room, including her drink of choice. She looked around as the other guests received their drinks. It was pretty stunning, the main building built of big logs with what looked like a thatch roof. It was all open, with steps leading up to a spacious interior, the center of which was occupied by a round bar. What looked like a receptionist area was to the left, and to the right of the bar was various seating, all built of tropical wood and upholstered in fabrics of tropical designs in vibrant colors like orange, turquoise, and lime green. The structure was quite large, and beyond the receptionist area Jena guessed were the kitchens, although she wasn't sure. Tropical wood seemed to be the main building material and it was stunningly beautiful, with contrasting wood grains of vibrant orange, red, gold and ebony. Chris would've loved it.

Beyond the main building were various pergolas that wrapped around an Olympic sized swimming pool, the entire area surrounded by beautiful concrete colored tiles, green grass, and palm trees. The pergolas were built over firepits with sitting areas. One was massive, big enough to cover a fourteen-chair dining table made of thick wood beams. There was another smaller building similar to the main one that looked to be a second bar. The swimming pool area opened up to sand so white that it looked like snow, the expanse of the flats stretching beyond that. There were a handful of guests enjoying the pool area while servers in white shirts made sure their every need was taken care of. All in all, it was a stunning tropical resort in the middle of nowhere.

Pierre ushered his four guests to a smiling brown-haired woman behind the long receptionist desk. She was pretty in an athletic sort of way, probably in her mid-twenties. Like the other staff, she was bronzed by the sun, and Jena couldn't help but notice the familiar scent of suntan oil. Four other receptionists helped the other guests get organized. Lorello, the receptionist helping them, wore a maroon vest over a white blouse, the hotel's logo on the upper left chest. She greeted them cordially and in no time had them all organized and ready to see their rooms. The other receptionists were equally efficient. It was obvious to Jena that they had done this many times.

By the time Jena had finished with her drink, Pierre had them back in the golf cart heading down another white gravel road. The vivid green palm trees and thick colorful jungle foliage flanked the road, the contrast with the white gravel stunning. The air was humid and warm and the cacophony of tropical bird calls soothed Jena's heart. She had been emotionally solid during the long flight, but now that she was here, and the reality of the once of a lifetime trip was settling in, the pain in her heart began to ache once again. Her calm heart suddenly began to tighten, a pain all too familiar, a pain that had been Jena's companion ever since Chris had passed. Occasionally it had taken a break, receding into the shadows of her consciousness, but more often than not it broke open the door to her consciousness in sudden bursts of emotional agony. It was in the present moment that the door had crashed open and a melancholy weight settled on her shoulders. She wanted more than anything to be sitting next to her husband driving down this gravel road, to see his exuberance as they viewed their surroundings, taking in the scenery and imagining the extraordinary moments the week would surely provide. But he wasn't there. He wouldn't experience those moments with her. She closed her eyes and leaned her head back, concentrating on the calming sounds of the jungle and the warm sun against her face. After a few moments, she was able to close the door and push the pain behind it, and although the ache was still there, she was able to somewhat control it.

She opened her eyes once again and studied the family riding with her. Jena had learned that the couple was on their twentieth anniversary and that the man, whose name was Gregory, was an avid fly-fisherman. They were renting a villa near the main lodge and when Pierre had dropped them off, there was another worker there to greet them and show them into their accommodations. Jena couldn't see it all, but what she did see looked extravagant. She remembered from their website that the luxurious villas were beautiful with their own dipping pool. She also remembered the price tag matched the opulence.

Pierre looked back at her. "Ready to see your place?"

"I'm excited," Jena said, doing her best to bring forth a sincere smile.

"You're going to love it." Then he took off, following the gravel road further away from the main compound. They passed three other villas before they entered a part of the island that was more open, the terrain manicured green grass and with only sporadic clumps of tropical shrubs and flowers. Palm trees peppered the land on both sides and the white sand beaches could be seen to her right. Pierre passed two beach bungalows; their A-frame structures built on concrete stilts a stone throw away from the beach. Jena had seen pictures of the buildings on the resort website, but as usual, the pictures did them no justice.

When they reached the third bungalow, Pierre turned down the gravel path and parked the golf cart next to the building. Just like at the villa, there was a staff member there to greet her, his own cart parked to the side. "Enjoy your stay," Pierre said.

"Thank you," Jena responded as Pierre smiled and put the cart in forward, moving back down the short driveway. The other resort employee approached her.

"Hello, Mrs., O'Malley, my name is Jon Steiner, I'm the Resort General Manager," he said, reaching his hand out. "Welcome to Lone Island Resort."

Jena shook his hand. "Thank you. It's really amazing."

Jon smiled. "Wait until the fishing starts."

"So I've heard."

"Let me show you around your place," he continued. "Please, follow me." Jon's silver-gray hair framing his well-tanned skin gave him a rugged handsome look. He wore tan casual slacks and a loose-fitting light white shirt; his gold name tag the only accessory. Each bungalow was surrounded by short grass interspersed with coconut palms, a green hedge of hibiscus separating each one to offer privacy. White wood steps led up to a front deck. The A-frame entrance was a set of double glass doors surrounded by more windows; the wood frames painted moss green. There was a welcoming set of wicker outdoor furniture, the frames light brown, the cushions a soft white. Jena could see through the front window that the whitewashed wood ceiling that covered the deck continued into the interior of the room.

"You have bikes under the deck for you to use," Jon said, pointing under the stairs as he led her to the bungalow's front entrance. "Since your fishing doesn't start until tomorrow, feel free to use them to explore the island. There are gravel paths all around the island. Use these to get to the main compound in the morning for your first fishing excursion."

Jena nodded as Jon led her through the front French doors. "So you have a lovely studio room," he continued, "the back deck of course leading out to the beach."

The room was neat and comfortable, a king size bed to her left, as well as a small gray linen couch, matching chairs, and a teak desk to her right. The floor had large gray tiles and the furniture and bedding matched, mostly shades of gray, white, and beige. Glass French doors opened onto the back deck and Jena could tell it was basically a mirror image of the front, the only difference being a large sun lounger as big as a twin bed facing the beach. "That looks lovely," Jena said, smiling as she pointed to the comfortable looking recliner.

Jon nodded. "Great spot to unwind after a fantastic day of fishing."

"I was thinking the same thing. Is that the bathroom?" Jena asked, pointing to a door on the left near the bed.

"Yes, please, follow me." Jon led her through the door into a luxurious bathroom, the vanity made of a lightly lacquered teak the color of copper. A charcoal gray concrete sink sat on a white quartz countertop. White towels of various sizes were rolled up neatly in open faced cupboards. There was a toilet and a clawfoot tub opposite the counter. "The bathroom already has everything you need, and there is an outdoor shower through that door."

"Outdoor?"

Jon smiled. "Don't worry, there is a wood privacy screen, and even at night, the temperature won't get below seventy-five. Take a look," he said, opening the door.

Jena went in and loved it immediately. Strips of tropical wood lined the floor horizontally and the privacy screen was a rustic construction of straight branches lashed together, evidently made from the same wood as the floor since they were the same reddish gold color. The wall was over six feet tall and there must have been another material on the other side as she couldn't see any light shining through the gaps. The branches of palm trees swayed above her dancing back and forth across the blue sky. It was the perfect place to relax under a cool shower. "It's lovely," she remarked. "Everything is perfect."

"I'm glad you like it," he grinned, leading her back into the main room. "So, there is a cabin phone if you need anything. Food and drink is available to you anytime, 24/7, so don't hesitate to ask. There is a small fridge near the table there that is already stocked with some of your favorite beverages. You can choose to eat here, or with the guests in the main dining room. Dinner will be served this evening at seven but feel free to come whenever you want. Food and drinks will always be available to you. Whatever you decide, everyone meets in the main lobby at six a.m. to determine the day's fishing schedule. Do you have any questions?"

Jena looked around, but nothing came to mind. "I don't think so. Thanks, Jon. I'm looking forward to this." She wasn't lying, but she also wasn't telling the complete truth. She was apprehensive, feeling a bit insecure about the fishing, knowing she was in a world class fishery with minimal skill. And, Chris's absence continued to weigh heavy on her heart. She hoped that once she got into the fishing, that perhaps the adrenaline rush of it all would distract her from those emotions. For brief times in New Zealand, the excitement of the fishing had done just that, and for those fleeting moments she was able to forget her sorrows. She hoped it would be the same here, and perhaps, over time, the pain would ease, and as Chris had hoped, she would be able to face life again with a sense of happiness, and that the memories of him would bring her joy instead of sorrow. It seemed impossible at the moment. But that was why she was here. That was why Chris concocted this crazy adventure. She would do her best to honor his wishes. And maybe, just maybe, he would be right.

"Well, your luggage is on the back deck. I'll leave you to unpack and relax. I hope you enjoy your stay with us."

"Thank you," she said, seeing her luggage on the back deck for the first time.

Jon nodded. "Remember, we want this to be a special experience. Don't hesitate to ask for anything."

Jena nodded. "I appreciate that."

He smiled one more time and left her to her thoughts.

A few hours later Jena had unpacked everything and had even strung up her two rods. She had decided to make another drink, mixing some Bombay Sapphire with tonic and lime, all of which had been conveniently stocked in the mini fridge. She was impressed with their thoroughness. All of her favorites were there, from champagne to chardonnay, and mixers for gin and tonics as well as vodka tonics. And they didn't skimp on the vodka, filling the fridge with a bottle of Belvedere, one of her favorites. She enjoyed the gin and tonic on the back deck while putting her two rods together, the soothing sound of tropical birds and small waves hitting the shore her companion. She had no idea what flies to use so she didn't tie any on, figuring all that would be done tomorrow with her guide.

Laying back on the lounger, she grabbed her leather-bound journal and decided to peruse her entries from New Zealand. The first thing she noticed was the life lesson she had written down from her previous trip...*Choose experiences over things.* Ron and Lilith, an older couple she had met at the New Zealand Lodge, had shared that little bit of wisdom with her. She really liked it, but she laughed to herself as she thought about the ridiculous amount of money she was spending to create this 'experience' in the Seychelles. But she didn't feel too guilty as she wasn't accumulating material things, she was simply spending an outrageous amount of money to indulge in a once in a lifetime fishing experience. She was buying memories. She rationalized that the trip did in fact support the phrase regardless of the material costs. She read her notes about Justin, her guide that had taken her to that stunning location where she had sprinkled Chris's ashes. He was a good man, and his words had given her hope, that perhaps, one day, she would be able to lessen the pain associated with thoughts of her late husband. If an ex-soldier suffering from PTSD associated with witnessing death in combat could do it, then she could as well.

After ten minutes of rereading her journal she decided it was time to do some exploring. She grabbed her backpack, filling it with sunscreen, her waterproof camera, and a bottle of water. Then she glanced at her rods and wondered if she should take one with her on her bike ride around the island. Thinking back to Chris's old adage, *it's better to have a rod and not use it, than to need one and not have it,* she decided to bring one. She filled her small pack with her neoprene wading boots and her small chest pack filled with flies, tippet, and snippers. Then she broke her eight weight four-piece rod down into two pieces and used Velcro strips to secure them together. The pack was made to carry rod tubes on either side so it wasn't an issue to strap the rod to the pack. It would stick up a bit high but she didn't think it would be an issue riding through the trails.

She found the bikes underneath the front stairs and picked the pink one. It was a charming bike, reminding her of a cruiser you might see on the strand in Manhattan Beach, California. She climbed upon the white banana seat and took off heading in the opposite direction of the lodge.

A Year of a Thousand Casts

The trails were smooth and covered in white gravel, contrasting sharply with the lush verdant green of the tropical vegetation. She wound her way through the dense foliage as palm fronds swayed above her. Other parts of the trail opened up into flat grassland sprinkled with sporadic palm trees. It was hot and she was glad she opted to wear her wading shorts, Teva sandals, and red bikini top. She was wearing one of Chris's fly-fishing hats to keep the sun from her eyes. She loved the worn and aged condition of the inside rim. It made her feel close to him. The breeze off the water felt good but did little to lessen the heat of the scorching sun pounding down on her when she broke from the cover of trees.

She had ridden for about a mile and was nearly at the southern end of the island when the trail turned sharply to the right, wrapping around a dazzling tranquil cove. She pulled over and hopped off the bike, leaned it against a palm tree and walked out onto the white sandy beach. The cove was magnificent, a peninsula beyond covered in palm trees swaying in the breeze. The blue sky above was void of clouds, the hot sun sparkling off the smooth surface of the water. She could see from her perch that the cove was no more than a football field wide and equally that long, narrowing to her right into a point. The water looked like a thick layer of glass no more than a few feet deep. She could clearly see the white sand beneath, tinged in spots with shades of green and black from the grasses that grew all around the atolls. She wondered if this particular cove had any fish. Well, she thought, there was only one way to find out.

She removed her chest pack from the backpack and strapped it around her body. Then she pulled on her wading shoes and spent a few moments making sure her skin was covered well in sunscreen. She worried a little about her back and reprimanded herself for not bringing her long sleeve 'flats' shirt, specifically designed to keep the sun off your skin while fishing tropical water. She would have to do her best to keep the sun facing her and off her back. She grabbed her rod and laid her pack next to her bike. Putting her rod back together, she picked a fly from the box resembling something that looked like a shrimp. It was tan and white with silver eyes, one of the flies that her local fly shop had recommended for bonefish, the most popular fish found in the flats.

She entered the shallow water and immediately pulled some line from the reel, holding the fly in her left hand. Moving slowly, she began to hunt the shallow flats, her untrained eyes doing their best to find any fish feeding within casting distance. Her polarized sunglasses did a good job cutting down the glare but the water was still brilliant from the intense sun. She walked a hundred feet or so, flanking a patch of grass. Suddenly there was some commotion on the surface along the edge of the grass as a group of small minnows skidded across the water. Something was chasing them.

A gray form bolted towards the minnows, scattering them further as it pursued them. She began to cast, leading the fish as it darted from her right to her left. It was nearly sixty feet away but the ocean wind was mostly blocked by the peninsula, so she thought she could hit that distance.

The fly landed about ten feet in front of it, right in its feeding lane. Her heart began to beat faster in anticipation of a possible strike. She let it sink a foot before she began to strip the line in, her short rhythmic jerks causing the fly to move erratically through the water. And in a flash the fish turned, zeroing in on the fly. Faster than she thought possible, the shadow shot towards the fly and a split-second later she felt a tug on the line. She instinctively lifted the rod tip high in an attempt to set the hook. But the line went limp as the fish turned and bolted away, disappearing in the crystalline waters.

"Damn!" she swore. She knew she had set the hook incorrectly. Even though she had never fished the flats before, she knew from YouTube videos that you never wanted to 'trout set' when fishing for most tropical fish species. The standard trout set, lifting your rod tip high, would generally not work here. You were supposed to do a strip set, which meant when a fish grabbed your fly, you were supposed to keep the rod tip low and simply pull the fly line hard and back with your free hand, setting the hook by yanking the fly in a forward motion rather than an upward one. She had no idea why but obviously the information she had learned had been accurate since her trout set had failed miserably. "Shit!" she added in frustration, reeling in the slack line.

She sighed in frustration and started slowly walking again, her eyes scanning the luminous water. An hour later she had nearly walked around the edge of the cove, and just when she was about to head back the way she had come, she spotted a shadow that looked like a fish. At first, she thought it was a log, the dark shape standing out against the white sand. But at closer inspection she realized it was a big fish, its body bluish gray. She caught glimpses of sparkling scales as they reflected the bright sun above. It looked like it was resting in a trough of slightly deeper water.

"I have no idea what you are," she whispered to herself, "but I'm going to catch you." She heard Chris whisper in her mind, *strip set...*don't forget to *strip set.* "I got this, honey," she answered back, starting to false cast. She repeated the mantra in her mind as she worked fifty feet of line out, the fly line zipping back and forth as she prepared to present the fly. Finally, when she guessed the distance to be correct, she lowered the rod tip and laid out the fly line. The seven-foot leader rolled out perfectly and the fly settled with a gentle plunk on the water. It was a great cast. She let the fly sink before stripping the line in, causing the fly to jerk forward like a shrimp moving away from the fish.

With a surge of power the fish bolted from its resting place, hitting the fly with lightning speed. This time Jena was ready and she set the hook by keeping the rod tip low and jerking the line back. There was a slight tug and then nothing. It flashed its tail and shot away like a torpedo.

"What the hell!" Jena yelled in frustration. She reeled in the line to look at the fly and realized there was no fly. The line had been cut. Whatever fish that was, it must have had some sharp teeth. "Shit!"

She tied on another fly that looked similar, but with some pink near the eyes. She looked up at the blazing sun and figured it was near four o'clock so she decided to make her way back to her bike. Edging the cove, she walked slowly, scanning the repetitious water for any signs of fish. She didn't see anything else, which of course didn't mean there weren't any fish. She had read that spotting bonefish was extremely difficult, their bodies blending in well with their natural surroundings. She was nearly back to her bike when she saw a small group of maybe ten fish moving away from her. They were not as large as the other fish she had seen, and still had no idea what they were. Picking up her pace, she hustled through the water to try and get close enough to cast to them. But they were moving away at a steady pace and there was no way she could cast that far.

Giving up, she headed back to her bike, eager to get home and shower and get ready for dinner.

A few hours later, showered and refreshed, she parked her bike near the steps that led up to the large open building that made up the main structure of the lodge. There were likely two dozen guests milling about, the men wearing shorts, flip flops, light loose shirts, and the women mostly wore summer dresses. Amiable chatter filled the room as the guests mingled, laughed, and smiled as they sipped their drinks. Jena knew that dinner was at seven and decided to grab a drink and head out to the pool to relax.

She walked up the steps and made her way to the circular bar that took up the center of the structure. A handful of people drank at the bar sitting in wood bar stools with orange cushions. Jena spotted an opening at the bar to order a drink. Approaching, the first thing she noticed was a long row of shot glasses filled with a dark liquid, behind each one a bigger glass filled with Red Bull. She recognized the blue and silver can immediately. Jena caught a whiff of coconut and banana, likely something to do with the drink ingredients behind the bar.

There was a young bartender pouring Red Bull in a glass behind the last shot in line. He looked up and smiled as she approached. "Just in time," he said. "Can I offer you a Jaeger bomb?" He looked to be in his mid-twenties with short brown hair and the ubiquitous tan, his gold name tag declaring him Antoine. He had a five o'clock shadow and various tattoos on both arms, giving him the look of one of those X game athletes. His genuine smile and charming French accent seemed to counter his rough exterior.

Jena was not a fan of Jaeger. "No thank you. But I'd love a vodka tonic with lime."

Antoine nodded. "Sure thing." He moved about with practiced efficiency preparing her drink. "So, did you come here for the diving, or just to relax?" he asked.

"Actually, I'm here to fly fish," Jena answered.

"Oh," he said, glancing up and appraising her once again. Her hair was pulled back into a ponytail and she wore a bright yellow summer dress which hugged her form just enough to be sexy and classy at the same time. It was one of Chris's favorites and she had to admit that when she was tan, which she was, she wore it quite well. She realized that it wasn't terribly common for women to travel alone to the Seychelles to fly fish so she didn't hold his obvious surprise against him. He quickly resumed his friendly banter and added, "Well, you've come to the right place." He set her drink on the bar next to her and continued. "The fishing here is so good that it's on most fly fishermen's bucket lists."

Jena's face suddenly paled as her emotions threatened to overwhelm her. Her eyes welled with tears as her thoughts returned to Chris. She grabbed the drink and looked away, quickly wiping the corners of her eyes. "Thanks for the drink," she said abruptly, her lower lip trembling as she fought back the tears.

"Hey, are you okay? Did I say—"

Jena looked back at him. His expression had gone from joy to worry in a flash. "It's not your fault. I'm sorry, I have to go," she added, walking away quickly as images of Chris walking beside her filled her mind. She walked by several sitting areas, all occupied by friends and families, and made her way down the steps on the backside of the lodge towards the pool. She needed to get away and calm her heart. There were at least ten tables and chairs positioned around the pool and she found one far away from anyone. The pool was spacious with sweeping curved edges. Its entire expanse was surrounded by four feet of concrete, and beyond that was manicured tropical grass and intermittent palm trees. Tables with white umbrellas were placed throughout the lawn area. Jena picked a table on the far edge closer to the white sandy beach and the water beyond.

She sat down and did her best to regroup, slamming half of her drink in one gulp. Taking a few deep breaths, she calmed herself, and did her best to blink away the tears. There were definitely times when certain triggers impacted her more. She had found that when she was busy fishing, that her mind became occupied with the task at hand. After doing some serious reflection, she had learned that it was the act of fly fishing that had allowed her to think of her husband in a way that was not bogged down with heavy emotion. Perhaps it was the intricacies of the sport that kept her mind focused, pushing Chris's image further in the background of her consciousness. Maybe that was the point all along, she mused. Maybe Chris had thought of all this, hoping that the sport would in fact be a conduit for her own healing while still holding onto him in a meaningful way. Just the thought of him planning everything for her before he died was enough to bring her emotions back to the surface. She felt alone, separate from everyone else. Everyone else seemed to be here with family, friends, and spouses. It made her feel more alone than ever. As she looked around, she couldn't help but wonder if this feeling of loneliness was ever going to go away. She finally decided to just let herself succumb to the feeling of aloneness, and allow herself to be sad. She sighed with resignation and downed the last of her drink, letting the alcohol soften the sharp edges of her grief.

"I thought you might want another," a hesitant voice came from behind her.

Jena turned and saw Antoine holding a second drink, his expression unsure. She did her best to force a smile. "Thank you, that was kind." She wiped the last of the tears from her cheeks, chuckling slightly. "And yes, I definitely need another."

"I also wanted to apologize. I'm sorry if I said something to upset you."

"Like I said, it's not your fault." She decided it would be easier to just tell him the truth. "I'm here because my husband recently passed away from cancer. This place *was* on his bucket list to fish, so when you said that, his absence just became more acute. He wasn't able to check it off his list," she added with a shrug. "So I'm here to do it for him."

"Oh shit...I mean, shoot," he stammered. "I'm so sorry."

"Listen," Jena said. "You couldn't have known. You didn't do anything wrong."

Antoine let out a nervous breath. "Well," he said awkwardly, "Is there anything I can do?"

"Just keep the drinks coming," she added with a wistful smile.

"I can definitely do that." He turned to leave but stopped short, looking back at her. "And I have to add, what you're doing is pretty cool."

The corners of her lips lifted in a slight smile. "Thanks."

Antoine nodded and walked away.

She spent a half hour sipping vodka tonics, her mind drifting, as it always did, to Chris. True to his word, Antoine had kept the drinks coming. After three cocktails she was feeling a bit buzzed and decided she would need to slow down on the drinks. The last thing she needed was an alcohol induced moroseness to cause her to lose control of her emotions. But she had had enough to cause her mind to wander, to focus on the things that she would not be able to do with her husband. She knew it was a dangerous place to be, but despite her best efforts she could not veer from the track she was on. She wanted so badly to look over at the chair next to her and see him, to share this experience together. She wanted to hear the excitement in his voice as he spoke of the day's fishing and their plans to come. But there was no one there, and she felt like she was falling into the void of his absence.

"Would you like another?"

She blinked and looked over at Antoine. "No thank you."

He nodded. "I also wanted to let you know that dinner is ready," he added.

"Thank you."

Antoine smiled and walked away.

She sighed, but had to admit she was thankful for the interruption. Standing up, she made her way towards the buffet that was placed under a ten-foot by thirty-foot pergola type building, the entire structure made of logs, the roof aged thatch. The hanging lights were beautiful. There were four that hung from the ceiling lighting up the delectable display of food underneath. Each one was a ball made from loosely woven sticks, three bulbs inside adding a warm ambient light throughout.

The line was already forming and Jena grabbed a plate and made her way through the buffet. As you might expect from a luxury resort, the choice of food was incredible. There were chicken skewers, shrimp, bacon wrapped scallops, and juicy prime rib. She saw a handful of cheeses, most she had never heard of, as well as breads ranging from various rolls to croissants. There were several salads to choose from, as well as three different pastas. On top of all that, there was a separate table stacked with desserts ranging from small cakes, specialty chocolates, three different pies, and even a small freezer offering fruit sorbet and two different Italian gelatos.

She filled her plate with some of the cheese and cracker choices, a slab of prime rib, Caesar salad, and a healthy helping of a penne pasta smothered in red sauce and parmesan Reggiano. Grabbing a glass of water she made her way back to her table. As she approached, she saw two women sitting there. Glancing around, she looked for another spot.

"Oh, I'm sorry, were you still sitting here?" One of them asked.

Jena smiled. "It's okay, I can find another."

The two women appeared to be in their early sixties. One had long gray hair that hung down to her mid back. She wore a modest dark blue summer dress with white flowers and wore little or no make-up. Somehow though, she still looked like she belonged at a fancy banquet. The other woman was short and a bit stocky, her dark hair cut like a boy, the tips frosted in silver. She wore a light white lose shirt Jena knew was popular with the fly fisherman. Her khaki linen shorts topped off a very masculine look. If Jena had to guess, she would bet they were a lesbian couple.

"Please," the long-haired woman suggested, "why don't you join us?"

Jena didn't want to be rude. Besides, she thought, this was a perfect opportunity to break out of her shell and have some friendly conversation. It would've been easier for her to sit alone with her own sadness. She was tired of brooding and it would be nice to meet new people. Perhaps this would be the couple she could tell her story to. Perhaps not. But she would never know if she didn't step out of her comfort zone.

"Sure," she said, making up her mind. "Thank you." She sat down and introduced herself. "I'm Jena," she added, shaking their hands.

"I'm Karen," the long-haired woman sad, "and this is my wife, Susan." They chatted and made small talk for a while. Jena shared just the basics of why she was there and she learned that they lived in Massachusetts and that Susan was an adult cardiologist at Massachusetts General Hospital while Karen was a practicing psychologist in private practice.

"I used to work at a pediatric cardiac office," Jena said, finishing up the last of her Cesar salad.

"Oh," Susan said. "What made you leave?"

Jena shrugged. "Just needed some change. I ended up switching to the peds ER and now I'm in the PICU. But I have to admit I miss the connections I made there. Over the years I was able to develop deep relationships with my patients and families as they navigated the difficulties of raising their children with cardiac defects."

"That can be a double-edged sword," Susan added.

Jena pursed her lips in agreement. "That's true. It makes it harder when you lose one."

They were all silent for a few moments as they ate.

"I don't know how you guys do it," Karen said softly. "But I'm glad you do," she added, looking at them both with respect. "It's one of the reasons I fell in love with Susan."

Jena's thoughts went immediately to Chris. He had told her on many occasions that very same thing. He had said that the things he loved about her the most were her compassion, her drive, and how she was able to help others. He had greatly respected the burden she carried, and had always made her feel loved and supported.

"Is everything okay?" Susan asked.

Jena looked up from her plate. She hadn't realized that she was staring at her food. "I'm sorry," she added meekly. "I was just thinking of someone."

They glanced at her inquisitively but neither of them pressed further.

"So," Karen asked, changing the subject, "are you here to fish, dive, or relax?"

"I'm a fly-fisherman," Jena said. "Actually, I'm not sure what to call a woman who fly fishes." She chuckled, realizing she had never really thought about it. "Fly-fisher person just doesn't roll off the tongue very well."

Susan laughed with her. "No, it doesn't. I like to say fly-fisher...no gender references necessary."

Jena nodded. "That works. I'm a fly-fisher," she announced with a smile.

"Me too," Susan added.

Jena looked at Karen expectantly. "Oh, not me," Karen added. "I just come along to bask in the sun and watch Susan."

"How long have you been fly-fishing?" Jena asked Susan.

"Just a couple of years," she answered. "What about you?"

"About a year."

"And you're here alone?" Karen asked.

Here we go, Jena thought. There was really no way to avoid discussing her husband's death. And besides, it was one of the stipulations Chris had required of her. But she was feeling a bit tired and emotional at the moment and decided that she would give them an abridged version. Perhaps she would have another opportunity to share more. But on this night, day one of her trip, she wasn't in the mood to dive into the details.

"Yes," she answered. "My husband recently passed away from cancer." She looked at them both. "His passing brought me here on a healing journey." She smiled weakly. "At least that is the hope."

Karen reached across the table and held her hand for a moment. "I'm so sorry. Thanks for telling us. It is good to talk about these types of things."

"Are you here to just get away then?" Susan asked.

Karen was obviously the more touchy feely of the two. She was a psychologist after all and Jena knew from firsthand experience that psychologists were trained to help people get through difficulties. At least the good ones did.

"Not exactly," Jena began. "My husband was an avid fly fisherman. He had a bucket list of locations he wanted to fish before he died." Jena shrugged, trying to be casual. "He wasn't able to complete the list. So I'm doing it for him."

Karen sat forward in her chair. "Oh, Jena, that is so amazing of you to take on such a task. I'm sure it's been quite difficult."

"It has...but at the same time I think it's been therapeutic. I don't know, the adventure has just begun so it's a bit early to tell how it will turn out for me."

"Is this the first trip?" Susan asked.

"No, the second. The first trip was to New Zealand."

Susan's eyes lit up. "You fished in New Zealand? You have to tell me about it."

"Now, honey," Karen scolded playfully. "You don't need—"

"It's fine," Jena interjected. "I don't mind talking about it. It was a great experience."

Susan looked at Karen with a *let her tell the story* look.

"Okay," Karen acquiesced. "But only if you feel up to it."

Jena smiled and began her story, sharing her New Zealand trip with many probing questions from Susan. The evening flew by, the comradery of the three building as they talked and got to know each other.

The next morning came quickly, and Jena, excited to start her first day of fishing, was at the main lodge by five forty-five in the morning. She wore tan hiking shorts, a light long sleeve turquoise shirt made just for fishing in the hot tropical sun, and black Velcro sandals. She brought her pack that contained her gear, including her wading boots, a water bottle and lots of sunscreen. She had also brought with her two rods, an eight weight and ten weight. Both had been broken down and lashed together with Velcro strips. Breakfast was served at six and Jena was sitting at the bar drinking coffee and finishing a plate of pancakes, sausage, and eggs. She wanted to make sure she had plenty of energy for a long day of angling.

"Jena O'Malley?" Jena turned to see a black man with unruly dreadlocks cut just above his shoulders. He smiled when she turned and his entire face lit up. He wore a shirt similar to her own, but orange, the color stunningly vibrant next to his ebony skin. "Hi, I'm Jean-Luc and I'm slated to be your guide today." His accent marked him as a local.

"Hi," Jena said, shaking his hand. "Nice to meet you."

"You excited for an amazing day?"

She returned his smile. "Very much so."

"Good. So, we don't normally have a single fisherman, and when we do, we try to pair them with another group. I have a couple—"

"She can fish with us."

Jena and Jean-Luc turned to see three men walk by, one stopping as he spoke. He appeared to be in his early fifties, with dark hair styled like a GQ model much younger, with a hint of silver streaked over his ears. Tan and quite handsome, Jena thought he looked like a younger Sean Connery. But that's where her appreciation stopped. His eyes looked her up and down and spent far too much time assessing her attributes. She was immediately turned off by him. He looked like a typical good-looking rich guy used to getting what he wanted.

"Come on," he urged, "join us. You're easier on the eyes than these guys." He laughed and the two men behind him joined in.

Jena glanced at Jean-Luc and she could tell he was just as irritated as she was. He jumped in before she could. "I think she will—"

"But do you know how to fish?" the rude man asked, abruptly cutting Jean-Luc off, his eyes still inspecting her body.

"She can come with us," Susan said as she walked up behind Jena and stood next her. Karen was just behind her. Susan challengingly eyed the man.

He looked them up and down, his expression reflecting his distaste. "Whatever," he said, looking back at Jena. "Suit yourself." His cheeky tone was unabashedly rude and to top it off, he turned and walked away, laughing with his cronies like a bunch of high school bullies.

"What a dick," Jena grumbled.

"God, I hate dicks," Susan added, chuckling.

"Silicone ones aren't bad," Karen sniped in.

Jena looked at them both and burst out laughing, Susan and Karen joining her. Even Jean-Luc joined in, clearly relieved that the situation had been diffused.

"Seriously though," Susan continued. "You should fish with us."

"It's pretty tough to have three fishermen," Jean-Luc said.

"Oh, I'm not fishing," Karen added. "I just like to watch."

He smiled. "Oh, good, that could work. Let me just confirm with my manager. I doubt it will be an issue, so why don't you guys head to the beach and I'll join you there. He looked at Jena's plate and back to the others. "Do any of you need more time to eat?"

"Give us fifteen minutes," Karen said, already moving towards the breakfast buffet.

Jean-Luc nodded. "No worries. When you are done, just head to the beach. I'll find you there."

Twenty minutes later and they were standing next to the shore as Jean-Luc loaded their gear onto a white skiff. The nineteen-foot boat was fifteen feet in the water, the bow and stern roped off to anchors, one buried in the sand on shore and the other further out into the water. Small waves tumbled in as their guide waded through the blue-green water to drop the last of the gear into the boat.

Looking around, Jena noticed that the beach in front of the lodge curved around a cove, the water deep, allowing the many boats owned by the resort to anchor there. She saw six other skiffs like the one they were taking, as well as four larger fiberglass boats with center consoles, Bimini tops, and dual outboard motors. There were even a few yachts anchored further offshore, likely for the divers or deep-sea fishermen. The beach was busy as guides moved about with their clients, loading gear onto various boats depending on the type of fishing they were doing for the day. Luckily, they did not see the group of adolescent men that had accosted them at the bar.

The skiff they were taking was made of white fiberglass, the rails low and the interior open for easy movement. There was a padded bench seat in the front as well as one in middle and back, the center of the boat occupied by a small console and steering wheel. The ninety-horse outboard was tucked under a tall flat platform, which Jena surmised was where the guide stood as he slowly pushed the boat through the flats with his long white pole. At least that's what she had seen on YouTube. It would be a great location to stand tall to spot the varieties of fish that called the flats their home. The front of the boat had a smaller platform, likely where the angler stood, the higher elevation allowing for better casts and sight fishing.

Jena and the women applied sunscreen as Jean-Luc talked with Susan and Jena about the type of fishing they wanted to do for the day, as well as their experience. He had told them that he would give them casting direction based on the clock, explaining that if he spotted a fish, he would guide their cast based on the position of a clock's time, as well as telling them the distance. They agreed that they wanted to stalk the flats and he said it was likely they would get into bonefish, trevallies, triggerfish, and perhaps milkfish. Jena knew about bonefish, but she was excited to learn about the other species of fish in the area.

Jena was apprehensive about her skills and voiced her anxiety. "Just so you know, I've only been fishing for a year," she said. "Don't expect too much."

Jean-Luc flashed her a dazzling smile. "Do not fret, Jena O'Malley. I am here for you both. You are to have fun, not to stress about your skill level. Either way, I will get you both onto some fish."

She returned his smile, feeling more at ease. Jean-Luc didn't seem to have any preconceived notion about what to expect from them. He just wanted them to have fun and his calm reassurance eased her anxiety.

"I can't cast very far though; will that impact my success?" Susan asked.

He smiled and shrugged his shoulders. "Perhaps, but do not worry, Susan Johnson, for I will get you close enough. Now, everyone ready?"

They all smiled, eager to get on the water.

The whine of the outboard was a dull hum in Jena's consciousness as they sped across the crystalline waters. Her mind had again drifted to Chris, and although she didn't feel the ache of sadness, there was still that sense of emptiness as she wished more than anything that he was here with her, sharing in her excitement as she remembered his eyes, his smile, and his windswept hair. But he wasn't here with her, and she determined to focus on having a memorable experience, one that he would have enjoyed. Karen and Susan sat up front while Jena sat next to Jean-Luc. She shook her head to clear her thoughts, and leaned in closer to Jean-Luc who was manning the wheel, guiding the boat around the edge of the island.

"I wanted to ask you something," she said loudly, raising her voice over the droning sound of the four-stroke motor. "What's the purpose of the strip set compared to a trout set?"

Jean-Luc nodded, expecting the question. "Bonefish have soft mouths. When they feed, they suck the food into the back of the throat where it's crushed with harder teeth located there. After they suck the food into their mouths, they move forward looking for more. When a trout or salmon feeds, they attack the prey and turn quickly away from it. Their jaws are hard, their teeth located along the gumline. So when you do a trout set, lifting the rod when the fish turns actually embeds the hook in the corner of its hard jaw, right where you want it. But when you trout set on a bonefish, you pull the fly up and away from the fish, generally right out of its soft mouth. Also, the trout set pulls the fly completely out of its feeding zone. With a strip set, you can more easily embed the hook in their mouth with a forward jerk. Not to mention, if you don't hook the fish the first time, you've simply pulled the fly further ahead in its strike zone. It may decide to grab it again."

Jena nodded. "That makes sense. But it's so hard to get used to."

"Yes, it is," Jean-Luc agreed. "But trust me, when you head back home, you'll be strip setting as your body will have adjusted to that style. You'll have to tweak your muscle memory to be able to return to the trout set."

He slowed the boat as he turned it into an enormous stretch of flat water located along an atoll a few miles from Alphonse Island. As the water shallowed, he turned off the motor and used the electric trim to raise the motor so the propeller was out of the water. The flat was expansive, most of it only a few feet deep over snow white sand that was mottled with various shades of green made by the different grasses that grew like moss in a rainforest.

Jena and Susan were instructed to get their eight weights ready as Jean-Luc removed the long two sections to form the sixteen-foot push pole. He screwed the two sections together and hopped up onto the platform over the motor. It wasn't long before he was standing tall, using the pole to guide the skiff slowly, and quietly, across the smooth vividly clear water.

It wasn't fifteen minutes before Jean-Luc spotted a fish.

"Three o'clock," he said. "It's seventy feet out and moving right." His voice was soft but held the energy of excitement. "It's a nice GT. Grab the twelve weight."

"I don't think I can cast that far," Susan said. "Jena, you go first."

Jena's eyes showed her eagerness tinged with uncertainty, but she grabbed the twelve-weight secured to the rod holders attached to the inside of the boat rails. She jumped onto the front platform and unhooked the fly from the hook at the reel. The fly was long and white and looked like a minnow pattern. She turned to face three o'clock but couldn't see anything. "I don't see it," she whispered, as if the fish could hear her.

"Four o'clock...sixty-five feet," he added. "It's there."

She let out a deep breath and started to false cast, each cast letting more and more line out. She had never cast a twelve weight and realized immediately that she would not be able to fish it all day. It was simply too heavy. It took her a moment to adjust to the weight of the fly and fly-line, but soon she had the fly zinging back and forth.

"Good, good," Jean-Luc instructed. "Next cast, lay it down."

Jena let the fly-line unravel behind her, and just when it unfurled, she started a hard forward stroke, whipping the fly towards the target. The cast was okay, but the presentation was awful. The fly smacked down hard onto the water. "Shit!"

"That's good," he said, his eyes glued on the fly. "He turned!" His voice rose in excitement. "Strip!"

Jena suddenly saw the fish, a gray form, barely noticeable as it bolted towards her fly. She stripped the fly in, long hard jerks, causing the fly to shoot rhythmically through the water like an injured baitfish. And in a blink, the gray form bolted for the fly. Jena's heart pounded in her chest as she readied for the strike.

"He's coming!" Jean-Luc exclaimed.

Then she felt the tug.

"Set!"

She had been reciting the mantra in her mind. *Strip set, strip set, strip set.* And when the fish grabbed the fly, she jerked back hard on the fly line, keeping her tip low.

The water exploded as a massive form surfaced, bolting away like a runaway truck. The twelve-weight bent as the slack fly line was ripped through the eyelets of the rod. She frantically guided the slack line through the eyelets so it wouldn't wrap around the reel seat or her feet. But the fish was moving so fast that she had little control as the slack line was gone in a flash. Luckily, it didn't get hooked on anything and almost immediately she had the fish on the reel, the drag zinging as the strong fish tore more line out. She could do very little to stop it. Jena had never felt a fish so strong.

"Holy shit!" She screamed.

"You got it!" Susan yelped.

"Well done!" Jean-Luc shouted. "Loosen the drag a notch."

It was all Jena could do to hold the rod with both hands as the GT, or grand trevally, ripped more line from the reel. Frantically she clicked the drag one notch back, loosening it some as the reel continued to scream.

Jean-Luc used the pole to push the boat as quickly as he could, following the fish as it raced back and forth across the shallow flats. A few times it turned back towards them and Jena had to strip in line frantically to pick up the slack line. You never wanted the line slack as it gave the fish an opportunity to shake the hook free. Once the fish stopped its run, she had to quickly reel in the line pooling at her feet to get the fish back on the reel in order to use its built-in drag. Just when she would get the fish back on the reel, it would take off again in powerful bursts that caused Jena's arms to shake from the strain.

"I can barely hold on!" she screamed, adrenaline racing through her body.

"You got this! He's starting to tire!" Jean-Luc shouted encouragement.

"It doesn't feel like it," she wailed, her strained arms flexed tightly as she struggled to keep the rod tip up against the tremendous strength of the fish.

Karen was snapping pictures and Jena found enough energy to turn towards her, the rod bent, her arms still shaking, but a huge smile plastered across her face.

"Wow," Susan said. "That is an amazing fish. Are the GT's all this strong?"

"Yeah, but this is a nice one." Jean-Luc smiled. "Wait until we can get you a milkfish."

Jena glanced at him, struggling to hold onto her violently shaking rod as the big GT raced back and forth through the shallow water. "They are stronger than this?" she asked, clearly finding that difficult to believe.

"Yup," he said simply. Just then the fish slowed, the zinging reel finally getting a rest. "Okay, he is getting tired. We're going to get out of the boat to land it. Follow me." Jean-Luc laid the long pole across the rail of the boat. Then he jumped into the water, holding onto its edge. The water only went up a few inches above his knees. Reaching into the boat, he took out a small anchor attached to the boat and dropped it into the water. Then he moved to the front of the boat and helped Jena get into the water.

Just as she positioned her wading boots in the sand, the GT took off again, its run strong and fast. Holding on with all her might, she ran through the shallow water as fast as she could to keep up with the powerful fish. Jean-Luc followed close behind her giving her encouragement the entire time. Jena's arms and hands were starting to cramp. "I'm not sure how much longer I can hold onto him." Her voice was strained as she gritted her teeth, struggling to hang onto the fish.

"Not much longer now," he whispered next to her. "You got this."

The fish again slowed as Jena started to reel in the line. This time, the fish turned towards her and went with the path of least resistance, its tired body not able to resist her pull. A couple of times it took off again in its desperate desire to escape. But in its exhausted state it managed only a few yards.

Finally Jena could see it. Its back was grayish, the hot sun reflecting off of silver-white scales as the fish struggled futilely against the pull of the reel. "I think he is almost ready."

"It's beautiful."

Jena turned to see Karen and Susan standing in the water behind her. In her battle with the fish, she hadn't even noticed their approach. Karen was still snapping pictures with her waterproof camera.

"Okay," he said. "I'm going to approach it from behind and tail it. Keep the rod tip high and keep doing what you're doing, bringing him in closer.

Jena nodded as he moved closer to the fish. She brought the GT in closer, her arms still cramping and her hands nearly ready to drop the rod. She fought the desire to let go and kept pulling steadily on the rod, easing the tired fish closer to her guide.

It turned lazily, angling its tail back towards Jean-Luc. And with practiced efficiency, he reached down and grabbed its narrow tail. "I got it!"

Jena relaxed her grip and nearly dropped the rod as the tension instantly disappeared. "Holy shit my arms are tired," she whispered wearily.

"I bet," Susan agreed.

"Come here for a picture," Jean-Luc said, smiling up at her as he squatted in the water, the fish secured by the tail while his other hand held it under the belly. "Bring the rod with you."

Jena's heart pounded as adrenaline raced through her body. It felt like she had just run a 5k as hard as she could, her body exhausted but filled with excitement. She squatted next to him as Karen got closer for a picture.

She marveled at her first GT. Its body wasn't much longer than a large salmon, but it was much thicker, like a muscle-bound torpedo. Its head was wide and blunt, its body tapering to a strong but narrow tail. It was built for speed and power.

"You know how to balance the rod around your neck?" Jean-Luc asked.

"Yes." She had learned that you could balance the rod on the back of your neck, the weight of the reel allowing the rod to settle on your neck so you could free your hands to handle a fish properly for a picture and release. It made for a good picture to be able to see the fish, the fly rod, and the big smile that was always present when landing a great fish. "I'm so tired though. I'm not sure I can even lift this fish out of the water."

"You can," he said. "The water will hold most of its weight. You'll only need to lift it for a moment." He removed the fly from the fish's mouth and glanced at her. "Ready?"

She took a deep breath as she balanced the rod on the back of her neck. "Yup."

"Okay, grab the tail, and when you're ready, hold it under the belly and lift her up."

Jena nodded and reached for the tail, gripping it just behind his hand. Once he released his grip, he stepped away as she used her other hand to hold its thick belly. She was still squatting in the water, and although the fish was mostly submerged, she could feel its great weight. Its tail slowly moved back and forth, its powerful jaw opening and shutting in the water. She could feel its strength and felt a strange connection to it. She had caught it with skill and tenacity. A year of casting and practicing had enabled her to land a grand trevally in a far-off land. She took a moment to marvel at her accomplishment, the feeling similar to that of conquering a tall mountain peak for the first time. Was this what Chris had meant when he said, *once you get it, you will get it?* She wasn't sure, but she was sure of how she felt. She looked up at Karen and beamed with pride. "Ready?"

Karen nodded.

Jena lifted the heavy fish out of the water, and although she was tired, she found the energy to hold it steady as Karen clicked a few pictures. Once the fish was out of the water, she was able to really appreciate its size and beauty. Its head was huge, with big round eyes, that, if she didn't know better, were looking right at her. "Thank you," she whispered to the fish as she put it back into the water.

"Let go of her belly and when she's ready to go, she will let you know," Jean-Luc instructed.

Jena did as instructed, and a few moments later it flicked its tail hard, forcing Jena to let go as it bolted away.

She stood, grinning from ear to ear. "That was amazing."

Jean-Luc gave her a high five. "Fantastic job! You're a natural." Then he looked at Susan. "You ready for one?"

"Hell yes!"

Jean-Luc led them back to the boat. Jena turned around and gazed out at the stunning flats that surrounded them. She had no idea if she would catch another GT, or if there would be another trophy fish. But there was something about the moment that just felt right. Reaching under her shirt, she lifted the thin rope attached to the small container holding Chris's ashes from around her neck. Unscrewing the top, she held it above the crystalline blue waters. "I love you, baby. I wish you could've seen that fight." Tears formed and ran down the sides of her face as she dumped his ashes into the water. She wiped the tears away, relishing this memory. She deeply inhaled the clean air, exhaling slowly as she took in the scene one more time, taking mental snap shots of it to file away. Then she turned and walked back to the boat.

About mid-day they met the other guides and fishermen for lunch at a scenic location just off one of the nearby atolls. The deep ocean water met up with shallow water no more than six inches deep, the entire bottom of the huge flat covered in white sand. All the guides had driven their skiffs up onto the shallow sand. Spread before them were tables and chairs, as well as cooks barbecuing fresh meat over hot coals. It was incredible. Jena and the girls had never seen anything like it. They ate a delectable lunch of Thai grilled chicken, sliced kobe beef, and prawns drenched in butter and grilled over a hot flame. There was various pasta and green salads, and they stuffed themselves all the while resting in chairs sitting in several inches of water. There was a large assortment of sodas, beer, wine, water, and cocktails. And the flat on which they dined was larger than any Jena had seen so far. As far as she could see the shallow water extended out like a desert, the only thing visible in the distance a lonely island, the green tips of palm trees barely noticeable. It was a luxurious way to relax for a bit after an amazing morning of fishing.

That evening Jena sat in a turquoise Adirondack chair, Susan and Karen comfortably relaxing next to her, all three chairs nestled in the white sand facing the picturesque water that surrounded Alphonse Island. It was dark but the outdoor lighting that shone up the trunks of the palm trees behind them added a soft ambient light. And out here, away from the lights of towns and cities, the Milky Way lit up the sky with a luminescence she had never before witnessed, countless stars like glittering diamonds filling the clear night. Jena's stomach was bruised and sore from the butt end of the fly rod pushing into her flesh as she fought fish all day. They had each landed at least ten bonefish, and Jean-Luc was able to get Susan onto a grand trevally. It was smaller than Jena's but true to its reputation it had put up an amazing fight.

They had already eaten dinner, which was equally incredible. The variety and quality of the food was quite impressive. There was perfectly cooked prime rib, seared scallops, yellow tail tuna served sushi style, and much more. They had all three decided to grab some cocktails and relax on the beach before they went to bed. Jena had really enjoyed their company thus far and looked forward to talking with them again. Perhaps it would be the right opportunity to finish her story.

"You know," Karen said, looking out to the ocean, "there is such beauty in solitude."

Jena smiled. It was just the thing that Chris would've said. Then she realized that Karen's words would make a great life lesson. She had to have one per trip, and if it could be applied to fly fishing then it was even better. *There is such beauty in solitude,* Jena whispered in her mind. It was perfect. Chris had always argued that humans were constantly inundated with the stimuli of the modern hectic world, and that it was absolutely necessary to unplug and surround yourself with the beauty and solitude of nature. He believed it could literally heal your soul. Jena never really thought much about it, but now, sitting with her two new friends, alone on some remote island off the coast of Africa, she thought he might have been onto something.

"I like that," Jena said, her thoughts flashes of Chris. She looked at Karen. "My husband would've said something similar."

Karen reached for her drink, a dirty martini, and took a sip before setting it back on the small table before them. "Will you tell us about him?"

"Sure. Would you mind if I just tell you the rest of the story?" Jena asked. "I think that would be easier for me."

"Of course," Karen urged. Susan nodded for her to begin.

So she told them everything; how he had died, how he had lived, ending with the tasks that he had put before her upon his death. She had already given them an abridged version of the story the night before, so all she had to do was fill in the gaps.

"I think I'm going to use your words," Jena said, finishing her story, "for the life lesson of the trip."

"What words?" Karen asked.

"There is beauty in solitude."

"Oh, I like that." She smiled. "I think I would've liked your husband a lot."

Jena smiled softly, nodding as she sipped her vodka tonic. She had told the story without crying, something she was quite proud of.

"That's an amazing story," Susan mused. "Did you sprinkle his ashes after you caught that GT?"

Jena nodded. "Yes. Something about that moment just seemed right."

Susan nodded, clearly agreeing as she sipped her whiskey sour.

"And how do you feel so far?" Karen asked. Being the psychologist, Karen always seemed to be the one who asked probing questions. Jena didn't take offense at all, in fact she liked it. Her questions were always respectful and gave her an opportunity to dig into her thoughts, and to possibly learn something.

She shrugged. "The pain comes and goes. Sometimes I can think of him and smile, but most of the time his image brings me a sense of loss so profound that my heart hurts. It's a deep wound that I just want to heal. I want it to go away."

Karen smiled almost maternally. "Honey, what you experienced is not the type of wound that will ever completely heal. What you experienced," she continued, "is not a scrape one gets falling off their bike. You suffered a traumatic injury, like a crushed femur, and although it will heal, you will always have a limp."

Jena began to tear up. "I don't want a limp," she lamented, wiping the corners of her eyes. "I want the pain to go away."

Karen leaned forward and put her hand on Jena's. "Listen, Jena. That limp is how you will always remember him. But you will learn to live with it, just as a soldier lives with losing an arm in battle. The injury will always be there, but life will go on. Don't wish it away, welcome it, and then find ways to live with it." Karen released Jena's hand and picked up her martini, cradling it in her hands as she leaned back in her chair. She smiled warmly. "You're a strong woman. You'll get through this."

Jena smiled weakly, "I know," she said. "It's just still so raw."

"That will be two hundred and twenty-five dollars," Susan quipped, "her hourly rate."

Karen playfully slapped Susan's shoulder. "Stop!"

Jena laughed. "Worth every penny."

Susan grabbed her drink and held it up. "To Chris O'Malley, a man who taught lessons in life and in death."

"A man who brought joy in life...a man mourned in death," Karen added.

"A man," Jena stammered, "who holds my heart both past and present."

A Year of a Thousand Casts

Jena smiled sadly as they clinked their glasses, drinking to a man whose existence was now nothing more than thoughts and memories.

Chapter 6

"Hi, my love," Chris said, sitting in his brown leather chair.

"Hi, baby," Jena answered, determined to hold back her tears. As usual, she was nestled comfortably in the corner of her couch, wearing pajamas and cradling a dirty martini. Typically she preferred wine, but on this night, she was feeling a stronger drink was necessary. She was really missing him. He looked more worn, she thought, a wave of sadness washing over her. Despite the cancer that continued to drain the life from him, Chris still managed to smile. His face was thinner, his eyes sunken and rimmed with dark circles. A knit black beany covered his bald head, once covered with thick lustrous hair. Jena hated seeing him like that. She could no longer hold back her tears as she thought back to those painful trying days.

"I hope your trip to the Seychelles was as amazing as I imagine it." He smiled as his mind drifted to images that only he could see. "I picture you standing in the clear shallow water, your hair tied back in a ponytail, sweat dripping off your cute nose as you try to land a strong trevally. I know the fishing there is world class, and the resort, well," Chris added, "you get what you pay for. I know it was expensive and I'm sure it killed you to spend that much money for only a week vacation of fishing, but I hope, in the end, that it was worth it."

"It was," Jena said sadly, smiling a bit as she remembered her wonderful experience. The fishing was so incredible that her stomach was still bruised where she had crammed the butt end of her rod fighting the strong fish of the flats. She had made good friends, hanging out with Karen and Susan most of the trip, even fishing with them two more times. They had exchanged their contact information and planned to see each other again. She had opened up to them, and them to her about their own struggles. Jena thought of that first GT she caught and the sprinkling of Chris's ashes just after. She thought of the life lesson she had learned on the trip and wished she could vocalize it to him. He would've liked it... *There is beauty in solitude.* On many occasions Chris had forced her to do things outside of her comfort zone, most of which required hard work consisting of bush whacking and hiking deep into the forest, the end result typically solitude, surrounded by the beauty of the wilderness. Every time she had fought him, trying to come up with excuses to do something else. And every time he had convinced her to hike into some remote fishing spot, she had learned that he had been correct, although she didn't always admit it to him. She was beginning to understand the power of unplugging and seeing the world through a clear, uncluttered lens.

Figuring out the 'experience' that Chris would've loved and she would not, turned out to be a bit more difficult. Finally she had picked scuba diving. The resort had offered world class diving, including beginning classes for anyone interested. Jena was always afraid of the open ocean, especially water that was home to sharks or other frightening creatures. On the few tropical vacations they had gone on together, Chris had always tried to get her to go snorkeling or to take a scuba diving class. Her trepidation had always elicited a firm no. But this time, she sucked it up and went scuba diving. She smiled as she thought back to how nervous she was. But she had done it, and once in the water, surrounded by the instructors and other divers, had actually enjoyed it. The vastness of the water was scary, but she also found it strangely calming, the muffled sound and stillness tranquil, not to mention the thousands of colorful fish and coral created a beautiful landscape. She's wasn't sure if she would ever pursue it again, but it definitely qualified as a proper task that Chris would've loved.

"So," Chris continued, "let's talk about the next trip. With fishing you have to plan according to the time of the year as most places are at their best during certain months. So I imagine for you it's probably around Christmas time." He smiled. "Say hi to my sister and the kids for me." Then his expression turned solemn for a moment. "I hope she is doing okay," he said with concern, his eyes focusing elsewhere for just a moment. Catching himself, he redirected his focus to the camera, his face all smiles once again. "I think the best spot to head to next is Chile to fish the fjords along the Andes Mountains. The setting will be stunning. Can you imagine the snowcapped peaks of the Andes in the background as you fish the river inlets of the fjords, not a single soul around you, only the desolate beauty of the landscape?" he asked excitedly. Obviously, it was a rhetorical question

so he continued without pause. "The best times to fish there are December through March so your timing should be perfect. I think you're really going to like this trip. You'll fly into Santiago, Chile, and from there you'll take a connecting flight to Balmaceda Airport where you'll be driven to the small town of Puerto Cisnes. Now, here is the cool part. You'll then board a sixty-foot Grand Banks yacht that will take you through the fjords to all the rivers that flow from the Andes Mountains. I've been told the area is incredibly beautiful. Rob has all the details about the company but I suggest you get busy reserving your spot as soon as you can. Now," Chris continued. "You'll be fishing for brown and rainbow trout so I'd bring rods ranging from four to seven weight. You'll likely be fishing in some deep water for bigger fish so you'll need the seven weight as well as sink tip lines. I'd bring seven and nine foot leaders as well as plenty of tippet material ranging from 1x to 4x. Typical trout flies will do just fine there." He reached off camera and brought a glass of golden scotch into view, the single square ice cube clinking around in the glass. *"To the joys of fly-fishing,"* he toasted, saluting the camera. He took a sip and smiled.

Jena held up her martini. "To the joys of fly-fishing," she repeated between sniffles, drinking deeply, hoping the strong drink would dull the pain of missing him. Seeing his face and hearing his voice on the video just seemed to magnify her loss.

"You know," Chris remarked thoughtfully. *"Besides you, my family, and fishing, I think I'll miss this the most."* He held the glass of scotch to the screen. *"I hope you are enjoying your scotch and smoking a cigar as instructed,"* he chided.

"I am," Jena sighed. When she was in the Seychelles she had decided to indulge in the scotch and cigar after she had caught the sought-after Milkfish. She had never heard of that fish before, but apparently it had recently become one of the most sought-after fish in the area. Fly fishermen had struggled for years to catch the fish since it eats algae, which makes it difficult to get the fish to take a fly. But, after years of experimenting, the guides in the Seychelles found a way by creating flies that look like algae clumps, their main food source. Jena's guide had spotted a pod of milkfish feeding as they were about to enter a new section of flats. They had spent an hour casting to them. Jena was not willing to give up even though they had eluded her the entire time. She eventually hooked up with one but it snapped her line, its powerful run stronger than anything she had yet experienced, even compared to the GT she had caught on the first day. Finally, two hours later, she had hooked into a second fish, and had learned instantly why they were one of the top sportfish in those waters. The fish was incredibly strong and fast, leaping from the water again and again in an attempt to spit the fly. And it didn't seem to tire, performing endless powerful runs that nearly kicked her ass. But they were finally able to land it. It had been an incredible experience that Jena deemed fitting for the obligatory cigar and scotch. It was just something Chris would've done; casting endlessly to a fish he could see, testing his skills against a very worthy adversary. She smiled as she thought back to the guide's look on his face when she told him she wanted to take a break while she lit up the cigar and sipped a nice scotch in ninety-degree weather.

"Oh, before I forget, there is one more thing. I don't want to give away too much but your trip after this is close to Chile, so it makes since that you will fly directly from Chile to your next destination, Manaus Brazil on the Amazon River."

"What!?" Jena exclaimed, unsure if she heard him right. "The Amazon River?" Jena had no idea what fish she would fly fish for on that river. When she pictured the Amazon River, she pictured a place so remote that no one even lived there, except indigenous people who had little connection with the outside world. Of course, she realized that her opinion of the Amazon basin was likely outdated, but just the thought of traveling there made her quite nervous as images of snakes, mosquitos, and piranhas filled her head.

Chris smiled. "Don't worry honey, it won't be like you imagine. You'll be fishing with an experienced outfit and it will be perfectly safe. The only thing you need to do is get a yellow fever vaccination. Normally, if you're flying from the United States you don't need it, but since you are flying from Chile, they might require you to show a record of the vaccination. Just get it before you go and you won't have to worry about it. When you go to Brazil bring my nine and ten weight rods for that trip. You'll find out why later. Rob has all the details but I'll tell you more on the next video."

"Oh, honey, what have you gotten me into?" Jena murmured.

"Remember, love, I want you to enjoy every experience. I want you to use them to remember me, but at the same time learn that life is simply experiences, one connecting to another until you die. Our time together was just that, one amazing experience after another, and although my part on your timeline is over, you will continue to create new positive experiences. It's quite simple really; as you continue your timeline of experiences, you can choose to wallow in pain and seclusion, or you can find another series of wonderful experiences until you too pass on, ending your timeline. I want this journey I put you on to be the conduit for your own realization, that you can, and must, move on. I will always be here, with you," he said, tapping the side of his head. "But you must open this up," he continued, moving his hand to his heart, "so that you are able to accept the love and joy that life can still offer you. I want this for you more than anything. I love you more than I can express," he said smiling, though Jena could sense the weariness in his eyes. He lifted his glass one more time. "To the joys of fly-fishing. Remember what I always told you, once you get it, you—"

"will get it," Jena sniffled. She had to admit, that simple sentence was proving to be quite accurate. The more she learned about fly-fishing and the more accomplished she became, the more she was able to understand his passion for the sport.

"May it forever add wonderful memories to your timeline," Chris continued as he took a small sip from his scotch. "I love you." Then he winked and reached off camera. His image disappearing.

Jena cried as his face disappeared, flashing to a black screen. "I love you too. I miss you so much," she softly wept.

* * *

Four weeks later Jena was standing on a dock looking up at the sixty-foot Grand Banks yacht. The boat's name, Thiare, was etched beautifully into a piece of teak and secured to the side of the boat. The boat was exquisite, with long sleek lines and teak wood edging white fiberglass throughout. The fly bridge was high up and the back was occupied by two cranes from which hung two silver zodiac boats. There were tinted windows below deck near the front that Jena assumed were the staterooms. Above the yacht a sapphire blue sky sported feathery white clouds drifting slowly along the calm breeze. The temperature was a comfortable seventy-one and it felt fantastic compared to the humid heat of the Seychelles. Lush vegetation covered the many mountains surrounding them. The taller peaks were brushed white with snow.

The little town of Puerto Cisnes catered to a variety of boating and outdoor activities. People from all around came to hike the mountains and explore the many bodies of water, canoeing the rivers and kayaking through the fjords surrounded by picturesque scenery and an abundance of wildlife. The town was built on the outflow of the Cisnes River and all around were fingers of water that made up the fjords before entering the expanse of the Pacific Ocean.

"What do you think?"

Jena turned as Mark approached. He grinned, clearly proud of his boat. "It's lovely," she said. "What does the name mean?"

Mark was one of the brothers that owned the yacht as well as the company that operated the fjord fly-fishing outfit. She had learned that they were both Canadians who had moved to Chile to open the business together. Their love of fly-fishing, guiding, and for the ruggedly picturesque lands of Chile led them to this chapter in their lives. Mark was in his forties, with jet black wavy hair and a nicely trimmed short beard that seemed to glisten like oil. His brother, Lance, looked quite similar, and although he was a few years older he still had the same dark hair, without a wisp of gray.

"Thiare was my wife's name," he said. "It has a Tahitian origin which means flower." He looked at her a bit sadly. "Unfortunately," he added. "We have something in common."

He was still smiling, but his expression reflected something else. It wasn't sadness. Perhaps it was just an expression of mutual understanding, Jena thought. She had spent many days on the phone with the brothers, trying to schedule a time to join them on her excursion. It had been difficult to get on the books as the boat only offered two state rooms, which meant it could only take four fishermen at any one time. The cost of such an expedition was 4,500 dollars a person. But each stateroom must be filled with two fishermen, which meant it was rare to ever take a single person as they would have to pay for double occupancy or room with another single fisherman. Their outfit was really set up for couples or men and women who were friends who didn't mind bunking together. After many discussions, Jena was able to fill an open slot, but they could only accommodate her if she was willing to pay the double occupancy sum. It was a lot of money, but quite frankly was no different than what she had paid for the Seychelles trip, and besides, Chris had left her with plenty of money and it would be nice to have a room to herself. In fact, after hearing her story, Mark had given her a discount for the master stateroom, dropping the price to eight thousand dollars to have the room to herself. Mark had been very accommodating on the phone and she had felt it necessary to explain to him her situation. She did not get into the details but once she told him of her husband's passing and what she was doing, he went out of his way to find a slot for her. One thing she had not been aware of was that he too had lost a loved one.

"I'm sorry, Mark, I didn't know that," Jena consoled.

"It's okay, how would you? It happened five years ago. It's one of the reasons I'm doing what I'm doing," he added. "But listen, let's not talk of this now," he smiled, switching subjects. "How about we board and get settled in? It's best to talk of such things after a fantastic day of fishing with a drink in our hand," he suggested. "Don't you agree?"

Jena nodded in agreement. "That I do."

"Please, after you," he said, indicating the ramp that led to the main cabin door.

Mark led her to the main stateroom. It was simply furnished but roomier than she expected. It came complete with a double bed, plenty of storage, and even her own private bath. Everything was creamy white accented with smooth red teak. It was immaculately clean and Jena could tell the brothers were going to provide top-notch service. She knew this room typically cost more. She also knew that Mark had purposefully set this room aside for her, despite the deal he was providing for her. She would make sure his generosity was rewarded with a large tip at the end of the trip. Her luggage and gear was already in the room and when he left, she spent a half hour unpacking and relaxing. When she heard the twin diesels kick on she made her way to the main cabin to take part in the departure.

Jena couldn't believe how lavishly impressive the boat was. Dark glossy stained teak steps led to a main room as opulent as any expensive hotel. The fully equipped kitchen was near the back with living space and an oval dining room table near the front of the boat. The carpets were freshly vacuumed and the color of light caramel. The L shaped couch was white leather and everywhere she looked was red stained teak that glistened in the bright fluorescent light. A steep set of steps led to the flybridge and the two doors opened out to the walkways that wrapped around the boat. Jena could see a small door near the kitchen that she guessed was the bathroom. And the kitchen was equally impressive. She had no idea what to expect from a yacht's kitchen, but it certainly wasn't this. It was small, as you would expect, but quite extravagant, with marble countertops, a breakfast nook with a small teak table surrounded by booth benches upholstered in creamy leather, as well as a small island with two teak and white leather bar stools.

Sitting at one the leather couches was Dagen and Amos, the two other guests that were joining her for the next six days. In the kitchen was Karmen, their chef for the trip. Her shoulder length hair was just as black as the brothers' hair, but she was clearly Chilean, her skin darker and her features more native. Her Spanish accent was quite noticeable. Jena had already met them all and she smiled when they saw her.

"Mrs. O'Malley," Karmen said, smiling, her white teeth bright against her caramel skin. "Would you like a margarita or a Marlborough Sauvignon Blanc?"

"I think I'll have a glass of wine," Jena answered. "Thanks, Karmen." Jena was learning that most high-end fishing outfits catered to your specific needs by having their guests complete a comprehensive questionnaire. It was one way to make sure they were happy with their food and drink choices. This particular outfit was no different.

"Of course," Karmen replied as she went about getting the wine.

"Please, join us," Dagen offered.

The couch was an L shaped sectional and Jena sat on the smaller section. "Thanks," she said, looking around some more.

"Pretty impressive boat," Dagen added.

Dagen and Amos were a father son team. Jena had learned they were both Palestinian and lived in the West Bank of Israel. Their skin was the color of dark walnut and they were both very handsome. Dagen's wavy black hair was short and streaked with gray. Jena figured he was in his sixties, but he looked healthy and fit with a hawkish nose and an aristocratic appearance. His son Amos could've been a model. He was tall with angular and narrow features. His coal black hair was a bit longer, with natural waves that gave him the look of an Arab surfer. But it was his eyes that drew Jena's attention. They were a sparkling jade green that contrasted beautifully with his dark skin. Jena guessed him to be in his late twenties. Both spoke English well but with an obvious Arab accent.

"It is," Jena agreed. "It's not quite what I was expecting." Karmen approached and handed Jena her glass of wine. "Thank you."

"Of course," Karmen replied as she looked at the other two. "How is your scotch?"

Jena glanced at their drinks and suddenly felt a jolt of nostalgia. Golden liquid filled their tumblers along with a sizable ice cube. It was just the drink that Chris would've ordered. She sighed and quickly subdued her urge to cry. It had almost gotten through her defensive wall. She was thankful for her many years practicing keeping her emotions behind bars. Of course she knew from experience that you could only hold them at bay for so long. It was only a matter of time before they eventually broke free. She just preferred that to happen in times of her own choosing.

"Outstanding," Dagen affirmed.

"What did you say it was called?" Amos asked.

"Isle of Jura, thirty-year-old," Karmen answered proudly. "There were only two hundred bottles shipped to the United States, so it's quite hard to find there." Karmen smiled. "Mark and Lance are quite the scotch drinkers and go out of their way to bring their guests the best they can find. But if I can be honest with you, I think it's more of a selfish gesture," she added with a wink.

Amos sipped some the amber liquid. "Well I'm glad," he replied in contentment. "It's really good."

The melancholy threatened to overwhelm her again. It was all she could do to overcome it. Chris would be in heaven, sitting her and enjoying expensive scotch and talking with people who clearly understood the various nuances of the distillate. There was little he enjoyed more than finishing a long day of fishing with a premium glass of scotch. She forced herself to put on her best smile.

"Would you like some more?" Karmen asked the two men.

"I'm good for now," Dagen replied.

"Perhaps in a bit," Amos added.

Karmen nodded and made her way back to the kitchen. She seemed to be preparing some appetizers.

"So how long have you guys been fly fishing?" Jena asked. Just then the boat began to move, slowly pulling away from the dock.

Amos smiled. "Here we go."

"I started pretty late in life, actually," Dagen began. "But I've been at it for around ten years. I tried to get my son into it at the same time but he was too busy chasing girls."

"Father, I was no more chasing girls than any other boy my age." Jena was impressed with Amos's use of language. He was clearly educated and well spoken.

"Perhaps," his dad muttered. But his expression was doubtful and Jena smiled.

Amos shook his head and looked at Jena. "I haven't been doing it that long. My father finally got me hooked a few years back. It's quite addicting, don't you think?"

Both of the men sounded very educated, and Jena wondered what they did in Israel. "It is," Jena confirmed. "I've been fly-fishing less than a year but it feels like much longer."

"That is because you have developed the fly-fishing itch, as I like to call it," Dagen replied. "If you don't scratch that itch, it just gets worse."

Jena laughed. "I like that analogy."

"What do you do back home? Dagen asked.

"I'm a pediatric intensive care nurse."

"Oh, wow, very impressive," he replied. "You must have thick skin to be able to do that job."

Jena hated getting into details about her work. His response had been quite typical, and although he meant no offense, she knew that it was unlikely he had any idea of the traumatic experiences she had endured in her line of work. And it was quite likely that he didn't really want to know. Who wanted to hear about kids that were so sick they might die? That was one of the reasons why first responders and nurses either held onto the pain and tried to bury it deep, or they had to talk with a professional. If they were lucky, they could unload on a fellow colleague who could in fact empathize with what they were dealing with. Luckily, there were enough successes to keep her showing up to work. There wasn't much better than being a part of saving a child's life.

"Yeah, it can be quite difficult. But it's also very rewarding. How about you two, what do you do?"

"I'm in medical school," Amos said proudly. "I'll be starting my residency soon. My father is taking me on this trip for graduation."

"Congratulations," Jena replied.

"I'm a professor at Tel Aviv University in Israel," Dagen said. "I teach history."

"History, in Israel...talk about thick skin," she said.

Dagen's lips curled up into a soft smile. "Yes, it is interesting to say the least."

"And whose history do you tell, Palestinian, or Israeli?" Jena asked.

Dagen lifted his eyebrows at that. "Are you a student of history, Jena O'malley?"

She frowned a little. "No, not really. My husband was though, and he used to talk about the Arab-Israeli struggle. But if I am honest with you, my questions must have made me sound much more knowledgeable about the subject than I really am."

Amos laughed. "Well, you just wound up the clock. I hope you're ready for a long dissertation."

Dagen shot his son a playful glare. "I will not bore our new friend with a dissertation. But, to answer your question," he continued, addressing her, "I try my best to present the history from both sides, letting my students form their own opinions."

"And my father is most suited to do this," Amos added. "You see, we are Jewish Palestinians."

"Forgive me for my ignorance," Jena replied, "but aren't Palestinians Muslims?"

"Most are," Amos agreed. "But there is a small percentage of Christian and Jewish Palestinians."

"Doesn't that throw a wrench in the conflict?" Jena asked.

"Not really," Dagen answered. "Keep in mind, the Arab-Israeli conflict is mostly about land, not religion. And although religion is a

184

major factor in who governs Jerusalem and the sacred sites located there, the main issue and cause of violence is who controls the land. I could talk for hours on the subject, but as my son said, I don't want to give you a dissertation."

"I wish my husband were here, he would love to talk with you about it over a glass of scotch," Jena added before catching her words. She didn't really want to talk about Chris's death but she had just brought it up herself. Jena looked away, hoping they would avoid the subject.

Amos was about to say something when Dagen touched his leg, shaking his head. "So, Jena, what do you know about the fishing we are about to experience?"

Jena turned back to them appreciatively. "From what I gathered we'll be targeting see-run browns and rainbows, although all I know is what I read on their website."

"That's true," Dagen agreed. "But I guess the fjords in this area also boast runs of coho, kings, and Atlantic salmon."

"I thought coho and kings were indigenous to the west coast of North America."

"That was my thought as well," Dagen added. "But supposedly they were introduced in raising pens and have now adapted to become naturally reproducing populations."

She lifted her eyebrows at that. "That will be quite a fight on my seven weight."

Amos smiled. "Sounds fun though."

They continued to talk for half an hour before Lance came down from the flybridge and welcomed them to join either him on the bow deck, or Mark on the flybridge. He informed them that they would be entering the fjords soon.

"How long will we be cruising in the fjords?" Amos asked.

"Most of the day," Lance replied. "We'll make our way deeper into the fjords today, then tomorrow we'll jump in the zodiacs and do some exploring and fishing."

"So no fishing today?" Jena asked.

"It's unlikely," Lance confirmed. "It will be dark before we get to our first destination."

A Year of a Thousand Casts

It was quite an enjoyable day. They ate a wonderful lunch of grilled lobster and salad, and although Jena wasn't much of a seafood eater, she very much enjoyed the lobster. It was light but rich in flavor. She hadn't had much lobster before, but something told her that this was some of the best, perhaps because it was so fresh. They drank pisco sours, a cocktail that Jena learned was the Chilean national cocktail. Jena loved the drink as it sort of reminded her of a margarita. There are of course different versions of the cocktail, but it was typically made with Pisco, which is a type of brandy, lime juice, simple syrup, egg white, and a touch of Angostura bitters.

They talked and watched the abundant wildlife that inhabited the fjords. They saw a few sea lions, albatross, and even a handful of the rare Chilean black dolphins. And the scenery was also incredible. Temperate rain forests blanketed their surroundings in lush green vegetation that climbed the southern Andes to mingle with snowfields, epic glaciers, and volcanoes. They saw waterfalls and birds everywhere, and no sign of human life. Jena felt so small and her mind kept drifting to the life lesson she had learned in the Seychelles...*there is beauty in solitude.*

"How did you guys find out about this place?" Jena asked Mark as she sat next to him on the flybridge. He was steering the yacht while she sat on the adjacent leather seat. She could see the others standing at the bow gazing at their surroundings with the same appreciation she felt.

Mark smiled. "I used to run an import export business with my brother. We did quite well but our hearts were always into adventure; it was one of the reasons we operated from this area. It's one of the most remote places in the world, one of the last frontiers. We had always been avid fishermen, something we had learned from our father. One day my brother came to me after he had visited Puerto Cisnes on a business trip. He said he had talked with a local about fishing and was told that deep in the fjords were rivers teeming with fish. So, we charted a boat and spent two weeks exploring it." He looked at her and smiled. "It's a trip I will never forget. When we came back, we sold our business, bought this boat, and the rest is history."

Jena was wondering how the passing of his wife fit into the story but decided that the first day was not the time to press the question. "Are there other outfits that do this?"

"There are now, but we were the first. These fjords expand hundreds of miles south and there are so many waterways and unexplored rivers that one could fish a lifetime here and only touch the surface of possibilities. It is unlikely we will see another soul out here."

"It sounds incredible."

Mark nodded. "It's changed my life. When my wife died, I wasn't sure what I was going to do. I couldn't work. I felt lost. This," he said, indicating his surroundings, "saved me. It's hard to explain but it's given me a new purpose. She had always been so supportive of my wild adventures." His expression warmed. "I see her smiling down on me every time I get in this boat."

She didn't say anything for a few moments, her mind drifting to her own predicament. She felt a rising anxiety as she thought about her unknown future. What was she going to do when all her trips were over? Was she going to be able to go back to work and be a nurse as if nothing happened? She was having a hard time thinking of herself as a nurse without Chris beside her. It was the unknown that frightened her the most. But as she glanced at Mark, seeing him content, she thought that perhaps there could be a new future. "I'm happy you've found this escape."

He shook his head. "No, no, you misunderstand me. This is not an escape. This is how I hold onto her."

"But how do you move on then?"

"Slowly," he mused. "I'm still a work in progress," he added, smiling wryly. "Listen," he continued. "I wish I could answer that question, but if I can be honest, I still have days where moving on seems impossible. And then there are other days where it seems a real possibility. The more time that passes, the more I feel positive about being able to move on, and all I can hope for is that over even more time, I will be able to hold onto her memories and move on at the same time."

"Yeah," Jena muttered, "it seems as if I'm walking up a steep mountain against a winter gale. Occasionally the wind dies down and I can rest, but reaching the top seems like an unachievable goal. I can't even picture what the top looks like."

Mark looked at her with apparent understanding. "I like that analogy. And I know exactly how you feel. How about this," he suggested. "Find a cave to rest in. Enjoy your break from the storm, and when you are rested you can try to conquer it once again."

"Let me guess," Jena laughed. "This fishing trip is one of those caves?"

He joined in her laughter. "Exactly!"

Later that evening Mark and Lance anchored the yacht in some calm water just off a huge rock face, over which a small waterfall cascaded dropping fifty feet to the deep water below. It was a spectacular scene and Jena was looking forward to falling asleep to the calming susurration of the waterfall in the background. Two nearby rivers nearby flowed into the fjords and they would be fishing them first thing in the morning.

Karmen had prepared them a hearty meal of creamy polenta and braised beef ribs accompanied by a salad of microgreens, beets, and gorgonzola. Everything was delicious. They talked incessantly about the fishing and Jena found herself holding her own in the conversation. Chris would've been so proud of her. By the time dinner was done it was just after eight o'clock. They had a five o'clock wake up time and Jena was feeling pretty tired. Her bed and book were calling her name.

Mark stood up from the table. "You are welcome to stay up and watch movies here if you'd like," he instructed. "The hot tub on top is hot and ready as well or you can relax in your staterooms. We'll be waking everyone at five for breakfast."

She stopped and looked at Mark. "I forgot you had a hot tub."

Mark smiled. "You did bring a suit, right?"

"I did."

"There isn't anything better than relaxing in the hot tub with a cold drink after a long day of fishing," Lance added.

"Now that sounds nice," Dagen concurred.

"I think I might take a soak now before bed," Amos said as he stood.

"Suit yourself, make yourselves at home," Mark added. "The steps to the top are in the back of the boat and you have towels in your room. You can leave your dirty towel here and Karmen will take care of it."

"I think I might just relax with a movie," Dagen said eying the couch and television.

"In the cabinet are all the DVD's," Lance instructed. "Help yourself."

"The hot tub sounds nice," Jena pondered, "but I think I'll save that for a treat tomorrow evening. A bed and a book sounds good right now. I'll see you guys in the morning."

She said her goodnights and headed to her room for the night.

The whine of the outboard motor seemed so out of place in the tranquil setting surrounding them. Jena and Mark skirted the edge of the fjord in a zodiac heading to a small river inlet. The sun was barely peeking over the tall mountain peaks and it was consequently a little chilly. Dagen and Amos had gone with Lance and they had planned to fish the outgoing tidal water of a river further south. Jena wore a life vest over a Patagonia coat tucked into her waders. She had her seven-weight fly rod strung up with a sink tip and Mark had a few rods ready to go as well. It was near six o'clock and in the mid-sixties. Mark said it would likely get into the seventies and there was no rain in the forecast. It looked like it was going to be a good day for fishing.

After twenty minutes Mark beached the boat near a small river flowing into the fjord. All around them were tall grasses and lush vegetation, but the river's edge was navigable providing narrow paths of river rock and downed timber on both sides. They were in a small valley with a few miles of fishable water before they reached the base of the steeper mountains surrounding them.

Mark tied the boat to a tree and put on his small pack. After withdrawing one of the rods and net, he looked at Jena, who was holding her own rod. She already had her small chest pack on and was ready to go. "Ready?"

Jena smiled. "Let's do this."

Mark led her along the river's edge where the ground was marshy and wet. She asked Mark about it and he told her that they were fishing the outgoing tide, and that when the tide was in, they would be standing in water. As it was, the river was slow and deep, resembling a large slough. They walked a quarter of a mile before the river started to look like a traditional river. There were some twists and turns and typical runs, some deep and slow moving, and others fast moving riffles. Mark stopped at the second bend, the water moving slowly but cutting into a bank on the far side. The top of the run was faster and more turbulent, eventually dumping into more slack water.

"Here we go," Mark said, indicating the spot. He had already tied on a muddler minnow and knew she was rigged and ready. "Start at the top and work your way down. Let the fly swing into the deep water and then strip it in."

She nodded and stepped into the water, preparing her fly rod for her first cast. Looking back, the area behind her was clear enough for the short distance she had to cast. It would be a simple cast in comparison to what she had had to do in the wind along the flats of the atolls in the Seychelles.

Her first cast was good and she let the fly swing through the deep water along the edge, stripping it in at the end of the swing.

"Faster on the strip," Mark instructed. "These fish are used to being in the open ocean and are quite aggressive to a fast strip."

She nodded and cast again, repeating what she had previously done but stripping faster. On the third cast something grabbed her line and she set the hook. The rod bounced tight for a second and then nothing. "Damn," she swore, looking at Mark. "It was there for a second."

He smiled. "Try again in the same spot."

She did as she was told and during the drift her line suddenly stopped moving.

"Set!" Mark yelled.

Jena hadn't been expecting a strike that soon in the drift and was slow on the set. Nothing. "Shit!"

"I think there are a couple fish in there. Try again in the same spot. Be ready, sometimes they'll grab the fly as the current pulls it quickly out of the strike zone. To the fish it looks like bait swimming away."

"Okay," she responded, readying her cast once again. The fly struck the water and literally a second later the surface exploded as a fish took the fly before it had even sunk a few inches.

"Set!" Mark yelled again.

This time she was ready and she lifted the rod tip. The line went tight and she felt the familiar tug of a fish, and it was a nice one. "Fish on!" she yelled excitedly.

"That's a nice sea run brown!" Mark shouted, moving closer to her as she stepped out of the water to fight the fish on land.

Jena felt the intoxicating excitement surge through her body as the fish leaped from the water. As it jumped aggressively several times, Jena leaned forward with the rod to cushion the tippet, the lighter line attached to the fly.

190

"Good job!" Mark encouraged, holding his net at the ready despite the fact that the fish was nowhere near done with the fight.

The strong fish surged up and down river several times, leaping from the surface twice more. By this time Jena had it on the reel, all the slack line having been taken out when it ran down river with the current. Eventually she was able to guide the tired fish closer to shore where she could finally get a close look at it. It was a great fish, likely twenty to twenty-five inches. Jena could see the dark spots along its back and realized that sea-run browns looked a little different than the brown trout she had caught in New Zealand. These dark spotted browns were more silver color in comparison to the yellowish bodies of the New Zealand browns.

Mark entered the water and readied the net. "Walk backwards and guide the fish into the net," he instructed.

She stepped back and angled the rod to her left, pulling the fish's head closer to the shore. Exhausted, the fish went with the least resistance, finding itself in Mark's net a few seconds later

"Yes!" Jena whooped.

"Nice job!" he congratulated her. "It's a big one...looks to be twenty-four inches."

"He was strong," Jena said moving closer to Mark.

"The fish here need to be to survive in the saltwater. Let's get a picture."

By this time Jena knew the drill, getting herself into position by balancing her rod on the back of her neck. She crouched down and took the net from Mark as he prepared the camera. He had already removed the fly from its mouth so all she had to do was tail it, and then lift it up towards the camera.

"I'm ready," he announced.

"Jena reached into the net and gripped its tail, careful to wet her hands first so as not to hurt the fish. She had learned from Hans that you never wanted to damage the delicate slime layer covering their bodies as that protects them from various diseases. Once she had a good grip, she reached under its thick body and lifted it out of the water, holding it before her with a big smile on her face.

Mark clicked several pictures, stepping closer for a few more. "Okay, I think I got it. Go ahead and release her."

She marveled at its weight and girth. "She is so heavy."

"They have a good diet of minnows, crustaceans, crawdads, and shrimp." Mark explained. "They get big here."

Holding her in the water by the tail, Jena waited a few moments before it got oxygenated, and when she did, she kicked her tail harder and Jena let go. She darted away like a rocket, disappearing in a blink.

Mark gave her a high five. "That was well done. Nice job leaning into the leaps."

"Thanks," Jena beamed. "I had a good teacher," she added, remembering Hans's words in her head that time she had lost the steelhead because she had not dropped the rod tip into the jump.

"Well, you ready to do it again?"

"Yes!"

They fished another two hours and Jena caught three more beautiful fish, one a nineteen-inch rainbow. The tide was starting to come back in so Mark led her back to the boat, which was now floating in a few feet of water. He pulled on the rope attached to the tree and dragged the boat to the ever-moving shoreline.

"Jump in, we're going to fish this brackish water and hopefully get a salmon," Mark instructed.

Jena was excited about that. She had caught a few salmon with Hans but that was the limit of her salmon fishing experience. The area around the mouth of the river was getting bigger as the tide was coming in and there was a slow-moving current that dumped the fresh water into the salt. Mark maneuvered them a stone throw out and put the boat in idle, handing her an eight-weight rod that was all ready to go. She checked the fly and it was some sort of a minnow pattern with a black line on its back and silver and white underneath, a streak of red along its side.

Mark saw her looking at it. "That is one of my designs," he said proudly. "I call it The Hammer."

Jena forced a laugh, a wave of melancholy suddenly resurfacing with memories of her husband proudly showing his flies that he had created. She heard him say in her mind, *any true fly-fisherman names the flies he creates.* Of course, he would always laugh when he said it. But his echoing laughter in her consciousness did nothing to alleviate her current sense of loss. But she shook off the feeling and did her best to hide her emotions.

"Why do you call it that?" she asked, looking away to hide any incipient tears that had appeared.

He was busy angling the boat in the proper position and didn't seem to notice. "Because the fish like it so much they 'hammer' it when they strike." He smiled, obviously thinking he was quite witty.

"Well," she added, "let's see if it lives up to its name."

"Okay," Mark said, pointing at the water near the mouth of the river. "When the tide comes in like it is now, small minnows move in to feed off anything coming down from the river. Not to mention, the tidewater covers other food sources like crustaceans and other goodies. It's not uncommon to have salmon move into this brackish water to feed. So just cast out towards the edge of the flowing water, let it sink, and strip the fly in. Some fish like it fast and others slower, so try a variety of speeds."

"Sounds good," Jena said as she stood and began to cast. They worked the water all around the river outlet without any luck. Just when they were going to pick up and try again, the water suddenly fluttered with small silver fish. Something had spooked them.

"There!" Mark said excitedly, pointing to the edge of the disturbance. There was some commotion on the water and it looked as if bigger fish were chasing the bait, their bodies creating a wake under the surface.

Jena's heart began to beat faster as she cast to the area, stripping the fly in with rhythmic jerks. Five casts later and nothing. The bait, likely small herring or anchovies, were moving around the outlet so Mark kicked the motor in gear to follow them.

"Right there!" Jena yelped, pointing to some more surface action.

"Here!" Mark said, quickly handing her another rod. "This rod has a dry line and a popper. Hopefully, that will get their attention."

She quickly set the rod down and grabbed Mark's. "I've never used a popper," she said.

"No worries," Mark answered, shutting off the motor. "Cast out like a dry fly. When it lands, strip it with quick jerks. The action is crazy and it might entice one of those salmon."

Jena glanced at the fly and saw that it had a white foam body with an upturned front. There were silver and black strands tied in the back like a tail. Moving quickly, she cast near the bait ball. It landed hard with a big wake. Jena swore, thinking she had made a mistake.

"No, that's good. Now strip it in hard, pausing in between." He was excited and his enthusiasm was contagious. Jena focused on the fly as she jerked it in. It was designed to float, but the upturned front caused it to plow though the water making a noticeable wake, allowing it to twist and turn across the surface like an injured bait fish.

Five strips later and the water exploded as a salmon slammed the popper. "Holy shit," she squealed as she set the hook.

"Fish on!" Mark yelled as the salmon took off like a bullet. The eight-weight rod bent hard as the fish shot straight down, trying to disappear into the dark depths. The reel whined as Jena kept the line tight.

"Oh my god, that was amazing!" she whooped as she struggled to hold onto the rod.

"That was a big fish! And there is nothing more exciting than a surface take like that!"

"I agree!" Jena beamed.

"I think that was a silver salmon."

Suddenly the fish turned and shot away from the boat, angling closer to the surface and pulling more line out. Five seconds later and Jena was into her backing. The strong fish had pulled all her fly line from the reel and was now working on the two hundred and fifty yards of thirty-pound backing. "Whoo hoo!" she cheered. A few seconds later it leaped from the water, shaking its body frantically in hopes of spitting the fly. She dropped the rod tip, leaning forward to keep the stress off the ten-pound tippet, the lighter line attached to the fly.

"Good job!" Mark yelled encouragingly. "And that was a big one. I'd say it's twenty plus pounds."

Five minutes later and a few more runs, Jena was able to get the fish close to the boat. The salmon tried a few more runs but didn't have enough energy to defeat Jena's endurance. Mark grabbed a long boat net and readied it as Jena brought the fish closer. A quick dive of the net and the fish was snared.

"You did it! Nice job!"

"Thanks," she replied happily as she wiped the sweat from her brow.

"Set the rod down and grab the net. Keep him in the water while I grab the camera."

"Okay." Jena took the net from him and removed the fly as the fish tried in vain to flop out of its protective folds to freedom.

"Now, give me the net," Mark said as he set the camera nearby on the seat. "I'll bring it in close. Reach in and tail it. Once you got it, lift him up and face me. He's not going to like it so I'll take a few quick pictures. If he flops out of your hands just let him go. We don't want to hurt him just for a picture."

"Got it." Mark drew the net in close and Jena leaned over the zodiac's soft edge, reaching in to grab its tail. A few tries and she had a firm grip on the tired fish. It was so big she could barely get her hand around the tail's girth. Mark held the net's handle between his legs and readied the camera just as Jena reached her other hand under its belly. Pulling the fish from the water, she quickly angled her body towards Mark and smiled widely, her hands still shaking from exertion as she did her best to angle the fish towards the camera. It was a beautiful fish, its scales a bright silver glistening in the sun. Black spots peppered the silver landscape along its back and it must've weighed at least twenty pounds.

Just as Mark predicted, the fish didn't like being out of the water. After two clicks of the camera, it flipped from her hands, the camera still clicking away as the fish landed in the water, disappearing in the dark depths with a flick of its tail.

"I got it, don't worry." Mark looked at the camera and smiled. "What a beautiful fish!" he exclaimed, giving her a high five.

"Thanks. That was a blast." She looked around at her surroundings, wondering if it was the right time to sprinkle Chris's ashes. She didn't really know if that fish was considered a trophy fish for the area, but it sure was a fun experience. And the setting was spectacular; tranquil water, lush vegetation, and snowcapped peaks reminiscent of a fantasy setting straight from a Tolkien book. But then again, she mused, the setting wasn't going anywhere. Making up her mind, she decided that day one was not the right time, the cold metal of the locket around her neck a reminder of the weight of the task set before her. She wanted each location to be perfect, and something told her there was still more to come.

"Ready for another one?" Mark asked.

"Of course."

* * *

It was on the third day that Jena and Mark had decided to go on a real adventure. Mark had been mulling over an idea of exploring a new area and asked if Jena would be up for it. He said it was a longer boat ride and there was no guarantee of fish, but he followed that up quickly with a counter argument that the unexplored area could be teaming with fish. Mark had been her guide since day one and Jena had gotten the feeling that he was monopolizing his time with her in some way. It wasn't the feeling a woman got when a man was flirting with her, it was more reminiscent of how a sister might feel under the protection of her big brother. She had a feeling it had something to do with what they had in common in losing a spouse. She was happy for it as she really liked him as a person and a guide. Lance, his brother, was great as well, but Mark seemed more personable and prone to smiles, something Jena needed more than she knew.

They had been in the Zodiac for nearly an hour before Mark took it into an inlet that opened into a peaceful lagoon. It was currently slack tide but Mark said the tide would start to come in within the hour.

"You see that?" he asked, pointing off in the distance.

Jena followed his finger and saw off in the distance a huge rock face, white water cascading from the top. They were too far away to hear it but it looked pretty impressive. "It looks like a pretty big waterfall."

"I saw it last time we came through the channel but I didn't have time to explore it. I'm glad you agreed to do this with me."

"What do you think we'll find?"

He turned, gazing back at the waterfall. "Well, if I'm right, we'll find the waterfall's outlet in this lagoon."

"You mean like a small river?"

"Exactly," Mark responded, his eyes scanning the edge of the lagoon as he skirted its shoreline. "There!" he cried as they came around a corner. As he predicted there was a small stream dumping into the lagoon. Since the tide was out, the water from the river was cutting a channel through the muddy bottom of the lagoon until it met with the shallow saltwater. Mark slowed the boat and used the automatic trim to raise the motor, stopping it just before the intake broke the surface.

"What are we going to do?" Jena asked.

"I brought the prop up and I'm going to take us up the river channel as far as I can. Then we'll tie her off and go exploring. Sound good?"

"Yup," Jena confirmed. "I'm excited to see this waterfall."

"I'm hoping we're going to see some fish too. My thoughts are that maybe the fish will congregate near the falls as they can't go any further. The area could be rich in food which might bring some of the big sea-runs in or even some salmon. We won't know until we check it out."

Jena thought of Chris and for the first time in a long while his image wasn't associated with sadness. She was thinking how excited he would be if he were here with Mark. Exploring an unknown stream ending in a waterfall was just the sort of thing that he would have loved to do. He had so enjoyed telling Jena his stories of adventure and she could still hear his voice in her head doing just that. Her heart sank momentarily as she wondered how long it would be before she couldn't remember the lines of his face or the tone of his voice.

Luckily, Mark's voice pulled her away from her thoughts. "Look there!" Mark said, pointing into the water as he slowly guided the zodiac upriver. Jena looked down and saw dozens of fish shooting around. They were all between three and six inches.

"That's a good sign, right?"

"It is," Mark agreed. "Where there are small fish, there are—"

"Big fish," Jena finished, a smile on her face.

"Exactly."

Five minutes later and Mark could go no further, the river was getting too shallow. He turned the motor off, jumped out, and pulled the boat close to shore to rest on the smooth worn rocks that covered the river's edge. He took the bow rope and tied it off to a nearby tree.

"Grab your seven weight," he instructed as he cinched on his pack, net, and grabbed the heavier eight weight rod. He turned to face her, his brows raised in excitement. "Ready?"

She thought he looked like a kid in a candy store and again her thoughts went to Chris. Her husband would've loved Mark. They were clearly kindred souls and it saddened her to know that Chris would never get to meet him and have this experience fishing, surrounded by the pristine wilderness of the Andes.

"I'm right behind you," she said, refocusing her thoughts on the present.

They hiked a few miles along the river. It wasn't easy going as occasionally the water was too deep and they had to hike into the woods, pushing through the dense foliage before dropping back down to the river. There were a few fishable spots but Mark suggested they push hard to the falls as they were on a tight timeline based on the incoming tide. He looked back at her a few times to make sure she was doing okay. She was in good shape and had hiked quite a bit over the last year, so she reassured him with smiles that she was fine.

As they hiked, Jena couldn't help but think of Chris. They had hiked a lot together, mostly at his insistence. But over time she had learned to love the joys of hiking, in working hard to find that secluded place where you could unwind and really relax without the stresses of life slapping you in the face. It was hard for her to walk along a riverbed, with a fly rod in hand, and not think of him. But she forced herself to maintain her composure despite the threat of tears.

"Wow," Mark said, his voice pulling her from her thoughts once again.

Jena looked up at his voice. They had just come around a bend in the river, and in the distance, no more than an arrow shot away, was the massive wall of rock and the cascading waterfall plunging to the river below. Jena had been so preoccupied with her thoughts that she hadn't even registered the roaring sound of the falls reflecting off the rock face.

"It's bigger than I thought," Jena announced.

"I agree." Mark looked back at her with a huge childlike smile. "Let's get closer."

She nodded, just as excited to see the falls. The terrain leading up to the falls was littered with rocks and boulders, likely having crumbled from the rock wall over thousands of years. After wading the river in spots and maneuvering around countless rocks, some half the size of a car, they finally made it to the falls.

Mark was speechless as he gazed up at the cascading water, the sound nearly deafening in the clearing surrounding the pool that had formed by the crashing water. Moss covered rocks ranging from the size of a baby to a Volkswagen bug ringed the large pool, the area near the falls turbulent as thousands of gallons of water hammered into it. As the current flowed away from the falls, the pool expanded and formed what looked like a little lake before picking up speed again as it formed the river that flowed into the fjords nearly three miles away.

Jena stood next to him; her eyes wide as she tried to take in the beauty of the pool and the falls that fed it. "This was well worth the hike," she murmured, her mind drifting to Karen's words from the Seychelles...*there is beauty in solitude.* The waterfall before her was a direct reflection of that phrase.

Mark nodded and looked at her, his exuberant smile turning serious. "Thank you for allowing me to take you here," he said. "I'm just hoping we can catch some fish, after all, you have paid for a fishing adventure."

"Even if we don't catch any fish, it was worth it," she announced. "This place is stunning. It's so serene that I almost feel like a trespasser."

He nodded. "I know what you mean. Okay," he added, his tone all business. "Let's watch the water a bit and come up with a plan."

"Sounds good."

They both walked around the edge of the large pool, scanning the water and looking for any signs of fish. It wasn't long before Jena saw a fish rise and slurp something off the surface. "There!" she said, pointing to the swirl left behind.

Mark moved closer to her. "Did you see what it took?"

"I didn't."

He squinted his eyes but couldn't see anything on the surface of the water. "Okay," he said, "Let's try the popper and see if we can get something to rise to it."

She smiled at that. She had really enjoyed catching the salmon on the popper and was hoping to experience that again. She leaned her rod against a big rock and took the eight-weight rod from Mark.

"Just start here at the edge and we'll move closer and closer to the more turbulent water," he instructed. The pool was large and deep, and they were starting at the end, where the water was much calmer. Mark clearly wanted her to work the edge of the pool and move steadily closer to the churning water created by the waterfall.

She nodded, unhooked the white and silver popper, and began to cast. Nothing took the fly as she moved slowly clockwise, edging the pool and getting closer and closer to the turbulent, more oxygenated water.

Suddenly, without preamble, just as the fly moved beyond the dark deep water to the visible, more shallow water, a shadow shot up from the darkness and hit the fly so aggressively that it shot out of the water.

"Fish!" Jena explained, the attack so sudden that she jerked backwards, causing her to trip on a rock. Falling to the side, she caught herself with her left hand as she held the rod tip as high as she could. Righting herself quickly, she leaped to her feet and stripped the line in hard, hoping to take up any slack. But the fish was gone, her line limp in her hand. "Damn it," she swore. "Did you see that!?"

"How could I not!" Mark yelped. "Are you okay?"

"I'm fine," she said, gritting her teeth in frustration.

"Try again," he encouraged. "And remember, fly fishing is all about learning humility."

Jena nodded. She liked what he had said, and thought that perhaps this could be the life lesson for the trip. She realized that fly fishing could definitely humble one. There was so much to know and learn about the sport, and the casting could be so frustrating that one often quite before they even began to scratch the surface of that knowledge. Chris had always said that no matter how good you were, or how much you knew about fly fishing, there was always something else to learn. She held onto Marks words, excited to write them down in her journal.

Starting again, she covered the water with her fly as she moved slowly to her left, her hand jerking the popper across the surface in short rhythmic bursts. The pronounced front of the fly splashed water into the air at every move, imitating something hurt swimming across the surface of the pool. Five casts later, the popper smacked down hard onto the water ten feet away from the white water created by the tumbling falls. She was just about to start her strip when the water exploded again in a vicious take. This time Jena was prepared and she set the hook perfectly. Her line went tight. Fish on!

"Holy shit!" Mark said, "that looked like a big rainbow!"

Just as he said it her reel screamed as the fish ran like an Olympic sprinter. It seemed like the fish had drank ten Red Bulls, running left and right and jerking its head back and forth so hard that Jena's rod bounced crazily in her hand. It leaped from the water half a dozen times before taking off towards the deep water by skimming its

200

body across the surface, all the while flipping around so aggressively that Jena could not believe it hadn't spit the hook.

"This fish is crazy strong!" she exclaimed, trying futilely to maintain control of it.

"That's a big pissed off rainbow," Mark said, his tone all business as he held the net at the ready. "Your drag is good," he added. "Let it run, he'll tire soon."

Jena nodded, gritting her teeth as she kept the pressure on the fish. Five minutes later, it seemed to suddenly run out of energy. She was able to reel it in slowly, keeping the line tight as the fish reluctantly moved closer to the shore. "I think he's finally given up," she said.

As if the fish heard her, it expressed a big 'F' you, bolting off one more time towards the deep water. Keeping the pressure on, she used her hand on the reel frame to slow it. It tired quickly and she began to maneuver it closer once again.

"I think now he might be done," Mark said, stepping into the water.

Jena didn't say anything, hoping not to jinx her chance of landing the magnificent fish. Turning the rod, she angled its head towards the shore as the fish finally complied. "Here he comes," Jena said, her heart pounding in anticipation of landing such a trophy.

And just like that, Mark expertly shot the net forward and scooped up the fish. "Yes!"

Jena relaxed her shoulders and arms and moved forward quickly, excited to see the fine specimen. "Holy crap," she said when she finally saw it. "That's big."

Mark looked up at her, grinning. "That is the biggest rainbow I've seen here," he effused. "It's at least twenty-seven inches. Damn," he continued, "I've seen smaller salmon."

Jena was mesmerized by the beauty of the fish. Its body was sleek but strong, with dark spots splattered across a silver body and a long brush stroke of pink running down the middle. This was a trophy fish. She knew in her heart that this was the place to not only sprinkle Chris's ashes, but to indulge in the scotch and cigar. It was perfect, the beauty almost surreal, and the fish, well, she was still shaking from the excitement of it all.

"Let's get a picture," she suggested. "After that, I have something I'd like to do."

He looked at her curiously, but didn't say anything.

After Mark took a few pictures, they both sat down on a log nearby and Jena told him the entire story. She gave him an abridged version but didn't leave out any of the important points. When she was done, he looked at her, his expression serious as he too seemed to be pondering his own situation.

"I'm sorry for your loss," he said softly. "But I'm also sorry that I never had the privilege to meet your husband. He sounds like an amazing person."

"He was," she agreed. "You would've liked him a lot."

He smiled. "So, do you sprinkle the ashes now or are you going to break out the cigar and scotch first?"

Jena knew that Mark and Lance loved scotch, their own collection on the boat quite impressive. She figured the ashes could wait. Reaching into the watertight zipper compartment on the front of her waders, she pulled out a zip lock bag, removing two snipped Cuban Cigars. She handed one to him.

"Oh," he said, a bit surprised. "I didn't know I would get one. And it's a Cuban."

"Of course. I'm not about to smoke one by myself."

Mark smiled. "It's an honor to join you."

She took out a lighter and got both the cigars lit. While Mark enjoyed his first puffs, she unzipped her chest pack and found the flask tucked away in one of the folds. She unscrewed the cap and handed it to Mark.

"What kind is it?"

Jena smiled. "Johnny Walker Blue Label."

"Wow!" he said appreciatively. "That's a five-hundred-dollar bottle."

"I know."

He smiled and took a sip from the flask, swirling it around in his mouth before swallowing it with relish, his eyes closed in enjoyment. Then he opened them and held the flask up. "To Chris O'Malley."

She took the flask and drank. It was smooth with a hint of vanilla and smoke, but it was still tough to swallow, burning on the way down. She had been working on acquiring a taste for it but still had a way to go. "To the best man I know," she added.

They sat together enjoying the scenic beauty surrounding them, the rich smell of cigar smoke drifted around them as they reminisced about their lost loved ones. Mark talked about his wife's love for animals, and that at any one time there would be a few stray dogs or cats at their house as she worked to find a safe home for them. Jena shared Chris's strong bond he had created with so many people, telling him stories of how he had helped a friend move, or come to their rescue with a household problem. Some memories brought them to laughter, and others to tears, but the ease with which they shared their stories softened the edges of their sadness.

When she finished the scotch, she silently stood and walked to the edge of the pool. The strong drink had warmed her body, and strangely, the bite of the cigar taste in her mouth made her smile as she thought of Chris standing at the edge of this very pool. His image smiled back at her, content in his world, and it oddly made her feel good. Holding onto that image, she reached around her neck and took off the necklace containing the small container holding his ashes. Unscrewing the top, she held the small gold container over the water.

"I love you," she whispered, dumping his ashes into the water. She smiled through her tears and fastened the necklace back around her neck. Then she turned towards Mark. He stood as he watched her, his face a reflection of concern, sadness, and understanding. She could easily see his eyes glisten with moisture in the sunlight. "This was a perfect spot. Thank you for taking me here."

He nodded. "Thank you for sharing it with me. I'm glad to have been a part of your story." He paused and looked up at the sky. "We have another hour before we need to head back. Do you want to fish more or head back now?"

Jena smiled, knowing the answer before he even finished his question. "What do you think Chris would do?"

Mark chuckled. "That's easy...he would fish until his arms fell off."

"Then that's what we're going to do."

* * *

That night Jena, Amos, Dagen, Mark, and Lance, sat in the jacuzzi, the hot water soothing her aching muscles. She was tired and sore. The long hike to the falls and back had worked her legs pretty good. The fishing at the falls had turned out to be incredible. She had landed four more great fish before they had to bail and head back to the zodiac. The trout had all given her a good fight and her arms and grip were pretty exhausted. But none of the other fish she had caught held a candle to the first one. And although the day had been physically and emotionally taxing, it had also turned out to be one of the best so far.

The hot tub was cramped but no one seemed to care. They had been talking about their day's adventures and Dagen and Amos were eager to check out the 'secret' falls. Everyone was well into two or three cocktails at this point and they were all feeling talkative. They had a few drinks during their wonderful dinner and were now finishing the night out under the stars with a well-earned soak. Mark and Jena had enjoyed rubbing it in that their little adventure had actually paid off. Mark had passed around his camera so they could all see the big rainbow that Jena had caught.

"I've never seen one that big around here," Lance said appreciatively. "That's a beautiful fish."

"Thanks," Jena replied. "He was so strong...I'm glad I was able to land him."

"And you got him on a popper?" Dagen asked.

"Yup."

"That's awesome," Amos added. "I can't wait to check it out tomorrow."

Lance looked at his younger brother and they both smiled, some inside joke passing between them.

Dagen picked up on it first. "What?"

Lance broadened his smile, looking at each one of them. "Anyone want to do a polar bear plunge?"

"A what?" Amos asked.

"It's when you jump into freezing cold water," Jena added, wondering why anyone would do that.

"Not just any jump," Mark added with a mischievous smile. "We jump from here, off the top of the boat."

"This water is glacier fed from the Andes," Dagen said. "It's freezing."

"That's the point. It's a tradition we started," Lance added. "It will forever connect you to this beautiful place."

"I'll do it!" Amos announced.

"Isn't it dangerous?" Dagen interjected.

"Lance will be in a zodiac to pull you from the water. We've done it many times," Mark reassured them.

"Where will you be?" Jena asked.

"I'm jumping," he said, grinning confidently. "What about you?"

"I don't know," Jena faltered.

Mark turned his head and looked at her seriously. "What would Chris do?"

She scrunched up her face in mock anger, then just laughed. "He would do a back flip off this boat and laugh the whole way down."

The others in the tub knew about her loss but they were not privy to the details. She had felt obligated to divulge to them that she had lost her husband. It was just uncommon for a middle-aged woman to be traveling around the world fly fishing these incredible destinations by herself. Her presence always seemed to generate questions. She had indulged them the other night during dinner but had kept the story short and to the point. None of them were aware of all the details that she had shared with Mark at the falls.

"So, *are* you going to join me?" Amos asked.

Jena absolutely did not want to join them. She hated the cold and she was not a fan of heights. There was nothing remotely appealing about what they were about to do. Which was exactly why it would count as an experience that Chris would have loved and she would not. But she was dreading it more than anything she had done thus far.

"You have to do it," Mark pressed. "Trust me...it will make you feel alive."

"Fine!" she snapped playfully. "Let's get it over with before I lose my nerve." She slammed the rest of her gin and tonic.

"That a girl!" Mark cheered.

"I'll get the boat ready," Lance added, jumping out of the hot tub.

"I can't believe I'm going to jump off this boat," Jena gulped.

"It will be fun," Amos declared, climbing out of the tub.

Mark joined the young man at the edge of the railing. The boat was lit up pretty well and it was easy to see the railing and the glistening water below. "Make sure you clear the railing," he instructed.

It was around sixty degrees outside so Jena stayed in the warm water of the hot tub until the zodiac was ready. "How far down is it?" she asked.

"It's about twenty-five feet," Mark replied casually.

"Oh god," Jena moaned. Then she heard the zodiac's motor start up and she really began to dread her decision.

"Okay," Mark said. "Get over here."

She grunted in frustration and pulled herself out of the hot tub. She was wearing a one piece but knew that it would do very little to protect her from the freezing embrace of the icy water. She approached the railing and was about to back down when she pictured Chris standing next to her. He would have been so excited, his wide smile plastered across his handsome face, his wet unruly hair stuck to his forehead. She wasn't kidding when she had said he would have done a back flip off the boat. She heard him speak to her. *You got this*, he said. *I'll be right behind you.*

"Amos, you want to go first?" Mark asked.

Amos let out a deep breath, readying himself. "Yup."

By this time Dagen had pulled himself from the tub to watch the spectacle. "Be careful, Son," he said, looking over the edge.

Amos laughed. "I got this, Dad."

"Stand on that fiberglass section," Mark instructed, pointing to a thick wall closer to the flybridge. Amos moved without hesitation and climbed onto the edge, balancing himself in a low squat before standing tall. "Push off hard," Mark added.

Amos looked at them and smiled. Then he launched himself off the railing, screaming all the way down. He hit with a splash, clearing the lower walkway easily and landing five feet from the zodiac. Within seconds he surfaced in an explosion of water. "Holy shit that's cold!" he screamed, frantically swimming to the zodiac. Lance was there to help him up while Amos gave a continuous litany about how cold it was.

"How do you feel?!" Mark yelled down.

"Freezing cold! But amazing," he replied. "You're right...I feel alive! My skin is tingling and my heart's about to jump out of my chest, but I feel refreshed!"

Mark looked at Jena. "I told you."

She looked at him doubtfully. "You go next."

"Okay," he said, pulling himself onto the railing and balancing in a low crouch before standing tall. Without preamble, he jumped, not making one sound on the way down. He wasn't so complacent when he resurfaced. The water exploded as he burst through the surface, frantic to get to the zodiac. Lance dragged him into the boat, draping a towel over his shoulders.

Jena could see that they were both shivering. But their excited laughter rang out in the evening darkness. She still didn't want to jump. But she knew she was committed, and she had to admit, it would make for a memorable experience to add to her journal. She looked at Dagen. "Will you help me up in case I slip?"

"Sure," he said, moving to the thick fiberglass railing with her. He held her hand, helping her get onto the edge. She squatted low, her body already shaking from fear and the cool night air.

She gave Dagen a frightened look. She really didn't like heights. "I don't want to do this."

He looked sympathetic. "Listen, any woman who can do what you're doing, can jump twenty feet into cold water. You can do this."

As if he heard him, Mark yelled from the boat below. "You got this!"

"Just stand and jump," Dagen suggested. "Don't think about it too much."

"Not sure I can get my body to move," she said, her jaw chattering. It might have been the cold, or her nerves, but she was afraid she wasn't going to be able to jump.

"Think of Chris," Dagen encouraged, still holding her hand to stabilize her. "Picture him next to you, leaping off with you."

She nodded and closed her eyes. She conjured up Chris's image, his body standing tall, balanced perfectly next to her. *This will be fun*, he said. *Let's do it together. I won't let anything happen to you.*

She smiled and slowly stood on wobbly legs. Dagen let go of her hand but held her calves to keep her balanced. She didn't even feel his grip on her legs as she looked at her husband in her mind's eye. He lifted his eyebrows playfully. *Ready?* He asked, reaching for her hand.

She reached out and could almost feel his hand in hers. Then he smiled and jumped, pulling her with him. Jena's eyes opened and all she saw was blackness before she slammed feet first into the cold water. Instantly her eyes widened and her body stiffened as the freezing water embraced her very soul. For just a moment she caught the image of Chris swimming next to her. The freezing water did nothing to diminish his excited grin as he looked at her through the water's dark haze, the light from the boat penetrating the blackness like fingers of the sun's morning light flashing through a canopy of trees. Then she blinked and he was gone. She was alone in the blackness, the water's icy fingers stabbing her skin. Like a bolt she shot towards the surface, bursting from the water with a shriek. "Holy shit! Get me out of here!" she screamed as she frantically swam to the boat.

Mark, Amos, and Lance laughed as she gripped the edge of the zodiac. She had swam so fast that one would've sworn that a shark was right behind her. Mark reached down and helped her into the boat. Amos took his own towel and wrapped it around her shoulders.

"Oh my god, oh my god, oh my god," she murmured through chattering teeth.

"Give it a second," Amos said. "Soon, your skin will warm and it will feel amazing."

"Get me back in that hot tub," Jena ordered.

Lance laughed, the others joining in. "You got it," he said, putting the boat into drive.

Thirty seconds later and everyone was on the yacht, the boat secured off the stern with the other zodiac. Jena had to admit, her skin was starting to tingle and feel alive. She was still shaking some, but strangely, her body was warming.

"How do you feel?" Mark asked, seeing her expression change.

"Actually, pretty good," she said. "All my soreness is gone. I feel refreshed...clean."

"You've been baptized in the waters of the Andes," Lance announced.

"I still want to get back in the hot tub," she said.

The others laughed as they followed her towards the jacuzzi.

Chapter 7

The screen clicked on and Chris was grinning, sitting casually in his soft leather chair in his office. His face lacked its typical luster, but he smiled nonetheless, as if it would erase his gaunt face and red rimmed eyes. His hair was long gone so he wore a black knit beanie to cover his head. "Hello, my love. I've missed you." He paused to clear his throat. "I know I don't look very good, but quite honestly I feel better than I have all week. So don't let my 'walking dead' appearance fool you into thinking I feel like shit. For whatever reason, today is a good day, which I guess is why I decided to film your next video clip. I have so many questions for you about Chile, but alas, it's impossible to ask them. In the end, the only important thing is that you had fun and that you learned something about yourself. And perhaps, you are one step closer to moving on with your life with more joy and peace. As I've said many times, I believe fly fishing will help you better deal with my absence, with being alone. I know you miss me." He paused again as he grew serious for a moment, his eyes glancing up at the ceiling as his mind went elsewhere. He wiped a lone tear from his cheek as he turned his eyes back to the camera. "I know this because I miss you. You know, once I came to the realization that I was going to die, it wasn't my death that became the most difficult thing to bear, it was the thought of losing you, of never seeing you again. As I sit here, recording this video, we are still together. But the connection is tenuous. I can feel it slip away as I'm getting weaker." He coughed to clear his throat, regaining his composure. "I'm sorry. I really hate to get emotional like this. But sometimes it's so hard to stay positive."

"I know," Jena wept. "I understand exactly what you mean." Tears were pouring freely as she watched her husband attempt to deal with the pain of not only losing his wife, but dying, leaving forever the world he loved so much.

Jena had just gotten out of the shower and was lying in bed in her state room, her head and back propped up with several pillows. She wore comfortable gray sweats and a soft Patagonia long sleeve shirt. She was, of course, cradling a cocktail, opting to go with a gin and tonic.

It was near nine in the evening on their last night fishing the fjords of Chile. The following morning they would head back to town and Jena would depart the magnificent Grand Banks yacht ending her third fishing trip. Next up was the Amazon River. Jena had to admit, she was more nervous about that trip. All she could think about were snakes, piranhas, and screaming monkeys.

Chris wiped the last tears from his eyes, forced a smile, then reached off camera and held up a drink that looked like a margarita, but it was on the rocks. "Today I decided on a Caipirinha, the national drink of Brazil in honor of your next trip. You're going to love it," he added as he took a generous sip. "It tastes similar to a margarita."

"Something to look forward to," Jena mumbled wryly. She had worked with Rob and they had planned the two trips simultaneously. She would stay overnight at Puerto Cisnes before flying out to Manaus, Brazil. She would stay three days in Manaus before taking a small plane to the remote lodge far up the Aqua Boa River, one of the many tributaries that feed the massive Amazon River. The Last Cast Lodge, built along the Aqua Boa, offered six bungalows, a huge swimming pool, and world class guide services, all in the middle of the most remote jungle in the world. She was pretty apprehensive about fishing in the jungles of Brazil. The last thing she wanted was to get eaten by a jaguar or get bitten by mosquitos, or other unknown vermin that might exist there. She hoped the experience would be different than what she imagined.

"It's really good," Chris continued, relishing another sip. "It's made with cachaça, sugar, and lime, giving it that margarita taste. But it's unique because cachaca is made from distilled fermented sugarcane juice, giving it a flavor unlike anything else. I think you're going to love it. And a lime-based cocktail is pretty refreshing after a long day of fishing in the heat, and word has it, the lodge will have one waiting for you every day you get off the skiff."

It made her miss him even more to hear him describe in detail this cocktail, reminiscent of all the times he used to discuss various cocktails and their particular characteristics.

A Year of a Thousand Casts

"Okay," he continued, "let's get into the fishing. I think you're going to find the Aqua Boa River absolutely incredible. From what I understand, if you plan your trip from December to mid-March, the water levels are the lowest, and that offers the best fishing. What makes this section of river outstanding for fly folks, is that it's very clear, offering, in many cases, sight fishing for peacock bass, giant arapaima, arowana, pacu, and a lot of other species. I'm sure you're going to learn all the different species but your main target fish will be the plentiful peacock bass." He paused and smiled. "Honey, these fish are so aggressive and strong that they are known as rod breakers. Bring rods ranging from nine to eleven weight, as well as floating tropical fly lines to withstand the jungle heat. Make sure you have at least two hundred yards of backing as well as a shock tippet ranging from thirty to forty-pound monofilament."

"Wow," Jena murmured. Typically, the tippet was the lightest line connecting the fly to the leader. It was designed to be invisible so the fish couldn't see the line. She knew that shock tippet was quite the opposite. It was tippet material designed to be strong and resistant, to take a shock, and was typically only used for fish with rough teeth or for large fish that were massively strong. Most fish that required a shock tippet were not leader shy. That meant that they would aggressively hit the fly regardless if they saw the line.

"As far as flies, bring the typical assortment of big fish flies tied with size 3/0 and 4/0 hooks. Bring plenty of poppers, Dahlberg Divers, Lefty's Deceivers, and Clouser Minnows."

Jena knew most of this already, having researched the lodge prior to taking off to South America. She knew she would be flying direct to Brazil from Chile and would need to bring the proper gear. Her Simms travel bag had been stuffed with tackle for both destinations.

Chris reached off camera and took another sip of his cocktail. He swallowed, closed his eyes, and took a deep breath. When he reopened them, his expression grew more serious. "I'm not sure how many more videos I'll be able to make with a cocktail in my hand. Already I can feel my body failing me, and anything I drink plays havoc on my system." He frowned. "I have to admit, my weak body is one of the most difficult parts of this journey for me. I used to pride myself on my endurance and stamina, and now," he paused, "I can barely drink a cocktail without feeling nauseated."

"I know," Jena cried as she watched her husband have a rare vulnerable moment. She knew how he had felt about the cancer eating away at his body. They had discussed it many times, his head laying in her lap as she massaged his bald scalp. He had, at times, cried openly, expressing his fear of experiencing his strength and vitality slowly fade away. She had tried to be strong for him, but on many occasions had just ended up crying along with him. For someone accustomed to taking on the world with his own physicality, his increasing and inexorable weakness was nearly as bad as death itself.

He took a couple more deep breaths and forced another smile. Jena could tell that it was difficult for him to do that, but in the end he almost managed to appear lighthearted again. "I know that you must've had an amazing trip fishing the fjords of Chile. I hope you experienced something unique and life changing. And now, you will be joining a select few in fishing in the jungles of Brazil. You will see virtually an untouched land filled with sights that most people will never have a chance to experience. I hope that your adventures have given you some tools to help you move forward...to help give you the desire to wake up in the morning and enjoy the life you still have." He paused as he gathered his thoughts. "I'm not sure what level of grief you are experiencing at this moment. If I had to guess, you are fluctuating back and forth between bargaining and depression, occasionally reverting to anger, although I bet that is one of the stages that doesn't impact you as much. My guess is your skilled and rational mind has dealt with so much death and dying, that anger is not an emotion that grabs hold of you as much as it might others. You are not going to get angry at me, or the doctors, or the disease," he added as he winked at her. "Jena, you are too hard on yourself. I know you better than anyone. I know you get angry at yourself for," Chris used his hands to give the quotation marks, "not doing enough. I can imagine you berating yourself for not learning to fish sooner, so you could experience these adventures with me before I died."

"Yes, I do...I'm so sorry," Jena smiled sadly at his perceptiveness.

"I can imagine you coming up with all kinds of irrational examples of where you think you failed me. I know you think about our infertility issues and blame yourself. I can only imagine your mind holding onto that thought now more than ever since my passing." He shook his head. *"Baby, don't let those thoughts eat you up. You have given me everything."* Chris blinked, his eyes pooling with tears. Quickly wiping them away, he continued. *"Our life together was amazing. I have been so happy. There is nothing I regret. We tried to have children and it didn't happen. It's okay. Please,"* he implored seriously. *"Let those thoughts go. Do not let them consume you."*

Jena put both hands to her mouth as she tried to subdue the waves of sadness crashing against her heart. "I'll try, baby...I'll try." He was right of course. She rarely felt anger at his death, but when she did, it was typically directed at herself, mostly focused on that fact that she could not have a child with him. Despite the fact that the doctor confirmed that they both, medically, had contributed to their infertility, Jena still felt a sense of maternal failure. Providing a child in a marriage was something society drove into the hearts and minds of all young women, and not being able to do that had created a deep sadness as well as, at times, anger. She knew deep down that she had to let go of that anger if she was going to move forward. The goal of fulfilling his bucket list was to advance through the stages of grief and eventually experience acceptance, the last stage. She desperately wanted to achieve that goal, but there were times when it simply seemed impossible. When would she be able to accept Chris's death? She still couldn't answer that question. But she had to admit that each trip she had taken thus far had seemed to put the answer a little closer to her grasp. She had to believe in that possibility. After all, that was his last wish. She would do everything within her power to try and make that happen.

"Promise me...promise me you will let go of whatever guilt you feel," Chris added, leaning forward to emphasize his words.

"I promise," Jena whispered.

"Good, now," he added, lifting his cocktail towards the camera. "To tight lines, jungle adventures, and healing." He drank deeply.

"Cheers, my love," Jena added, lifting her own glass before taking a sip.

Chris smiled. "I love you more than anything. Oh, I forgot to tell you, don't piss in the water." Then he winked. Reaching up, the screen went black.

What did he mean, *don't piss in the water?* She figured his meaning would show itself at some point. Taking a deep breath, she closed her eyes, images of Chris playing through her mind. She had a feeling that sleep was going to elude her, her mind constantly playing a depressing romantic comedy. She wanted the movie to be over. But then again, she didn't, the risk of losing her memories of Chris more than she could bear. She would find a way to deal with the loss. After all, she wasn't the first person to lose a loved one.

* * *

The Last Cast Lodge looked just like the pictures from their webpage. Jena had been a bit leery as they had neared the compound. The landing strip in the distance looked like nothing more than a dirty road cut through the jungle. But as they flew closer, the concrete landing strip appeared well-manicured, providing at least a small sense of security. The landing was smooth and so was offloading. There were ten other guests, not including herself, and they were met by two cheerful men, and a beautiful dark-haired woman holding a tray of cocktails. The taller of the two men appeared to be in his forties and Jena thought she recognized him as the lodge owner, a Canadian who had purchased the fly-fishing enterprise back in 2008.

"Greetings everyone, and welcome to Last Cast Lodge," the tall man said loudly as everyone gathered near him. "My name is Larry Stanbecker and I'm the lodge owner." He looked just like he did in the pictures Jena had seen on the lodge webpage. He was a big man, easily a few inches over six feet, with a protruding belly and warm smile. He introduced the man at his side. "This is Daniel, our lodge manager. If there is anything you ever need, he is the man you want to talk to." Larry and Daniel welcomed the guests, shaking each one's hands as introductions were made.

A few moments later, Daniel addressed everyone. "Welcome to the Last Cast Lodge." His English was good but his Portuguese accent was thick. He was dark skinned, clearly a local, with dark hair trimmed short. He looked almost Arabic to Jena, a striking angular jaw and sincere smile creating quite a handsome image. "Would anyone like a glass of champagne?" he asked, indicating the lovely woman to his left holding the tray of drinks. "This is Aline, our kitchen and bar manager."

There was a murmur of excitement as Aline made her way to the guests, everyone grabbing a glass of champagne from her tray as she made quick introductions.

"Do not worry about your luggage," Larry said. "We will take care of that for you. Why don't you follow me and we will give you a tour of your new home for the next six days."

Jena looked around and was quite impressed. The entire compound was built along the river's edge. The main lodge looked like something from the southwest. The structure was built of what looked like a smooth plaster or clay. There was a wraparound concrete paver deck covered by a roof supported by rough cut logs and thatch. The plaster-like walls was painted a tan color and the windows and trim were constructed of natural tropical wood. There were paths of concrete all surrounded by a nicely manicured lawn. But the best part was the immense round swimming pool that was located only forty feet from the river's edge. A fifteen-foot solid natural rock wall framed the Aqua Boa River and consequently protected the pool and compound from flooding during the rainy season. The pale blue water in the pool reflected the clear cerulean sky, a welcoming sight as she stood sweating in the tropical heat. She felt as if she just emerged from a steam bath. She had been in hot weather before, but the humidity here was something else altogether.

Larry showed them the pool, pointing out the cabana where one of the lodge servers would be making them evening beverages after a long day of fishing. He walked them down the path, a trail cut into the natural rock formation that protected the lodge, to the dock at the river's edge. She could see eight different blue painted skiffs, each one a flat bottom boat with an outboard, and a platform above the motor for either the guide or a fisherman, along with a lower casting platform at the front It was a similar set up to the skiffs she used in the Seychelles. The water was calm and clear, the edges of the river surrounded by dense green foliage. It meandered slowly, twists and turns visual in both directions. Where the dense green foliage didn't grow to the water's edge, sand as white as snow dusted the shoreline. Jena was pleasantly surprised. The entire area had a tropical feel about it similar to the Seychelles. For some reason, she was expecting something different. The sounds of the jungle were abundant, strange birds and monkeys adding to the remote feel of the lodge.

Continuing on, Larry showed them the main lodge and introduced them to the chef, a young man named Luis. He was all smiles and had caipirinhas ready for them as well as several expansive charcuterie plates filled with delicious meats and cheeses local to Brazil. Everything was tasty and the caipirinha, true to Chris's word, was really good, similar to a margarita but with a unique flavor that Jena had never tasted. The main lodge was open and spacious, the center of the room occupied by a big dining room table made of magnificent red stained Brazilian Torowood polished to a glossy shine. It was so big it could easily fit all twelve of the guests. There was a quaint sitting room on one side, a leather loveseat and matching cushioned chairs positioned around a wood coffee table offering a great place to sit and read a book. The arrangement was facing a large bookshelf filled with popular books both past and present for the guests to enjoy. She noticed a large bouquet of yellow and orange orchids sitting on the coffee table, fragrant and beautifully arranged, they were welcoming after her long day of travel. There were a few other smaller sitting areas offering guests some private spots to read or enjoy a cocktail, all with views through the large windows of the pool and lawn. The other side of the room was occupied by a small fly shop. Jena could see various rods positioned vertically in rod holders, tables stacked with fly lines, fly boxes, and reels. A small desk with a fly-tying vice and a smattering of fly-tying materials scattered across it was nestled in the corner.

She chuckled at the memory of the many times she had scolded Chris for keeping his office so messy, especially his fly tying desk. His desk had been constantly littered with fly tying materials that she had no idea how he managed to find what he needed. But he had always told her not to mess with his stuff, that all artists had some degree of sloppiness. She pictured his wry smile as he articulated some bull shit about how so much of his brain was centered around artistic greatness that he couldn't be expected to be clean at the same time.

She pushed away the memory and continued to look around. She remembered reading on their website that the fly shop offered any gear necessary for fishing the local waters. The last thing Jena noticed, and characteristic of any high-end fishing lodge, was a bar in one of the room's corners. The curved bar was built of polished Honduran mahogany and the wall behind it was lined in shelves filled with numerous bottles of liquor, enough to satisfy any guest's fancy.

There were a few other servers about and once the tour had ended the guests were all led to their own bungalows to unpack and relax. Larry was the one who led Jena to her own accommodations.

"So," he began as he led her from the main lodge to the row of bungalows outside, the other lodge workers doing the same for the other guests, "I was hoping to get a few private words with you," he smiled warmly.

"Oh, why is that?"

He laughed good naturedly. "It's not often we get women coming to fish here alone and are willing to pay the double occupancy rate. Your presence has intrigued me."

Jena chuckled with him. Seeing it from his viewpoint, she could understand his curiosity. She had just paid over eleven thousand dollars to fish alone in one of the most remote places in the world. She imagined that was something he rarely saw in men, let alone women. There likely were very few people in the world who could, and would, do something like that. "I can see why, I guess. Let's just say that my last year has been life changing. I think for now I'll leave it at that. Perhaps later in the trip we can talk in more detail."

Larry nodded as he came to the first row of bungalows, stopping at the door. "Fair enough. Inside you'll find simple but comfortable accommodations. Your luggage is already inside. We have solar power and a big diesel generator, so hot water and electricity is not a problem."

"That's great," Jena replied, looking around. "Your lodge is fantastic. I have to admit, it's more than I expected."

He nodded. "Let me guess, you were picturing grass huts and jaguars."

Jena laughed. "Well, I had seen the pictures online, so no, but," she nodded, "I was imagining it more rustic. I don't even see any bugs."

Larry laughed. "The no see ums will come out this evening, so wear your bug spray later. But I'm glad you are surprised. And you're going to love the fishing."

"I can't wait."

"Speaking of," Larry added. "Will you want to relax today or did you want to get a half day of fishing in?"

Jena flipped both palms in the air in a *come on* gesture. "I didn't come here to relax."

He smiled and winked at her. "I knew I was going to like you. Fishing it is. You know" he said, "I just might take you out myself."

"Now I feel really special," Jena laughed.

"You should," Larry quipped, turning to leave. Then he stopped, turning back to her. "Oh, I forgot to tell you, don't pee in the water." He chuckled softly and left her alone.

She laughed, but inside was wondering what was so bad about peeing in the water.

A few hours later and Jena was sitting in one of the skiffs, the ninety-horse jet outboard pushing the boat quickly over the smooth water of the Aqua Boa River. It was hot and humid, typical Amazon weather. She wore a light short sleeved Simms fishing shirt, board shorts, as well as a cap and scarf to protect her head and neck from the sun. Larry sat in the back manning the tiller while Jena sat in the middle of the boat on one of the two padded seats. Larry had told her that they wouldn't be going far since they had to be back by six, which was only four hours away. The scenery was vibrant. They were surrounded by dense green foliage and taller tropical trees, the tops of which created a thick canopy above the forest ground. Despite the hum of the four-stroke motor, Jena could hear the sounds of the jungle. Chirping and cawing birds in addition to other squeals and howls made for quite a jungle song.

He slowed the boat, turned off the motor, and stood up tall on the platform over the motor, the long skiff pole in his hand. Before them was a narrow tributary no wider than two boat lengths, the thick green brush growing right up to the edge.

"The Aqua Boa has hundreds of small tributary streams pouring into it," Larry explained. "There are thousands that feed the mighty Amazon itself before dumping twenty-eight billion gallons into the Atlantic. Did you know that the Amazon accounts for twenty percent of the world's fresh water?"

"I did not," Jena replied. "That's amazing."

"It really is," Larry agreed. "This little waterway will take us into a lagoon teaming with fish. Get your ten-weight ready."

Larry had already checked her gear and after a few changes had helped her pick out the flies she would be fishing with. One rod had a popper and another a white and chartreuse clouser, which was basically a minnow pattern.

"So do I use a traditional set or a strip set for these fish?"

"You can use either but a traditional trout set works just fine. Just set it hard." Larry smiled. "They have tough mouths."

She nodded. "So were you serious about pissing in the water? You're not the first person to tell me this."

Larry chuckled. "I was just joking. But there is an old indigenous tale that has spread amongst the populace, turning into sort of an urban legend. Who told you beside me?"

Jena didn't want to get into it but neither did she want to lie. "My husband." Her affect was guarded and Larry somehow picked up on it, deciding to not push her further.

"Well, there is a small parasitic fish that swims in these waters called the Candiru. It attaches itself to the gills of fish and feeds off their blood. It is believed that they can taste the traces of ammonia and urea that is expelled through the gills of other fish. As the legends go, the fish sometimes can't tell the difference between a human peeing in the water and the urea being expelled from gills, swimming into the urethra where it injects its small spikes and sucks the blood from its victim. The fish engorges itself and gets lodged in the victim's urethra. This of course ends in a painful surgery or some special tribal remedy."

Jena's spine shivered as she imagined such a ghastly scenario. "That is not a true story, right?"

Larry shrugged. "I've never seen it, nor have any of my local guides. But a few swear they have heard stories of the Candiru whispered amongst their tribal elders. For me, I think it's an jungle legend."

"Do you pee in the water when you go swimming?"

"Hell no!"

They laughed as Larry used the long pole to guide the boat from the narrow waterway into a big open lagoon. The water was a bit cloudier than it was near the lodge, and she could only see a few feet into its dark depths. Thick forest surrounded them and the cacophony of the jungle seemed even louder in the calm of this freshwater lake. A deep guttural sound jerked Jena from her reverie. The loud noise was very close and sounded like a hurricane, or a chant from a demon possessed choir of monks. It was quite eerie.

"It's a howler monkey," Larry said casually, pointing over her shoulder.

She looked up and sure enough, a big hairy monkey was hanging from the branches of a nearby tree. The monkey howled loudly a few more times before leaping back into the canopy, disappearing as quickly as it had arrived. The sound however, did not go away, as other monkey's in the distance picked up the chat. "They certainly live up to their name," Jena said.

Larry nodded. "He was welcoming you to his home."

Jena laughed. "If that was a welcome screech, I'd hate to see him angry."

"You definitely don't," Larry added. "They are darn right ornery. Okay," he continued, his tone turning business-like as he pointed to the edge of the water at about two o'clock. "This area is pretty fishy. Start casting towards the shore and strip it in quickly."

"Popper, or streamer?"

"Try the popper."

"Good," Jena added. "I love fishing poppers."

"Well, then you came to the right place," Larry grinned.

She stood on the front platform; the metal floor lined with a black sandpaper material for a better grip, and began casting, the heavy popper and sink tip flying through the air with practiced skill. She was quite proud of herself; her casting having improved significantly from when she had left Hans's side. Laying the line out, the popper landed with a splash two feet from the dense vegetation hanging over the water's edge. She began to strip the popper in, the rush of adrenaline causing her heart to pound in anticipation of a possible strike. She couldn't help but think that this was the feeling Chris had talked about. Hans had said it as well. Fly fishing wasn't about catching fish. It was about the process, the culmination of skills coming together to build the anticipation that you *might* catch a fish. It was that anticipation, that excitement, that made the entire experience worthwhile. It was that anticipation that became the drug that she craved. Had she just figured it out?

Suddenly the water exploded. Her mind, although elsewhere, registered the strike, sending waves of impulses to her hands. She set the hook hard, the weight and power of the fish nearly pulling her into the water. There was an audible snap. Green, red, and orange flashed across the water's surface as the fish took off.

Jena's rod had broken. "Oh shit!" she screamed as the fish fled for the cover along the water's edge. With the fly still in its mouth, the fish yanked the line from the reel, the broken end of the rod dancing around like a marionette. "What do I do!?"

Larry was just about to respond when the line snapped.

The entire event happened in a few heart beats. Jena, her eyes wide in shock, looked back at Larry, her snapped rod held helplessly in one hand.

He just smiled. "Welcome to the Amazon," he said, chuckling.

"Oh-my-god," Jena stuttered. "That fish just broke my rod."

Larry nodded. "They tend to do that. My guess is your connection at the rod section was loose, making a weak point. Plus, that was a big fish."

Jena's eyes were still wide and her mouth hung open. Her heart was still pounding. "Let's try it again."

"That's what we are here for."

She grabbed her second rod, a ten weight, a big colorful streamer tied onto the shock tippet. She unhooked the fly and prepared to cast once again.

"Check the section connections," Larry advised. "Make sure they are tight."

She smiled knowingly, doing just that. She could afford another broken rod, but that didn't mean she wanted one.

That evening Jena was cooling off in the pool with several other guests after a half day of fishing. She hadn't met all the guests yet, but she had introduced herself to the pool goers and they were all hanging out near the cabana sipping cocktails. There was a father with his twin sons, who looked to be in their late twenties. Jena found it interesting that they were traveling with their grandma, their father's mother, and she was lounging nearby in a sun bed. Her skin was aged and the color of coffee. She wore an expensive looking maroon swimsuit trimmed in gold. Three gold bracelets adorned her right hand and nearly every finger sported ornate gold rings set with diamonds and other gems. Her silver-gray hair was cut into a stylish bob which complimented her refined, although sun baked, appearance. Jena couldn't tell, but she looked to be in her late sixties. There was also a group of four friends who were celebrating the fiftieth birthday of one of them. Everyone was friendly and excited to be on a once in a lifetime fishing trip. They were already telling stories of their first fish on the Aqua Boa.

"Your first fish broke your rod!?" Jack exclaimed, shaking his head in amazement.

Jena had told them the story of her rod snapping. She had fished the rest of the day, catching three peacock bass as well as one arowana, a long strange fish that sort of looked like an eel with big scales. Larry had told her that they were traditionally pretty spooky and hard to catch. He had spotted the fish cruising and instructed her to cast fifteen feet in front of it, trying to minimize the splash caused by the fly. Her cast had been perfect, the fly landing gracefully in the water. When the fish got close, he had told her to strip it in much slower than what she had been doing for the peacock bass. He also wanted the strips shorter. She had followed his instructions and the fish had zeroed in on the fly, hammering it like an apex predator. It had been a lot of fun. But the story of her broken rod seemed to overshadow the landing of the arowana.

"I think one of my ferrule's was lose," she said. "It snapped right at the joint. But it was a big fish."

"I bet," Jack said as he sipped his rum and coke.

Jack was short and a little big around the waist. He sort of reminded Jena of a smaller James Gandolfini from the Sopranos. "How did you guys do?" she asked his two boys. They were spitting images of each other, although they didn't look much like their father. Both were taller, close to six feet, in good shape and pretty handsome. Where Jack was balding, his two boys had thick brown hair shaved short on the sides, the top longer and combed over. They more likely resembled their mother.

"It was amazing," Jason said, although Jena couldn't tell them apart. He was drinking a beer in a plastic cup. "We got into a school of peacock bass and it was lights out for half an hour."

"I've never caught fish so strong," Jaylin added, shaking his head in wonder, a huge smile plastered across his face. "And they hammered the flies!"

"I know. I recently fished the Seychelles and I thought I wouldn't find a fish stronger than the milkfish I caught." Jena chuckled. "I was wrong. Although," she added quickly, "the peacock bass don't have the stamina of a milkfish."

"I've never heard of a milkfish," Jack said.

"I hadn't either until I went there. They feed on algae so they are tough to get on a fly."

"Did you catch any GT's while you were there?" Jason asked.

Jena nodded. "They were amazing. So aggressive. They were definitely the peacock bass of the Seychelles."

Jack looked at his boys. "Maybe we can get Grandma to take us there next," he said, raising his eyebrows in jest.

"Only if you're good!" the grandma chirped; her eyes closed but clearly listening in on their conversation.

Jena laughed. They clearly had an interesting relationship. She wondered where the mother was. It was obvious that the grandma was the matriarch of the family, and likely had money. She glanced at their grandma and caught her staring back. She winked and smiled, closing her eyes once again as she soaked up the sun. Jena liked her immediately.

It wasn't long before the crew of men on the birthday trip joined them as they all swam up to the bar. One of them ordered four caipirinhas. They all appeared to be in their fifties and they joined into the fishing conversation easily enough.

Richard, a tall and gangly man with a bright smile directed his attention to Jena. She had learned earlier that it was his birthday. "I heard you say you went to the Seychelles." He smiled even wider, if that was possible. "Man, that place looks amazing. It's definitely on my bucket list."

As Jena became more quiet, the pain resurfaced, remembering how much Chris had wanted to do the same. She would never get to see Chris casting to cruising trevallies', and that thought alone crushed her heart. She did her best to push the pain below the surface, but Richard seemed to notice her demeanor change, although he didn't say anything.

"It's pretty incredible. I highly recommend it. So, do you guys do these fishing trips often?" she asked.

Richard shook his head. "Not as often as we'd like. We are all married with kids. It makes it tough to find the time. But we try and do it for the big life moments."

"Like a fiftieth?"

Richard smiled. "Exactly."

Scott, one of Richard's friends jumped into the conversation. "Okay," he said, "I have to ask. We've all been wondering what brought you here." It was clear he had been enjoying the drinks as his words were a bit slurred.

"Brought me here?" she asked, scrunching her brow in confusion. "The fishing of course."

Scott chuckled. "I know that. It's just," he continued, "well, it's not often you find a woman fly fishing alone in some far-off place."

"So I've heard...many times," she replied. She was a bit annoyed at that sentiment but she didn't hold it against them. After all, she knew it was quite rare indeed and they were likely just curious.

Scott was a bit more intoxicated and didn't pick up on her tone. But Richard was more perceptive. "Sorry about that," he said, smacking Scott playfully on the shoulder. "Scott didn't mean to pry."

"Oh, I'm sorry, was that offensive?" Scott asked, finally picking up on Jena's reluctance. "You don't have to—."

"It's okay," Jena interjected. "I know you didn't mean to pry. It's just hard for me to talk about it. Let's just say that my story might ruin the vibe of a vacation like this."

"Fair enough," Richard added.

"Oh man, now you really have me curious," Scott chuckled. "But I understand."

"For now, let's just talk fishing and enjoy the drinks."

"Sounds good," Richard confirmed, saluting. "To fishing and friends."

Everyone nearby joined in, toasting in turn and returning to their fishing stories.

Jena gave herself a proverbial pat on the back for changing the conversation in a different direction. Although she had felt the pain of loss rise to the surface, she had been able to subdue it quickly. She wasn't sure that would've been possible just months before. The danger of course was that she might tire of wrestling the sadness down over and over again, and that eventually it would overpower her defenses and bust through the wall as it had done before. But maybe that wasn't a bad thing. One thing she had learned over the last six months was that every time her sorrow overcame her, she had learned something about herself and how to better deal with her loss. Facing the pain created more opportunities for learning. It just wasn't much fun.

Later that evening everyone sat casually at the big dining table as Luis served up a delicious meal. The meal began with wine or a beverage of your choice, and a tray of savory coxinhas, deep fried meat balls made from chicken and some cream cheese mixture. They were absolutely amazing and they reminded Jena of mac and cheese balls. Those disappeared quickly and he followed it up with the main meal, succulent and tender braised short ribs accompanied by a pinto bean dish called feijao tropeiro, beans sautéed with cassava flour, scallions, egg, and bacon. Everything was fantastic, the cuisine as well as the fishing stories. Jena was actually enjoying herself, and although she thought of Chris often, the comradery of the group helped keep her attention focused on the conversation and not on what she was missing. Chris's absence was always there, but she found if she had somewhere else to look, the void he left behind was less apparent. It was when she was alone with her own thoughts that she had the hardest time. He was always there in her mind. And that was good, she thought. She didn't want to forget him. Chris's hope for her, was that she could live with his memory in a positive way.

She was seated next to Jack's grandmother and learned that her name was Stella. They had talked briefly during dinner but since Stella didn't fish, the fishing conversation around the table had monopolized her attention. She did have a chance to get to know the other four guests a bit more. There was a husband wife duo from England. They seemed to be around Jena's age, athletic and full of energy. The youngest guests, besides Jack's twins, were two guys from Montana, a fly-fishing guide, and his buddy. Collin was tall and quite good looking, his brown wavy hair and short scruffy beard reminding her of Chris. But he didn't have Chris's vibrant smile. No one did. She had almost succumbed to her sadness, when his friend, Lars, managed to distract her.

"Jena, tell us about the Seychelles," he asked. "I've wanted to go there so bad."

Jena forced a smile as she looked at Lars. He was short and stocky, but lean. He looked like a middle weight wrestler, or perhaps an MMA fighter. There seemed to be no fat on his body. His jawline was angular, and he had a pronounced brow ridge. Jena even noticed his cauliflower ears, something she never would've noticed if she hadn't been married to Chris. Chris had been a state wrestling champion and he often watched college wrestling on ESPN. Whenever they came across someone with cauliflower ears, he had always pointed it out. Chris had always respected other wrestlers, seeing them as both mentally and physically tough, a culmination of skills derived from hard work and tenacity. She had thought that their cauliflower ears were disgusting and often laughed at Chris as he saw them as a badge of honor. According to Chris, cauliflower ear is caused by the ear being hit repeatedly, forming blood clots, that if not drained, forms hard deformations of the ear. She had to admit, Lars looked like he could pin a grizzly.

"It was amazing," Jena replied. "Everywhere you looked were schools of bonefish. And it wasn't uncommon to have quite a few shots at GT's, triggerfish, and even milkfish."

"Did you get a milkfish?" Collin asked.

"I got one. But it took me nearly three hours casting to the pod to get one to take the fly." She paused and smiled. "I've never felt anything that powerful."

"Three hours," Collin murmured. "Very tenacious of you." His tone reflected respect.

"Stronger than a peacock bass?" Lars asked incredulously.

"Not exactly," Jena added. "They don't strike as hard, that's for sure. But they have more stamina and can pull just as hard, maybe harder as they can get much bigger."

"Sounds incredible," Lars added. "And you went by yourself?"

It was obvious that he, and likely everyone else, was wondering why a middle-aged woman, who was still wearing her wedding ring, was by herself fishing some of the most renowned places in the world. She couldn't blame them really and it was doubtful that their questions stemmed from anything other than curiosity. She figured she might as well tell them while they were all at the table. She worried that opening up about her husband's death might lead to her breaking down in front of them. The last thing she wanted was to get emotional in front of a table of strangers who were there to enjoy a once in a lifetime fishing experience.

She let out a deep sigh. "Yes, I was there by myself. And I just returned from Chile fishing the streams that dumped into the fjords. And before that I was fishing the South Island of New Zealand."

"You're kidding," Collin said incredulously. She knew that for a fly fisherman, those locations were the crème de la crème, the most sought-after places in the world for someone who slings a fly line.

"Nope, I'm not." She got right to the point. "My husband was an avid fly fisherman, just like all of you folks." She could feel the energy of the room change when she used the word *was*. But she pushed on, wanting to get it over with. "He passed away nearly a year ago from cancer. It was quite sudden. Chris, my husband, had a bucket list of places he wanted to fish before he died. He was not able to complete the list, so he asked me to do it for him." Jena forced a smile. "That is it...that is why I am by myself fishing the most wonderful places in the world."

The room was silent for a moment.

Oddly enough it was one of the young twins who spoke first. Jena thought it might be Jason but she could not be sure. "Did you know how to fly fish before he died?"

She shook her head. "I did not. I learned from one of his fishing buddies."

Lars let out a deep breath. "I'm sorry I asked. But wow, what a story. It's incredible you are doing that for him."

Jena pursed her lips, fighting back the emotion. She didn't say anything, afraid her voice would shake.

"Let us move on," Stella chimed in as she held up her wine glass. "To forging new paths and adventures!" she toasted, smiling at Jena. Everyone lifted their glasses and toasted.

Luis interrupted their toast by bringing them all dessert, a lovely dish called mousse de maracuja, made from passion fruit. It had been cut in squares and topped with a passion fruit glaze and strawberries. It was a lovely way to wrap up a fantastic meal. Jena ate her mousse in silence, doing her best to control her emotions. Although everyone was really friendly and outgoing, she felt isolated and alone. Everyone had been tactful and respectful, and she was thankful for that. But it just made her feel even more alone. She knew Chris would have loved the dinner banter, immersing himself in the conversations and perhaps forging lasting friendships with some of them. It was something he did. It was something she would dearly miss.

* * *

The next few days were occupied by some of the most memorable fishing Jena had ever experienced. The Seychelles had been incredible, but the Amazon was filled with such a numerous variety of some of the hardest fighting fish she had ever caught. In the Amazon, the fish had to be strong and fast, or it died. Every species was trying to eat or not be eaten, making a breeding ground for the toughest fish on the planet. She had caught so many fish that her stripping fingers were cut in several places, band aids a visual reminder of her battle wounds. She had caught a variety of peacock bass and had learned that there were three main types. The butterfly peacock bass was the most numerous and also the smallest, ranging from two to eight pounds. The spotted and temesis peacock bass were the big boys, sometimes reaching twenty-five pounds. They were the strongest and the most aggressive of the species. Jena figured it had been one of those two species that had broken her rod on that first day. She had caught a ton of pacu right in front of the lodge. The fun part about the pacu was that they were taking trout flies off the surface. Each evening you could find them rising and feeding off the surface all around the lodge. And if you had enough energy after a long a long day of fishing, you could have a blast catching the silver dollar fish no more than a stone's throw from the pool. They were aptly named as their bodies were round and silver, reminding Jena of a permit found in tropical waters. One of the craziest looking fish she had caught was the payara, or vampire fish. She had never seen a fish so scary looking. They generally ranged between two and ten pounds but it was their forbidding teeth that gave them such a frightful reputation. Their big mouths were filled with sharp teeth, but it was their long two to three-inch front teeth that earned them the vampire nickname. She had also landed a bicuda, which was a ton of fun as they swam extremely fast, reminding her of big bonefish. Bicuda were shaped like torpedoes, with a long big mouth filled with small razor-sharp teeth. They were pretty elusive so she was happy she was able to land one. They were not only fast, but strong, like the trevally she had landed.

A Year of a Thousand Casts

It was on the fourth day of the trip that she had her first opportunity to catch the famous and elusive arapaima, known to the locals as pirarucu. Her guide for the day was Carlos, the head guide for the lodge. He was native and spoke decent "fishing" English, as the lodge owner liked to call it. Carlos could communicate well enough to get his clients into fish, but having an in-depth conversation about religion and politics was out of the question.

They had motored far upriver where Carlos had proceeded to guide her through a maze of tributaries, some no wider than the boat with tree branches forming a canopy of shade over the water. Once they broke free from the narrow waterway, they emerged onto an expansive lagoon, large enough to qualify as a small lake. They had been cruising the edges, casting for peacock bass, when there was a tremendous splash about sixty feet to the right of the boat.

"Pirarucu!" Carlos shouted as he reached down and handed Jena the twelve-weight rod that had been secured against the inside rail.

All the guests had been talking about the elusive arapaima so Jena felt she had a pretty good understanding of the strange fish. She had learned that they were air breathers, having to come to the surface to breath. Larry, the lodge owner, had told her that they were the largest freshwater fish in existence, sometimes reaching four hundred pounds. He said it was very difficult to get them to take a fly, and if you did, getting a strong hookset was nearly impossible. According to him, their heads were nearly all bone, and their jaws were lined with a tough skin layer that resembled sixty grit sandpaper. And if you were lucky enough to get one to take the fly, as well as getting a good hook set, then it was not uncommon for a huge fish to bend the hook shank. Needless to say, they were seldom caught. Jena knew that if she could pull it off, then it would be her trophy fish for the trip. It might even be her trophy fish for the entire adventure.

Her heart was pounding as she stood on the casting platform, gazing into the semitransparent water. A few moments later Carlos directed her. "There! Three o'clock...fifty feet," Carlos instructed in his choppy English. "When fly land, strip slow."

She nodded as she began her cast. Her skills were improving and it wasn't long before the line unfurled across the water, the big red and black fly landing softly.

"Good good," Carlos praised, his eyes glued to the water. "Slow strip, slow strip."

She began to strip as instructed. Her hands were shaking and her heart sounded like war drums in her ears. Suddenly the water exploded about fifteen feet from the fly. It was so violent that it startled her. What looked like five or six arapaima splashed erratically across the smooth surface. But they were nowhere near her fly. "What do I do!?"

"They chasing bait!" Carlos's said excitedly. "This good. Strip faster now!"

She began to strip a bit faster, trembling with excitement. Everything seemed to slow down. All of her senses were electrified as she anticipated a massive strike. And then it happened. Her fly suddenly stopped, a second later her rod was nearly ripped from her hands.

"Set! Hard!" Carlos ordered.

Jena screamed as she strip set harder than she ever had, pulling her left hand back hard as she jerked the fly line towards her hip. She kept her tip low and extended her line hand far behind her in an effort to really embed the hook in the fish's mouth. The rod shook violently and an arapaima burst from the surface, its huge body contorting powerfully.

And then it was gone. It had spat the hook.

"Shit, shit, shit!" she screamed as she nearly threw the rod into the water in frustration.

"Ok," Carlos said, his voice soft now. "Hard mouths...hook not stuck."

"I set it as hard as I could," she said, exasperated. She normally didn't get so mad when she lost a fish, but she wanted this one more than any she had lost before. But she didn't want it for herself, she wanted to catch it for Chris. She couldn't explain it, but in her head, she recognized this fish as a gift to her husband. Something to honor him, to show her love, to represent her thanks for forcing her on this crazy fishing adventure. Then she remembered one of the lessons she had learned from Mark in Chile...*fly-fishing is all about learning humility*. Holding onto his words, she calmed down a little.

"It good set." Carlos shrugged. "It happen." Carlos looked at her intently. "Patience," he said tapping his heart, "come from here. It necessary."

Jena was still angry. "Necessary for what?" she snapped, instantly regretting her sharp tone.

But Carlos didn't seem to mind. He calmly tapped his heart. "For fishing. For life."

"Patience is necessary for fly-fishing and life?"

He shook his head, tapping his heart again. "Calm."

"A calm heart is necessary for fly-fishing and life?" she asked again.

Carlos smiled. "Yes."

By this time Jena had relaxed some, thinking that perhaps Carlos had just taught her another life lesson.

Suddenly there were another series of turbulent splashes. It sounded like a three-hundred-pound person had just done a cannon ball. Jena jerked her head around and glimpsed flashes of silver and red across the surface of the water. They were seventy feet away. Arapaima scales were big, the edges tinted red, creating a brilliant display of silver, pewter, and crimson.

"Still feeding! Good!" Carlos exclaimed as he used his long pole to propel the boat closer. "Cast...sixty feet, nine o'clock."

Jena had already began casting and moments later she laid the fly line down. "You see them?"

Carlos shook his head. "Strip, just like before."

She started to strip in the fly, giving it a jerky movement as her right hand gripped the rod like a race car driver clutching the steering wheel. "You see anything?" Her voice quivered with excitement.

"Yes...it turning. Be ready."

Her mind focused on the strip set. She was ready, and when it hit the fly, she would set harder than she ever had. She wasn't worried about breaking the line as the rod she was using was outfitted with hundred-pound shock tippet. There was no way she would break the line by setting too hard.

Suddenly it felt like her fly had just hooked onto a car racing in the opposite direction. She screamed and set the hook, jerking her left hand back while stepping backward with her left foot to get more power. She was so focused on the hook set that she didn't realize she was standing near the edge of the platform. Her foot slipped off the edge and all of her momentum propelled her backward. She felt herself falling and frantically looked back to try and cushion her fall. But there was no way she was going to let go of the rod. Her will to catch the fish was so strong that she would not allow herself to release the line or the rod. Unfortunately, that meant she was going to smack her back hard onto the metal bench in the boat.

She screamed as she fell, her rod tip snapping up and back as she struck the metal bench seat behind her. Luckily, most of her body hit the cushioned seat, but she still felt a sharp pain in her elbow and knew she would have bruising along her back and legs. But she ignored the pain and scrambled to her feet, her left hand frantically guiding the line as it was ripped through the rod's eyelets.

The fish was still on!

Breaking the surface like an attacking great white, the arapaima leaped from the water, its huge long head shaking back and forth in hopes of spitting the fly. But this time the heavy fish stayed on, and when it landed back in the water it took off like a freight train. Her reel screamed and so did she.

"Let it go!" Carlos shouted, his excitement palpable.

The arapaima didn't pull as fast as a bonefish or a GT, but what it lacked in speed it made up for in sheer power. It felt like she was trying to stop a runaway train. Carlos pushed the boat and followed the fish as it swam all around the lagoon, all the while Jena holding on like her life depended on it. She wondered how long she could hold on.

"You fall...set hook good," Carlos said, smiling wide.

She laughed. Was that what happened? When she fell and her rod jerked up and back, did it set the hook hard enough to bury in its tough jaw? Her falling weight would certainly have helped. It was definitely possible. And if so, the aches and pains caused by the fall would be worth it. But she needed to land the fish first.

"It's so strong," Jena growled as the arapaima pulled down, trying to hide at the bottom of the lagoon. It felt like she was trying to keep a semi-truck from sinking.

"Let it tire," Carlos instructed.

"How big do you think it is?" Jena gasped, looking back at him.

Carlos shrugged. "Over hundred."

She had never caught a fish that big. Just the thought of it caused her anxiety to skyrocket. She didn't want to lose the fish. For just a moment, she pictured Chris in the boat cheering her on, his exuberant smile plastered across his face. She heard him laugh in excitement as he instructed her. She would never get to experience that in real life. All she had now was flashes of images she would never experience firsthand.

It made her mad.

Growling, she redoubled her efforts as the fish moved from the bottom and took off again. Surfacing to get air, it launched from the water as it tried to distance itself from the boat. But this time she could feel it tire, its pull and jump lacking the same power it had previously.

"I think it's tiring!" she yelled, her hands aching as they struggled to hold the rod.

Carlos nodded and used the long pole to push the boat closer to the shore. He was heading towards a weedy shoreline, a ten-foot niche covered in tall grass, the dense jungle surrounding it.

"We will land fish on ground," Carlos instructed.

Jena glanced back before returning her efforts to fighting the fish. "Okay," she said, her voice strained. The fish was still pulling hard and she was afraid she was going to drop the rod into the water. Her hands throbbed and sweat dripped off her brow. Again the monster fish broke the surface, frantically shaking back and forth as it struggled to escape, her rod threatening to tear itself from her hands.

She felt the boat lurch and glanced back to see that Carlos had slid it onto the grassy shoreline. Sensing the shallow water, the angry arapaima took off again toward the safety of the darker depths. Her reel screamed as the line was ripped from it. She wanted to let go with one hand to give it a rest, but she didn't dare, afraid her other would give out and the rod would be yanked from her grasp. She gritted her teeth and held on.

For fifteen more minutes she struggled to hold on. Finally the fish was pulled near the boat, its body floating across the water as it slowly swam back and forth in exhaustion. It was obviously spent, but so was Jena.

"I don't know if I can hold on," she moaned.

"Not much longer," Carlos said. He was already standing in the water ready to help land and release the fish. "Reel in more...get to back of boat."

She took a deep breath and dug for more energy. Then she lowered the rod tip and reeled in more line, using the last of her strength to pull the fish towards the shore as she carefully stepped towards the back of the boat. It felt like she was moving a whale, it was so heavy. But the fish was finally tired and it went with the path of least resistance, which was towards the shore.

The arapaima lifted its head from the water and made a strange gulping sound. "Did it just breathe?" Jena asked.

"Yes," Carlos said as he stepped aside, providing a path for the big fish. "Keep pulling."

Jena got to the end of the boat. "Should I get on shore?"

"Yes."

She carefully stepped out of the boat onto the mushy grass, keeping her rod tip up, grunting with the effort.

Carlos knew she was fatigued and he tried to encourage her. "Almost...you do great."

The arapaima lazily moved next to Carlos, its huge five-foot-long body nearly grounded as it rested on the thick grass that grew in the shallow water. He reached down and smacked the side of its body. In response, it shook its tail, but didn't take off or thrash about much. Looking up at Jena, he smiled and gave her a thumbs up. "It tired."

Kneeling in the shallow water, he reached his hands under the huge fish and held it still. The arapaima lazily flipped its tail back and forth but was too tired to bolt from his grasp.

"What should I do?" Jena said, eager to drop the rod.

"Come in water...hold fish. I quickly take picture."

"Should I set the rod down?"

"Yes, yes," Carlos confirmed as he wiggled the hook from the corner of the fish's mouth. It had gone in so deep that it looked like he was trying to remove a hook from a piece of thick wood. He struggled momentarily before it finally popped free.

With great relief Jena set the rod down and moved quickly into the water. She couldn't believe how big it was. The fish was nearly her size, with a thick powerful muscular body. Its tail looked more similar to an eel, and what they had told her about their heads was very true. They were long and felt like bone, with huge wide mouths, almost like a lizard. But it was the most beautiful thing she had ever seen. Its scales were large, like armor on a knight, the ends brushed a brilliant crimson. As the fish undulated in the water, the Amazon sun reflected off its body, flashing colors of silver and red.

She knelt in the water next to Carlos and reached her arms under its huge body. Then Carlos moved away quickly, finding his waterproof camera along the edge of the boat.

"It's so heavy," Jena groaned, doing her best to keep the fish still.

"Lift up more," Carlos suggested as he readied the camera.

She looked at him with a *you're kidding* look. "I couldn't tie my own laces right now and you want me to lift it higher. The thing weighs as much as I do."

Carlos had already taken a few pictures. He smiled warmly. "Do best."

She took a deep breath and lifted with all her might, smiling wide towards the camera. The huge arapaima's body rose a few inches higher, exposing more of its brilliant body as Carlos snapped more pictures. Suddenly the fish lifted its head and made a gulping sound again.

"He is going—" Carlos started to say before the fish thrashed violently.

Jena screamed as the monster fish kicked its tail hard, knocking her back into the deeper water where she was completing submerged. Bolting from the surface, Jena swam to the side as she felt the arapaima swim past her into the deep water. She stood in the shallows, blood dripping from the cut at her elbow from when she fell, water cascading from her face. But she was all smiles.

Carlos smiled back. "Good pictures."

"You like scotch and cigars?"

* * *

That evening Jena was still riding the high from catching the arapaima. Her exploit was the talk of the lodge while everyone was outside eating a traditional Brazilian barbeque, called churrasco, prepared by Luis, the lodge chef. There were six tables with five chairs each scattered across the lawn and a handful of staff were barbequing a variety of meats and serving up cocktails, beer, wine, and soft drinks. A large main table was set up for the buffet from which guests could choose a wide assortment of dishes.

The meat was to die for, all cooked traditionally over an open flame on long skewers called swords. There was steak, which had been coated in salt for a few hours before cooking, as well as chicken and pork, which had marinated all night before hitting the fire. They served a fingerling potato dish with peas and a cilantro pesto that was incredible. Jena particularly enjoyed the hearts of palm salad with cherry tomatoes. It was light and fresh, a delicious accompaniment to the rich meats.

After she had stuffed her belly, she found herself staring with uncertainty at a few dishes that sat on a small table off from the main food area. Jack stood next to her looking equally apprehensive. On the table were a few traditional native foods. Luis thought it would be fun and educational to introduce the guests to some of the local cuisine. There was grilled chayote, a green vegetable that had originally been cultivated by the Aztecs and Mayans. There was also an interesting dish called Peruvian juane, which was a mixture of chicken, rice, and spices wrapped in banana leaves. But it was neither of those dishes that had given Jena pause. She was staring at a shallow plate lined with skewers of suri palm grubs, the large fat grubs of the palm weevil, each one the size of a toe. The skewers rested in some sort of liquid, perhaps a brine, or soup base.

Luis stood behind the table smiling. "You going to try one or just stare at it?"

She had already tasted the chayote and juane, but she did not think she could get herself to touch one of the grubs, let alone eat one. "I don't think I can."

"If you eat one, I will," Jack said next to her.

Jena had yet to find something that qualified as an activity or action that Chris would love but she would not. In New Zealand it was flying in a helicopter. In the Seychelles it was taking a diving class. While on the yacht in the Chilean fjords it had been the polar bear plunge, jumping off the top of the boat into freezing cold water. And now, she was staring at a plate filled with worm-like insects and contemplating eating one. She knew that if Chris were here, he would jump at the opportunity to try something so unique. And he would definitely push her to try one with him.

She looked at Jack. "I'm not sure I can," she whispered apprehensively. It was clear to both Luis and Jack that she sort of wanted to try one. She just needed a push.

"Listen," Jack said. "I'm not looking forward to it, but we'll never have an opportunity to do this again. It will make a great story."

Jena nodded in agreement, chuckling. "That's definitely true."

Jack smiled, grabbed a skewer, and pulled two grubs off before setting the rest back in the bowl. He held his palm towards her, two grubs perched there, their fat bulbous bodies nearly making her retch. "Let's do this."

She looked up, past Jack, picturing Chris standing behind him, a teasing smile and raised eyebrows urging her on. She knew, if he were with her, that he would pop one into his mouth without hesitation. Which meant that her own act of eating weird stuff would definitely count as something to journal.

"You okay?" Jack asked.

She blinked and Chris's image disappeared. "Yeah, sorry, was just thinking of something."

Jack knew about her situation and smiled encouragingly. "Come on," he urged. "You'll regret it if you don't."

Jena knew that was true. If she backed out now, she would be upset with herself later. "Okay, I'll do it," she said sternly, trying to find the courage. She plucked a grub from his hand.

"Ready?" he asked.

She looked at the table to make sure her gin and tonic was still sitting on the edge. She had a feeling she was going to need it. "Yes."

"On three," Jack instructed. "One...two...three."

He popped the grub into his mouth.

Jena closed her eyes and did the same. She had contemplated just swallowing it without chewing. But she knew Chris would have given her shit for doing that. The thought of biting into the fat grub made her almost nauseous, but she also knew in her heart that if she took a shortcut now, she would be mad at herself afterwards. So she found her resolve and bit down on the grub, ready to quickly swallow whatever she would encounter.

Its skin was tough, like rubber. Once it split, the grub exploded in her mouth, a pudding like texture that tasted similar to cashews. It actually didn't taste that bad, but the consistency nearly made her vomit. She quickly swallowed, grabbed her gin and tonic and downed the entire thing.

When she opened her eyes, she saw Jack staring back at her. Unbeknownst to her, they had attracted a mini audience. Jason and Jaylin, Jack's twin boys, stood next to him.

"Well, what did you think?" Jack asked.

Jena shivered, disgusted. "It wasn't the taste," she said, "it was the texture."

"That's what she said," Jason quipped, laughing at his joke.

"Good one bro," Jaylin chuckled, smacking his brother's hand as they walked away.

"Sorry," Jack said, embarrassed by his boys but laughing, nonetheless.

Jena laughed as well. "Oh, I've heard worse." Chris and his fishing buddies were grand masters at *that's what she said* jokes. She looked at Jack. "Thanks for doing that with me," she said sincerely.

He reached up and squeezed her shoulder, giving her a brotherly smile. "You're welcome." Then he left, leaving her to her thoughts.

After a few moments of quiet contemplation, she decided she wanted to journal the day and the recent grub eating incident. She grabbed her leather-bound journal, another cocktail, and made her way down to the sandy beach to enjoy the setting sun. The entire lodge was protected by a rock face, a natural bulkhead to the Aqua Boa River. It wasn't the rainy season so the river was lower, exposing many sandy beaches along its meandering course. She noticed a particularly lovely beach to the left of the dock, complete with three sets of tables and chairs set up in the sand for the lodge guests to relax in river side whenever they wanted.

She sat in a white chair with blue cushions, her cocktail on the table, her journal in her lap. She had thought about sitting on the dock and dangling her feet in the cool water. But it was a fleeting idea when she remembered some of the dangerous creatures that called the river their home. Piranha were abundant, but it was really the black caiman, or freshwater crocodile that kept her out of the water. She had seen a twelve-footer around the dock on many occasions. The beach was a much safer spot to relax.

Fifteen minutes later she wrote down the life lesson she had learned from Carlos, as well as her recent experience eating local cuisine. Glancing at her list, she went over the lessons she had learned, ending with Carlos's words...*A calm heart is necessary for fly-fishing, and life.* She smiled, thinking of Mr. Miyagi from The Karate Kid. As luck would have it, she had her own Mr. Miyagi guide her today. It wasn't so far from the truth, she thought. Carlos had been calm and zen-like the entire day. Jena now wished she would've made more of an effort to communicate with him. Perhaps she could have learned more.

"You mind if I join you?"

She glanced up from her journal to see Stella, two wine glasses in one hand and a bottle in the other.

"Before you say no," she continued with a smile. "I have in my hand a very special bottle of Chateau Lafite Rothschild Pauillac, 2006." She lifted her eyebrows enticingly.

Jena smiled and set the journal on the table. "All you had to say was free wine."

Stella laughed and sat down, poured two glasses of wine, and handed one to Jena. "This was one of my husband's favorites." She lifted her wine glass. "To the ones we love."

Jena pressed her lips together in a soft smile, her eyes taking on a slight sheen. Stella noticed of course, but said nothing. They both drank from their glasses.

Leaning her head back in her chair, Jena closed her eyes and savored the wine's nuances. It packed a lot of flavor for such an old bottle. It was jammy but still had a strong tannic backbone. She could taste cedar and a touch of spice. It was very complex, which surprised her for such an aged vintage. She opened her eyes, swallowed, and looked at Stella. "Wow, that is really good. Thanks for sharing it with me."

"You're welcome."

"You mentioned your husband, are you still married?" Jena asked.

"He died five years ago," she replied.

"I'm so sorry."

"He smoked like a chimney. Knew it was going to kill him but he just couldn't stop." She paused and took another sip. "Drinking his favorite wine is one way I can hold onto him."

Jena nodded, understanding that sentiment. After all, the main reason for what she was doing was just that, to do something that would keep her memories of Chris as solid as stone, so they wouldn't blow away with the winds of time.

"Well, he had good taste," Jena added, lifting the glass of wine.

Stella smiled. "Of course he did, he married me after all."

Jena laughed.

"Tell me about your husband," Stella asked, settling back in her chair.

Jena had yet to tell someone here her entire story, which of course was one of the stipulations. When she had first met Stella a few days ago she had thought that perhaps she would be a good person to share her story with. She was glad to have that opportunity now. So, she started from the beginning, telling Stella about Chris's death and the path he had laid out for her this last year. Jena talked about the fishing, the life lessons, the cigars and scotch...everything. She shed a few tears, but all in all was able to stay in control.

Stella was a good listener, asking a few probing questions here and there, but mostly she just listened and sipped her wine.

"And now," Jena finished, "I'm here, in Brazil, fishing the Amazon basin."

"Bet you never thought you'd say that," Stella chuckled.

"Nope, not even close."

"That is quite the story. Thanks for sharing it," she said sincerely. She paused, refilling each of their glasses. "Tell me," she continued, "what do you regret the most?"

Jena sighed, her mind fluttering through possible answers. But every response led to one thing. "Not being able to have children with Chris," she said, her voice cracking as she relived the emotions of their infertility. Her eyes misted while she cleared her throat, trying to maintain her composure. "I'm sorry," she whispered.

Stella nodded thoughtfully as she looked away. Jena noticed her own eyes glisten with fresh tears. She looked back and wiped a tear away before it fell. "I want you to know something before you tell me your own experiences. I too was not able to have children." She paused. "We tried everything. But nothing worked. It was the hardest thing I've ever experienced besides my husband's death. So I understand your pain."

Jena reached out and touched Stella's arm. "So Jack is adopted?"

"Yes," she replied, "It was the right choice for us. I'd love to hear more about your struggles if you're willing."

Jena nodded and continued. "We tried IUIs nine times. None of them worked. Every time we got our hopes up," Jena paused as the pain returned. Her throat constricted as she tried to control her emotions. Sniffly, she pushed through the feelings of regret. "Every time the results came back negative it was like a kick in the stomach. I tried acupuncture, I gave myself shots in my car, we tried different drugs. Two years of trying, nine IUI's, I finally said I can't do it anymore." By this time Jena's chin was quivering and her voice was shaking. She wiped the fresh tears away and paused as she thought of the fact, that prior to Chris's death, she had been able to speak of their infertility without getting too emotional. They had gotten through it together, their love for one another enough to override the pain of not becoming parents. But now he was gone, and this was the first time she had spoken about their infertility since his death. His absence had caused the pain to resurface.

Stella dabbed tears away from her own eyes. She took in a deep breath. "And you regret not trying something else?"

Jena nodded. "Yes," she choked, the knot in her throat returning. "Chris was willing to try *invitro*. But I said no." She stopped and looked away, working to shut the door to those painful memories. "I...just...couldn't...do it anymore," she stammered, wiping her nose. "But now, I would do anything to have had a child with him. I could forever see his smile in our little boy, or his twinkling eyes in our daughter. But now," she continued, "I have nothing." She looked down and put her hand over her eyes, willing the sense of regret and loneliness away.

Stella silently wiped her own tears. "We tried *invitro*. Three times actually. Nothing worked."

Jena looked up. "At least you tried," she said softly.

Stella leaned forward and put her hand on Jena's knee. "Listen to me," she said firmly. "You *did* try, a lot by the sounds of it. Don't let regret poison your heart. From what I've learned about your husband, my guess is he supported you in the decision you made. And you don't need a child to hold onto a loved one. There are other ways."

Jena wiped more tears away, regaining some control. "What do *you* do?"

Stella smiled. "Every year my husband and I would take Jack and his family on a big trip. It was a tradition. I am continuing that tradition after my husband's death."

"What is your late husband's name?" Jena sniffled.

"Bart. It was short for Bartholomew. At every trip," Stella continued, "I take all the letters that Bart wrote to me during the fifty-three years we were married, and read them over and over again."

"That must be hard."

She nodded. "Yes, it is, but it's gotten easier over the years. I used to cry nonstop, and I still do sometimes. But now, I find myself smiling more often than not as I remember the man he was. I miss him

241

dearly. That will never go away. But I've found a way to live with his passing."

"I hope I can," Jena lamented.

"Oh, honey, you are already on the right path."

Jena wiped her nose again and took a sip of her wine. She was feeling a little better and she gave Stella a weak smile. "Thank you for listening."

"Of course."

"I was wondering. What happened to Jason and Jaylin's mother?" Jena inquired.

Stella's face crinkled in disgust. "Oh, he kicked that money hungry bitch to the curb."

Jena nearly spit out her wine. "Seriously?"

"My dear, we are quite well off," she said casually, more matter-of-factly than arrogantly. "She was a young model who just wanted our money. Jack fell for it of course." She shrugged. "Well, you've seen him...he's not much to look at, but he has a big heart and she took advantage of it. But I saw right through her shit."

"I hate her already," Jena said emphatically.

Stella laughed. "But she gave me two gorgeous grandsons." She winked at Jena. "Luckily, they both got her looks."

Jena laughed as Stella refilled their glasses with the last of the wine.

Jena held up her glass. "To good men."

"And to strong women," Stella added.

They clinked their glasses in comradery.

Chapter 8

The computer screen was black for a moment before it flashed a few times, settling on Chris's image sitting in his leather office chair. He didn't look much different from the last video, Jena thought, but nonetheless his gaunt and pasty complexion took her breath away.

"Oh, baby, I miss you," Jena moaned softly.

Chris smiled as if he heard her. "Hey, honey. I hope your Amazon trip was incredible. Again, making these videos is so hard. I want to ask you so many questions," he lamented, shaking his head, "but I can't. But I can only assume that the frustration and difficulty I go through in making these videos, is nothing compared to the pain you feel when you watch them. That of course was never my intent. Causing you grief is the last thing I want." He paused as he reached off camera. Jena heard the clinking of ice before she even saw the glass of scotch. He smiled, holding the glass up. "I decided to make this video soon after the previous. At this moment, despite my zombie apocalypse look, I feel pretty good. I figured it would make sense to film the last video while I felt fairly well," Chris said. He held up the scotch. "I still feel healthy enough to have a few sips of scotch. This, by the way, is the finest bottle I could find. It took me a while to find it but I've been saving it for the last video. It's Gordon and MacPhail Macallan Speymalt 1973. I paid two thousand dollars for the bottle."

She put her hand to her mouth in surprise. "Oh wow, is it good?" she asked softly. She had slowly been acquiring a taste for scotch. She wasn't sure why, but she had her theories. Each time she had tried his scotch, it was after landing a trophy fish. In a strange way the drinking of scotch was always associated with her memories of Chris, seeing the moment through his eyes, similar to how a certain smell could bring back memories of a particular event. Tasting scotch now, elicited memories of Chris and trophy fish. It was a solid link to him, and because of that she began to appreciate the nuances of its flavor. She wasn't sure if it was all in her head, but the reality was she was starting to enjoy it.

Chris took a small sip and closed his eyes with pleasure. A few moments later he opened them and smiled. "It's so good," he affirmed. "Do me a favor. I want you to take this scotch with you on your very last trip. And no, it's not the next one. If you recall, I am sending you back to where it all started. I am sending you back to Hans to end the adventure by spreading my ashes at my secret fishing hole, you know the one," he added with playful grin.

"Chris's hole," Jena sniffed, her eyes welling with tears as the finality of her adventure began to hit home. "Baby, I don't want this to end." Sadness clouded her features as the tears began to fall.

"Now listen. I know this talk about this being the last video and your last destination is likely causing you grief. But I know you are doing better now. I have no idea if you have reached the acceptance level yet, but if you have not, you will soon. You are an incredible woman who deals with things that no one should have to. If you can handle holding a six-month baby that was beaten so bad by the mom's boyfriend that every bone in her body was broken, then you can handle my death. If you can handle holding that child while you take her off life support, the mother nowhere to be seen, then you can handle my death. You are the strongest woman I know. You got this, baby."

Jena was now openly crying, her body racking with deep sobs as she came to terms with the fact that she was presently watching the last video she would get from him. "I just want to see you again," she cried. I need to hear your voice."

Chris smiled and took a sip. "Listen, if you need to, you can simply re-watch the videos." He laughed, but buried beneath the levity Jena could see the sadness, the melancholy drifting behind the eyes. "Okay, enough of this 'last video' talk. Let's go over your next trip. So, I wanted to end your adventure with a place that I've been dying to go." He laughed, "that is pretty funny now actually." He chuckled as he sipped more scotch. "Sorry, but you have to admit that was serendipitous. Okay, the fishing. As you know, I've been to several places in Alaska, but this particular lodge is in a location that I never got a chance to explore. What drew me to it was its remoteness and its access to small, remote rivers filled with big rainbows. The place is called Big Tree Lodge and it's located on the Talachulitna River. Back in the seventies there were a few lots for sale in the area and the lodge owner, Gary Foster, bought one of the parcels. Soon after that the state of Alaska designated the area as a restricted park so no other settlers were allowed. It's so remote that when you see footprints along the riverbed, you'll know they were yours from three days ago." He shook his head and smiled. *"Can you just imagine, small, pristine rivers teeming with fish, and not a single person around, your only company the wildlife that thrives in the area."*

Jena wiped her nose, grabbing the box of Kleenex on the coffee table to dab her eyes. "I can, baby. It sounds wonderful." Then she reached over, paused the video, and jumped up from the couch. She went to the sideboard in her dining room, on top of which was Chris's wet bar covered with bottles of liquor, bitters, tasting glasses, shot glasses, everything a craft style bartender would want. Chris had built the side bar, even including an ice maker built into the top. Every guy that visited their house was envious of it. She searched around and found the bottle of Gordon and MacPhail Macallan. She had decided that she was going to drink some with him as she finished the video. Taking a tumbler, she filled it with a few cubes of ice followed by two fingers of the expensive scotch. She quickly returned to the couch and reached over to restart the video. Just before she hit the play button, she decided to taste it. Before bringing the glass to her mouth she caught the aromas of vanilla, and of course alcohol, then as she paused and held the glass to her nose, she though she detected some smokiness. Next, she put the glass to her mouth, taking a small sip. It was smooth and silky, the flavor a mixture of vanilla and malt. It went down smoothly and didn't burn at all. She was still a novice scotch drinker but she somehow knew that this one was special. "That is really good, babe," Jena agreed as she pressed play on the video.

"So the really cool thing about this lodge is that for five of the six days you will be heli-fishing, flying into small remote rivers with your guide. It's going to be remote and personal, the lodge only allowing eight fishermen for each trip. You'll have your own little cabin and, like all high-end lodges, you'll be wined and dined after each day of incredible fishing. But because of its remoteness, the experience will

245

be much more rustic with the lodge being tucked away in a remote forest deep in Alaska's interior."

Jena had gotten a hold of herself and was already thinking of the fishing. She smiled to herself as she thought about how far she had come. Remembering the first video, the last thing she had thought about was the fishing. She had been overwhelmed, frustrated, and even a little angry. Now she listened intently and was really looking forward to the next trip. Chris had been right. Fly fishing had become a conduit for her own healing. And even though she still felt the sting of Chris's death, she was beginning to see a way to accept her loss, to hold on to the memories of her husband while making more new memories along the way. Perhaps she had climbed the ladder to the top, reaching the rung of acceptance. She wasn't sure if she was quite there yet, but she did know that she was improving. Things were getting better.

"Now, I had to reserve a spot way ahead of time as the lodge books quickly. I planned the reservation based on your other trips so I hope the timing will work out. If I had to guess, it is sometime in the spring for you, perhaps April or May. I booked your trip for mid-July so you should have plenty of time to plan and prepare. During that time you can catch almost all species of salmon, as well as fat rainbows and artic grayling. So bring a wide variety of rods ranging from five to eight weight. I think by now you know what flies to bring. Also, bring your bug spray, after all, you are going to Alaska." He smiled again and held up his drink, taking a sip and savoring it, a look of utter enjoyment plastered across his face. *"Now, you knew the time would come. But I'm afraid I have to say goodbye."*

Jena suddenly felt a pain in her chest, a weight sitting right on her sternum. She couldn't breathe or swallow as she remembered when she had to say goodbye to her dying husband. She could still smell the sterile hospital room. She could hear the hospital paging system in the background as Chris's distressed breathing amplified in her ear as she hugged him close. She could still hear him whisper, *I love you,* the last words he spoke before his fingers relaxed in death, releasing her hand. The pain returned like a tidal wave, releasing a deluge of tears as she sobbed uncontrollably.

"Honey, now listen. I know this his hard for you. I know you already said goodbye to me when I died, which is weird to say now as I'm still alive." He tried to laugh to lighten the mood, but it came out as a feeble attempt. *"This is hard for both of us. But I will never really be gone. You will think of me every time you touch a fly rod, every time you tie a fly, every time you drink a scotch or smell the earthy rich smoke of a cigar. Eventually, you will think of me in a way that elicits a smile, your joyful memories erasing the painful ones. I hope you feel, right now, that that is a possibility. If you do, then this entire adventure has been worthwhile, as that has been my goal all along."* He lifted his glass. *"One more toast for the road,"* he added.

Jena was still crying, her body shaking as she tried to regain control. She reached her shaking hand towards the table to grab her own glass of scotch.

"To us," he said. *"To the love of my life. To the woman I am proud to call my wife. To the timeline of memories we created together, and to the timeline you will create without me."*

He took a final sip as Jena's trembling hand brought her own glass to her mouth. Her eyes were glued to the screen, not wanting Chris's face to disappear. She swallowed the liquid but didn't taste it, her mind holding onto his image.

"You got this, Jena O'Malley. I love you." Then he smiled and winked.

She blinked, shedding the pooling tears. And when she reopened them, the screen was black. Her tears continued to fall as she felt her world come crashing down for a second time.

* * *

The smell of fresh tomatoes, garlic, and thyme rose from the simmering pan as Jena poured three glasses of an expensive cabernet. Tesa, her mother, and Brook, her best friend, sat at the breakfast table adjacent the kitchen talking as Jena's favorite cooking music, bossa nova, played through Pandora. She brought them each a glass and grabbed her own, sitting next them as they enjoyed the music, comradery, and the beautiful charcuterie plate she had laid out before them.

Brook cocked her head as she eyed the glass of wine. "Did I just see you pour a Faust?"

Jena smiled. "Nothing but the best for the best," she said, lifting her glass to toast.

All three clinked their glasses together and drank.

Tesa tasted the wine, pressing her lips together, her forehead scrunched in thought as she attempted to analyze the wine's nuances. Jena looked at Brook and they shared a smile as her mother tried her best to enjoy the cabernet. "It's good," Tesa said. "But—"

"It's wasted on you," Jena and Brook said in unison.

Tesa laughed. "I'm sorry. I just can't tell the difference between this and my—"

"Two buck chuck," Jena and Brook said again in unison.

"Am I really that predictable," Tesa chuckled.

"Well..." Jena said mockingly.

"Okay, okay, I get it." She held up the wine. "But thanks for continuing to try and educate me."

"You're welcome."

"So, your next and last trip is Alaska. Where abouts exactly?" Brook asked.

"I don't really know," Jena responded. "I will fly into Anchorage, and from there I'll take a bush plane to the lodge. It's in the middle of nowhere surrounded by protected lands."

"Sounds dangerous," Tesa added. As her mother, she tended to worry about her.

"If being far away from any convenience is dangerous, then yes, I guess it is. But, mom, I'll be fine. The only real danger is bears."

"Oh dear, I don't know about this. You're going to be around bears?" Tesa asked.

"Of course," Jena responded casually. "It is Alaska. But these people have been doing this for over thirty years. It's family owned and operated. I'll be perfectly fine."

"What about the helicopters?" Brook asked.

Jena gave her a *shut-up* look but it was too late.

"Helicopters?!" Tesa explained. "They are really dangerous, honey. I hear they crash all the time."

"Where did you hear that?" Jena inquired.

"Well...just...around, I guess. I've seen crashes on the internet."

"Mom, I'll be fine. But yes, I'll be taking a helicopter to different fishing locations."

"I don't like that," Tesa said stubbornly.

"I know," Jena said, drinking more of her wine as she glared at Brook.

Brook flashed her an *I'm sorry* look before sheepishly drinking from her own glass.

"How are you feeling with all this?" Tesa inquired motheringly. "I know you just watched the last video." She reached over and touched her hand. "That must've been hard. You doing okay?"

Jena held back her tears, but her eyes glistened in the soft glow of the dimmed lights. But she held on, not allowing the sadness to take control. "Yeah, it was really hard actually. It almost felt like I was reliving his death." She wiped the corners of her eyes. "But I'm getting stronger," she added, nodding her head. "The pain is losing its sharp edge."

"That's good, Jena," Tesa added. "I am so proud of what you've done. I'm not sure I could've done it."

"Oh, I know I couldn't," Brook blurted. "I'm not that strong."

"It's been really hard," Jena agreed. "But Chris had been right all along. Somehow, these fishing trips have helped me work through his passing." She shook her head in bewilderment. "I never would've believed it a year ago." She looked at them both. "And both of you *could* have done it. You would just need someone like Chris to encourage you, as I did."

"Perhaps," Brook said. "Chris sure was an amazing man. He was an old soul, wasn't he?"

Jena smiled as more tears pooled in her eyes. "He was."

Again, Tesa reached over to hold her daughter's hand. "So, what's next after all this?"

Jena let out a slow breath, grappling with her apprehension once again. "Well, I'm not totally sure yet."

"Are you going to get your job back at the hospital?"

Jena sighed. "I'm not really sure. I can't imagine not being a nurse. It's who I am."

"And you are so good at it," Tesa added proudly. "I don't know anyone more perfect for the job."

"Thanks, mom," Jena replied with a thoughtful smile. "It's just that I feel so different. Honestly, I'm not yet sure what I'm going to do."

"Well," Brook added. "You have enough money that you don't have to work at all."

"Yeah," Jena replied. "I guess that's always an option." Then she shook her head. "But I will need to do something. I can't just sit around and do nothing."

"I got an idea," Brook mused. "Why don't you pay my bills, and I'll sit around and do nothing with you." She laughed. "You could give me a friendship stipend and teach me how to fly-fish. Maybe I could meet a good guy on the river."

Jena picked up a cracker and threw it at her. "You wish! You know, you would be a hit with all the cute fly-fishermen, that's for sure."

"Something to think about."

"If that's the case, maybe I should pick up the sport as well," Tesa added.

They all three chuckled and drank more of the lovely wine.

"Well," Tesa said, "You have the luxury of taking your time to figure everything out."

Jena nodded. "Yes I do."

"Maybe this last trip will give you some more insight," Brook announced as she lifted her wine glass. "To new paths in life, may they open new doors for us."

Jena smiled and lifted her glass. Tesa did the same, gripping her daughter's hand as they toasted to new adventures.

* * *

Jena was wheeling her carry-on to baggage claim when she noticed a young girl hiding behind a large support column at one of the gates. The Anchorage airport wasn't overly busy, but there were enough people milling about that it was unlikely one young girl would have caught her attention. It wasn't her presence that gave her pause, but her facial expression. She was obviously frightened.

Jena stopped and looked around but couldn't see anyone near the girl. She made up her mind and pulled her luggage towards her, slowing when she neared as the girl looked up. She looked about eight years old, with black hair tied into two cute ponytails. Her large blue eyes looked like those of a frightened deer, and she had clearly been crying. Her eyes were puffy and her cheeks were wet with moisture.

Jena squatted down so she was looking eye to eye with her. The girl pressed her body closer to the column when she saw Jena. "Honey, are you okay?" The girl looked at her, but didn't say anything, her eyes blinking fresh tears. "Did you lose your mommy?"

Jena noticed she was looking intently at her, and when she had said the word *mommy*, she looked hopeful. Suddenly her hands moved in quick sign language. Jena recognized the movements as she had learned basic sign language years ago. She had a patient in the PICU that was a frequent flyer. She was deaf and had cardiac issues. Jena had developed a close relationship with her parents, as well as creating a strong bond with the little girl. In doing so, she had learned basic sign language from the family, as well as taking it upon herself to take lessons.

Jena thought the little girl had said, *I need to find my mommy.*

Jena smiled warmly, trying to ease the little girl's concern. *Did you get lost from your mommy,* she signed back.

The little girl lit up like a Christmas tree when she saw that Jena knew sign language. *Yes. I don't know where they are.*

Jena imagined it was pretty easy for a deaf child to get lost, especially in an airport. Her parents must be worried sick and frantically looking for her. *My name is Nurse Jena,* Jena signed. *Do you know what a nurse is?*

Yes, I see nurses for my ears

Jena smiled, figuring it was likely with her ear issues that the little girl was a permanent fixture at her local hospital. *I help little kids, just like your nurse helps you. What is your name?*

Laura

Hi, Laura, Jena signed. *Do you want me to help you find your mother?*

Jena could tell that Laura was torn, likely wanting her help but leery about taking it from a stranger. *My papa says never go with strangers,* she signed reluctantly.

Jena smiled reassuringly. *Your papa is right,* she signed, getting an idea. She reached into her purse and pulled out her wallet. Inside was her hospital ID card. It had her picture as well as her hospital insignia. She wasn't sure if Laura could read, but thought perhaps the badge looked official enough if she couldn't. She showed Laura the badge. *This is my badge as a nurse. Do you know what a badge is?*

Laura took the badge and looked at it, nodding her head. *Police officers have badges,* she signed. *And my nurse has a badge too.*

They do, Jena signed back. *I am like a police officer. I help people. Can I help you find your family?*

Laura looked at Jena. Then she nodded, signing *Yes Please. Can I hold your card?*

Jena stood and smiled wide. Of course. *Will you hold my hand while I take you to your family? I don't want you to get lost again.* She held her hand out.

Laura sniffed, wiping the remaining tears from her eyes. Then she nodded, reaching up to hold Jena's hand, cradling Jena's badge to her chest.

It took her a bit of searching, but twenty minutes later Jena found the airport police station. She didn't get within thirty feet when she saw a frightened mother scream Laura's name and come running towards her. There were a few police officers about talking to a dark-haired man, but when he heard his wife scream, he came running as well.

Laura let go of Jena's hand and she was scooped up by her mother. "Oh, honey, you had me so scared." She wasn't signing knowing full well that Laura wouldn't see her doing so while she was crushed in a bear hug.

Then she set the girl down and looked at Jena. Just then Laura's father arrived and grabbed her in a hug as well.

"Thank you so much for bringing her here," the woman said, her eyes moist with fresh tears.

Laura's dad was still holding her tightly. "We really appreciate it. I'm surprised she came to you. Normally she is very frightened of other adults."

"You're welcome," Jena said. "I'm just glad I noticed her hiding behind one of the support columns. I probably would have walked right by but she looked so scared."

"We can't thank you enough," the mother repeated.

Laura wiped the tears from her eyes and signed, *thank you for bringing me to my mom and dad.* Then she handed Jena her badge back.

Jena smiled and took the badge. *You're welcome,* she signed. *Promise me next time you'll stay close to them.*

Laura nodded vigorously and buried her head in the father's neck.

"You know sign language," the father said.

Jena nodded. "Yeah, I'm a pediatric ICU nurse," she said, holding up the badge. "I learned it years ago as one of my frequent patients was hearing impaired."

"Well, thank her for us next time you see her," the mom said, smiling.

"Sure," Jena said. She didn't have the heart to them that the little girl died two years ago. "Well, I better get going. You guys have a safe trip."

"You too," the father replied. "And thank you again."

Jena nodded and left the two holding tightly to their daughter's hands.

Well, Jena thought, *I did my good deed for the day.* She felt good, knowing that her skills as a nurse had played a role in getting the girl to come with her. She had always been good with children, and perhaps this event was the universe telling her that the nursing profession still needed her. She remembered something her mom once told her when she had given up on having a baby. She said that perhaps a child was not in her cards as she was meant to take care of other people's children. Tesa had said that maybe her role in life was to be a caregiver of children who needed more than what their families could provide. Jena was not a religious person, or even someone who believed in fate, but she did like the idea. And even now, as she headed to baggage claim to grab her bags, that thought made her feel better about her allotment in life. She pictured Laura's smile of relief when she saw her parents. *Sometimes,* she thought, *you just need to hold onto the little victories to get you through the day.*

Did she just have an epiphany? Did she just come up with her own life lesson? She loved that idea and promised she would hold onto it if nothing better presented itself. Even if it did, she would still journal the idea.

The airport was small and she found her bags at the baggage claim carousel easily enough. Making her way outside to find an Uber, she thought of her epiphany again. *Sometimes*, she repeated in her head, *you need to hold onto the little victories to get you through the day.* She smiled as she pulled her luggage through the double doors, breathing in the cold, fresh, Alaska air. She was ready to take on her last adventure.

* * *

The Lodge was just like she pictured, remote, rustic, quaint, and comfortable. A float plane had landed her on a sizeable lake, its calm waters surrounded by Alaska's mountains capped in thick white snow, while the mountain bases were covered in green, untouched wilderness. From the shore of the lake she was picked up by helicopter, the lodge owner himself piloting it. Gary was just as she imagined him. He was lively and filled with excitement. It was obvious that he was elated to show her his life's work. He was a big man, with strong shoulders and thick fingers, messy wavy brown hair and an unshaven face completed the look of a stereotypical mountain man.

As Gary positioned the helicopter for landing, he quickly went over the lodge layout as if he were a practiced tour guide. He pointed out the main building where everyone gathered to eat, drink, and tell stories. He showed her the four cabins sprawled around the main lodge, including his own home tucked away a quarter mile from the grounds. Jena had learned from the website that he had built everything. She loved how proud he was, and by the looks of the structure, it was definitely something to be proud of. There were green grass paths lined with wildflowers, courtesy of his wife, connecting all the structures. Everything was built of stout logs taken right from the property. It looked just like a remote fishing lodge should look. Despite all the wonderful and unique places she had been so far, she was still excited to see what Big Tree Lodge had to offer.

Gary touched down expertly on an open grass patch just off the main property. There was an off-road golf cart with a small trailer behind it and it wasn't long before Gary had all her gear loaded up and they were headed toward the lodge.

"What's it like here in the winter?" Jena asked, imagining ten feet of snow everywhere.

"Cold and snowy," he replied. "Which is why we don't stay here."

Jena had assumed that they lived here all year long. "Where else do you live?"

He lifted his eyebrows and smiled. "We have a small home in Belize."

This time it was Jena's turn to smile. "So you hook into rainbows and salmon all summer and then chase bonefish on the flats of Belize all winter? Now that sounds like a life."

"A lot of hard work got us to this point. But yes, it is amazing. A fly-fisherman's dream."

Jena looked around as they neared the main building. The logs used to the erect the structure were huge. The building was the epitome of a log cabin pictured in a ski lodge brochure. "I don't doubt you deserve it," Jena agreed. "This place is really cool."

"Wait until you experience the fishing," Gary remarked

"That's why I'm here," she replied.

Jena could tell that Gary wanted to ask her something, likely why she was fishing alone at a remote fishing lodge. But he held his tongue. She figured the question, as it always did, would arise at a later point.

He drove her past the main lodge being careful to stay off the grass paths. Jena noticed that there was a gravel path that led around the main grounds, circling behind the structures. Jena guessed Gary's wife would not appreciate the golf cart trampling on the grass paths. And Gary seemed wise enough to stay off them.

He drove by three cabins and stopped at the very last one, pulling to the side of the building. It too was made of logs, but much smaller ones than the trees used to construct the main lodge. It had a steep roof, likely to shed the large quantities of snow that piled up in the winter, and it was built on stilts, the deck and front door at least six feet off the ground.

"Why is it built on stilts?" Jena asked as they jumped off the golf cart.

"For the snow," Gary answered, reaching for her bags. "The steep roof sheds the snow and it piles around the cabin. If it were built on the ground it would get buried and you could never get in or out."

Jena nodded, understanding the logic right away. "I thought you weren't here in the winter."

"I'm not. But we sometimes rent the cabins out to hunters."

She helped him grab a few bags and he led her up the stairs onto the high deck. It was a good-sized deck, with a small table and chairs all made from logs and milled lumber likely taken from the property. And when she got to the top and looked around, she noticed she could see the tall snowcapped mountains in the distance. It was beautiful, a great spot to relax after a hard day of fishing.

Inside was just what you'd expect. Everything was made of wood, except for the river rock fireplace and the Formica kitchen countertop. There was a comfortable looking couch and matching side chairs. Each piece had soft cushions with some sort of Native American print, and a big fluffy sheep's skin draped over the back of the couch. The furniture faced the huge stone fireplace and fresh chopped wood was piled high in a metal wood holder to the side. A small round dining table sat in the dining area and was adjacent to the living room, and the kitchen, although small, had everything one needed. Jena saw a small fridge, a gas stove, and enough cabinets to hold the basics. A small hallway off the dining area led to the bathroom and bedroom.

"Down the hall is the bathroom and bedroom. Both are small," Gary added, "but comfortable."

She looked around. "I really love it. That stonework around the fireplace is stunning."

Gary's face lit up. "I laid those stones myself."

Jena had a feeling he was going to say that. "It's amazing. I can't wait to light a fire and drink a nice glass of wine after catching rainbows all day."

"Now that sounds like a good day."

Jena decided to wiggle the worm a little bit, hoping to get some of the conversation out of the way. "My husband would think so too." Just six months ago Jena would have avoided the conversation at all costs. But now, although not welcoming it, felt more comfortable talking about her husband's death.

"If you don't mind me asking, where is your husband?" Gary asked.

"I don't mind," Jena replied. "He died a year ago of cancer. I still think of him as my husband, which can be quite confusing for people when I talk about him. I guess I should start saying my late husband." Jena pursed her lips. "It's not so easy to do though."

Gary's expression changed to one of concern. "I'm so sorry to hear that." He paused for a moment, his own mind somewhere else. "And yes, I can imagine how hard it must be to say out loud, *ex-husband*." He shook his head. "If my wife died that young, I don't know what I'd do."

Jena nodded. "It's been a tough year." She felt tears began to well, but amazingly enough she didn't feel the deep ache in her chest. Wiping her eyes, she smiled, feeling pretty good that she could broach the subject and not lose control. "It's quite a story actually."

Gary looked thoughtful. "Well, if you ever feel up to it, I'd love to hear it."

Jena nodded. "We might have to do that."

He smiled and added, "Okay, I'll leave you to unpack and get settled in. There are snacks, as well as beer, wine, and bottled water in the fridge. I'll be bringing the rest of the guests in over the next few hours." Then he grinned, displaying bright white teeth against the backdrop of his dark scruff on his face. "But get that fishing gear ready. I'm going to take you out for an evening of fishing."

"You guide here as well?" Jena asked. She had seen Gary's list of guides on his website and figured she would be working with them the entire week. One was a cute blonde in her early thirties. She had yet to work with a female guide and was excited by the prospect. She didn't think Gary would have had the time to guide as well as oversee the functioning of the lodge.

"Not typically," Gary answered. "But by the sound of it, you deserve some personal attention."

Jena smiled. "Ahhh, thank you. But if I didn't know any better," she added, looking at him sidelong, her expression playful, "my guess is you have an ulterior motive, like perhaps hearing a particular story that intrigues you."

Gary continued to smile, "What...me? Of course not." Then he winked at her. "Until this evening."

Then he left her, and as usual her thoughts went to Chris. "Chris, you would love this place," she whispered to herself. The only response was the front door shutting as Gary left the room. But this time the emptiness didn't crush her. She smiled and looked around, eager to start this final episode of an extraordinary journey.

Later that evening she was flying low over a dense green forest of Sitka spruce, western hemlock, and cedar. The whooping blades of the helicopter would have frightened her just a year ago. For a while she had wanted to be a flight nurse, but the dangers of flying had always steered her from that course. Now though, the thought had crossed her mind that perhaps a career shift was a possibility. The whirling of helicopter blades now signaled something different. They were like a dinner bell, the rhythmic slapping blades announcing fly-fishing at its best. She wore a headset so she could easily talk with Gary over the sound of the engine. They had been in the air for just under fifteen minutes.

"Where are you taking me?" she asked, as she stared at the landscape below. Suddenly she caught some movement down below near the riverbed and looked more closely. "Oh shit," she exclaimed. "There is a bear down there."

Gary chuckled. "Yup, that's why I carry Big Bess." He tapped the holster strapped at his chest just above his wader belt. It was leather and looked custom built. The gun looked huge, aptly named of course.

"Have you had to use it before?"

"Never had to actually shoot a bear. But yes, I've had to fire it to scare a few off. As you can imagine, she is loud." He looked sidelong at her. "Don't worry. They are there for the fish, just like us. And if there are plenty of fish, they have no reason to see us as food."

She nodded but still looked apprehensive. Bears were nothing to take lightly, that much she knew. "Where are we going?"

"Not much farther," he answered. "Just a small tributary stream called the Kylie. I named it after my daughter."

Jena had met Kylie for just a brief moment before they had boarded the helicopter. She was nine and had the same high energy as her father. "Does she like it up here?" Jena asked.

"For the most part," Gary replied. "But she is starting to get to that age where lack of available friends is starting to become more problematic." He smiled at her. "Her mom and dad are no longer enough, if you know what I mean. But she loves the lodge. I swear she can do anything here. She helps my wife with the household chores. She helps our chef, our guides, everyone. She even knows the ins and outs of working on this helicopter."

Jena smiled. "If I didn't know better, she is turning into her father."

He looked at her with an 'I know' smile. "Exactly. But her mother is worried she is too much of a tomboy."

"Can there be such a thing?" Jena asked rhetorically.

Gary picked up on the sarcasm. "Exactly!" Looking down, Gary pointed to a flat expanse of riverbed. "There she is," he said, turning the bird towards the Kylie River.

It looked more like a small creek, much smaller than Jena had imagined. He set the chopper down expertly and turned off the motor. While the engine was winding down, he glanced at Jena. "Get your five weight and gear. Ready to have some fun?"

"Let's do this."

Ten minutes later they were walking the riverbed. Gary had instructed her to put on a stimulator pattern, which was a dry fly that didn't really mimic any particular bug, but could be viewed from a fish's perspective as any number of dry fly patterns, from caddis flies to stone flies. It was aptly named as it stimulated the fish to rise to the surface and strike. The Kylie River was small, but picturesque, with great little pools of clear water tinged with the blues and greens of the reflected sky and forest. One side dominated by an open rock and debris strewn riverbed, the other dense brush and trees.

The holes were deep and crystal clear. And all of them held fish. She could see the fat rainbows at the bottom, and as it had turned out had no problem getting them to aggressively take a fly from the surface. The first half hour she landed four fish, not one under seventeen inches.

"These fish are so strong," she said, releasing her fifth fish. In the last year, she had caught some truly impressive fish. But catching these powerful rainbows on a five-weight fly rod just felt right. It was an intimate experience. The river was remote, the rod and flies light, and the fish aggressive and strong. Landing a big twenty-inch rainbow on a medium action five-weight fly rod was just as fulfilling as landing the hard fighting milkfish in the Seychelles.

"Everything is wild here," Gary agreed. "These fish have to be tough to survive. Pound for pound you won't find anything stronger." He shrugged. "Well, maybe bonefish."

She nodded, knowing firsthand how strong bonefish were. "Do salmon run in this river?"

"Yup. There are probably a few already in here. The main river has them now and in a few weeks, they will be loaded in here."

"And the rainbows then feed off their eggs?"

He nodded. "In a month, these rainbows will be even bigger."

They walked a little further down and fished a long deep hole. Gary had tied a dropper off the main fly. A dropper was a second fly tied to the curve of the dry fly hook. It was usually a nymph of some sort designed to sink a few feet under the dry fly. But this time Gary had tied on a salmon egg pattern. Jena cast on the inside seam, letting line out as the gentle current took the dry fly slowly towards the deeper water.

Gary was watching intently. "Remember, your dry fly is now the strike indicator. If it drops below the surface, that means a fish took the dropper fly."

Jena nodded, already aware of this. But she appreciated the reminder as she hadn't really fished a dropper rig very often. Suddenly the dry fly was yanked under the surface. Jena quickly raised the rod, setting the hook. Instantly the rod shook violently as a fish pulled hard towards the bank. It wasn't huge, maybe fifteen inches. But it was strong. It didn't take her long to battle the fish closer to shore, but that's when something surprising happened. There was a sudden explosion of water as a huge fish shot from the depths of the pool and engulfed the smaller fish.

"A bull trout!" Gary shouted. "And a big one."

Jena screamed as the big bull trout shot back towards the deep hole, ripping line from the reel at the same time. Her eyes were wide and she was laughing. The bull trout was as big as a salmon and had just swallowed a fifteen-inch rainbow. She couldn't believe she had just witnessed that.

"That was crazy!" she yelped, holding the rod tip high as the bull trout bent the five weight dangerously close to breaking. "What size tippet is this again?" she asked, leery of the line snapping.

"3x, 9 pound," Gary said. "Should be good as long as you don't reef him in."

Jena nodded, battling the fish as it swam up and down river. Forcing a big fish in with a nine-pound tippet could easily end with a snapped line. As long as she fought the fish with the proper drag and technique, the line should hold. A few minutes later it had decided that the deep hole was not protection enough, and took off down river. Her reel zinged as the bull trout caught the faster water down river.

Jena looked at Gary with a 'now what' expression.

"Better follow it down!" He said, already moving down river.

She ran across the rocks, keeping the line tight as the fish took off. It was much too big and heavy for her to tighten the drag and try to slow it down. If she did that, it would likely break the line. So she kept the line taut and followed the crazed fish down river.

"My god, this fish is strong!"

"I think you just hooked into a fifteen-pound bull trout," Gary beamed, watching the fish swim further down river, his eyes sparkling with excitement.

They followed the fish for over a hundred yards before it settled into another hole, the run longer and a bit shallower compared to where she had hooked the fish. But it was tiring and it used the slower, deeper water, to rest, its heavy body near the bottom. It was just deep enough that she couldn't see it.

"What exactly is a bull trout anyway?" she asked. She had caught a few on the Skagit with Hans. Hans had taught her about lots of fish but she couldn't remember what it was that set bull trout apart from other trout.

"They aren't actually trout," Gary said, his eyes still glued to her tight line. "They are part of the salmon family known as char. This big guy likely just migrated from the lake into the river system. As you just saw, they are predatory and mostly eat other fish. Although it's not uncommon to get smaller ones on dry flies or egg patterns."

"How big do they get?" Jena asked, her seasoned arms holding the heavy fish easy enough.

"Well, they can get big, ranging between trout size all the way up to ten pounds. I've seen bigger in the lakes of course." He looked at Jena and smiled. "But I've never seen one this big in the Little Kylie."

"So this would be a trophy fish for this river?"

Gary nodded. "Oh yes. But don't count your ducks yet," Gary added. "He's got a lot of energy left I think."

Just then the bull trout again pulled hard down river. Her reel whined but she let it go. She really had no choice. The fish was too strong for her light rod and tippet. All she could do was hold on and hope it tired out. Once the fish got to the end of the deep water, it shot back upriver, this time heading towards the tree lined far bank.

"Shit!" Jena growled, seeing the fish pulling towards a downed tree hanging over the water, its long branches dangling deep into the river.

"Don't let it get near those branches!" Gary shouted.

"I can't stop it!"

"Tighten the drag one turn and lower the rod tip! Try pulling its head towards us!"

She turned the knob of the drag until it clicked once. Then she quickly did as he instructed, taking her left hand and moving it up the rod just above the reel, all the while lowering the rod tip to the side. Then she pulled the tip back, and using her left hand as leverage she gently pulled harder. The zing of the reel slowed but still the fish pulled dangerously close to the entanglement.

"He's still pulling!"

"Keep up the tension!" Gary shouted encouragement.

She held tight, using her palm to put a touch more tension on the reel, trying her best to keep the fish from the branches. If it got there, it would surely break off.

The pull on the fish's head must have worked as it slowly backed off, turning towards Jena to ease the tension and find the path of least resistance. It was likely tired by now but Jena knew all too well that you had to always expect another burst of power.

"Good job," Gary coached.

"I feel like I'm dragging a log off the bottom," Jena gritted.

Gary nodded. "Keep 'im coming."

It shook its head violently, trying in vain to shake the hook. It gave it a few more tries, pulling hard up and down river, but in the end, Jena's tenacity paid off and the big bull trout was slowly guided into the shallow water.

Gary was ready with the net, a big smile on his face. "Walk back some," he instructed. Jena stepped back, angling the rod tip to move its head away from Gary. "Good job," Gary added just as he swooped the net under the fish. "Yes!"

"Woo hoo!" Jena shouted, pulling slack line from the rod before moving next to Gary to look at her prize. "Wow, look at that thing." It was at least fifteen pounds. Its body was fat and its head long, with a cavernous mouth, much bigger than most trout. Jena couldn't even see the fish it had eaten.

"I can't believe he didn't just spit the fish out," Gary said. "He actually swallowed it. We'll have to cut the line to release it."

"Tenacious fish," she agreed. "Guess that's why he's so big."

Gary nodded. "Let's get a picture."

By this time Jena was a pro at setting up a good picture and it didn't take them long to get a few good shots. The fish's belly was so big that when she held it, it squished over her fingers, nearly making her hand disappear. It was so beautiful, its dark green body covered in large spots ranging in colors from yellow to pink.

She released it quickly and Gary gave her a high five. "Well done," he beamed. "I can see you know what you're doing."

She smiled. "As of a year ago I was clueless about fly fishing. Let's just say that I've gained a lot of experience this last year."

"Well, it shows. That was a trophy fish...the biggest I've seen in this river."

"In that case are you in for some scotch and a cigar?" Jena had yet to meet a fisherman who wasn't.

He smiled and looked up at the sun. "We have about an hour before we have to head back. You sure you don't want to fish more?"

She shook her head. "I have all week. Besides, this would be a good time to fill you in on why I'm here. And the story starts well after a trophy fish accompanied by a scotch and cigar."

Gary lifted his eyebrows at that, clearly even more interested. "In that case, we have plenty of time."

* * *

Three days later Jena was sitting on a bench nestled amongst a bed of flowers, her perch atop a gentle hill giving her a great view of the snow-covered Alaskan mountains. It was a beautiful spot, carefully planned by Gary's wife, Eve, creating the lookout spot off a short path from the main lodge. Even though it was summer, the temperature was brisk, morning lows in the fifties and daytime highs in the mid-sixties. Jena knew that the lodge and surrounding river system was a bit higher in elevation than the coastal area. Even a few hundred feet made a difference when it came to weather systems in Alaska. But they had no rain, which was fantastic, and the mosquito activity had been nearly non-existent. Much of what she had read about Alaska had always paired fishing with annoying mosquitos, so she was enthusiastically happy that Big Tree Lodge had so far been free of the pesky bugs.

She was wrapped comfortably in fleece, her leather-bound journal in her lap. She had had a great day of fishing and thought it would be a good time to peruse her journal, going over all she had learned this last year. She had forgotten to write down her previous life lesson, and decided to do that now. *Sometimes you have to hold on to the little victories to get through the day.* She nodded, writing it down. She hadn't yet learned a life lesson for this trip, but she was content surmising her own wisdom if that didn't happen. Looking up, she thought about the trip so far. The fishing of course had been incredible. She had caught big, strong rainbows, bull trout, and one day she had targeted salmon, getting even a few silver salmon to rise to a popper dry fly that she had stripped across the surface. The guides had been knowledgeable and a lot of fun to fish with.

Her first day with Gary had been the best though. Landing that big bull trout had provided her an opportunity to share her story with the lodge owner. They had sat on a log looking out at the river, sharing an expensive scotch and smoking Cuban cigars. Gary had been a good listener, and Jena found he was quite emotional. He was a good empathetic listener. Jena had done well, telling the story smoothly with few tears. She felt good talking about Chris's passing. It was a safe place, and they had shared a nice moment together.

Looking up at the mountains, she used the edge of her sleeve to wipe her eyes as she recalled the event.

"Why are you crying?"

Jena jumped, looking behind her. It was Kylie, Gary's daughter.

"Oh hey," Jena said, quickly wiping the wetness from her cheeks. "Sorry, I was thinking of something."

Kylie walked closer and stood by the edge of the bench. She looked concerned, which was so cute. "Was it something sad?"

Jena nodded. "Yes, it was."

Kylie held a small yellow box and she held it out to her. "You want some Milk Duds?"

Jena smiled. She had not had Milk Duds since she was a kid. It was one of her favorite candies to get when she had gone to the movies. "I would love some. Thank you," she replied as Kylie dumped a few into her hand. "Want to sit down?"

Kylie shrugged. "Sure."

"What are you doing out here?"

"I'm visiting Remy's grave," she said, pointing ahead towards the edge of the forest.

Jena followed her finger and saw a big rock sticking out of the ground right where the grass met the forest. Written on the rock in white paint was *Remy*, and all over the rock were various child drawings of rainbows and butterflies. And scattered around the rock were plantings of colorful flowers. She had been so preoccupied with her own thoughts that she hadn't even noticed it.

She suddenly felt ashamed. "Was Remy your dog?"

Kylie nodded, tossing a few Milk Duds into her mouth. "He died last year. My mom and dad built this little area for him. I get sad when I come here too."

"Is it okay if I'm sad here with you?"

Kylie nodded. "I guess so." She looked intently at Jena. "Did your dog die too?"

Jena wasn't sure what to say. She was clearly old enough to understand death, but at the same time she didn't want to burden her unnecessarily. She decided to keep it simple. "Well, yes, I did lose my dog a few years ago. My husband and I were really sad as well. But I'm crying now because I lost someone close to me, someone more recent."

"You mean someone close to you died?" Kylie asked.

"Yes."

"I'm sorry," Kylie said, looking away towards Remy's grave. "My dad told me something when Remy died? It helped me. Maybe it will help you. Want to hear it?"

"Sure," Jena encouraged. "I would like that."

Kylie pushed her lips out as she thought of what her father had told her. "My dad said that Remy filled part of my heart..." she scrunched up her face, clearly trying to think of the rest. "And," she continued, "that part of my heart will always be his." She smiled, remembering the rest. "But I have room in my heart for another dog to love."

Jena looked at Remy's grave and smiled. She remembered their dog, Macallan, dying, and how it had impacted them both so much. Since they were not able to have children, they had dumped all their love into their little puppy. They had read books on how to raise a puppy. They watched videos on how to train them. They did everything a young couple does to prepare for a new child. When they came home from work, they talked and played with Macallan. They taught him games and how to fetch. And when he got sick, they cared for him, took him to vet appointments, and administered medications and special food, hoping that they would get a few more years with him. But when he was three years old, he had died of cardiomyopathy, a disease of the heart muscle that makes it harder to pump blood throughout the system. It leads to an enlarged heart and then heart failure. He had died of a big heart.

Jena dabbed her eyes and looked at Kylie. "Thank you for telling me that."

"But you seem sadder," Kylie added.

"I know, honey, but it's okay," Jena sighed. "Your words did help."

And in fact they did. She realized that if Chris had been there, he would say that she could hold onto him in her heart, that he would always be there, but she still had room in her heart to love again. Just the idea of it seemed preposterous, but Kylie's words were true enough. Jena knew that many people had learned to love again. Perhaps, in time, she would as well.

"Are you going to get another dog?"

Kylie smiled and nodded. "Yes. Papa promised this year."

Jena smiled back. Well, she thought, I now have a life lesson for this trip. She restated it in her mind so she wouldn't forget it...*the ones you love fill part of your heart, and that's how you hold onto them, but there is always room in your heart to love again.* She sort of made up her own wording, but the gist was the same.

"Want some more Milk Duds?"

Jena smiled and nodded. "As a matter of fact, yes, I do."

Kylie dumped a few more into her hand as they sat silently, enjoying the soothing quiet of the Alaskan wilderness.

A Year of a Thousand Casts

* * *

The next day Jena finally got to fish with Ella, the only female guide at the lodge, well actually, the only female guide in any of the fishing destinations she had been to all year. She was twenty-eight years old and quite pretty, and Jena was angry at herself for being surprised at that. She had pictured Ella as a short haired tom boy type. She had fallen into the typical stereotype that if a female performed traditionally masculine jobs they would appear more 'masculine'. She berated herself for stumbling into that societal trap. A pretty feminine woman was just as capable as a man of being a fishing guide...of being most anything actually. Jena knew she was no swimsuit model, but she also knew that men generally found her attractive. And she herself, a single woman, was traveling on her own, fly fishing some of the most remote and exotic destinations in the world. And still her immediate thought was that Ella was going to be stout, rough around the edges, and manly, whatever that means. She hated that society had preconditioned her to think those misogynistic thoughts.

Ella was upbeat and just as excited to meet and fish with her as Jena was. They hit it off immediately and Jena loved her story. She had been born and raised in Alaska, her father the captain of a crabbing boat. She was raised with a gun and fishing rod in her hand, although a cute and petite blonde, she could turn a wrench or perform with the best of them at a shooting range. She was dating one of the other guides and they worked as a guiding team at Big Tree Lodge for five months out of the year. She spent the rest of the year on her father's crabbing boat during the winter and made enough money to travel and fish all over the world with her boyfriend. It sounded like quite the carefree life.

Ella had decided to take Jena grayling fishing. It was one of the few species in Alaska that she had yet to catch so she was very excited. Ella had told her that they were part of the salmonid family and are found in Europe, Russia, and the western portions of North America. The silver-gray fish were known for their long, high dorsal fin. Though similar to trout in size, most in the Alaskan rivers were between one and three pounds. Jena was excited as they were using light tackle, three and four weight rods, and targeting them mostly with dry flies, which was her favorite technique next to poppers.

Gary had dropped them off on a bed of grass adjacent to a tributary stream known for its grayling fishing. Ella wore waders, a backpack, a net strapped to the pack, and she also carried a rifle. Jena had noticed that all the guides had carried guns; whether it was a big handgun or a rifle was based on personal preference. They all had said that the fishing was safe, but always followed it up with you were crazy to enter the Alaskan frontier without a gun.

Ella and Jena had talked and fished all day, catching more grayling than she could count. She was really enjoying Ella's bubbly personality as well as her pool of knowledge regarding the fishing and the Alaskan wilderness. Jena hadn't talked so much in months. It was her first experience talking fashion while reeling in a two pound, leaping grayling. They chatted about recent world news and gossip as well as their favorite television shows, both finding solace in the fact that they shared a love for all the housewives of all the counties. They even agreed that The Real Housewives of Beverly Hills was the best of them. Chris had hated those shows, and every time Jena started to watch one, he would disappear, often mumbling his criticisms as he made himself busy in his office.

They were chatting noisily as they walked a narrow trail adjacent to the river. There was a huge rock face the river had cut through, and Ella was leading her around it where they would converge with the river a quarter mile later. The path, strewn with pine needles, meandered through a forest of tall pine trees.

Ella was leading as they crested a small rise, her chatter suddenly stopping as Jena felt her hand reach back, the flat of her palm touching her chest like a stop sign. She immediately felt the tenseness in the air. Then she heard the growl.

"Don't move," Ella whispered, lifting her rifle to her shoulder.

Jena looked past her, and down the path, no more than forty feet away, was a big brown bear.

"Is that—"

"A dead deer...yes. Shit," Ella whispered nervously as the bear stepped over the bloody carcass, roaring aggressively as it tried to defend the carcass. Jena flinched, instinctively wanting to run. "Don't run," Ella snapped. "Stay still." Ella pushed Jena behind her further and repositioned her stance, her left foot forward, the big rifle braced against her shoulder.

The bear stood up on its legs and roared louder. Blood was splattered across its jaws and Jena thought it looked absolutely terrifying. She blanched and her heart pounded with fear. "Is it going to attack?" Jena whispered.

"Generally I'd say no," Ella whispered, her tone tense as she stared calmly down the barrel. "But we approached its kill. It might charge us to scare us away. If it does, do not run. Just back up slowly. If I fire, don't run."

Jena nodded, not sure if she could control the urge to not run if the bear charged. Suddenly the bear dropped to its legs and barreled towards them, roaring as it ran at them with wild ferocity. Jena's body jolted. "Don't run!" Ella shouted as she fired the rifle above the animal.

The noise was so loud that she had to cover her ears. The gun's kick was impressive, but Ella expertly took the impact, quickly using the lever to inject another round into the gun's chamber, stepping back slowly as she did so.

Jena saw the bear skid to a stop, roaring loudly in defiance. Clearly the noise had startled it. "Did you hit it?" Her voice shook with fear.

"I wasn't aiming to hit it," Ella added coolly, stepping back again. "I'm just trying to scare it. Keep stepping back." She was all business and Jena did exactly what she said.

Slowly they moved backward as the bear angrily postured further, roaring and pawing the ground, churning up the earth like a rototiller. They continued to walk backwards, dropping slowly behind the gentle rise of the hill. They could no longer see the bear, but they could still hear it. "Should we run now?" Jena asked hopefully.

"No," Ella replied, her tone still tense. "But pick up the pace some." They moved a little faster, Jena following Ella's lead as she continued to walk backwards, her gun raised and ready. Thirty feet further, the bear stopped roaring. "Damn," Ella swore.

"What?" Jena asked nervously.

"Now I don't know where it's at. Just keep going."

They walked another twenty feet when they saw the bear at the top of the rise, now about fifty feet away. "Shit," Jena swore, her voice still shaking. All she wanted to do was run.

"Keep moving slowly," Ella instructed.

The bear rose up on its back feet and roared defiantly again. Then it plopped back down, turned, and disappeared over the crest.

"Good," Ella said. "Now, we can move faster. Let's jog back to the river."

Jena needed no further encouragement. They jogged back to the main river, Ella stopping occasionally to listen or watch for pursuit. But there was nothing. They were in the clear.

Getting back to the river, Jena felt a bit safer, the open rock-strewn riverbed allowing a clear vantage point to the forest's edge. If the bear did follow and charge them again, Ella would have a clear shot.

They were both panting, not from exhaustion, but from the adrenaline rush. Ella leaned over, took a few deep breaths, then looked up at Jena and smiled.

"What's so funny?!" Jena blurted.

"That was tense!" Ella exclaimed. "But pretty cool."

"What are you talking about! I think I peed in my waders," Jena countered.

"Even if you did," Ella laughed, "just think about the story this will make. That was an event that few will ever get to experience." She was still smiling. "You feel your heart?"

Jena's heart was pounding and her hands were just beginning to calm. "Of course. I'm still shaking."

"Exactly. The rush feels good. Besides, we were never really in danger," Ella added nonchalantly. "That bear didn't want to attack us. That charge was just posturing. He was just trying to scare us away from his food."

"Well it worked," Jena said. Then she looked at Ella, a small smile lifting the corners of her mouth. "And that *will* make a good story."

Ella laughed. "There you go...that's the silver lining."

Jena shook her head, exasperated. "You're crazy. But thank you."

Ella nodded, letting out a deep breath to calm the flowing adrenaline. "Still want to fish?"

Jena looked around. "Will that bear come back?"

Ella nodded. "These bears are well fed. We are definitely not on their menu. The only reason that one charged us was because we walked in on its meal. It's pretty rare for them to eat anything other than salmon this time of the year. That one must've gotten lucky and come across that dead deer."

"You mean it didn't kill it?"

"It's unlikely. Deer are not so easy for a bear to bring down, unless they are hurt or small. Hard to say with that particular deer. Perhaps it was sick, or injured, either way that bear does not want to leave the carcass. We are safe if we stay away. But we can move back down river if that would make you feel better."

"Yes, I think it would," Jena said. She had already begun to think that she could use this event as one Chris would have enjoyed and she definitely did not. Well, she figured it would be a stretch to say he would have enjoyed it, but it was likely he would have had the same reaction as Ella when it was all over. She had yet to find something she could check off the list for this last trip. This could definitely count. Chris would have been scared, for sure, but he also would have been excited that he had gotten to experience it. She, on the other hand, felt no such emotion. Seeing a bear in the distance is one thing. But being charged by one, a shot from a high powerful rifle likely the only thing stopping it, was quite another. She definitely could have done without it. The more she thought about it, the more she confirmed that she would indeed journal the event.

Ella had checked her rifle to make sure everything was good. "Ready to move down?" she asked.

"More than you know."

She laughed as she slung the rifle over her shoulder, leading Jena down river.

Epilogue

It was a beautiful summer morning when Jena decided to get on the road and head back to where it had all started. She was overcome by a wave of nostalgia as she navigated the long meandering road to the Skagit River. She was excited and apprehensive about heading back to the spot where her adventure had begun. She was looking forward to seeing Irma and Hans, but at the same time a bit apprehensive about returning, her arrival marking the completion of her great fishing adventure. She had one more task. To sprinkle some of Chris's ashes in the river where she first learned to fish. The finality of it filled her with a deep sadness.

It was July second, the summer sky sporadically filled with puffy white clouds, some dark, like a bruise, possible rain moving in. But it wasn't unusual for Western Washington. It always seemed to rain, or at least sprinkle near the fourth of July. It was still warm, however, in the mid-seventies, and the crisp air blowing through her lowered window smelled fresh, like pine trees and earth. She was glad she had decided to leave town for the holiday, eager to be casting again in the secluded mountains, away from the noises of Independence Day. Typically, she loved the holiday. In fact, it had been one of her and Chris's favorites. They loved to hang with friends, drink beer, barbeque ribs, and watch the fireworks, the typical American Fourth of July. Despite her emotional growth since his death, she still was not ready to hang out with their friends without him. But, she thought, the possibility of socializing again seemed less and less foreboding. She *had* grown. She *had* learned. She did feel that it was possible to create another timeline, one without Chris's presence. In fact, she thought, perhaps she had already started to do that.

Looking up, her eyes caught the silhouette of a dangling fly stuck into the visor, the sun breaking through the clouds, its light shining behind it. It was an old worn out grasshopper pattern, the body made of orange foam with orange and black striped rubber legs and white synthetic hair for a wing. It was likely a fly Chris had tied. Thinking back to what he always said, *any true fly fisherman should always name the flies he creates,* she analyzed the fly again, wondering the name he would have given it. She smiled as a name came to her...the Orange Creamsicle, named of course after his favorite ice cream bar. He would have liked that name.

The drive went by quickly as her thoughts drifted through the events of the last year. She thought of all the wonderful destinations she had experienced, and all the friends and incredible people she had met. Images of trophy fish and emotional moments filled her mind. She went over the life lessons in her head, having memorized them, the words chiseled in her consciousness. She laughed as she thought of the events she had to experience through Chris's eyes, and cried when she thought of the moments she shared when telling her story. It was an adventure she would never forget, searing in her mind a connection with her late husband that would forever stay with her. She knew that was the point, after all, to remember him while trying to heal and move forward. That was what he had wanted for her. She had done her best to honor his wishes, and in the end, knew that he had been right in asking her to complete the journey. But now it was almost over. Now she had to figure out how to use what she had learned to actually move on. Intellectually, she thought she could do it. But emotionally taking action, she knew, would be more difficult, and likely take more time. But she was okay with that. She was fine with taking her time.

Suddenly Han's little store materialized on her right and she turned into the parking lot next to another car, a beat-up station wagon parked near the door. She glimpsed Irma's white Ford Ranger behind the building and smiled, knowing she would be at the counter just as surely as the sun rose every morning.

She parked and made her way to the entrance, the old wood door opening as she neared as a rather large woman exited. The familiar *ding ding* of the bell gave her a sense of belonging, more so than she had expected. She thought of the many mornings where she had heard the front doorbell signaling Hans's entrance and a long day of fishing and instruction. She pursed her lips in a fond smile as she envisioned Irma prepping the coffee, the fragrant aroma of ground coffee that had greeted her every morning. Basking in the memories, she entered the store. Immediately she saw Irma look up from her magazine, her eyes widening in recognition.

"Jena, what a pleasant surprise!" she exclaimed, setting the magazine down and coming from around the counter to greet her. They hugged warmly.

"Sorry I didn't call, but I wanted to surprise you."

"Well you did," she smiled. "Are you done with your journey?"

Jena's face turned a little somber. "I am. Just one more task to complete."

Irma understood. Jena had explained to her that she would be returning to spread Chris's ashes one last time, where it all started. "I can't wait to hear all about it."

Jena looked up. "Is the apartment rented?"

"Nope. You want it?"

Jena nodded. "I was hoping to stay a few days."

"It's yours."

"Thanks. Where is Hans?"

"Where do you think?" Jena asked, chuckling.

"On the river." She laughed along with her, knowing that it was a dumb question. Jena could not think of a day when Hans had not got his line wet. It was part of his routine. He would likely be back by mid-afternoon. "I was hoping that maybe we could have a fire down by the river tonight. I have a lot to tell you both."

"That sounds wonderful," Irma agreed. "Hans and I are so excited to hear about your adventure."

"Good," Jena beamed.

"Want to get settled in?" Irma asked, moving behind the counter to grab the keys to the apartment.

"That would be great," Jena replied, grabbing the keys from her. "I think I'll hit the river for a bit while you work."

Irma smiled. "Of course you would."

* * *

It was a comfortable summer evening, the temperature dropping to sixty-seven degrees as the day's sun had just disappeared behind the mountain peaks. The backdrop was the tranquil sound of the river, at the very same hole where Jena had caught Sparky the first day she had come to Han's store. She had had no idea what she was doing, and Hans had reprimanded her for it. She smiled, thinking how much things have changed over the last year. Hans, Irma, and Jena, sat in camp chairs around a crackling fire, glasses of scotch in their hands. It seemed fitting that Jena would share the rest of the thousand-dollar bottle that Chris had bought before he had succumbed to cancer. It wasn't too cold, but they were bundled up in warm pants and coats, and Irma even had a blanket draped over her legs.

"Honey," Irma said, "this scotch is wasted on me. I just taste strong alcohol."

Jena laughed. "I know what you mean, although I will say I've acquired a taste for it over this last year."

"Well, at least I know you learned something," Hans quipped, smiling.

"A smile looks good on you," Jena said, ignoring his comment, but smiling with him.

"I have had to give him moisturizer daily so the skin on his face won't crack," Irma said. Hans was shaking his head. Irma chuckled.

They all laughed and sipped their drink, their eyes drawn to the dancing fire. It was nearly dark and Jena thought it was a good time to tell them what had happened to her over the last year.

"Well," she began, "my journey is nearly over."

"We can see that," Hans interjected, waiving his cup impatiently. "Tell me about the fishing."

She smiled and began her tale, starting with her adventure in the South Island fishing the remote rivers of New Zealand. She recounted meeting Lilith and Ron, as well as the emotional connection she had made with Justin, one of the guides at the lodge. She related the exciting experience catching the powerful milkfish in the Seychelles and the friendship she had made with Susan and Karen. Her descriptions of the Chilean Fjords made Hans and Irma feel like it was a place from another world. When she told them about the remote waterfall and the adjacent pool filled with big rainbows, Hans jumped into the story.

"That sounds like a place Chris would've loved," he said as he recalled the fishing with his friend.

Jena nodded. "I thought that too. It was the type of place for which he lived to find." Her choice of words hit her hard, the others catching it as well. She looked into the fire, concentrating at holding back the tears. She was proud she was able to keep them in check. Looking up again, she continued. Hans and Irma asked a lot of questions about her time in the Amazon. It was such a unique place and even Hans had little knowledge of all the various fish species one could catch there. They both laughed when she told them about eating the palm grub. But the story of the arapaima really got Han's attention.

"You caught a fish over a hundred pounds, on a fly rod!?"

She nodded. "It was amazing. That fish was so strong." She shook her head in bewilderment, still wondering how she had managed it. "Their jaws are so tough that I couldn't set the hook hard enough to embed it. It took me falling on my back to stick the hook in far enough."

"I want to see a picture of that fish," Irma added.

"I'll show you the pictures tomorrow."

Jena spent some time talking about Alaska and her discussions with Gary and Kylie, his daughter. Hans particularly loved the story of the big bull trout that ate the rainbow she had caught. That very same thing had happened to him on the Skagit, but not quite on the same scale. It was Irma who interrupted her story when Jena got to the part about running into the big bear.

"You mean the bear actually charged you?!"

Jena nodded. "I was so scared."

"How did you keep from running?" Irma asked.

"I had a good guide."

"And she actually had to fire off a round?" Hans asked.

"It was so loud," Jena added. "Stopped the bear in its tracks."

"Good thing," Hans muttered.

Jena nodded, and they all paused as they gazed into the enticing red embers of the hot fire. After a few moments, she reached to the side of her chair and picked up a paper bag, handing it to Hans.

"I have a gift for you," she said as Hans took the bag.

"You didn't—"

"Just open it," Jena interrupted playfully.

He frowned but reached into the bag, pulling out something in a black frame. He stared at it a moment before looking intently at Jena. "What is this?"

"Those are all the life lessons I learned." She looked at Irma, who was not privy to all the guidelines Chris had given her for the journey. "One of the things Chris wanted me to journal, was one life lesson that I learned at every location." She nodded to the frame. "I had them all written down."

Irma smiled. "Hans, read them out loud."

Hans looked up from the picture. "Okay," he said, his voice cracking a little.

Irma looked at Jena and smiled, both sharing a moment as they realized how much Hans had changed over the last year.

"The title is *Life Lessons Learned from Fly Fishing*. Number one, from...Hans paused as he looked up smiling, "Hans on the Skagit." He shook his head chuckling.

Jena returned his smile. "Well, it all started with you. Of course you have to have provided one of my life lessons."

"Just read it," Irma said, eager to hear what he had said nearly a year ago.

He looked back down. "Fly fishing builds friendships based on a common comradery." He glanced at Jena. "I said that?"

"Well, not those exact words," Jena conceded. "I couldn't remember it exactly so I had to tweak it some. But you were talking about the friendship you and Chris had created around fly fishing. Throughout my travels I realized that your words rang true. I met so many people that had deep and lasting friendships, and the common narrative was fly fishing. It was the glue that held them all together."

Hans nodded thoughtfully as he looked back at the frame.

Number two," he continued a few moments later, "from Ron in New Zealand. *Choose experiences over things.*"

"I like that one," Irma whispered, urging him to continue.

"Number three, from Karen in the Seychelles. *There is beauty in solitude.* Number four, from Mark in the Chilean Fjords. *Fly-fishing is all about learning humility.*" He looked up. "Aint that the truth," he added. Glancing back down, he read, "number five," he continued, "from Carlos in Brazil. *A calm heart is necessary in fishing, and in life.*" Hans paused, nodding his head, obviously finding a deeper connection to those words. After all, his heart had been in pain for the last thirty years after he had lost his daughter. He knew he had to find a way to calm his heart, to live a better, more enriching life. Jena had opened him up to the idea that that was in fact possible. He took a deep breath and continued. "Number six," he said, looking up at Jena. "You have your own in here."

Jena shrugged. "I learned a lot."

He smiled and looked back to the gift. "Number six, from Jena in Alaska, *sometimes you have to hold onto the small victories to get through the day.*"

Irma pressed her lips into a knowing smile. Reaching over, she squeezed Jena's leg.

Jena's eyes glistened but she said nothing, thankful for Irma's support.

"Number seven, from Kylie, a nine-year-old," Hans looked up to make sure he was reading it correctly.

"She was so cute," Jena said. "The lesson she gave me technically came from her father when her dog, Remy had died." Jena shrugged. "I converted it a little."

"Okay," Hans said, looking back down. "Kylie said *when a loved one dies, they fill a part of your heart, but there is always more room in your heart to love again.*"

Hans pressed his lips together and looked up at the night sky, the sparkling stars gazing back. He dabbed the corners of his eyes, pausing until he felt he could continue.

Jena sniffed, wiping the wetness from her eyes before they turned into tears. "I think you should hang that in your office, or your store. What do you think?"

He looked down, nodding. "I think I'll hang it above my rod rack in the store." He paused. "Thank you for this."

She smiled. "You're welcome."

"What's the plan now?"

Jena took a deep breath. "I complete the journey Chris made for me. I go to Chris's fishing hole tomorrow to sprinkle his ashes. After that, I don't know."

"One step at a time, my dear," Irma coached.

Hans nodded. "We're all in this together." He lifted his scotch for a toast, the others doing the same. "To friends, comradery, and fly-fishing."

They tapped their glasses and drank.

Irma held her glass up again. "Losing expectations makes a happier heart."

They clinked their glasses and drank again.

"You know," Jena said, "that would make another good life-lesson."

"I could scribble it on with a marker," Irma added playfully.

"We have a lot of time," Hans added thoughtfully, "perhaps we can make another list."

"I like that idea," Jena agreed.

The three spent another hour talking about her journey and what might come, drinking scotch and enjoying each other's company and shared experiences. As they talked, Jena's mind drifted to something she had learned. Everyone, at some point, was going to experience the pain of loss. It made her realize that she was not alone, that she, like many others before her, and many more to come, would get through the pain. It was a comforting thought, the idea warming her almost as much as the scotch and the crackling fire.

* * *

The next morning Jena left early for her hike up to Chris's fishing hole. She kept her rods in their tubes remembering the difficulty of climbing down the rocky cliff using little more than the rope that Chris had left behind years ago. And she was glad she did as the descent was much easier with two unobstructed hands, her rod tubes strapped to either side of her backpack.

Returning to Chris's fishing hole after nearly a year brought to the surface many emotions. She was sad, mostly because her fly fishing timeline with Chris as her virtual guide was nearly over. She was angry that she would never get to experience this place with Chris. But she was also happy that this destination would forever solidify the deep connection with her late husband. It made her feel good knowing that she could come here and always remember who he was. Nostalgia hit home as well. She had fond memories of learning to fish here with Hans. Images of hooking into her first steelhead still rose to the surface as if it had happened yesterday. *Steelhead dreams* Hans had called it.

Once she made the decent to the rock-strewn riverbed, she made her way towards the waterfall and the long deep run known as Chris's Hole. But she hadn't gotten more than a hundred yards upriver when her heart sank. Standing at the end of the long run was a fisherman, his line unfurled behind him as he shot a perfect cast to the far bank.

What the hell, she thought. This was her hole, her place. Well, technically, it was Chris's find first, then Hans's, then hers, but she couldn't help but feel angry at seeing another person fishing her waters, especially considering why she was there. She had come to sprinkle his ashes into the water. She was supposed to have one final moment with her late husband. Now it was ruined.

He was stripping in his line when she approached, her wading boots knocking the river rocks around warning him of her approach. He turned and smiled when he saw her.

"Oh, hi," he said. "Didn't think I'd see anyone else here."

"Why is that?" She asked, her tone a bit harsher than she wished.

He picked up on it. "I'm sorry, are you the one who put that rope out? If so, thank you. I never would've been able to get down here. And man," he jabbered, "this place is awesome. I was lucky to have even found it. I heard the waterfall, bushwhacked to it, and realizing I couldn't get down I spent an hour skirting the edge. And that's when I found the rope." He looked back at the beautiful pool. "What a great spot," he added. "I've landed two great rainbows and a huge bull trout all within forty-five minutes." He grinned sheepishly. "Sorry I'm blabbering, its been a good morning."

Jena lightened up some, his excitement contagious. After all, she didn't own the river. And what he just described was likely what Chris had done to find the hole so many years ago. How he originally had gotten down without the rope was still something she wondered. But Chris had been the type of person to not let a rock cliff get in his way of fishing unknown waters. "It was a friend of mine who put that rope there," she replied. "Sorry I was snippy. I don't normally find others here."

He lifted his rod tip and grabbed the dangling fly, attaching it to the hook near his reel. "I understand. Secret fishing holes are few and far between." He smiled warmly, trying to ease her tension. "I'm Scott."

"I'm Jena," she replied. He appeared to be close to her age, maybe a bit younger. He was tall and lanky, his forearms bare and sinewy, strong looking in an *I work with my hands for a living* kind of way. His brownish blonde hair was cut short, military like, and he sported a trimmed goatee. Jena thought he was handsome, but where Chris was ruggedly good looking, Scott looked more proper, like he had just returned from a tour in Iraq. But his lighthearted smile and enthusiasm warmed his sharper features and Jena's anger at his intrusion fizzled away. "There is plenty of room for us both to fish."

Scott put up his hand in a placating gesture. "Oh no, this is your hole. I've already fished the run anyway. I'll leave it to you."

She nodded. "Suit yourself. But if you want to stay, you're more than welcome." She moved to a big downed log and took off her pack, prepping her gear and stringing her rod.

Scott sat on the other end of the log, breaking his rod down. "I think it will be easier climbing up that rope without holding onto a rod," he said, looking over at her. "Have you fished here much?"

"Just a couple of times," she said.

"This is my first time here. What a great place," he effused. "Let's just say I needed it."

Jena chuckled. "I know what you mean."

"Yeah?" Scott asked. "Work or family?"

"Both I guess."

"What do you do?" he asked as he pulled his rod apart and began to put it back into its tube.

"Pediatric Intensive Care Nurse," she replied, running her fly line through the eyelets of her five-weight rod. As soon as she said it, she realized she missed her work. Her interactions with the young deaf girl at the Alaskan airport, and Kylie, Gary's daughter, had stopped her life's compass from spinning. She was excited to get back to work.

Scott paused, looking more intently at her, his expression one of respect. "Well, you definitely deserve a day on the river. I know that from firsthand experience."

She glanced at him. "Oh yeah?" She did not want to press any harder as she didn't know where he was going with that response. What if he had a son or daughter that had gotten injured, or even worse, died, and his knowledge of the PICU was connected to the worst time in his life. She didn't want to probe any further.

"I'm a paramedic," he responded. "I've had the pleasure of working with PICU nurses before."

"Well," Jena added. "Sounds like we both deserve a day on the river."

"Yup," Scott added, tucking his gear into his pack while Jena tied on a streamer. A minute or so later, he cinched his pack on and looked over at her. "I'm going to leave a fly on this log for you," he said. "I nailed all three fish with it. I tied it myself."

Jena's eyes were on the knot she was tying so she did not look up. "Oh thanks, but you don't have to do that." She wondered why he didn't just bring it to her, but dismissed the thought quickly as she focused on the knot.

"I call it the McTavish Missile."

Jena wet the knot with her mouth before cinching it tight. Looking up she smiled. "You named it that? Is McTavish your last name?"

He lifted his eyebrows playfully and smiled from ear to ear. "Yup, Scott McTavish. And of course I named it. Any serious fly-fisherman names the flies they tie."

Jena's heart suddenly felt heavy, but then she chuckled through it, pushing past the immediate sadness. She couldn't believe what she was hearing. For years those were the words she heard from Chris. She had repeated his mantra in her head many times over the last year. And now, at the end of her adventure, she meets some random fly-fisherman, at *his* hole, repeating *his* own words. It was almost too much.

"You okay?"

She blinked, refocusing her attention on Scott. "Yeah, sorry, I'm fine. You just reminded me of someone."

"He must be handsome," he said jokingly.

Jena flashed him an awkward smile and looked away.

He sensed her unease and redirected the conversation. "Well, give it a try," he said, setting the fly down on the log as Jena connected her fly to the hook near the reel.

"I will. Thanks," she replied, still thinking of Chris. But she pulled her thoughts to the present and looked at him. "Nice to meet you Scott McTavish."

"You too, Jena..."

"O'Malley," she said.

He gave her a lingering smile, nodded, and left.

She looked back to the river, the weight of the little gold container holding Chris's ashes heavy against her chest. She let out a deep breath, figuring she would fish a little first before depositing his ashes. That's what Chris would want.

Looking back to the log, her curiosity about the McTavish Missile, drew her attention to the spot where the fly sat. She made her way to the end of the log and saw a black and white streamer, nicely tied, sitting on top of a little piece of paper. She picked them both up and smiled. On the paper was written Scott McTavish, his phone number, and a little note that said, *look me up if you want to blow off some steam on a river sometime.*

She looked at the river and was surprised at how she felt. She had no idea if she was ready to call Scott, or anyone for that matter. But it felt good knowing that the idea of calling him wasn't unfathomable. She felt optimistic that simply entertaining the idea didn't make her feel like she was cheating on Chris's memory. Perhaps, she thought, I can do this. Perhaps, unbeknownst to her, the journey Chris had sent her on had actually given her the tools to enable her to move on. As the adage said, she thought, time will tell.

"Thank you, my love, for everything," she whispered. "I love you. I will always love you." She wiped the fresh tears from her eyes, unhooked the fly from the reel base, and made her way to the river.

She had some fishing to do.

Looking for something else to read?

The Life of Ely is Jason L. McWhirter's first non-fantasy book. Twenty-five years in the classroom and half those years as a coach has given him a unique perspective on the trials and tribulations that some students experience as they attempt to survive their adolescence. This story, although fiction, is inspired by these experiences.

Look for it on Amazon!